'Popular author Tricia Stringer returns [...] tale of friendship, family drama and cha[...] again demonstrates why she is one of the best chroniclers of small town Australia.'

—*Canberra Weekly* on *Keeping up Appearances*

'...another great story of family and friends with Tricia, [who is] a master at producing authentic and real people and places that take you right to the centre of the community.'

—*Great Reads and Tea Leaves* on *Keeping up Appearances*

'"Masterful" gets used a lot in reviews, but Tricia Stringer really is. With *Birds of a Feather*, she firmly takes her place as one of Australia's most accomplished writers.'

—*Better Reading*

'Warm, sincere and thoughtful, *Birds of a Feather* is an engaging contemporary novel sure to delight readers, new and old.'

—*Book'd Out*

'A good, warm-hearted read with relatable and empathetic characters.'

—*Canberra Weekly* on *Birds of a Feather*

'*Birds of a Feather* is the latest offering from Aussie favourite Tricia Stringer. Her books always strike a chord with her faithful following. On this occasion, Tricia gives us a multi-generational family drama but with the emphasis on what exactly is family? A fantastic theme to ponder in these new and uncertain times.'

—*Great Reads and Tea Leaves*

'A book you can't put down ... Stringer's skill is in weaving the experiences of different generations of women together, with sensitivity and familiarity, gently showing how context can shape women's decisions ... A moving, feel-good, warm read about strong, loving women ... the exact book we all need right now.'

—*Mamamia* on *The Family Inheritance*

'... a polished family saga ... all delivered with intelligence, wit and emotion in equal measures ... Perfection!'

—*Better Reading* on *The Family Inheritance*

'Tricia Stringer is an intuitive and tender-hearted storyteller who displays a real ability to interrogate issues that affect families and individuals. *The Family Inheritance* is another gratifying read from Tricia Stringer.'

—*Mrs B's Book Reviews*

'This book is the equivalent of a hot bath or a box of chocolates, it's comforting and an absolute pleasure to immerse yourself in ... If you enjoy well-written family sagas, look no further. *The Model Wife* is perfect.'

—*Better Reading*

'Tricia Stringer's *The Model Wife* is a beautiful multi-dimensional family saga.'

—*Beauty and Lace*

'Tricia Stringer excels at two things: strong, empathetic characters; and finding an experience or emotion shared by many, then spinning that small kernel of commonality into an engaging novel. *The Model Wife* is no exception ... Stringer's prose is warm and friendly. She pulls you in with an easy and flowing writing style that quickly has you absorbed by the action. It's easy to read, but that doesn't mean it's shallow.'

—*Other Dreams Other Lives*

'[A] heartfelt saga.'

—*Herald Sun* on *The Model Wife*

'I would highly recommend this novel and hope that readers will gain what I have from it. *The Model Wife* is a beautiful story with familiar challenges and a strength of a family who are connected via their life experiences together.'

—*Chapter Ichi*

'A well-written, engaging story of the everyday challenges of life and love ... a wise, warm, and wonderful story.'

—*Book'd Out* on *The Model Wife*

'Delivers a gentle satisfaction that makes it a great choice for a lazy Sunday afternoon read.'

—*Books + Publishing* on *Table for Eight*

'A witty, warm and wise story of how embracing the new with an open heart can transform your life.'

—*Herald Sun* on *Table for Eight*

'... a moving, feel-good read ... a warm and uplifting novel of second chances and love old and new in a story of unlikely dining companions thrown together on a glamorous cruise.'

—*Sunday Mail* on *Table for Eight*

'A wonderful story of friendships, heartbreak and second chances that may change your life.'

—*Beauty and Lace* on *Table for Eight*

'Stringer's inviting new novel is sprinkled with moments of self reflection, relationship building, friendships and love.'

—*Mrs B's Book Reviews* on *Table for Eight*

'Tricia has no trouble juggling a large cast and ensuring we get to know and connect with them ... captivated me start to finish; if it wasn't the wishing myself on board for a relaxing and pampered break from reality, it was connecting with the characters and hoping they managed to find what they were looking for. Definitely a book I didn't want to put down!'

—*Beauty and Lace* on *Table for Eight*

'A heart-warming novel that celebrates friendships old and new, reminding us that it's never too late to try again ... If you enjoy stories that explore connections between people and pay tribute to the endurance of love and friendship, you will love Stringer's new novel. *Table For Eight* is a beautiful book ... If you're look-ing for a getaway but don't quite have the time or funds, look no further – this book is your next holiday. Pull up a deck chair and enjoy.'

—*Better Reading* on *Table for Eight*

about the author

Tricia Stringer is a bestselling and multiple award-winning author. Her books include *Keeping up Appearances*, *Birds of a Feather*, *The Family Inheritance*, *The Model Wife*, *Table for Eight*, seven rural romances and a historical saga set in the unforgiving landscape of nineteenth-century Flinders Ranges.

Tricia grew up on a farm in country South Australia and has spent most of her life in rural communities, as owner of a post office and bookshop, as a teacher and librarian, and now as a full-time writer. She lives on the traditional lands of the Narungga people, in the beautiful Copper Coast region, with her husband Daryl, travelling and exploring Australia's diverse communities and landscapes, and sharing her passion for the country and its people through her authentic stories and their vivid characters.

For further information and to sign up for her quarterly newsletter go to triciastringer.com or connect with Tricia on Facebook or Instagram @triciastringerauthor

Also by Tricia Stringer

Table for Eight
The Model Wife
The Family Inheritance
Birds of a Feather
Keeping up Appearances

Queen of the Road
Right as Rain
Riverboat Point
Between the Vines
A Chance of Stormy Weather
Come Rain or Shine
Something in the Wine

The Flinders Ranges Series
Heart of the Country
Dust on the Horizon
Jewel in the North

back *on* track

TRICIA STRINGER

First Published 2023
First Australian Paperback Edition 2023
ISBN 9781867247722

BACK ON TRACK
© 2023 by Tricia Stringer
Australian Copyright 2023
New Zealand Copyright 2023

Published by
HQ Fiction
An imprint of Harlequin Enterprises (Australia) Pty Limited (ABN 47 001 180 918), a subsidiary of HarperCollins Publishers Australia Pty Limited (ABN 36 009 913 517)
Level 19, 201 Elizabeth St
SYDNEY NSW 2000
AUSTRALIA

® and TM (apart from those relating to FSC®) are trademarks of Harlequin Enterprises (Australia) Pty Limited or its corporate affiliates. Trademarks indicated with ® are registered in Australia, New Zealand and in other countries.

A catalogue record for this book is available from the National Library of Australia
www.librariesaustralia.nla.gov.au

Printed and bound in Australia by McPherson's Printing Group

MIX
Paper | Supporting responsible forestry
FSC
www.fsc.org
FSC® C001695

For Joy and Andrew

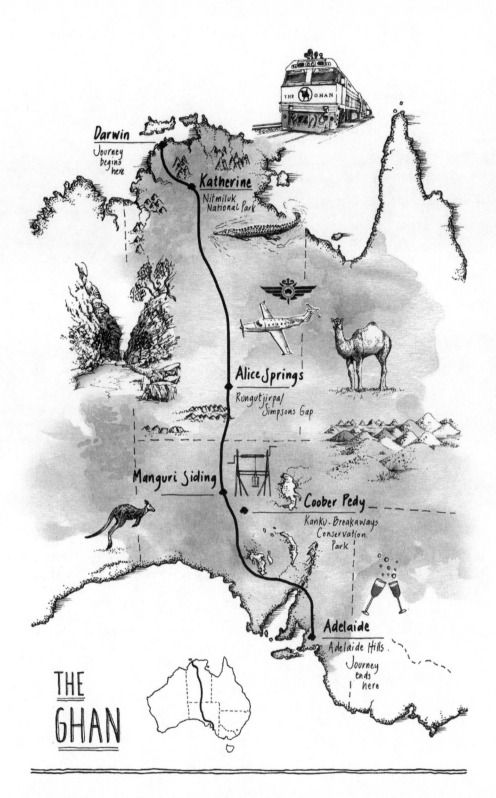

Darwin
Journey
begins
here

Katherine
Nitmiluk
National Park

THE · GHAN

Alice Springs
Rungutjirpa/
Simpsons Gap

Manguri Siding

Coober Pedy
Kanku-
Breakaways
Conservation
Park

Adelaide
Adelaide Hills
Journey
ends
here

THE
GHAN

one

One night in February – Paddington, Sydney

The deep blue of evening slowly descended over Sydney, creating a momentary lull as the day departed and the night took over. In Paddington a small group were gathered for drinks under the pergola at the back of Ketty Clift Couture. Jazz played and, as the light faded, fairy lights winked and blinked to life. They momentarily distracted Ketty from the speech she'd been about to make. She loved fairy lights. There was a certain kind of magic in them that even at seventy-one still filled her with the frisson of anticipation.

She gazed up at the twinkling strands looped beneath the vines covering her courtyard and followed the trail of one string that wound down the verandah post and stopped beside a pot containing a lush green tomato plant. It was covered in small fruit, round and bright red like the baubles on a Christmas tree, that matched the colour of the silk dress she wore.

The gentle clearing of a throat brought her attention back to the women gathered before her. Tien, one of her seamstresses, was looking at her closely. "Are you all right, Miss Clift?"

1

Tien had been seventeen when she'd first started working at Ketty Clift Couture. Now at forty-eight, no matter how many times Ketty insisted she call her by her first name, her employee stuck with the formality.

"Of course."

Ketty ignored the disbelief in her smile and swept her gaze over the group before her, each with a glass of their preferred drink.

Her second-in-command, Judith, stood to one side stiffly holding a glass of wine, and at the other side of the small group stood Lacey, Ketty Clift Couture's young designer and deft jack-of-all-trades. Funny how their drinks reflected their personalities. Judith could be as crisp as the pinot grigio she gripped while underneath dwelled a kind heart. Lacey was as sparkly as the champagne she held but could never be described as frothy.

Between them stood the three women Ketty called her engine room – these were the women who cut and sewed with careful precision. Ketty's three long-serving seamstresses smiled back at her. Ning, who'd been with her from the early days of Ketty Clift Couture, held a glass of icy lemon squash. Tien, who was approaching twenty-eight years of service, held a glass of apple juice, and Birgit, who'd been there nearly half as long, had champagne like Lacey.

Ketty cleared her throat. From the moment she'd made her decision she'd been planning this Friday night get-together; from the drinks and nibbles to the carefully packed brown-paper bags, one for each woman, the raffia handles tied with a ribbon of their favourite colour. She wanted her staff to hear it from her while they were all together and then to give them the weekend to digest her news. She knew it would be a surprise, perhaps even a shock, and now that the time had come to make her announcement she felt a little nervous.

"Thank you, my friends, for your dedication and talent and your service to our business. Last year was one of the most successful in the history of Ketty Clift Couture and it's because of all of you." She lifted her glass, putting off the moment a little longer. "Join me in a toast to you all. To us." She raised her glass higher. "To Ketty Clift Couture."

A chorus of voices joined her. Patch, Ketty's old black-and-white cat, startled from his position on a chair by the door and ran inside. They sipped their drinks and all that could be heard in the brief pause was Norah Jones serenading them with 'Come Away With Me'.

Ketty savoured the easy intimacy of the gathering. They'd worked together a long time and she was concerned that the old saying 'familiarity breeds contempt' had somehow been infiltrating the previously harmonious working environment she'd fostered. She'd noticed some of the cracks prior to Christmas. She'd been sure it was simply that they were all in need of the break over the festive season, but they hadn't been back at work long before it was more than scissors that snipped and needles that stabbed.

Not only had Ketty Clift Couture survived and evolved over the last few tough years, but each of these women had been integral. They'd been right beside her doing their part, but now something was wrong.

"We've worked together a long time." She met Ning's gaze. She'd been with Ketty since the early days, when the building that now housed the business and upstairs apartment had been little more than an empty relic of Paddington's bygone era.

"I have something to tell you that may come as a surprise but I—"

"You're retiring, aren't you." Tien's words cut through Ketty's.

"Oh, no," Birgit wailed. "You're not selling?"

"She is over seventy, you know," Tien sniffed.

Judith frowned, Lacey paled, Ning cried out and then they all started talking at once.

"I'm not retiring or selling." Ketty's words were lost in the kerfuffle. She put down her glass and clapped her hands. "Ladies!"

They fell silent and turned back to her. In the background Norah crooned on.

"This is something else—"

"Are you taking time off?" Birgit's eyes shone with excitement. "I know! You've booked a cruise."

"That's fabulous, Ketty," Judith said. "You didn't ever do anything special for your seventieth."

"You haven't been away in a long time," Tien said. "It's good you're doing another trip before it becomes too hard for you."

Ketty struggled to keep the smile on her face. Once more her speech had been hijacked. And what did Tien mean, 'too hard'! The last four years had been about keeping her business afloat in a constantly changing and difficult world, though she hadn't lied about the past year being their most successful. It didn't mean she hadn't longed to go on another cruise but the fact that it hadn't been possible had been beyond her control.

"That's so wonderful, Miss Ketty." Lacey beamed at her.

It was enough to snap Ketty from the sudden regret that had enveloped her. After all, not taking a cruise for years was hardly something to wallow in self-pity over. Cruising had begun again and while Ketty had kept her eyes firmly averted from the tempting offers, it didn't mean she wouldn't go again one day.

She lifted her shoulders, ready to address the group again. This wasn't going how she'd planned at all.

"That's not what I want to tell you. It's been a difficult few years but we've survived it. You've all helped to ensure Ketty Clift

Couture has survived as well. And I do wish we could all go on a cruise."

Ning shook her head and Tien looked horrified.

"Careful what you wish for." Birgit grinned

"I have a surprise for you," Ketty said. "Lacey, would you please hand out those bags." Ketty indicated the brown-paper bags she'd prepared earlier, packed with an assortment of travel treats, brochures and a mock-up of a ticket.

"What are you up to, Ketty?" Judith's look was wary as she took the bag Lacey handed her.

Once more there were murmurs from the others.

"I've booked us on a train trip," Ketty blurted before they could cut her off again. "On the Ghan from Darwin to Adelaide."

The women lifted their gazes from their bags. Five sets of surprised eyes locked on hers.

"Which I'm paying for, of course," Ketty added quickly. "We depart mid-April."

"Doesn't that take a few days?" Birgit gasped.

"Four days and three nights plus two nights in Darwin before we get on the train."

Judith glanced at the others then back at Ketty. "By 'we' you mean…"

"The whole staff of Ketty Clift Couture."

two

Lacey unlocked her front door and let herself quietly into the house. Once inside she stopped and listened. There was no snoring, so it was unlikely her dad had drunk himself to sleep yet as he often did on a Friday night. She couldn't wait to tell him the news about the train trip. She paused then realised nor was there a radio going, the background noise that, along with the pervasive smell of cigarettes, always announced his presence. For now it was just the usual lingering smell of stale smoke and silence that greeted her, but he might be dozing.

She stepped carefully along the passage. Even though she knew where the worst of the creaking floorboards lurked beneath the stained carpet it was impossible to miss them all.

It was almost dark outside and with the first two bedroom doors shut the windowless passage was gloomy, but she didn't turn on a light. The third room along had been her gran's but her dad had taken it over. It was the biggest of the three, and when Gran had renovated many years ago she'd included an en suite. The

6

door was wide open, revealing an unmade bed, clothes strewn about and cluttered surfaces that included overflowing ashtrays. The stench of cigarette smoke was strongest there. Gran would be dismayed but not surprised.

Lacey pulled the door shut and stepped into the open-plan kitchen–living area at the back of the house. There were only floorboards so there was nothing to muffle the sound of her boots but it didn't matter. It was obvious her dad wasn't in the house and he rarely went out the back. Didn't even bother to go out there to smoke now that Gran was gone.

Lacey opened the fridge and peered in. She hadn't eaten many of Miss Ketty's savouries and now she was hungry. She knew there was little in the fridge but she always lived in hope her dad might have shopped without her. She glanced around but there was no note to say where he'd gone. Probably at the pub with his mate Watto.

She told herself she didn't care. It was better at home without him, but since her gran had died the old house felt so empty and even a drunk dad was better than no company at all. And she wanted to share her news.

She flicked on the light. At least the house was still tidy and even though the fresh air coming through the permanently jammed-open window was hot, it helped dispel the odour of cigarettes in this room.

Lacey's phone vibrated on the table and made the special sound she'd chosen for video calls. Her spirits lifted immediately and she tapped to accept. Her sister's bright smile filled the screen, froze, flickered then steadied.

"Happy week's end, Freya."

"And to you, little sis."

Lacey sat on a kitchen chair, the one that didn't wobble, and leaned in. "How was work?"

"Great as usual. I'm so lucky to work with these people. They're amazing. One day you'll have to come and meet them all."

"One day I will." Lacey wished she could afford to visit Freya in New Zealand sooner.

"I can see you're in the kitchen," Freya said. "You on your own then?"

"Yes. Dad's out."

"Is he contributing to the bills yet or still spending his money on booze, fags and pokies?"

"I had a chat with him like you said. He's giving me money for groceries now and some extra towards bills." Lacey said it with a smile.

"How much?"

"Enough." It wasn't much and it was intermittent but Lacey didn't want to spoil her conversation with her sister by dwelling on their dad's shortcomings. Freya never saw any good in him no matter what he did. "He got a mate to fix the roof for us so it's not leaking any more. Only cost us the materials and a carton of beer."

"Bloody hell, Lace! He should be contributing far more than that. The house needs maintenance and—" Freya's head wobbled back and forth on the screen before it froze again, the problems with the house and her tirade against their father silenced for a moment, then she was back, her lips curved up in a gentle smile. "Dear Gran, it was good of her to leave me the money. You got the short straw with a house that's falling down around your ears."

"It's not that bad."

"You should sell it. A developer would buy it and you could get yourself something better."

Lacey sighed. They'd had this conversation before. Her run-down house would fetch a decent amount if she sold it; she had to weigh that against the pluses which were convenience to work, she was only a thirty-minute bus ride away, she had a small back-yard and the house was roomy – she and her dad had plenty of space for the two of them.

"The house might be a bit run-down but—"

"A bit!" Freya scoffed.

"I've got something else to tell—"

Freya's excited yelp cut her off. "Someone's at the door. Friday night pizza at our place tonight. We worked late and we're all starving. Sorry, Lace, but I have to go. I'll ring you tomorrow, okay?"

"Sure."

A blast of noise came from behind Freya and the image on the phone wobbled as she moved away.

"Sorry. They've got the music going already. Must go. Love you."

Lacey's screen went black and in the sudden silence the old house pressed in on her. She glanced around. The ceiling was stained and paint flaked from the walls. Gran always said it had good bones, but the bones were in need of nurturing and that cost money that Lacey didn't have.

Her gaze returned to the table and Miss Ketty's paper bag. She'd been so shocked by the the gift of a holiday she'd not really looked inside. She pulled out the contents. Besides the mock-up of a train ticket, there were brochures about the train journey and some about Darwin, a pretty tin of mints, travel-sized packs of tissues and hand cream, a pen and small notepad, and a fancy bag tag. She looked again at the message on the page. Miss Ketty was the kindest person.

The ticket slipped through her fingers at a thud on the front door. Then she relaxed as she heard keys jingling. It would be her dad. There was another thud, muffled swearing and then some sharp knocks. Lacey hurried up the passage. He was obviously having trouble with his key.

She opened the door and he tumbled in. Lacey put out her hands to stop him from falling. His arms wrapped her in a hug.

"Hello, love."

She let out a breath. He was drunk enough to be happy. It was always a fine line.

He clung to her, his frame scrawny beneath her grip. He was little more than a bundle of bones, smelling of booze and cigarettes.

"Hi, Dad."

He wobbled away from her, studied her through narrowed eyes, then staggered backwards against the wall.

"I thought you'd be out with that fella of yours."

"We both had things on tonight."

"'Bout time you brought him round so I can meet him, don't you reckon?"

"Soon." Lacey's relationship with Dean was still very new. She wasn't ready to bring him home yet. "I had some exciting news at work today."

He patted her cheek gently and grinned. "I've got news too." He lurched around and made his way along the passage, bouncing from one wall to the other like a pinball seeking a slot. "Anything for dinner? I could eat a horse and chase the rider."

"I'll get changed and make you something to eat," she called after him. "Might be just cheese on toast and baked beans tonight."

He waved one hand in the air but didn't look back. "Sounds good, love." The words whistled over his crooked teeth.

Lacey hurried into her bedroom. The stale smell of smoke infiltrated, despite her best efforts to keep it out. She turned on her small oil diffuser and while she changed the gentle floral scent of bergamot wafted through the room. She was glad her dad had come home happy. They could have a relaxing time together, so rare these days. Often he drank just enough to fill him with regret for all the things that had gone wrong with his life – his wife dying, moving from the country, trouble finding work, being beholden to his wife's mother for putting a roof over their heads, and the final barb that had hurt more than all the rest was Lacey being left the house instead of him. It made him a nasty drunk. Tonight she'd take him as he was, way too intoxicated to remember it tomorrow but happy at least, and she could tell him about Miss Ketty's offer.

The smell of a fresh cigarette reached her before she'd made it back to the other end of the house. She stepped into the kitchen, gasped and rushed forward. Her dad was face planted on the table, one arm dangling with a freshly lit cigarette that slipped from his fingers just as she got close. She snatched it up, stubbed it out in the sink and put it in the bin, trying not to think of the money she was tossing away.

She turned back to him. His right cheek was squashed side-on against the tabletop and a strand of hair had fallen across one eye. She reached down and gently tucked it back.

"Oh, Dad," she mumbled then batted angrily at the tears that rolled from her eyes. She was done with crying over him. As Freya often told her, he was an adult responsible for his own actions and a father who should be trying to help his daughter, not make her life difficult.

Lacey thought of the great day she'd had at work, and the icing on the cake had been the exciting news of the train trip. Miss Ketty was always so kind. She was nothing like Lacey's gran in looks or stature but was a cup-half-full type of person, always seeing good in others. Gran had been like that except when it came to Dad. He'd lost one job too many in her opinion and needed to pull his weight.

His deep breaths changed to ragged snores. Lacey gripped him
by the shoulders and gave him a gentle shake. "Come on, Dad.
Let's get you to bed."

Judith went straight upstairs as soon as the taxi dropped her off.
Her shoes clacked loudly on the steps and her front door clunked
shut behind her. After Ketty's announcement and the excitement
that had followed her apartment seemed empty, every sound
amplified and echoing in her tidy kitchen.

The plastic bag of containers rustled crisply as she lifted it to
the bench. Ketty had insisted she take some of the leftover food
with her. Judith placed it in the fridge and as she went to close
the door her hand hovered over a bottle of pinot grigio. Perhaps
Dean would like a nightcap. He was much younger than her and
moved in different circles, and she was only the woman who lived
upstairs, but they were good friends nonetheless. She hadn't seen
him much lately, but his light had been on as she'd approached
the front door of the apartment building. And she was sure Lacey
wouldn't be there. She'd rushed out the door after Ketty's gathering to make it in time for the next bus home.

Judith looked at the stack of containers Ketty had given her.
Dean would appreciate some as well and Judith had far too much
for herself.

She plucked out the bottle along with two of the containers
and made her way downstairs again. Dean wasn't a wine drinker
but he always had beer in his fridge. She wondered what he'd
think about Ketty's train trip.

He took a while to answer her knock, not unusual, but when
he did he had his phone tucked under his chin and pressed to his
ear. The door was propped against the wheel of his chair.

"Yes, Mum, I was at a work dinner so I couldn't talk then."

He rolled his eyes at Judith. She knew when his mum called he'd be tied up for ages.

"Just brought you some food from our after-work get-together," she whispered and held out the bag.

Thanks, he mouthed as he sat it on his on his lap. "I've already told you it was work, Mum." He wheeled back and the door swung shut.

Judith was left outside gripping her bottle of wine. She waited, momentarily stunned, then made for the stairs again, her feet like lead weights.

"Hey, Jude!" Dean sang out, his deep melodious tone keeping perfect pitch. "I thought you'd followed me inside. Was that bottle of wine a decoration or did you fancy a drink?"

She looked back over her shoulder. He was propped against the doorframe, his stick in one hand and his cheeky grin masking the effort he would have made to leave his chair so quickly.

"If you're not busy?"

"You know I'm not. And you saved me from a long call with Mum. She was happy to end the chat knowing you were here to look out for me."

Judith followed him inside. His place was usually messy but tonight it was tidy – one of the better things that had come from his going out with Lacey. His apartment was smaller than Judith's but more open plan, better suited to a wheelchair or manoeuvring on sticks like he was now.

"Find yourself a seat," he called from the kitchen. "I'll bring you a glass."

Judith moved the abandoned wheelchair to one side and sat as Dean returned with a glass for her and a beer for himself. He settled opposite her in his favourite chair.

"Haven't seen you in a while," he said. "What's the goss?"

"You know I never have any gossip."

"You were late home. I saw your taxi pull in. Was it Friday drinks at work?"

"Yes, Ketty asked us all to stay on. We haven't done it in a while." Judith relaxed into the chair. "She had a special reason, as it turned out."

Dean leaned forward. "You do have goss. Come on, spill."

"Ketty's booked a staff holiday, on the Ghan."

"The train? Really?"

Judith nodded.

"How good is that? She's a special woman, that Ketty."

"She is." Judith took another sip of her wine. Telling Dean and seeing his excitement made her feel a bit more comfortable about Ketty's train idea. Judith hadn't been keen to begin with but it was growing on her.

"Will Lacey be going too?"

"We're all invited."

Dean blew out a long, slow whistle. "That's so cool. Lacey will love it."

Judith sat back as he told her all about the previous weekend, when he and Lacey had caught the train to Woy Woy and had lunch at the pub. Lacey and Judith never indulged in idle chatter at work so it was only from Dean that Judith heard the details of their blossoming relationship. Tonight he was full of excitement – not that he divulged anything too personal but he was obviously happy.

Judith lifted her glass. It was empty. Like her life, really. Dean was family to her even if he didn't know that. She hoped Lacey wasn't going to let him down.

He stopped talking and drained his beer, then waved a hand at her glass. "Another?"

"I'd best be off." Judith rose from the couch.

"Good to see you and thanks to you and Ketty for the food." He followed her to the door. "Good night."

His door clunked shut behind her, the sudden silence weighty. She strode forward and up the stairs to her apartment, her steps clacking loudly again.

Once inside she closed the door, leaned back against it and shut her eyes. Her body felt heavy, the combination of too much wine, fatigue and something else she couldn't quite put her finger on, an unrest that stirred in the pit of her stomach.

She pushed away from the door and dragged herself into her little kitchen, replacing the wine in the fridge. The cupboards were old but they gleamed under her care. The curtains at the window were only new. She'd made them last year. Ketty's gift of a violet in a pot from last Christmas was a bright splash of purple on the well-worn bench.

Judith refolded the dish cloth that sat on the sink. Not a thing was out of place. She flicked on the kettle to make a cup of tea, then stared into the cup as she slowly jigged the bag up and down. The people she counted on were moving in different directions, leaving her behind. After the exciting evening at Ketty's then drinks with Dean, her home felt hollow and she with it.

three

Day One – Darwin Berrimah Terminal

Ketty paused on the edge of the shade thrown by the terminus verandah. People surged around her. She stepped to one side and slipped on her sunglasses. In front of her a single sign stood atop a pole on the platform. *Darwin* was printed on it in large letters and in small print above, *The Ghan*. Beyond the sign, the famous train itself stretched out like a giant serpent basking in the sun pounding down from a cloudless blue sky.

Finally they were there. Ketty sent a silent thank you to her travel agent. The woman was worth her weight in gold. Somehow out of all the chaos of the last month she had cobbled together their bookings and constantly changing plans and pulled off a holiday for Ketty and her five staff. She should be excited but a combination of lack of sleep, concerns about whether she'd done the right thing – Judith had questioned her sanity after she'd announced the trip – and the undercurrent that still simmered beneath the surface at work had kept her spirits in check.

Added to the mix would be the presence of her old friend Carlos. They'd first met many years earlier on a cruise, Ketty as a passenger and he a head waiter. They'd kept in touch and had been on the same cruise ship several times over the years, with Carlos working his way up to maitre d'. Their last cruise together had been aboard their beloved *Diamond Duchess*. He'd retired just before the cruise industry had been decimated by the pandemic, but then between that and his parents needing him he'd been unable to get to Australia as he'd intended. At last things had fallen into place for him. Over the previous Christmas and into the new year he'd spent some time with Ketty and some with his cousin in Brisbane, but then his mother had died and he'd had to go back to Spain. He'd planned to return to Australia mid-year, but when Ketty had told him about the train trip he'd brought forward his plans and had booked a cabin with them on the Ghan.

Then his poor father had died just two weeks before he was due to fly out to Australia. Carlos had deferred his travel plans once more, but his sister had found out and insisted he not put his life on hold any longer. There was nothing more but paperwork to be done in Spain so he'd agreed. But then the airline had changed his flights and he'd only landed in Darwin that morning. Ketty had received a text from him as she'd been going to breakfast at the hotel to say he had indeed arrived, albeit without his case which he was trying to track down and he'd meet her on board.

She looked again at the train that was to be their home for the next three days and nights; the red of its large locomotives a brilliant contrast to the sleek silver carriages that continued down the track, around a slight bend and beyond her sight. Although they weren't in the same carriage, Carlos had been told their cabins were close and that they could dine together.

"Ketty!" Birgit's call shrilled along the platform, making heads turn.

Ketty glanced around. Her ladies were standing in a mismatched group near the front of the engine. They'd arrived in Darwin two nights earlier, and even though they had enjoyed their brief visit, there was still a subtle tension that hadn't completely gone. Ketty had hoped being on holiday would act like some kind of magical fix-it elixir but so far that hadn't happened and she had work to do.

Birgit was beckoning wildly at her and the others were all waving for her to join them.

Ketty had only taken a few steps in their direction when Tien hurried forward and reached for her case.

"Let me take that for you, Miss Clift."

"It's small and on wheels."

"But your arm..."

"Is well and truly healed now." Ketty glanced at her wrist where there was still a faint difference in skin colour since the plaster had been removed a few weeks earlier. No matter her protest, Tien wrestled the handle from her grip and they joined the others.

"We're having a group photo." Birgit's Irish brogue deepened. "I've lined up this fine Irishman to take it for us."

Ketty glanced across at the young man holding up a phone, smiling brightly. Even though Birgit had been born in Australia and as yet never set foot in Ireland, she'd learned the accent from her family. Only in her early thirties, Birgit was a fine seamstress, completing garments with the high standard Ketty expected but recently there'd been a few mistakes. Birgit had accepted responsibility and made them right but extra expensive fabric had to be sourced in one case and had cost them a customer in another.

"Come on, everyone," Birgit called. "Get organised. Let's give Rory our best look."

Tien, who was beside Ketty, tutted under her breath.

"Sunglasses off," Birgit commanded.

There were several groans. Ketty squinted in Rory's direction. He snapped a few shots, suggested they put their sunglasses back on, took some more then and passed the phone back to Birgit.

"Oh, Tien," she said. "You had your mask on. Please take it off for a photo."

Tien complied and Birgit handed Rory her phone again. He snapped more photos and handed back the phone, the sun reflecting from the glass of the screen and the ring on the finger of his outstretched hand.

Ketty adjusted her sunglasses. Even with them on she felt as if she was squinting in the intense light.

"Oh, no!" Birgit waggled her phone in the air. "We forgot to do a funny one. Would you take some more for us, please, Rory?" She was being charmingly cheeky and Tien tutted again.

"Sure." He grinned, and while Birgit had them standing on one leg, pulling faces and waving their arms about, he snapped several more.

Once Birgit was satisfied Ketty suggested they start walking. "Our carriage is towards the end of the train." She quickly took control of her bag or Tien would be trying to wheel it for her. Ketty gave a brief yearning thought to the extra case of clothes and accessories that she'd had to hand over to be stowed in the baggage section, not to be seen again until they reached Adelaide. She hadn't given a thought to the size of the cabin. When she cruised she always took two cases. There was often someone she'd meet who'd enjoy the fun of a Ketty makeover so she tended to take extra, but even though she had her train cabin to herself, they were only allowed one large piece of luggage per person.

Tien called out the carriage letters as they passed. After several carriages and with the rest still stretched out a long way ahead of them, they paused.

A small buggy passed them with two passengers, a man and a woman. They both wore hats and sunglasses, and he was slouched back in his seat but the immaculately dressed woman held herself elegantly poised, a stylish walking stick gripped in one hand.

"How do we get a ride on one of those?" Birgit groaned.

Judith shook her head. "You're young and fit, you don't need a ride."

"I didn't expect it to be so hot." Birgit fanned her face.

"Nor did I," Lacey said.

While Birgit was blonde and Lacey brown haired, both had very fair skin.

"Surely you checked the weather ahead," Judith said. "And you should be wearing hats."

"It's not even…" Birgit looked at her phone. "Not quite nine in the morning."

"Boots are probably not the right footwear for the tropics." Tien looked pointedly at Lacey's Dr Martens boots.

Lacey's flushed cheeks turned deep pink.

"Once we're on board we'll be able to freshen up," Ning said.

"We will." Ketty smiled at her, glad of Ning's positive out-look. "Let's continue." Ketty gripped the handle of her bag a little tighter and set off again so the others would be forced to fol-low. Dotted along the way were clipboard-wielding staff wearing crisp striped shirts and broad-brimmed Akubra hats who smiled encouragingly, assuring them they were getting closer to their carriage.

Ning had been the cause of some last-minute changes and Ketty was glad it had worked out. When Ketty had first told them about the trip back in February and given them the weekend to decide, on the following Monday Ning had been adamant that she wouldn't come. Ketty had been sorry but she couldn't force anyone, and so two double cabins and one single had been booked for the staff of Ketty Clift Couture. Ketty and Judith were to share one double and Lacey and Birgit the other while Tien had opted for the single.

Then a couple of weeks earlier Ning had stayed on after work and broken the news that she planned to retire. Ketty had been taken by surprise. It was the last thing she'd expected, and when Ning had confessed that was the reason she hadn't accepted the offer of the holiday, Ketty had worked hard to get her to change her mind. The ever-patient travel agent had rearranged things yet again, but there'd been no single cabins available, only a double. Ketty was so keen to have Ning with them she'd been prepared to pay the extra, although with airfares, hotel rooms and their Darwin tour, this holiday had well and truly blown her budget.

Once the additional cabin was arranged it had meant a re-shuffle. Judith had insisted Ketty take the double for herself and Ning could share with her. That, along with the uncertainty of the experience ahead and the early morning heat, had created a tightness across Ketty's shoulders and in her temple. She rarely had headaches but she felt as if she was working towards one now. She ran her fingers up the back of her neck, lifting her short bobbed hair away and letting the air cool her damp skin.

"Are we there yet?" Birgit groaned.

"Nearly." Tien was still keeping a close eye on the carriage letters.

Finally they came to a raggedy stop in front of a small set of steps leading up to the open door. A young woman with *Caryn* printed on her name badge checked their paperwork and assured them that they were indeed in the right place.

"Once you're settled I'll be in to explain how everything works and ask for your off-train experience preferences."

Ketty was first up the steps onto the train. Now that they were there she was eager to get aboard. The entrance was tight and steep but she took it with ease. Her bag was passed up and she moved forward along the narrow passage so the others could follow. Behind her Caryn was giving Tien directions to the next carriage on from theirs to find her single cabin.

Ketty passed a small kitchen and moved on around a dogleg corner to discover a corridor stretched out before her. It was nowhere near as spacious as a cruise ship, of course, but the eucalyptus-green carpet, low lighting and venetian blinds at the windows made the polished wood-panelled walls glow. There was definitely a certain ambience. And just as on a cruise ship, every surface gleamed. She closed her eyes, inhaled the lingering trace of eucalyptus scent and anticipated the trip ahead. Her spirits lifted.

On a cruise ship she'd remodel herself, become part of the intrigue of shipboard life and help bring some sparkle to anyone in need. Unlike her cruising days she couldn't take on a new persona – the journey was short and she was travelling with people who knew her well, but that didn't mean she couldn't use some of her magic. The whole purpose of this staff holiday was to refresh and renew. Somehow in the chaos of the last few years they'd all lost their mojos. And Ketty was determined they should get them back.

"Are you all right, Ketty?"

She glanced behind her. At first Judith and then Ning peered around the corner.

"Just taking it all in." She moved on, checking the numbers on the cabin doors as she went. "This one's mine."

She reached for the handle but it wouldn't budge. Ketty frowned. The cabin doors didn't have keys. She tried the handle again then took a quick step back as the door was flung open. A tall man, his thinning grey hair askew, glared at her.

"I'm sorry." Ketty glanced at the number again. "I thought... think this is my cabin."

"You think wrong then, madam." The man's strong accent contorted his words. She couldn't quite pick it, Dutch maybe or Afrikaans? He tapped the number two on the door. "This is my cabin."

"What's happened?" Judith asked.

"Who is that man?" Ning whispered.

"I'm not sure." Ketty took the ticket with her cabin allocation from her bag.

"Hello, everyone." A man approached from the opposite direction. He wore the smart navy trousers and striped shirt under a beige jacket that appeared to be the uniform for the train staff. "Are you finding your cabins all right?"

"I have." The man who was claiming Ketty's cabin huffed. "This woman is confused."

Ketty took offence to that but held her tongue and showed the staff member her ticket. As he perused it she took in the deep crinkles around his eyes and the sprinkle of grey in his neatly clipped moustache and beard. She guessed him to be several years older than the other staff members she'd met so far.

"Ah, I may know what's happened." He smiled at Ketty and then at the man. "Do you have your ticket handy, sir?"

The man huffed again and spun on his heel. The door shut behind him and then just as quickly swung open again. He pushed his paperwork towards the attendant.

"Thank you, Mr Visser." The attendant nodded. Ketty caught a glimpse of his badge. His name was Matt. "Yes, I see there's a small mix-up. It's something that happens from time to time."

"Am I in the right place?" Ketty asked demurely, aware of Mr Visser's angry glare.

"You are not," he snapped.

"I'm sorry, Mr Visser." Matt's tone was calm, his smile fixed. "Miss Clift *is* in the right place. You are in cabin two but in the next carriage."

Mr Visser snatched the paper back from Matt and jabbed at it with his finger. "Carriage P, cabin two." He tapped the number on the door.

"That's right." Matt nodded. "But this is carriage Q. You may have turned left instead of right when you came aboard."

Mr Visser's ruddy complexion went a deeper red.

"Can I help you shift your bags, sir?" Matt asked.

"Nee." Mr Visser shook his head, sounding and acting like a disgruntled horse. He turned away and once more the door shut. There were scuffling sounds beyond then the door was flung open again. This time Mr Visser had a cap covering his unruly hair, a backpack slung over one shoulder, a suitcase in one hand and a shopping bag in the other.

"Do let me help you, Mr Visser, and I'll show you the way." Matt managed to wrestle the case from the man's hand and headed along the corridor.

"Sorry." Mr Visser gave a stiff nod of his head and strode off after Matt.

Ketty paused a moment then stepped inside. The cabin was narrow and most of the space was taken up by the three-seater lounge extending from inner wall to outer, like a traditional train seat. A quick glance showed everything was in its place. Mr Visser had obviously not had time to unpack so he may not have been there long. She took another step as Judith crowded closer, peering anxiously into the cabin.

"They're not very big, are they?" she said.

Ning stuck her head around the doorframe. "Where are the beds?"

"The seat turns into a bunk bed and the top one folds down from above."

"Hope it's not too tricky to do," Birgit called from behind.

"You won't have to worry." Ketty turned back. Judith, Ning, Birgit and Lacey were all jammed in the corridor looking in. "The staff will do that." Ketty spoke confidently. She'd never travelled on a sleeper train before but she assumed that would be the case.

"Everyone all right here?" a voice called from behind.

"We're blocking the way," Lacey said.

They moved off along the passage. Ketty stuck her head out. "Let's meet in the lounge car once we've unpacked. After our steward has been and spoken with us perhaps?"

"I'll message Tien," Birgit said.

Ketty waved a hand in acknowledgement, stepped back into her cabin, closed the door and leaned against it.

"Well," she murmured. "Here we are." She stood for a moment running her eye over every detail; from the bottled water and sunscreen to the many nooks and crannies to stow her belongings. She opened the door to the bathroom, which was an all-in-one toilet and shower with a generous array of toiletries and plump white towels. The space was small but there was a curtain to keep the area beyond the shower dry. She'd experienced similar in motels and her earliest cruise ship travels.

Ketty sat on the couch, put up her feet and ran her hand along the soft fabric. "I think this will do very well."

She wondered if Carlos had arrived yet and what he'd make of the cabins. He'd been the one to set her on the path of taking the train journey. His Christmas gift to her had been a travel voucher. She'd said it had been far too extravagant for a gift but he'd said he had an ulterior motive.

She closed her eyes, recalling his arrival at her apartment two days before Christmas. She'd been pondering her to-do list for her Christmas luncheon but it had been hard to concentrate when her staff were foremost in her mind. The buzz of her downstairs entry intercom had been a welcome distraction.

four

The previous December – Paddington, Sydney

Ketty got up to check the monitor – perhaps it was one of her neighbours popping in for an afternoon drink. She'd be happy to put her feet up and have a chat.

She peered at the small screen of the intercom. It was a wonderful invention that her nephew Greg had installed to save her going down the stairs and across the courtyard to see who was at the gate. A man stood with his back to the camera. He was tall, broad-shouldered with darkish hair. So not one of her neighbours then – Maurice was almost bald and Klaus's thick thatch was snowy white.

She pressed the mic button. "Hello?"

The man turned. He clutched a bunch of flowers in one hand. Ketty frowned. His face was partly covered by a moustache and beard but there was something about the smile.

"Ketty?" he queried.

She blinked at the screen.

"I have got the right place, haven't I?" he said. "Ketty Clift still lives here or maybe she's—"

"Carlos," she croaked.

His smile widened.

She pressed the lock release. "Come in!"

Unable to contain her excitement she hurried down the stairs and met him at the downstairs door. "It really is you." She drew him into a hug then stepped back and held him at arm's length. "It's so good to see you, Carlos. How did you get here? I wasn't expecting you till Christmas Eve."

"My flight was changed. I arrived in Brisbane last night, but of course my cousin wasn't expecting me and he's away up the coast with family so I thought I'd come here a few days early. I should have called first, I know, but my phone died as I arrived in Australia and I've been in airports ever since so couldn't do anything about it. I hope my turning up ahead of schedule won't mess with your plans."

"Not at all. I'm so glad you're here." She hugged him again. "Where's your luggage? Have you got a place to stay?" Ketty peered around him. Carlos had only the small leather bag lying at his feet.

"I left my bag just inside your gate." He waved across the courtyard behind him. "There's a little boutique hotel on Oxford Street. It's not far away."

"I know the one – it's lovely but I thought you'd stay with me."

"Yes, but I'm early."

"Your room's ready. You must stay here. Bring your case upstairs."

"Are you sure?"

"Of course. I couldn't have you in a hotel when I have a room for you here." Ketty faltered. "Unless, of course, you'd rather have your own space."

"I'm looking forward to catching up with you, my dear friend."

He handed her the flowers, went back for his case then followed her up the stairs. "This looks amazing." He glanced around her living area. "You've made a lot of changes since my last visit. I thought perhaps I had the wrong address."

"Good heavens, that was so many years ago." Carlos had visited her once a few years after they'd first met. "I've renovated my living quarters and the shop twice since then." Ketty put the flowers in a vase. "They're beautiful, thank you."

"What am I interrupting?" Carlos glanced at the notepad on the table.

"Nothing important. I was actually feeling a bit weary but seeing you has given me a boost." The warmth of his smile lifted her spirits further. "It's so good to see you, Carlos, and you've grown hair on your face."

He stroked his beard. "One of the benefits of retirement."

Ketty clapped her hands gleefully. "I can't believe you're actually here."

"Three years later than I'd planned, but here I have arrived at last."

Ketty studied him. His thick dark hair was more salt than pepper, but his cheeks were not quite so ruddy and perhaps he'd lost a little weight. "You look well." She waved him to a lounge chair, plucked her cat Patch from his preferred seat and sat down.

"I feel it." Carlos slid the leather crossbody bag over his head and lowered himself to the chair. "You, on the other hand, are looking a bit pale, my dear Ketty."

"I've no make-up on for a start. You're not used to seeing me without it." She patted her face. "It's been a busy end of year and I had our staff party here last night."

"Ha! Don't tell me...you danced on the tables until late."

"Nothing quite so exciting." She reached out and clasped his hand, reassuring herself he really was there. Patch jumped from her lap and stalked away. "I've been looking forward to you coming for so long." She squeezed his hand gently. "I'm sorry your parents haven't been well. How are they doing?"

"Failing in health but good in spirits."

"It must have been hard to leave them."

"They're being well cared for and my sister insisted I come. Between the pandemic and my parents, I couldn't go anywhere for a long time."

"What strange times we've lived through in the five years since we last caught up."

"Your business has survived?"

"Not only survived but grown and become stronger." A small niggle of doubt wormed inside her when she thought of her staff. She rolled her shoulders. "I'm so glad you're here, Carlos. I'm in need of the distraction. Have you eaten lunch?"

"No."

"Then let's go to one of my favourite little eateries. I'm sure they'll find us a table and it's just around the corner."

At the small local cafe Ketty loved she proudly introduced Carlos to the owners, Anna and Felix. They fussed over him like a long-lost friend and insisted he and Ketty have the table by the window. Felix chatted to Carlos about his work as a maître d'. The tiny cafe space filled up and Anna dashed off to serve and finally had to call Felix away to help her.

"They're a nice couple," Carlos said as he sat next to Ketty. "I feel as if they know me."

"I told them you were coming and that we'd visit."

They both chose the linguine that Anna was famous for and settled back with a glass of wine.

"I have something for you, Ketty." Carlos picked up his bag and lifted the flap. "I can't wait till Christmas Day to give you this." He drew out a long envelope and handed it to her.

She eyed him suspiciously. There was a gift for him already wrapped under her tree. "I remember the last gift you gave me. It was for my birthday. That beautiful little sewing case. I use it often and it reminds me of you." She tapped the envelope against her fingers.

"Ah yes, that was the birthday you celebrated on the final journey of the *Diamond Duchess*."

"It seems so long ago." Ketty sighed. "I know you said once you retired you never wanted to cruise again but I miss it, Carlos."

"Open the envelope."

Ketty did as he asked and drew out a piece of paper. She unfolded it. It was a gift voucher from her local travel agent. Ketty's name was on it followed by a large monetary figure. She dropped the sheet of paper and looked up.

"Carlos!"

He held up his hands. "Let me explain. We've talked about travelling together and now that I'm here—"

"Yes, but you're not paying for me. It's too much, Carlos." She eyed him closely.

"What if we shared it?"

Ketty looked at the page. The idea of cruising again was so alluring. "You said you'd never cruise again."

"I know your heart is set on it, and of course you'll go again if you wish, but what about you and I taking a train journey together?"

"Trains don't have quite the same appeal."

He sat back. "What do you love about cruising?"

"The people, the destinations, fine dining and being spoiled." She smiled. "Dressing for dinner…and not having to unpack more than once." Ketty drew in a breath and closed her eyes, picturing herself aboard a cruise ship. "It's an adventure, something special always happens."

"You've just described a train journey."

She opened her eyes. "I'm really not sure if train travel is for me."

"You once told me anything was possible."

"Did I?"

"The last time we were together farewelling the *Diamond Duchess*."

Carlos rummaged in his bag again and this time he pulled out a brochure. He opened it, ran his finger over the text, then paused and began to read. "*Iconic Australian experiences.*"

Ketty took a sip of her wine. "I like to go further afield than Australia."

"Have you seen it all?" He raised an eyebrow. "You're not being a snob about your own country, are you, Ketty?" He glanced back at the brochure and continued to read. "*Capturing the rich tapestry… romance and adventure…we take you there in style.*"

"Where?"

"There are several destinations with fine dining and exclusive off-train adventures."

"And you want me to go with you?"

"Most certainly, if you'd like to." He studied her hopefully. "We could plan it together."

Anna arrived at that moment with their linguini. As she fussed over them, bringing cracked pepper and extra parmesan, Ketty and Carlos took their first mouthfuls and murmured their appreciation.

Anna nodded her approval and moved off to greet some new customers.

"This is delicioso," Carlos said, scooping some of the sauce into his mouth.

"It's Anna's addition of vodka to the creamy tomato sauce that sells it for me."

"It reminds me of Venice." Carlos twirled more linguine onto his fork. "But I'm so happy to be here in Australia with you at last."

"I'm so happy you are too." Ketty smiled and took another mouthful of the delicious food. Life had changed so much in the last few years and she'd rolled with it but even this brief time with Carlos reminded her how much she'd got into the habit of managing rather than living. Perhaps he was right about a train journey. It would be something to look forward to. She imagined a cabin, the gentle rolling motion of a train and the view from the window, a changing vista over land instead of the ocean, dressing up for dinner, elegant cuisine, a new group of people to meet...a little shiver of anticipation ran through her.

"Tell me more."

five

Day One – On board the Ghan

Ketty was startled from her reminiscing by a sharp rap on her door. Surely Caryn wasn't there already – she hadn't even looked at the excursion brochure.

"Miss Clift?"

As Ketty opened the door Tien burst in.

"Oh, Miss Clift." Her eyes were wide with alarm.

Ketty glanced over her shoulder to see if someone was chasing her. "What is it?"

"I can't do it." She wrenched her hands. "I've tried but I can't."

"Sit down and tell me what you can't do."

Tien sat, then immediately jumped up again. "That cabin…it's too small."

Ketty felt her shoulders ease a little. She'd thought perhaps Tien was going to say she couldn't stay on the train.

"And that man who took our photos."

"Photos?"

"At the front of the train." Tien flapped her hands. "He is there with a friend."

"Surely not in your cabin?"

"No, they are further along the carriage but they are men."

"Yes." Ketty nodded.

Tien leaned closer and lowered her voice. "We have to share a bathroom."

Ketty placed a reassuring hand on Tien's. "But not at the same time." She'd forgotten the single cabins weren't en suite and Tien would need to use one of the shared bathrooms at the end of the carriage.

Tien's worry turned to horror. "I can't do it, Miss Clift. I can't."

There was another knock on Ketty's door and this time Judith and Ning were there. They both peered in anxiously.

"We thought we could hear Tien," Judith said. "What's happening?"

"Are you all right?" Dear calm Ning took her hand and Tien who never cried began to.

Next Birgit and Lacey appeared, the brochures they held quickly tossed aside when they saw all the serious faces.

"What's happened?" Birgit asked.

"Tien's cabin isn't suited to her," Ketty said carefully.

"Why?" Lacey bent down and offered Tien a clean tissue.

"Too claustrophobic," Tien said. "When I shut the door it was so confining, so…awful." She shuddered. "And I don't want to share the bathroom with men."

"What's wrong with that?" Birgit's eyes sparkled cheekily.

"You're not in the bathroom at the same time," Ketty explained again.

Tien wiped her eyes and sat stiffly upright. "I do not like it."

Ning sat next to her and put a protective arm around her shoulder.

Ketty quietly said goodbye to the room she'd thought she'd have to herself. "You can share with me."

"That's not fair, Ketty," Judith said. "You've paid for us all to come on this holiday." She looked pointedly at Tien. "Ketty is entitled to her own space."

"I don't mind taking the single cabin," Birgit said. "I live in a sardine can as it is with two cousins."

"But hadn't you moved in with—"

"I'm with my cousins again."

Ketty's head spun. She was sure Birgit had moved in with her boyfriend over the Christmas break. She'd shown them all some of the soft furnishings she'd sewn for his apartment.

"Having a room to myself would be grand." Birgit gave Lacey an apologetic look. "Tien could take my place."

"You're very kind." Tien looked up but leaned against Ning. "I don't know that I can share either. I...I'm so sorry, Miss Clift."

"Tien, you can't back out now," Ning said. "We would all be so disappointed without you. And you were the one who...who convinced me to talk to Ketty and come."

Ketty forgot about Birgit and glanced between the two women huddled together on her couch. Ning had asked Ketty to keep her retirement to herself until after their holiday but perhaps Tien knew about it too.

"You'd be okay sharing with me, wouldn't you, Tien?" Lacey smiled encouragingly. "You'll be able to fill me in on the latest *Amazing Race* episodes. I've missed the last two."

"And Judith and I will be right next door." Ning gave Tien's shoulders a gentle squeeze.

Ketty blew out a breath as Tien agreed, pleased a resolution had been reached. She was grateful to Lacey, who she was sure would be disappointed not to be sharing with Birgit.

"How are you all settling in?" Caryn called out from the corridor. "Are you ready with your off-train selections?"

"No," Birgit said. "We were just trying to decide before all this happened, weren't we, Lacey? And we've made a few room swaps."

"Oh?"

Ketty caught sight of Caryn's hat and, through a gap between Lacey and Birgit, a striped sleeve and a clipboard.

"Perhaps if you'd all go to your assigned cabins and you can tell me what's going on," Caryn said.

Ketty kept out of the way inside her cabin. Birgit was more than excited to take over Tien's single cabin and Caryn was doing her best to be accommodating of all the changes. It took a while to sort everything out, and due to the narrow space they all had to manoeuvre in Ketty thought it best to leave her to get on with her job for the moment. She sat back on the couch she'd only managed to sit on for five minutes and her phone rang.

She glanced at it reluctantly but then accepted the call quickly when she saw the name on the screen.

"Carlos! Are you on your way?"

"No."

"Why not?" Ketty glanced at her watch. It was almost nine thirty and the train left at ten.

"There's been a bit of a mix-up." Carlos paused, the usual assurance lacking from his voice.

"What's happened?"

"It seems my ticket wasn't postponed and then reinstated but cancelled instead."

"Oh no, Carlos. Surely there's been a mistake."

"There has, and unfortunately not in my favour. I have been on the phone ever since my name didn't appear on the hotel-to-train transfer list. But it seems there's nothing to be done. My cabin has been rebooked and the train is at capacity." He continued on, telling her about the whole difficult situation.

Ketty flopped her head back against the seat, only partly listening. She'd hijacked his idea of the train journey and made it a staff holiday then been delighted when he'd said he'd be able to join them and now that he definitely couldn't come the wind went from her sails. Or should it be she felt derailed. Somewhere nearby she heard Caryn's voice.

Ketty glanced at her bag, still not unpacked, and up at the bunk folded away overhead. The idea came to her with such force that she stood up suddenly and spun with light-headedness. She grabbed the table for support. Heat did that to her sometimes when she moved quickly.

"Carlos!" She cut him off just as he said the travel agent was putting him up in a fancy hotel as an apology.

"I can spend a few days here and meet you in Adelaide," he said.

"Nonsense. This whole journey was your idea. You're coming on this train." Ketty glanced at her watch. There were thirty minutes until departure.

"I told you, Ketty, I—"

"Can you get a taxi to bring you here immediately?"

"I suppose but—"

"Please, Carlos. Get your things – at least you don't have to worry about your case – check out of that hotel and come to the train. I've had an idea."

Judith sat back on the couch and stared out the window. She looked past the railway tracks and red dirt to the green of the vegetation beyond the railyard and wondered again how she'd given in to this. She'd been wary of Ketty's notion of a train trip from the start but as it had drawn closer she'd warmed to the idea. It was hard to ignore Ketty's joy at taking her staff on holiday, Birgit's open excitement and even Tien's regular updates on the places they would visit, but now that she was there and had seen the size of the space she was sharing with Ning, Judith was a little uneasy. She hadn't shared an apartment let alone a room with anyone since she'd left her failure of a marriage all those years ago. It wouldn't have been so bad if she was with Ketty.

Still, of all the other staff members she was pleased it was Ning she'd be with. They'd known each other the longest, being the first staff Ketty had employed in the early days of her business. While their personal lives were poles apart, they were of a similar age and, besides herself, Ning was the neatest person Judith knew.

They'd both unpacked, found a space for their items and stowed their cases, and the cabin was tidy. The only thing that might get annoying was the amount of time Ning spent on her phone. It pinged with a message every five minutes. At least it was quiet now. She'd gone off to help Tien shift her things. Judith thought it best to keep out of the way for a while and make the most of some time to herself.

Of course she'd have opted to share with Ketty but it seemed only right the person paying for this holiday should be the one to have a bit more space. And Judith had thought perhaps Ketty might like to entertain in her room like she'd said she had sometimes on her cruise holidays. Judith glanced around the small cabin. There was really only room for two, three would be a squeeze, but she and Ketty could enjoy a cup of tea together, a pre-dinner drink or even a nightcap and settle in for a chat. Judith was looking forward to that. She wanted Ketty's opinion on a pressing matter.

Ketty called from outside the door then there was a tap.

Judith stood. "Come in."

Ketty's head appeared around the door, her flushed cheeks a pretty pink contrast to her grey hair. "You'll never guess what's happened." She entered the small space. "Carlos's cabin has been double-booked."

Judith swallowed the small surge of excitement that whooshed inside her. Having Carlos along on this trip had been one of the things she hadn't been happy about. She knew he was Ketty's friend and she trusted Ketty's judgement on most things but there was something about the man she didn't like, with his smooth manners, ever-ready smile and that accent. She knew some women found a European accent attractive but he seemed too perfect to her – *smarmy* was how she'd describe him, and she didn't like the way he'd ingratiated himself into Ketty's life. Ketty was a push-over when it came to Carlos. Judith simply didn't trust him.

"That's a shame," she said and hoped she'd layered it with the right amount of disappointment.

"I couldn't bear him to miss out. The train trip idea started with him and he's travelled all this way after such a sad time. It will mean more swapping around but I'm going to see if Birgit would mind moving back, perhaps Tien could move in here with Ning and you could move in with me…if you didn't mind."

Judith took a moment to process Ketty's suggestion. It seemed they'd still be stuck with Carlos but at least she'd be sharing with Ketty.

"Of course not, if it's okay with everyone else."

"Thank you, Judith." Ketty gave her a brief hug. "I'll go and talk to Birgit now." And she was gone. Judith closed the door again. She looked at her case stowed up above the bathroom and sat down, a small kernel of warmth unfolding inside her. Carlos might still be on board but Judith would be Ketty's roommate and there'd be plenty of time for cosy chats – something rare since Carlos had first arrived to visit.

Ketty had seen several men in the time Judith had known her but none had held her as enthralled as Carlos seemed to, rendering her blind to the parts of his character that Judith questioned.

Voices sounded outside in the corridor and a door closed further away. Judith looked around the cabin and didn't know if the squirming in her stomach was due to excitement or trepidation. She'd never been outside New South Wales, let alone taken any kind of journey like this. She didn't know whether to be grateful to or annoyed at Carlos for sowing the seed of this train holiday. At least she would be sharing with Ketty. She lifted down her case and began to repack.

Her thoughts drifted to the first time she'd met the man who seemed to have woven some kind of magical spell over her friend. It had been two days before Christmas. Judith knew Ketty was creating a special luncheon and had refused any help. With nothing to do at her own place, Judith had decided to simply turn up and offer her services.

six

The previous December – Paddington, Sydney

Judith was hot and sweaty by the time she reached the side gate that gave private access to Ketty's living space above the shop. The afternoon was much warmer than she'd thought. The walk across the park from Randwick had tested her, but then on the final trek from Oxford Street down the winding narrow roads cluttered with vehicles, the humid air had pressed in on her.

Mail poked out from the letterbox. Judith tucked it under her arm and pressed the doorbell.

"Judith, what a lovely surprise. Come up." Ketty's voice crackled from the intercom and the gate clicked unlocked.

Ella Fitzgerald's perfect cadence singing 'How High the Moon' drifted down from the upper floor as Judith reached the stairs. She paused on the bottom step at the louder sound of a deep male voice followed by Ketty's laughter. Judith remained stationary. Ketty already had visitors by the sound of it, and they were in fine form. Judith hadn't heard that happy, carefree lift in Ketty's voice for a while. Often at the end of the week they'd

42

retire up to Ketty's living room or go out onto the balcony and share a bottle of wine. They'd relax and review the week, but the last few years had changed Ketty. The weight of the challenges that had come, first keeping the business afloat, and then keeping up with it once it expanded, and a pandemic, all had taken a toll on her.

Judith strode up the stairs and paused again as Ketty, reclining in her favourite armchair, raised the glass she held in her hand. "My dear friend Carlos arrived yesterday. We've been as busy as fleas and we've decided to put our feet up and have a drink a bit early. Carlos, this is Judith."

A tall, broad-shouldered man unfolded himself from the chair beside Ketty. He smiled. "Hello, Judith. I've heard so much about you. I understand Ketty wouldn't survive without you."

He kissed her on both cheeks.

"Oh, I don't know about that…" She fanned her face, suddenly feeling warm in the cool of the air-conditioned apartment.

"You look hot." Ketty sat forward. "Did you walk over? You need a drink."

"It's a bit early…" It was barely three o'clock.

"It's nearly Christmas," Ketty cajoled.

"Let me get you something." Carlos sauntered to the kitchen where the benches were stacked with signs that they had indeed been busy preparing for Ketty's upcoming Christmas luncheon.

"There's a jug of water in the fridge and plenty of wine. Judith prefers pinot grigio," Ketty called after him and waved a hand at the glasses on the coffee table containing something red. "Unless you'd like to try this?"

Judith shook her head. "I didn't think you liked red wine."

Ketty chuckled. "I do when Carlos makes it. It's chilled and has soda with a dash of lemon juice. Tinto de Verano, or we call it poor man's sangria. It's our favourite cruise drink, isn't it, Carlos?" She screwed up her nose. "Or was."

"Luckily you don't have to cruise to drink it." Carlos, who'd moved easily around Ketty's kitchen as if he belonged there, returned with a glass of water and another of white wine for Judith, both refreshingly chilled.

She drained the water glass then remembered the letters she'd slid into her handbag on the way up.

"There was mail in your box." Judith handed the three envelopes to Ketty.

"How lovely. I do enjoy Christmas cards."

Judith settled on the couch trying not to stare at Carlos, who she'd heard so much about. She was sure Ketty hadn't been expecting him yet. The spare bedroom door hung ajar behind him and she could see an open case and a jacket on a hanger.

"When did you arrive?" she asked.

"Yesterday. My flight was changed."

"And I insisted he stay here rather than a hotel." Ketty smiled at him. "Mind you, he's earned his keep helping me prepare for Christmas lunch. He's dusted the courtyard and got down those cobwebs and added some festoon lights. Not that we'll need them for lunch but they look festive."

Judith swallowed a mouthful of wine.

Ketty slipped on her glasses and began opening the cards, reading out names that meant nothing to Judith, nor to Carlos, she presumed. There were already several Christmas cards decorating Ketty's dresser. There were none at Judith's house. She didn't send any so she didn't expect to receive them.

"This one's not a card, it's an invitation," Ketty called excitedly as she opened the last one. "Oh, how wonderful! It's a wedding celebration invitation from Celia and Jim. I met them on a cruise and we've kept in touch." She looked up. "Do you remember them, Carlos? They were at my table on the last cruise of the *Diamond Duchess*. Both single – he was a widower, she a divorcee."

"It would be hard to forget the incident reports."

Ketty gave him a querying look.

"If I remember rightly, she was the woman who rolled down the stairs and landed spreadeagled outside my dining room and he was the man who was unaccounted for and a missing persons procedure was activated."

Ketty laughed. "Goodness, I was thinking more about how wonderful it was that they met and became such good friends on the cruise." She glanced at Judith. "They've been inseparable ever since and planned to marry, but like so many weddings these last few years it was delayed. They ended up having a simple cere-mony last year and now they're planning to celebrate with a wider group of family and friends at a winery in the Adelaide Hills." Ketty hunched her shoulders and grinned. "I do love a wedding."

"You're incorrigible, Ketty." Carlos sat back in his chair, smil-ing benignly.

Judith studied him over the rim of her wine glass. He was a good-looking man and his accent added to his allure. She could see why Ketty might be charmed by him but Judith was always wary of smooth-talking men with accents. Her rat of an ex-husband had lacked the accent but he'd been a smooth talker. And she had to admit to being a little surprised that Carlos was staying with Ketty.

"How long will you be in Australia, Carlos?" she asked.

"My visa is for twelve months."

"That's a long time."

"I want to see more of your wonderful country. My cousin encouraged me to apply for a year. It will be good to spend time with him and his family, and of course I'm hoping Ketty will show me a few sights."

"I will." Ketty beamed. "And your cousin has plans to take you around too, doesn't he?"

"Yes, but I don't want to outstay my welcome there or here."

"My spare room is yours any time you like and we can do lots of short trips. I'm sure I can take the odd long weekend away."

Judith felt a prickle of jealousy. It sounded like Carlos might take up quite a bit of Ketty's time. Patch wandered out from the spare room and jumped to Carlos's lap.

"He's probably been on your bed again, the old devil," Ketty said.

Carlos stroked the cat's head. "I don't mind."

Patch blinked at Judith, leaned against Carlos and began to purr. Even the cat was taken with Ketty's visitor.

"You'll never guess what Carlos and I are planning."

Judith shook her head.

"A train trip!" Ketty raised her glass. "To travelling again."

Carlos raised his. "Salud."

Judith followed suit. She pulled her lips up in what she hoped was a smile. Travelling was not something she'd ever aspired to. She'd always been too busy earning enough to meet the day to day. A small part of her was envious of their obvious delight in their plans. She had money squirrelled away these days but it was in case of emergency. Travel wasn't an emergency.

There was a brochure on the table. Judith picked it up. On the front, a train stretched across a desert landscape. She studied it and sipped her wine. "I thought you were keen to cruise again."

"I am, but Carlos has reminded me there's still so much of my own country I haven't seen, and of course neither has he. And a train trip would be a more relaxing way to do it."

The look that passed between Ketty and Carlos was intimate, as if they held a secret Judith wasn't privy to. The wine soured in her mouth.

"You certainly deserve a holiday. You haven't taken one in a long time."

"We shall see," Ketty said. "We're only talking about it at this stage, aren't we, Carlos?"

seven

Day One – On board the Ghan

Judith pressed her fingers to her ribs, rubbing to dispel the strange niggle that pulsed there. That had been the beginning of Carlos worming his way into Ketty's life. He'd spent Christmas with her and New Year with his cousin in Queensland, and then he'd returned to Paddington. He'd been there most of January, then had taken a trip to Perth with his cousin and had arrived back just after Ketty had broken her wrist in early February. Judith had been there to help Ketty but had once again been sidelined by Carlos's arrival. Then his mother had died and he'd returned to Spain, but Ketty hadn't returned to her senses. She'd announced this train trip and been caught up in all the plans ever since, barely keeping her usual finger on the pulse of Ketty Clift Couture.

There was a tap on the cabin door then Caryn poked her head around. "How are you going with your off-train experience choices?"

Judith leaped up. "I'm sorry. It's been so busy I'd forgotten. Do you mind giving me a few minutes? I'd like to consult with my colleagues next door."

"No problem. I was going in there next but I'll call back once I've seen the people at the other end of the carriage."

Judith followed her into the corridor but stopped at the cabin beside hers. The door was ajar and Tien was saying something about the small bathroom.

Judith opened the door further. "How are you getting on in here?"

Ning and Lacey were sitting at either end of the couch. Tien's almost-empty bag was on the seat between them and Tien herself was just closing the bathroom door.

"Everything all right?" Judith asked.

"There's no place to put the last of my things." Tien waved her hand at her case. "I'll just have to get the case down if I need them."

"Judith, Lacey and I have done the same," Ning reassured her.

"They're things we might not need anyway," Lacey said.

Tien closed her bag and with Judith's help put it in the over-head space. Judith didn't have the heart to tell them arrangements were going to change again. She'd leave that to Ketty.

"Caryn wants to know what off-train experiences we'd like." She tapped the booklet she'd brought in with her.

"Oh, we'd forgotten about that," Lacey said and looked around. "Where did I put that brochure?"

"I left mine in my cabin," Ning said.

"I don't know where mine is." Tien flapped her hands.

"Found it." Lacey's head bobbed up from under the little table, the booklet in her hand.

"We can share two between us," Judith said. "Can we squeeze onto the couch together?"

"There's only a choice of two gorge tours," Ning said, looking over Judith's shoulder.

"Unless you pay extra for the helicopter?" Judith tapped the page.

They all shook their heads at that idea.

"The first tour says less walking and there's rock art to look at," Judith said.

"There are crocodiles and snakes in Katherine Gorge," Tien yelped. "I've googled it."

"I'm sure the guides will keep a watch," Lacey said.

"Crocodiles are huge and aggressive."

"We'll be in boats," Judith reassured her.

"They can swim." Tien vaulted up, causing Judith and Lacey on either side of her to topple inwards. "I'm going to check with that train steward before I commit to anything," she said, and before any of them could stop her she shot out of the cabin, closing the door firmly behind her.

"For goodness sake," Judith muttered.

"She's a bit anxious still," Lacey said.

Judith stared at the door a moment then straightened herself against the back of the seat. "I think the rock art tour for me."

Ning stood up. "Perhaps I'd better go and see Tien's not bothering that nice young staff member too much."

"But we have to decide—"

Ning's phone began to ring.

"Can't you turn that off!" Judith snapped.

Ning's eyes widened but she didn't speak. She pressed the jangling phone to her chest and let herself out the door.

Judith shook her head. Beside her on the couch she sensed Lacey pressing away from her. She stood and paced the small floor space. "It's like herding cats."

"Everyone's a bit uncertain," Lacey said. "I'm sure they'll settle once we're on our way."

Judith bristled. "What would you know?" Advice from Lacey was the last thing she needed.

Lacey hesitated then spoke softly. "I know that Tien has never been outside the city," she said. "And even though she grew up in Australia she feels anxious about the outback."

"None of us have been in the outback," Judith snapped. "But we're on a paid tour. I don't expect we're going to be attacked by wild animals."

"We make jokes about crocodiles, snakes, spiders and all those scary things but Tien takes it all very seriously."

"Luckily she has you to keep an eye on her then." Judith took a step towards the door.

"And please don't be tough on Ning. She didn't want to come on this trip. Her sons were against it."

"Phht! She's a grown woman, a widow. She doesn't have to answer to anyone." Judith was a divorcee but since Ning's husband had died she'd felt they had a little more in common.

"That's not quite true. She has sons and they're very close. I'm not sure exactly why they're messaging but if she needs to keep in touch then we shouldn't hassle her about it."

Judith flinched. There was no-one for her to keep in touch with. She spun back. "That's enough, Miss Carslake. I will not be lectured by the likes of you on how to manage staff."

To Judith's surprise Lacey's eyes gleamed and she sprung to her feet. "The likes of me! What exactly does that mean, Mrs Pettigrew?"

"You haven't worked long enough to understand the ins and outs," Judith blustered.

"I've been with Miss Ketty for seven years."

"And you think that makes you an expert on staff iss—?"

The door flung open behind her and Tien hurried in.

"I can't find the steward."

Judith sidestepped around her. "You don't need to," she snapped. "The tour people wouldn't be taking us anywhere that put us in danger of being attacked by a crocodile. It wouldn't look good on the news."

The door opened again and this time it caught Judith's elbow. "Oww!" She gripped it as tingles shot down her arm.

"Sorry." Ning edged into the cabin.

"It's so squashy." Tien slid onto the seat.

"Have you decided about the tours?" Ning asked.

Judith pressed her elbow to her side, and glanced at Lacey's shocked expression then Tien's worried face before turning back to Ning.

"Caryn will be back soon. Make sure you've made up your minds." She spun on her heel and narrowly missed Tien then winced as her elbow brushed the doorframe. Without another word she marched back to her cabin and began to fling things into her case.

Ketty finally found Caryn exiting a cabin at the other end of the carriage. She strode forward to meet her, catching a glimpse of a Louis Vuitton case on the seat and a walking stick lying beside it before the door closed. Ketty explained the situation. Caryn was very empathetic but didn't have the authority to grant

Ketty's request. She suggested they check with her supervisor. Ketty wondered if that was Matt. There'd been an air of authority about him.

Caryn led the way to the lounge car. The door to cabin two in the next carriage was closed as Ketty passed. She hoped Mr Visser had resettled without incident.

They moved on along the corridor, through another gangway and into the lounge. Caryn's supervisor wasn't Matt but a woman. She was behind a workstation frowning over some paperwork but she looked up and smiled as they approached. She was several years older than Caryn with the calm reassurance that comes from experience. Her name was Jade, and once more Ketty explained the need to get Carlos aboard. She added in his recent bereavements. His mother dying only a few months before his father, the cancelled booking that hadn't been Carlos's fault, his desperate dash across the world to arrive in Darwin in the early hours only to find he had no bunk. She may have stretched the truth a little – Ketty wasn't Carlos's only friend in Australia, and he had the cousin in Brisbane – but by the time she'd got to the part where there was a spare berth among her party, Jade was ready to go all out to help. She said she'd need to talk with the train manager but she was sure something could be arranged.

Leaving it in Jade's hands, Ketty set off back down the train again to find Birgit, hoping she'd agree to the plan. There was no way Ketty was allowing Carlos to be left behind. She classed him as a dear friend. He'd come all this way, he'd given her a significant amount of money towards the trip and it had been his idea, even if he would be the odd one out.

They'd met when she'd been on her first cruise aboard the *Diamond Duchess*. Carlos had been a head waiter. He was both charming and mischievous and Ketty had taken to him immediately. The cruise line he'd worked for had been her favourite and so their paths had crossed several times after that.

Of course, staff were not meant to fraternise with passengers but the two of them had managed many a discreet catch-up, usually over a late-night drink when he'd finished work or on a rare day off. He'd met up with her once, many years ago when he'd visited Sydney, but their relationship had remained platonic. Not that she hadn't been tempted, but they were good friends and living different lives.

On several occasions while cruising he'd aided and abetted her in her endeavours to add a little magic to someone else's life. Now here she was, about to embark on a train journey she had never experienced with a group of women she needed to support. The timeline was short, only three nights, and Ketty needed all the help she could to make sure she got her staff back on track.

Ketty heard Birgit before she saw her. She followed the curving corridor of the single-cabin carriage. Unlike the straight corridor in her carriage, it swept slightly left and right, back and forth like a meandering river and finally revealed Birgit chatting animatedly with Rory, of taking-photo fame, and another similarly smart-looking young man.

"Ketty, this is Rory and his cousin, Rhys. I'm calling them 'the double Rs'." Birgit lathered the Rs with her Irish accent. The younger woman had never lived in Ireland, never even visited, but she'd been raised by Irish parents and a swag of Irish aunties and uncles and often sounded more Irish than the Irish.

"Hello, Ketty," Rhys said while Rory hugged her close. Too close for Ketty's liking.

"Birgit said you're over seventy!" Rory beamed at her as he stepped back. The look on his face was as if he was beholding some amazing treasure. "You look so good for your age."

There was a beat before Ketty spoke in which she noted Birgit's guilt-stricken look. "So do you," Ketty replied.

Rory's eyes widened and then he laughed. "And you're funny too." He winked at Birgit. "We'll meet you in the lounge car later."

The two men squeezed past, heading in that direction.

Birgit pressed her fingers to her mouth. "I'm so sorry, Ketty, I didn't expect—"

"No need for you to apologise." Ketty glanced over her shoulder. "Is this your cabin?"

"Yes, come in and see," Birgit gushed, obviously happy to change the subject. "It's perfect."

She opened the wooden door with a flourish to reveal a snug cabin. Ketty could see why Tien's fear of small spaces may have been engaged once she was inside and had shut her door.

"The seat's so comfy." Birgit urged Ketty to try it and then sat opposite on the ottoman. "There's enough room for two, and lots of little storage cupboards. And look at this." She pointed to more cupboards with a basin and a mirror. "I can wash my face, do my teeth in here. And look at all the room for luggage." Birgit indicated the space above, where she'd already stowed her bag and backpack.

"This has worked out really, really well. Lacey helped me bring my stuff down and met Rory and Rhys here. They're keen to do some of the sightseeing with us. I hope you don't mind." Birgit lowered her voice and leaned in. "I'm sorry about Rory's comment earlier but there don't seem to be too many our age so far. There's a man in the end room past the fellas who looks about a hundred."

Ketty raised her eyebrows.

Once more Birgit baulked and flapped her hands. "You know what I mean."

Ketty dismissed the ill-chosen remarks with a wave of her hand. "I want you to enjoy yourselves." She'd been going to ask Birgit to give up her cabin for Carlos but she didn't have the heart to any more. Her thoughts whirred with other possible cabin combinations, spinning as fast as a roulette wheel. When she'd come to find Birgit, she'd imagined Carlos could have the single, Judith could move in with her, Tien and Ning would be together and Birgit could be with Lacey again.

"Lacey and I will still do some things with you and the others, of course."

"It's worked out well," Ketty said, her mind already on the next spin of the roulette wheel. "I'll see you in the lounge car once we're underway."

Back in her cabin Ketty took her phone from her bag. She selected Carlos's number.

"Are you here yet?" she asked as soon as he answered.

"About five minutes away."

Ketty gave him the name of the person he needed to speak to at the terminus and the carriage number. "It's quite a walk. Almost to the end of the train. I think most people are aboard now. Jade, the supervisor, said she'd ask the staff to watch out for you." Ketty paused, cleared her throat. "And we're going with plan B rather than plan A."

"What's plan B?"

"You'll be sharing a cabin with me."

eight

Day One – Travelling South

Judith was outside Ketty's cabin. The door was slightly ajar then suddenly flew open.

"Oh, Judith, I was just coming to find you," Ketty said.

"I've packed my things. I thought I'd better see if you were here before I moved in." Judith was still bristling from her aggravation with the other three women. She was looking forward to sharing with Ketty, hopeful there'd be time for the pleasant camaraderie they'd enjoyed in the past.

Ketty took her arm and drew her inside. Judith winced.

"Sorry. Are you hurt?"

"It's nothing." Judith tucked her bruised elbow to her side. "I bumped it earlier. What was it you wanted?"

"I'm sorry to be a nuisance but plans have changed again."

Judith frowned as Ketty sat and patted the seat beside her.

"Birgit's staying in the single cabin," Ketty said while Judith lowered herself to the seat.

"She didn't refuse to move, surely?" What was it about this train that seemed to have switched the staff into Jekyll-and-Hyde characters?

Ketty shook her head. "She was so excited about her new accommodation I didn't have the heart to ask her."

"But—"

"Carlos will share my cabin."

"But I've…surely that's not…" Judith's cheeks heated.

"Good heavens, look at you getting all prim and proper on me. I had a hard enough time convincing Carlos."

"And rightly so."

"We're sharing a cabin, Judith, not a bed. And even if we were, I don't think that's anyone's business but our own. Anyway, look at the size of these bunks." Ketty's lips twitched and she tapped a finger to her cheek. "Maybe once upon a time but I think Carlos and I are both past single-bed hopping now."

Judith's cheeks burned harder. She pressed her fingers against her skin to cool them. It wasn't as if she was a starry-eyed child with no idea of the ways of the world. And Carlos had stayed with Ketty in her apartment for part of the summer, but she couldn't come to terms with them sharing this tiny cabin.

"How will you change? Or use the bathroom?"

Ketty waved a hand in the air. "I'll just strip off when I feel like it and then of course we can shower together to save time."

Judith's eyes bulged.

Ketty burst into laughter. "Look at you," she said when she drew breath. "You've seen the size of the bathroom. It's only meant for one at a time. Jade said there's an extra toilet down the corridor as well as the shared single-cabin bathrooms and a small kitchen for tea and coffee. We'll have a bit of extra space to use and, as for the rest, Carlos and I are old friends. We can work out an arrangement for dressing et cetera." Ketty's eyes sparkled, the smile on her face stripping years from her age. "The train trip was Carlos's idea and he's had such a sad time losing his parents. I don't want him to miss out."

"Are you sure there's no other way to find him a berth?"

"I haven't asked if there's a space in the baggage compartment." Ketty's smile dropped away. "I'm not leaving him behind, Judith. The train staff are okay with it. I know it will be a surprise for some of the others but you're my good friend – I thought you'd be supportive."

Judith pictured the bag she'd just repacked thinking it would be she who was moving in with Ketty. Instead she was to be discarded for Carlos again. She swallowed the bitterness that rose in her throat.

"Of course I support you. Just as long as you're sure."

"I am."

There was a tap on the door. Caryn stuck her head in. "I really need to get your decision about your tours now, Miss Clift."

"I'm sorry." Ketty glanced around. "With all this running around I haven't had a chance to look."

"Ketty?"

The three of them turned. Carlos was standing in the corridor. Judith was pleased to see he looked harried at least. He'd caused no amount of bother for everyone else.

"Thank goodness, Carlos. You made it." Ketty looked as if she was about to launch herself into his arms.

Judith stepped between them. "Hello, Carlos. I'll get out of the way so you can get settled." She edged past him and Caryn then grimaced as her sore elbow caught the doorframe. "I'll see you in the lounge car in a while."

Her last words were ignored as Ketty and Carlos both began talking at once, with the ever-patient Caryn hovering. Judith returned to her cabin. She cradled her sore arm to her side, used her other hand to put her case on the seat and began to unpack once more.

Lacey looked down at the screen of her phone. Of course the balance in her bank account hadn't changed since the last time she'd checked just before they'd left the hotel. Thirty-two dollars and forty-five cents was all she had until next payday, almost a week away. Her dad had promised that he'd transfer some money during their last chat but he hadn't come good on that promise.

She sagged back against the couch. Miss Ketty had been most generous covering the cost of flights, hotel accommodation and the train trip itself. She'd assured Lacey there'd be no need for money once they were on the train but she couldn't help the worry that constantly swirled in the pit of her stomach and gripped her chest in its prickly grasp.

Yesterday while they'd been on their Darwin tour, they'd had coffee from a lovely little shop in Parap and later lunch at a cafe in the botanic gardens, and at several of the stops the others had bought souvenirs. Besides the food, her only purchase had been some bargain clothing items from the op shop. And then at the end of the day they'd gone to Cullen Bay and had bought pizza to share as they sat on the lawn to watch the sunset.

The spectacular changing colours of the sky had been magnificent but Lacey hadn't been able to lose herself in the wonder of it like the others had. Not even the excitement of the locals at the clouds of dragonflies signalling the start of the dry could distract her for long. Nor could she eat much pizza. All she could think about was the hole in her meagre finances that her share of the pizza had made. She worried now that these off-train excursions she'd had to commit to would involve more unforeseen expenses. She was a long way from home and her lack of funds frightened her more here.

And she was still smarting from her run-in with Judith. The other woman had often been censorial but these last few weeks she'd got to the point of rudeness on several occasions. If it wasn't that she adored Miss Ketty, loved her job and needed the income, Lacey would seriously think about looking for another position but she knew it wouldn't be easy to find another such perfect opportunity.

Lacey really didn't know why Judith Pettigrew had grown to dislike her so much but the feeling had become mutual. When Lacey had first started working at Ketty Clift Couture she'd been grateful for the opportunity and in awe of everyone. Miss Ketty had taken her on for a trial period and Lacey had fallen in love with the place at once and had done everything she could to make herself essential. While everyone else had been friendly and welcoming, Judith had been aloof and a little starchy. Lacey hadn't been bothered by it then. She'd put her head down and worked hard.

Eventually Miss Ketty had confirmed the job was hers and not long after that Lacey had got up the courage to ask her about updating their online presence. Miss Ketty hadn't been so interested in that side of the business back then but she'd listened and given Lacey the opportunity to work with her IT friend to build a new website for Ketty Clift Couture.

Then there'd been Lacey's suggestions to declutter the shop interior and to design and sew a ready-made holiday range from some surplus fabric. It had taken off and was selling quite well, until the lockdowns of the pandemic when Lacey had pivoted the range to high-end leisure wear. If women couldn't go out they still wanted quality and comfort in their 'at home' clothing. Miss Ketty had been delighted, singing Lacey's praises. It hadn't been long after that the first of Judith's barbed comments had upset her.

Lacey and Judith had been in the confined space of the staff kitchen, and Lacey had accidentally trodden on the older woman's foot. Judith had unleashed.

"You and your clodhopper boots," she'd snapped. "It's not just the business you're stomping all over but you have to squash my toes as well."

Lacey had been shocked. Judith's words had been pure venom. Lacey had apologised but Judith hadn't been finished with her.

"You're putting too much pressure on this business. Miss Clift is being generous. You have made some improvements, the online shop for one, but it's important the business keeps its valuable reputation. Miss Clift shows some indulgence for your crazes but she's getting to an age where she'll have to retire and she'll need reliability and steady financial figures to make a good sale. She's my dear friend and I won't let you ruin her reputation for fine couture garments with all your fanciful ideas. Next you'll have us making pyjamas."

"What's going on in here?" Ning had come in, a questioning look on her kind face.

"Just business talk." Judith had drawn herself up and coasted from the room.

Lacey had ducked her head and hurried to the bathroom where she'd had to fight back tears. The last thing she'd wanted was to hurt Miss Ketty's business. Not all of Lacey's ideas had been a continued success but it was hardly her fault that a pandemic had all but destroyed sales of their ready-made holiday apparel. Surely her employer wouldn't indulge her ideas on a whim as Judith had suggested. Judith must know more about the business finances though. She was Miss Ketty's personal assistant and right hand. After that Lacey had doubled her efforts to toe the line, keep to herself, be obliging and smiling and Judith had gone on as if nothing had been said. But lately—

"There you are."

The phone slid from Lacey's hand as Tien stuck her head around the cabin door, bringing her back to the present.

"We're going to the lounge car now." Tien paused and studied Lacey as she retrieved her phone. "Are you feeling okay?"

"Yes." Lacey's voice squeaked. She cleared her throat. "I'm fine."

"You look a bit pale. You're not feeling sick, are you?"

"No."

It wasn't only large, scurrying or slithery creatures that frightened Tien but those she couldn't see too. She was a fastidious clean freak. Since the pandemic she'd continued to wipe every surface, question every tiny cough and always wear a mask in public places. She'd brought a box of masks with her and they were wedged behind the rail of the small recessed cupboard opposite. Lacey was surprised she hadn't put one back on since their photo.

She drew in a breath and smiled, not wanting to give Tien more to worry about now that Caryn had calmed her. After Judith had left them open-mouthed in her wake, the friendly steward had come back to get their tour bookings. Caryn had been very sensible and reassuring when Tien had voiced her fears about crocodiles and snakes. Once they'd all made their selections Ning had convinced Tien to take a walk with her down to Birgit's cabin.

"Is Birgit settled in?" Lacey asked when they returned.

"Yes. She likes that little cabin. She said to tell you she was going to the lounge car."

Lacey stood. "Let's go then."

Tien stepped away and then back quickly, almost bumping into Lacey. She took a mask from the box and put it on, then led the way along the corridor towards the lounge car. She stopped suddenly and again they almost collided.

Tien put her hands out to the walls on either side. "We're moving," she gasped.

She was right. The floor below their feet vibrated gently. Lacey bent to peer through the blinds in time to see the train station slowly slip past.

"We are. You can hardly feel it."

Voices sounded behind them as more passengers left their cabins.

"We have to keep going," Lacey urged.

Tien continued to use the wall as support, making progress slow. The train picked up speed and they began to sway a little with the movement. At the end of the corridor they turned left into the dog-legged space that led to the gangway which joined the next carriage and once more Tien stopped. The door to the gangway was shut.

"Open it," Lacey said.

"Are you sure?" Tien glanced back, her face full of worry. "Maybe we're not meant to go this way."

Lacey put a hand on Tien's arm. "There's no other way to get to the lounge and dining cars. They probably shut the doors once the train's moving." People were filling the space behind them. Lacey reached around her and opened the door. Tien squealed as warm air rushed in and the noise of the train clacking along the tracks rumbled around them.

"Is everything okay?" a man asked from behind them.

"Fine, yes," Lacey said. "My friend's a bit of a nervous travel-ler." She glanced back at the man. His round face, full of concern, was almost hairless but for his eyebrows and moustache.

"Let me help." He squeezed past Lacey and slid an arm under Tien's elbow. "My name's Warren and this is my fourth train jour-ney in as many years. What's your name?"

"Tien."

He leaned down, his body dwarfing Tien's. "Say again."

"Tien." Her voice was almost lost in the noise of the train, which was moving much faster now.

"Ten!" Warren said. "That's a fine name. Now, there's noth-ing to be worried about, Ten. I know it sounds noisy but it's quite safe."

Before Lacey could blink Warren had propelled Tien forward across the gap of the gangway that wheezed and shook like a giant accordion, and flicked open the opposite door. Lacey was one step behind them, holding the door for the woman behind her to catch. They continued on into and along the next carriage. Like a giant centipede they rippled forward, with Warren as the large head leading the way, Tien tucked firmly behind him, and then Lacey followed by a string of other passengers, their arms and legs wiggling with the motion of the train.

They arrived in the lounge car where several people had settled in ahead of them. Birgit was already seated with the two guys she'd befriended. Lacey admired her bravado. She'd made friends so quickly.

"Here we are, safe and sound." Warren released his grip on Tien's arm.

"Thank you." Tien's eyes crinkled in a quick smile.

"Tien! Lacey! Over here." Birgit waved a glass in the air. It looked like it may have contained champagne but there was little left in it.

"Your friend's got the right idea." Warren grinned, his big face as round as the moon. "Get a drink under your belt and you'll be right."

"Warren, let these young ones be." The woman who'd been right behind Lacey when they'd entered the carriage was tugging on his arm.

"Just helping them out, pet." He smiled again at Tien. "This is my wife, Val. We love our train travel."

Val tugged on his arm again. He waved cheerily as his wife led him towards the bar.

Birgit slid along and Tien and Lacey squeezed onto the lounge seat beside her. The two men sat on tub chairs pulled to the other side of the table.

"The boyos and I were having a drop to get us started," Birgit said, then leaned closer and lowered her voice. "Everything's free, can you believe it? Unless you want something fancy but their champagne's a good one."

"Another?" Rory reached for her glass.

"Why not?" Birgit drained the dregs and handed it over.

"What can I get you?" He looked at Lacey and Tien.

Tien sat up stiffly. "Nothing for me, thank you."

Lacey had never known her to drink alcohol. "I'm fine too for the moment."

"You'll like the champagne, Lacey," Birgit said.

"It's not even eleven o'clock yet." Tien's tone was disapproving.

"We're on holiday." Birgit nudged Lacey. "Live a little."

Lacey avoided Tien's glare. "Okay, thank you."

Rory headed to the bar and Birgit asked Rhys what his excursion picks were.

Tien leaned in towards Lacey. "Don't let her influence you," she muttered. "She's far too free and easy, that one. You don't want to do anything you'll regret."

Lacey wasn't sure she'd regret one glass of champagne before lunch but Tien's words dulled the brightness of the occasion. Rory had just returned with their drinks when Ning and Judith teetered into the carriage. Everyone walked with a slightly staggered gait to combat the sway of the floor beneath them. Ning collapsed to a couch opposite while Judith raised her eyebrows at the drinks in their hands.

"They've got a great selection of white wines," Birgit said.

"It's a little early for me." Judith sniffed and lowered herself beside Ning, who edged away. Tien tutted under her breath.

Birgit was oblivious to the tension and asked everyone about their excursion choice for after lunch when they reached Katherine. It seemed they were all going on one of the Nitmiluk Gorge tours.

"It will be very beautiful there," Ning said.

"And we're safe from crocodiles," Tien said enthusiastically.

Rory grinned. "Good to know."

"We're hoping to do the helicopter flight," Rhys said. "We're just waiting to hear from Jade if there's a place for us."

"That sounds amazing," Lacey said.

"It's a lot of money." Judith folded her arms and sat back scowling as Rory and Rhys, whose backs were slightly turned to her, talked animatedly about their choice of tour.

Lacey took a sip of her champagne. The bubbles hit the back of her throat and exploded in a fruity tingle. She sipped again.

It wasn't fair of Judith to snap at Tien who was naturally cautious. Lacey understood how the cabin changes, the newness of the train journey and Tien's fear of scary animals might make her anxious. Lacey had her own permanent worry over money gnawing away at her, and the heated exchange with Judith back in the cabin had left her with a niggle that flared to anxiety when they were together. Lacey took a bigger swig from her glass. She'd been dubious about Warren's advice but now she thought the champagne was just what she needed.

"Are you okay, Lacey?" Birgit's hand waved in front of her face. Rory and Rhys had vacated their seats and Judith and Ning were moving to take their place. "I thought the champagne must really have gone to your head. We lost you there for a moment."

"Sorry." Lacey looked at the almost-empty glass in her hand. "I was thinking about something else."

"I need your attention." Judith glanced around the table and rested her gaze on Lacey. "All of you."

Lacey swallowed the last of her drink. What was Judith going to speak her mind about now?

"There's been a slight change to our holiday plans and I want you to be prepared," Judith said.

"What is it?" Tien wailed.

Lacey glanced around and her heart sped up. Miss Ketty wasn't in the lounge carriage yet.

"Don't panic, Tien. It's just that our generous employer has taken a guest into her cabin."

Lacey blew out a breath. She'd been worried something bad had happened to Miss Ketty.

"A guest?" Ning frowned. "But all the staff are here."

"The guest is not a member of staff." Judith leaned in closer. "You may remember Ketty's friend..." her nose wrinkled, "Carlos was also booked on this trip."

"I thought he went back to Spain," Birgit said.

"His poor dear parents died." Ning nodded sadly.

"Yes, well, he's cut his mourning period short and rebooked."

"Ketty will be pleased." Birgit grinned.

"Not exactly. Unfortunately there was a mix-up with his cabin and it wasn't rebooked as he...well, as he'd thought." Judith glanced at each of them in turn. "The only way he could be on this train journey was to take a berth in Ketty's cabin."

Lacey bit her lip so that she didn't gasp like Tien and Ning. There was a surprised pause and then Birgit laughed. "Go, Ketty," she said. "She's the oldest of all of us and already has a man sharing her room."

"You shouldn't speak about Miss Clift in that way," Tien hissed.

"It's just a bit of fun," Birgit said. "Ketty's a woman of the world."

"And your employer." Judith spoke as if there was a full stop after each word.

She glared across the table and Lacey didn't know whether to be relieved not to be the recipient of that dagger look for a change or to feel sorry for Birgit, who was trying hard to inject some fun into the moment. Something Miss Ketty would encourage, she was sure. Lacey glanced to the door but there was still no sign of her.

Judith's glare unlocked from Birgit and slowly moved from woman to woman. "You all know how wonderfully generous Ketty is." She spread her hands wide. "Here we are on this special holiday. She didn't want her friend Carlos to miss out. They are simply good friends sharing a cabin, just like we are. I'm telling you now so that you don't get a shock later."

Lacey thought the way Judith had made her announcement was providing the shock value rather than the situation itself. She wondered if Miss Ketty knew this was being discussed.

"But how will she…" Tien frowned. "How will he change?"

"Oh, for goodness sake." Birgit flung herself back against the seat.

"Being brazen with men might be something you accept," Tien said, "but—"

"What do you mean 'being brazen with men'?" Birgit's nostrils flared. "What are you insinuating?"

"You're flirting with those men," Tien huffed. "Don't you have a boyfriend at home?"

"My personal life is none of your business." Birgit folded her arms tightly across her chest.

"Ladies, please." Judith gave a soft clap of her hands.

The two women scowled at each other.

Lacey had to admit she'd wondered the same thing about Birgit, who'd been so excited to move in with her boyfriend earlier in the year. Now that she thought about it, Lacey hadn't heard Birgit mention him for a few weeks. At that moment the door opened and Miss Ketty entered, followed by Carlos.

"They're here," Lacey murmured.

"Right. Now remember what I said, ladies." Once more Judith's dagger look swept the group. Lacey's eye was drawn to the other passengers who were also looking towards the door. Even though their entrance had been low-key, Miss Ketty and Carlos made a striking couple. She was dressed in a stylish out-fit from Ketty Clift Couture's old travel range, a three-quarter sleeved cotton-linen top in a light shade of red that was a striking contrast to her grey hair. Beneath the shirt she wore wide-legged pants in a taupe-grey linen and on her feet flat espadrilles with jute rope trim. At her side, Carlos wore a two-tone blue striped polo shirt, neutral chinos were rolled up to reveal his ankles and on his feet were tan slip-on shoes.

Lacey waved to catch their attention. Miss Ketty had an anxious look, unusual for her – perhaps she was worried about what they'd all think of her cabin arrangements. Lacey pulled a wide smile, and as Miss Ketty made her way along the carriage she smiled back.

nine

Day One – Travelling South

"Here we go," Ketty whispered through clenched teeth and was reassured by the warmth of Carlos's hand against her back as they moved forward.

"They don't look too scary," he murmured back as they came to a stop beside the group.

"I'm sorry I've been so long," Ketty said, then gripped the back of a lounge chair as the train swayed. "It gets a wobble up every now and then, doesn't it? I haven't got my train legs yet."

Tien leaped from her seat. "You must sit down."

Ketty shook her head and waved her back. "You stay there. We'll find a seat in a minute. You all remember my friend Carlos who visited over Christmas?"

There were a few muttered responses, which Ketty found odd, then Birgit shot out her hand. "Of course we do. Welcome aboard, Carlos."

They shook hands and Carlos acknowledged the others with a brief inclination of his head. "Hello, everyone."

"We hear you nearly missed out on the trip," Birgit said. "Glad Ketty had a spare bunk."

Ketty glanced at Judith. Her lips were pursed in that look she got when she was trying not to speak but judging by the range of expressions from startled to shocked, it was too late. She'd obviously already filled in the others. Beside her, Ketty sensed Carlos's unease. He hadn't been keen on her plan to share. He'd never been prudish but today she'd had to do a lot of talking to stop him from leaving the train once he'd seen the cabin they were sharing. Thankfully the train had departed the station and she'd talked him round.

The women around the table glanced from Ketty to Carlos but no-one spoke.

Ketty had turned seventy-one a few months prior and yet she felt as if she'd just been chided by her father for being disrespectful, as if she were a little girl again caught poking her tongue out behind her mother's back. A knot of defiance formed within her. She was not about to be judged by her employees.

"Have you been taking in the scenery?" she asked and stooped a little to look out a window.

"Yes," Lacey said brightly. "It keeps changing so much."

Judging by the empty glasses Lacey and Birgit had enjoyed the free champagne but there was no sign the other three had partaken.

"After the morning we've had I think we're due a welcome-aboard drink." Ketty looked to Carlos.

"Good idea," he said. "Champagne?"

"I can recommend it." Birgit tapped her empty glass.

Ketty glanced around the group. "Can we get anyone else one?"

Before they could answer Jade called for everyone's attention and Carlos and Ketty found vacant seats a little further away along the opposite wall of the carriage.

Jade explained the seating arrangements for lunch. Ketty was dismayed to realise there were only tables of four.

"But there are seven of us," she murmured to Carlos.

"Trains are configured differently to cruise ships, dear Ketty. Perhaps we can be a table for three and a table for four opposite each other."

"Oh, that's a good idea. Should we ask Jade?"

"She looks a little under pressure at the moment. She's asked us to wait to be called."

Indeed Jade had, but immediately she stopped speaking several people had approached her clamouring for attention. Ketty was surprised to see Judith was one of them.

"Why don't we go with the flow for lunch?" Carlos said. "And then see what can be done for dinner."

"The words of experience." Ketty grinned. "Oh, Carlos, don't you miss those first nights of a cruise? It was always such a buzz to arrive and be met by you, to have a waiter guide me through a fine dining room with those immaculately set tables, the white tablecloths, the sparkling glassware and the gleaming silver cutlery. The discreet table decorations, the glamour and attention to detail." Ketty squeezed her eyes shut and imagined herself there.

"Ha!"

Ketty opened her eyes. Carlos was shaking his head.

"I miss the enchanting ambience," she leaned closer, "and meeting new people."

They were interrupted by Jade calling Birgit and Lacey's names.

"Looks like some members of your team are doing just that."

Ketty glanced over in time to see Rory and Rhys, the double Rs as Birgit called them, filing along with her and Lacey towards the dining car.

Judith made her way to Ketty.

"Takes a bit of getting used to walking with the train in motion, doesn't it?" Carlos said as Judith reached out and grabbed the back of the seat.

"I assume we'll acclimatise," she said primly then focused on Ketty. "Since the tables aren't bigger than groups of four and you have Carlos for company, the steward said she'd seat Ning, Tien and I together for lunch."

"Yes, of course," Ketty said, feeling a little as if she'd been picked last for the team. "That makes perfect sense. I'm going to ask her later if she can work us a bit closer together for this evening perhaps."

Judith nodded then turned back as her name was called along with Ning's and Tien's.

"See you in there," she said and moved off with the other two women. Ketty watched them go.

"You look worried," Carlos said.

"I am worried. They're so much more to me than staff and they each seem bothered by something. I'd hoped we'd get to spend enough time together on this holiday for me to figure it out."

"Perhaps they're just jittery or excited. This journey's a new experience."

"They've been like it on and off for months. Since before Christmas. Up until last December I thought of Ketty Clift Couture as a well-oiled machine, with dedicated, happy customers and staff. Recently I've lost a couple of long-time customers and there's something not right with my staff…an undercurrent I can't explain." Ketty stared in the direction they'd all gone for lunch.

"You can't do anything about it right at this minute. How about I get us that drink?" Carlos suggested.

"Thank you, yes. Definitely champagne for me, please."

He rose and made his way to the bar. It was strange and yet oddly comforting to have someone to share her concerns with. Ketty's original ideas about how this holiday would go were being tossed aside layer by layer. First Ning not wanting to come and then agreeing to at the last minute, the many changes to the cabin arrangements, Tien being so edgy, Lacey acting like a deer in the headlights, Birgit acting the opposite, Carlos nearly missing out altogether, Judith being on the verge of rudeness at times. And now they couldn't eat together around the one table. That's where Ketty found out so much about people, as they wined and dined. She'd wanted to be able to have that with her staff, hoping the holiday and the food and wine would loosen their tongues. Of course, all her plans had been based on her cruising experience and so far train travel was very different, despite Carlos's assurances.

She wondered if she was expecting too much. Perhaps she should have kept this train experience to just her and Carlos, another of his Australian adventures they could have chalked up together.

The two of them had been more apart than together over the years but when they did meet up it was as if the time and the distance had been nothing. She'd loved having him to stay the previous Christmas and into January, and then again on his brief return in February. He'd fitted in to her life easily, making friends with her friends, and she'd enjoyed taking him to parts of Paddington and greater Sydney that were favourites of hers, seeing them all afresh through his eyes. It made her smile to recall their trip to the fish market.

ten

The previous December – Paddington, Sydney

On the morning of Christmas Eve, Ketty and Carlos were on the footpath outside her gate waiting for her neighbour Maurice to arrive with his car. They were heading to the fish market.

Maurice and his wife, Lee, had called over for drinks the previous night and Maurice and Carlos had hit it off straight away. It was during the evening that Ketty's visit to the market had come up. She'd been annoyed at Maurice at first, suggesting it was too much for her to be getting the bus to the market – she didn't have a car, had never needed one. His comments often challenged her independence but he'd gone on and reminded her how it was one of the busiest days of the year and he loved to drive his car so it was a win-win. Now as they stood in the shade waiting, Ketty realised Maurice had been right. The temperature was already uncomfortably warm and it would be easier to bring her purchases home in the car.

Lee's little blue Suzuki slipped from the lane at the back of Ketty's and pulled up in front of them, Maurice's large frame crouched over the steering wheel.

Ketty opened the back door. "Good morning. I'll sit back here so Carlos can have the front seat."

"I'd rather be taking my car but we wouldn't all fit," Maurice grumbled.

"I must admit I was hoping to see your red Jaguar coupé," Carlos said.

"I'll take you for a spin another time, Carlos."

"I look forward to it."

Ketty settled into the back seat as Maurice whisked them away. He loved his Jaguar as much as his wife – more, Lee often quipped. He drove it nearly every day. He'd retired from his role as chief financial officer of a strata management business about six months prior and he hadn't found being at home all day easy. Neither had Lee, from what Ketty gathered.

"Ketty tells me you've done a lot of travel, Carlos," Maurice said.

"Working on cruise ships has taken me many places. And I've also toured on my own."

"Any hints for more unusual destinations? Lee and I have travelled extensively but we want to find something a bit more off the beaten track with more rustic accommodation."

Ketty wondered about that. Only the other day Lee had grimaced at a picture of a glamping tent in one of Ketty's magazines. "They might call it four star," she'd said, "but I want solid walls, a proper roof and easy access to all facilities when we travel next."

Carlos started talking about a trip he'd taken to South America.

While they chatted Ketty thought about the items on her list. Yesterday had been spent making the desserts and nibbles, cleaning and decorating; today she was purchasing the seafood that would be the entree and mains for her Christmas lunch. They'd start with oysters and then individual terrines of smoked salmon with avocado salsa and prawns, and the main would be baked fish. She was hoping for ocean trout, which she'd serve with beans, peas and mint.

"Traffic's not too bad today," Maurice said.

"No tunnels?" Carlos asked.

"Not along this route."

"I like being at ground level," Carlos said. "You get a better look around."

They stopped for a red light on the Hyde Park corner of Elizabeth Street.

"We'll have to come back here for a wander another day, Carlos," Ketty said.

"To Hyde Park?" Maurice scoffed.

"It's a pretty space and St Mary's Cathedral is just over there. Carlos has a thing for gothic architecture."

"How did you remember that?" He twisted to look back at her.

"Years ago in Noumea on your day off, remember? I went with you to look at the various examples of architecture."

"I do remember."

The light changed. Ketty glanced up at the glass skyscraper on the corner as they passed on into the city. Too modern for her. She shuddered to think how many people worked in such a huge office tower. She leaned forward. "I think I tried to interest you in the colonial-style buildings."

Carlos chuckled. "You did."

"You two have known each other a long time," Maurice said.

"Since our twenties." Ketty patted Carlos's shoulder gently. "So long ago."

"Are you taken, Carlos? Ketty could do with a man in her life."

Maurice was of the opinion a woman needed a man to take care of her. He'd tried to set her up more than once with one of his work colleagues. Ketty tried not to take offence but today it irritated her.

"Carlos and I are good friends. That's the best kind of man. No strings." She pressed her lips together as she realised how prim that sounded. Maurice brought out the worst in her sometimes.

"I find Ketty is nearly always right in her assessment of relationships," Carlos said.

"Very diplomatic." Maurice laughed then beeped the horn at a taxi who cut him off as he approached the motorway that would take them to the markets. "Wouldn't happen if I was in the Jaguar. Hope you're staying a while, Carlos. I'll take you for a ride along the coast. Nothing better than travelling with the canopy down and the wind in your face."

"I look forward to it."

Maurice began suggesting places he could take Carlos. Ketty settled back in her seat. She could rely on Carlos's assessment of situations too. They'd known each other since their twenties and even though they hadn't spent long periods together over that time, they understood each other.

The idea of a train trip together had grown on her. They'd put a hold on discussing the specifics when Christmas lunch preparations began in earnest but she hoped the two of them would be able to spend a day or two together after that and before they went to their respective families for New Year. She was motivated by the thought of holidaying with Carlos. He'd always been working when she was cruising so it was never a break for him. Any real time spent together had been on his brief days off. And Carlos was right about the train. It would take them to parts of Australia she'd never visited either.

Her phone pinged with a message. Lacey's name appeared on the screen and Ketty smiled as she read. When she'd realised Lacey was to be alone for Christmas lunch she'd invited her to her place and the text was an acceptance.

"An extra for our Christmas lunch," she said as she put her phone away. "My receptionist, design assistant and IT guru, Lacey."

"Splendid." Maurice slapped the steering wheel. "She'll be a bright foil to po-faced Judith. Is that young chap of hers coming again? The one in the wheelchair."

"Dean is Judith's neighbour and he will be joining us, yes."

"I don't know if you're aware, Carlos, but Ketty likes to gather lame ducks." Maurice glanced at her in the rear-view mirror. "What's the bet Lacey will be wearing all black with those army boots she favours?"

"They're Dr Martens."

"She's such a pretty young thing and she hides under layers of black."

"Judith and I wear black. It's the standard for my front-of-house staff."

"But you and Judith are old fogies."

Ketty's temper rose.

Maurice jagged a thumb in Carlos's direction. "You don't seem like one though, Carlos."

"One?"

"Lame duck."

"Oh?" Carlos didn't understand the idiom.

His English was so good Ketty forgot sometimes it wasn't his first language.

"Someone who's a bit inept...a hopeless case." Maurice drummed his fingers on the steering wheel. "Ketty has a few she gathers. There's Klaus from over the road as well. Lives alone. No family left in Australia. Moved here to be close to his daughter and she up and died. He's a bit of a sad, grumpy old thing. Likes to hang onto his German heritage."

Ketty cringed at Maurice's description of Klaus. "He's only just turned sixty and prefers his own company since his daughter died. He has a sharp mind and makes interesting conversation. He carves wood and builds clocks, loves music and theatre and walks every day."

"And when it comes to social interaction Ketty fits him in," Maurice said.

"I see." Carlos studied Maurice a moment before turning his gaze to the window.

Ketty's lips twitched in a quiet smile to herself. She enjoyed a variety of company. Maurice might call them lame ducks but he was oblivious to the fact he was including himself in that. He was bombastic and outspoken and she could only take him in small doses. Now that he'd retired it was his long-suffering wife, Lee, she felt sorry for. Ketty accepted the odd ride because it got him out of Lee's way for a while.

"And here we are." Maurice manoeuvred the car close to the entrance gate. "I'll have a coffee with my friend down the road. Text me when you're ready to go."

"Thank you, Maurice." Carlos was out of the car and opening Ketty's door before she'd finished collecting her bags.

They waved him off.

"Interesting man," Carlos said. "Do you think he's including me as one of your lame...?"

"Ducks. I doubt it. He's summed you up and found you worthy of his interest. I'm offended on behalf of my other guests though." She stared after the little blue car as it wound back around the car park towards the exit. "I always used to find Maurice an interesting conversationalist but since he retired he's become more judgemental, picky about things I'd never thought bothered him before."

"Perhaps he has too much time to think about it. I had a plan for when I retired. Of course things didn't work out exactly but I hadn't factored in a pandemic. It's a bit of a surprise to be at home with nowhere you have to be and not a lot to fill your time. Perhaps Maurice isn't managing his retirement well."

"Perhaps."

Carlos raised his head. "I can smell the market."

Ketty turned her back on Maurice and the disappearing Suzuki. "Let's go fishing."

Within half an hour Ketty had made her purchases but Carlos, who insisted on carrying the bags, lingered, exclaiming over the variety of fish, asking about the names and species and chatting to store holders. He stopped at the tanks of live crabs she always hurried past. He marvelled over them with such open delight she couldn't help but smile. Usually her trips to the market were a mission she carried out without lingering.

"Look at these oysters." Carlos tapped his finger on the glass in front of trays of the carefully arranged plump shellfish. "Where is Smoky Bay?"

"South Australia. They raise large and very tasty oysters there. I've already purchased some for our lunch tomorrow."

"We could try some now."

Ketty frowned. "We've got fish to get home."

"They're well packed." He held up the two fridge bags they'd added ice packs to. "A little longer won't hurt."

"It's barely past ten o'clock in the morning."

"What does the time matter when there's such delectable fresh oysters to be had?"

"A dozen to share, sir?" The man behind the counter smiled knowingly.

"Come on, Ketty. The sun is shining – we shouldn't give up this chance to enjoy the bounty of the ocean."

She thought of the list of jobs still to be done and then thought how much easier they'd be with Carlos's help. Both men were beaming at her.

"A dozen oysters to share," she said.

Carlos paid and took the tray.

"Let's find a seat out by the water." Ketty led the way.

They stepped out from the market hall and were met by a wall of humidity.

"Goodness, it's heated up a lot while we've been inside." She found them a table under the shade of an umbrella. "This is such a good idea," she said once they were settled.

Carlos waved a hand briskly at the plate of oysters. "You first."

She selected one, tipped the oyster from its shell and closed her eyes in delight as she chewed, the tender flesh exploding in a burst of salty juiciness in her mouth.

She opened her eyes to find Carlos studying her, his look bemused.

"That good?" he said.

"As if they've just been plucked from the ocean." She dabbed the paper serviette to her chin. "Even though they've come all the way from South Australia."

Carlos took one and soon they were both reaching for a second, laughing at their eagerness. Ketty had many friends but in that moment she realised how easy it was to be with Carlos, as if they'd lived their lives in each other's company rather than mostly oceans apart. She was so glad he was there.

eleven

Day One – Travelling South

Carlos had a glass of champagne in each hand. She smiled as he offered her one then tapped his glass gently against hers.

"What should we toast to?" he asked.

"You actually being here. I was so worried you were going to miss out."

"I'm worried my case will be permanently lost."

"Surely it will be found and forwarded, and if not you'll just have to buy new clothes."

Carlos frowned.

"You didn't have anything precious in it, did you?"

He hesitated a split second before shaking his head. "No. And I should be able to manage with what's in my carry-on bag, at least until Adelaide."

"I'm sorry. I don't suppose there's anything of mine I can lend you, a pashmina perhaps?" Ketty's lips twitched.

Once more Carlos shook his head, worry creasing his face. "I'm still not sure how we're going to manage this sharing cabin business but—"

"I'm not hard to get along with." Ketty cast her hand out. "Look at all the wonderful times we've already had on the first part of your Australian adventure."

His smile returned. "I'll drink to that."

They both sipped from their glasses.

"And then there's Celia and Jim. I'm so delighted it all worked out for them. Their celebration in Adelaide will be the perfect end to our train journey."

"Another of your match-making successes."

"I didn't do anything really. A cruise was perfect for them."

"With no interference from you." There was just the slightest quirky upturn of his lips.

"Not at all. Once they let go of their grief, poor Jim for his late wife and Celia for her divorce, then they realised for themselves that they were so well suited."

Carlos's eyebrows raised and he grinned. He was laughing at her but she didn't mind.

"All they needed was a little nudge from me."

He held up his glass. "To Celia and Jim."

Ketty echoed his words and added, "And speaking of friends, I had a text from Felix at the cafe wishing us a great journey and asking me to pass his number on to you. Something he wants to talk to you about." Ketty waited but Carlos didn't respond. She remembered Felix mentioning something about a visa when she and Carlos had last lunched together at the cafe. "You haven't had a problem with your visa, have you?"

A startled look crossed his face before he quickly shook his head. "No."

"I'll text his number when we have signal next," she said.

They lapsed into silence. Ketty studied Carlos, who was staring into his glass. His beard wasn't so neatly clipped and his hair was tousled as if he'd dragged it back with his fingers.

"How are you feeling, Carlos?" Ketty asked. "You must be tired. You've had a long journey to get here."

"All right at the moment. I'm annoyed about my missing case but at least I'm here. Like you I wondered if I'd ever make it. It's been a chaotic time since I saw you last."

"I'm sorry you lost both your parents so quickly but at least you were there when your father went."

"He was inconsolable when Mami died. He'd become so frail in the short time since I'd seen him last. They say you can die of a broken heart and I believe it." Carlos looked down at his hands.

"So now we are both orphans," Ketty said.

He tilted his head, his mouth twitching sideways in a quirky grin. "At our age I don't consider us to be orphans."

"Does it matter your age? When you lose your parents you become untethered, perhaps even the oldest of your generation. My nephew Greg delights in calling me the matriarch of the Clift family. Perhaps I feel it more because I don't have a partner or children."

"You have a brother, friends...have you been lonely, Ketty?"

"Far from it. I live alone but I'm not lonely. The last few years have been strange times for everyone but it's actually made my business grow and become stronger. My employees are more like family. Judith and I have a close relationship and I have wonderful neighbours. You've met them all."

"Christmas and then January with you was very special. I enjoyed meeting the people who are important to you."

"Even my brother? He can be a bit pretentious."

"Funny, that's how my sister describes me."

They both laughed.

"Excuse me a moment." Carlos put his glass on the table. "I'll slip to the bathroom before lunch."

Ketty nodded and sat back, taking in her surroundings once more. The atmosphere in the lounge car was not unlike the start of a cruise. She delighted in the choreography created by people when they were in a new place and meeting new faces. The light banter, the short silences, the over-enthusiastic laughter as they tried to settle in to the new experience. By the end of a cruise, after spending time together over food and drinks and shared tours, they became like old friends who'd divulged life stories. She hoped this train journey would be the same.

Two people entered the lounge car. She was leaning on a walking stick and he solicitous at her elbow. Ketty smiled at them. It was the couple she'd seen on the buggy at the Darwin terminal. The man smiled back. The woman still wore her sunglasses and her response was dismissive. She was perhaps Ketty's age but the man, even though he was younger, had a weariness about him that made it hard to tell his age. He settled her on the lounge recently vacated by Ning and Tien and asked if she'd like a drink. She replied that she could wait until lunch. He glanced towards the bar, hesitated a minute then sat on the couch next to her, a small space between them. The woman muttered something Ketty couldn't hear. He nodded and took her walking stick, sliding it to the floor out of the way. She plucked at the sleeves of her fine cotton shirt, her long nails a deep pink contrast against the white.

"I hope they won't keep us waiting as long for lunch as they did to get us to our cabin," she said.

"We had to wait for a buggy to be available."

She sniffed and he half-turned away from her to look out the window behind them.

Ketty tried to look as if she wasn't eavesdropping but something about the woman's voice had sounded familiar. There was no chance to hear more as Carlos arrived back just as their names were called for lunch. Ketty reluctantly rose to her feet. She could already tell there was something interesting going on with those two and she hoped she'd get the chance to find out what.

"Ketty?"

She shifted her gaze to Carlos who was waiting a few steps ahead.

"Was that someone you knew?" he asked.

"I'm not sure. Hopefully I'll see her again and find out."

They passed through another rattly gangway and arrived at the dining car where the doors opened automatically as Carlos approached. He stood aside, indicating for Ketty to go first. When she stepped into the dining car it was as if she'd entered another world and the couple were immediately forgotten. A smiling waiter greeted them. He was dressed in the same smart uniform as the other staff but with a navy apron tied at his waist.

"Would you like to sit alone or with company?" he asked.

"Company, please." Perhaps it was the two sips of champagne she'd managed on the way in or the intriguing couple she'd observed but Ketty felt brighter with each step and looked forward to meeting someone new.

The dining car pulsed with enthusiastic diners and elegant charm. On the walls there was more of the polished wood panelling she'd noted in the other carriages but here it was augmented by sections of padded fabric in rich tones and strips of etched glass that ran the length of the carriage bulkhead, trimmed with gold that toned perfectly with the pressed metal ceiling overhead.

Even more exciting for Ketty were the tables covered with crisp white tablecloths and set with elegant glassware and gleaming cutlery. For a touch of intimacy, partial partitions made of delicately curved etched glass extended from the wall and along the seat back and divided each table from the next.

Lacey gave them a tentative smile as they passed but Birgit was so enthralled by her conversation with the two chaps she didn't notice them. A few tables further along on the other side, Judith was engrossed in the menu, Tien was staring out the window and only Ning gave a small wave as they continued on along the aisle.

The waiter stopped at the last table. Ketty chose the seat with her back to the wall giving her a view down the entire carriage. She slid in close to the window. The blind was up and the plush fabric curtains hooked back so they had a full view of the ever-changing landscape as they rolled south towards Katherine.

"This is delightful," Ketty said as Carlos slid in beside her. "The seats are so comfortable." Ketty swept her gaze around the carriage again. "Almost like one of your ship dining rooms but for the shape."

"You have a grand imagination, Ketty."

She slipped on her reading glasses and picked up the menu. "A compact but fine array of choices, and look..." She tapped the map of Australia printed on the first page. "It even shows our approximate position. What a lovely touch."

"I'm glad you're impressed."

Ketty removed her glasses and met his gaze. "You did try to tell me, didn't you?"

Carlos smiled, raised his glass and tapped it against hers. "Here we are at last." He was nothing if not diplomatic. Ketty felt a little giddy. Perhaps it was the champagne so early in the day but she was more inclined to think it was due to the effervescent happiness that bubbled inside her.

"To a wonderful journey," she said and they both sipped their champagne.

"Thanks to you for letting me share or I wouldn't be here." His smile slipped away. "I'm still not sure how I let you talk me into it. We're good friends, Ketty, but—"

"We are good friends and I'm sure we'll work it out." She took in his serious expression. "You're not too bothered by our arrangement, are you?"

"I'm fine with it..." Carlos stared into his glass and fiddled with the stem.

"Sounds like there's a but coming."

"I get the feeling your staff aren't very impressed. You have a reputation to maintain."

"Fiddle! Surely at our stage of life we're beyond caring what other people think."

"You said yourself they're already off their stride." His face softened. "They're your friends as well as your staff."

"And they have to take me as I am." Ketty lifted her chin and met his gaze. "As I do them."

Another waiter brought water for the table. Ketty paused, watching as he filled their glasses then moved away.

"Carlos, we're good friends," she continued. "I feel that even more so since last Christmas when you spent time at my apartment and met everyone. And then video calling your delightful sister and seeing your Spanish family. I felt as if I knew them all well by the end."

"I feel the same. It was good to get to know the people who love and care for you. That's why I'm preocupado...you know, troubled by this current circumstance. People will read more into this cabin arrangement no matter what we say. I'm concerned for your reputation even if you're not."

Ketty took a mouthful of the water, uncertain how to proceed. Her relationship with Carlos would remain platonic. Several years earlier she'd thought she'd been given a second chance with Leo, the man she'd fallen in love with as a young woman. He'd hurt her badly back then. When she'd run into him again on her last cruise she'd thought perhaps they had a chance to try again. It had been foolish. Turned out Leo had been the same self-centred man he'd been in their younger days. Thankfully she'd seen through his smooth charm and attempts at romancing her and walked away. Carlos was nothing like Leo but she didn't want to spoil their relationship. She wanted nothing more than friendship and she felt certain the feeling was mutual.

"You're planning something," he said, drawing her attention back to him.

"No." She shook her head. "Just thinking about us."

"I like the sound of that." A brief cheeky smile creased his face and then was gone.

Ketty faltered, her thoughts from seconds ago fading already. Was he flirting with her? Carlos had always kept her at arm's length, treated her as a friend.

"We're sharing a cabin but there's no more to it," she said firmly. "We'll be like brother and sister. If anyone wants to think anything else, let them. You and I know the truth and that's all that matters. Besides, this makes me think of cruising, when I left behind plain, boring Ketty Clift—"

"My dear Ketty." He grasped her hand. "You could never be described as plain or boring."

She withdrew her hand from his. "I'm serious, Carlos. On a cruise no-one knew me. I could be like a chameleon changing my colour to suit the occasion. You of all people know how much fun I had. I can't very well be someone different when my travelling companions are all people I work with and know me so well. Sharing a cabin with you at least gives me a point of difference to reality."

Before he could reply their first waiter was back with a man and a woman who slipped in opposite. Ketty was a little disappointed it wasn't the couple she'd observed earlier but she smiled widely.

"Hello," the man boomed. "I'm Warren and this is my good wife, Val."

"I'm Carlos." Somehow the two men avoided all the glassware as they shook hands.

"And I'm Ketty."

"My sister." Carlos spoke so quickly Ketty thought she'd misheard.

She glanced at him but his gaze was fixed on the couple opposite.

"You look nothing alike." Val stared at one then the other.

"We're adopted." Carlos was smiling now in that agreeable way he'd used to soothe many an upset passenger in the past.

"Oh." Val sat back in her seat.

Ketty bit her lip to stop herself from laughing.

"I've worked overseas a lot so we haven't seen much of each other," Carlos said. "We thought we'd holiday together so we could enjoy a catch-up."

Ketty couldn't believe he was still going on with the charade.

Warren's huge grin split his round face in half. "What a good plan. Val and I are celebrating fifty years married. That's why we're on this trip."

Val's smile seemed more like a wince to Ketty. She wondered if the train trip had been a joint idea or only Warren's.

"Congratulations," Ketty and Carlos said in unison.

"Have you done a train journey before?" Warren asked.

"I have in Europe," Carlos said. "But not long journeys like this and Ketty hasn't either."

"This is our fourth trip," Warren said. "We toyed with the idea of a cruise this time but Val thought the train would be fun." He gave his wife a nudge. "Isn't that right, pet?"

Val made her wincing smile again and just below table level her finger prodded Warren's side. This time it was he who grimaced. Already these two held more attraction than the couple back in the lounge car. Ketty's people radar quivered into action. It had been such a long time since she'd left behind her cares and travelled she almost didn't recognise the sensation. She leaned a little closer.

"Where's home for you?" she asked, and then had to say little more as Warren told them all about the small town in Victoria where they'd both lived all their lives, how they'd been childhood sweethearts, the electrical appliance business they'd run there after taking it over from his father and how their son was now doing the same. Val interjected every so often to correct something Warren said and then they'd have a little squabble over who was right before he took up the story again.

When the waiter came to take their food order none of them had had a chance to decide.

"Stop talking, Warren." Val bared her teeth this time. "We want to eat."

"We sure do, pet." He glanced at the waiter. "Sorry, can you give us a minute?"

Ketty picked up the menu again, eager to select something and keep her gaze averted. She still couldn't make eye contact with Carlos for fear of laughing out loud.

Lacey took another big mouthful of water. The one glass of champagne had gone straight to her head and even though she'd just eaten a delicious lunch she was still feeling a little spun out. Some of it because the conversation around the table had become quite outrageous, at least from what she could comprehend. Sometimes Rhys's and Rory's accents made it difficult. And Birgit, now on her fourth glass of champagne, was getting harder to understand as well. With each glass, her Irish accent became more pronounced. Every so often the two guys would laugh at her words but they were odd about it, glancing at each other as if they were laughing at Birgit rather than with her. And there was something evasive about their answers to personal questions that seemed at odds with their jokey manner.

Evidently they were cousins, they'd been happy to share, and were in Australia for three months, seeing as much of it as they could. They'd been saving for years and the Ghan trip enabled them to go from top to bottom, as Rhys had mentioned several times. Lacey understood him then and liked the way the words "top to bottom" sounded as they rolled from his tongue. Occasionally he'd asked her a question and when he did his green eyes fixed on her so intently she stumbled over her answers.

She'd never been confident with men, or at least not with any that showed interest in her, with two exceptions. There was Marcus from her TAFE days. They got on really well and Lacey could talk easily with him but he was gay so there was never going to be anything more than friendship between them. And then there'd been Judith's neighbour, Dean. She'd thought they were getting along well but it had fizzled out. She still thought about Dean every day, about how happy she believed they'd been, and wondering what went wrong.

"Have you been to Katherine before, Lacey?" Rhys asked.

Letting go her thoughts of Dean and his deep brown eyes, she focused on the green pair studying her now across the table.

"No, but I'm looking forward to it."

Jade, who seemed to be in charge of most things, arrived at their table. "Excuse my interruption but I've got good news for you gentlemen. You've got your helicopter flight."

"Deadly!"

"That's bleedin' rapid." They both spoke at once.

From the looks on their faces Lacey gathered they were excited, and it was infectious. She glanced out the window at the trees flashing by and the blue sky beyond and imagined herself taking a helicopter flight.

"Come to the counter in the lounge car as soon as you finish your lunch and you can make your payment," Jade said.

"We're finished." Rhys tapped Rory on the arm. "We'll come now and get it sorted."

They both eased out from behind the table.

"Thanks for your company," Rory said.

"It was great." Birgit's words were softly slurred as she made goggle eyes at him, which he ignored.

"Let's meet for drinks when we all get back. Compare our adventures." Rhys smiled at Lacey and winked. He seemed like a nice guy but the wink didn't have the impact of Dean's and she couldn't help but feel a little deflated that she wasn't doing a helicopter flight.

"Great idea," Birgit gushed. "I'll come with you. I need to use the bathroom. Back in two ticks, Lacey."

Lacey settled back in her seat feeling a little despondent. She didn't have Birgit's talent when it came to chatting easily with men. Rhys was friendly but she didn't feel relaxed with him. Not like she had with Dean.

She pictured Dean the first time she'd met him at Miss Ketty's Christmas lunch, with his colourful Christmas shirt, his curly hair still damp from the shower and his cheeky grin. Lacey had been smitten straight away. They'd been placed next to each other and had immediately hit it off. She couldn't help but think Miss Ketty's seating had been well planned.

twelve

The previous December – Paddington, Sydney

Lacey glanced around the table, where all Miss Ketty's Christmas lunch guests were finishing their entrees, and then down at her partly eaten seafood terrine. She rarely ate smoked salmon or prawns but they went perfectly with the avocado salsa. They'd already had nibbles with their cocktails and this was only the entree. She'd found it filling and she knew Miss Ketty would have plenty more food. On either side of her Carlos and Dean had devoured theirs. She lay her knife and fork across the top of the last portion.

"Don't you like it?" Dean murmured beside her.

Her cheeks burned. "It's delicious but I find it very rich and I know there's so much more to come."

"Do you mind if I finish it off?"

"Oh, no, please do." Lacey tried to slide the remains of the entree onto his plate without being noticed by the others who were all engaged in conversation but as she set her empty plate down again, Judith gave her an appraising look. It was hard to know if it was in approval or displeasure.

"There are more in the fridge, Dean," Judith said. "I could have got you another."

Probably displeasure then, although Lacey couldn't see why it would matter. Food wasn't so plentiful at her house that it could be wasted. She folded her serviette in her lap.

"I don't mind eating Lacey's leftovers." Dean winked at her as he popped the last forkful in his mouth and Lacey's heart skipped a beat. It was conspiratorial, something just between him and her.

Judith sighed and began to collect plates. Lacey lifted hers but it was swiftly taken from her hands by Carlos.

"Please sit back and relax." His smile was wide and lit up his face. "Judith and I are in charge of dining."

Dean leaned closer. His wavy hair was damp and smelled of citrus. "It's as if Ketty has her own butler."

Lacey understood what he meant. Carlos was wearing a cream linen open-necked shirt, tan shorts and a pair of loafers but his manner made her think of one of the butlers in the *Downton Abbey* show her gran had been so fond of. It wouldn't have surprised her if Carlos had been dressed in a black suit, bow tie and white gloves. "He was a maître d' on a cruise ship for a long time. It's probably his nature."

"He's got an accent I can't pick. Is he British?"

"From Spain," Lacey murmured. Carlos was at the other side of the table but she didn't want him to know they were talking about him. "I think he speaks a few different languages. He spent a lot of time working on cruise ships."

Carlos passed them with a pile of plates and arrived at the door as Judith did. He stopped and tipped his head. She strode ahead of him and Carlos followed.

"I can see why Judith's got her knickers in a knot."

"Has she?" Lacey glanced sideways at Dean. He and Judith had been chatting like old friends when they'd sat down. She'd thought they were close but his wink earlier and his words now made him seem a little disparaging.

"Surely you've noticed her fussing over Ketty?"

Lacey gave a non-committal shrug.

"What was it, about two months ago, when Ketty had that nasty chest infection?"

"Yes, she was off work for a week and even then it took a long time for her to shake the cough. Judith stayed at her place for a few nights."

"Judith loves to have someone to fuss over. She was so happy. Not that Ketty was unwell but that she needed Judith's help," Dean continued. "Normally Judith would spend days helping Ketty prepare for Christmas but Carlos has kind of sidelined her. He seems like he's settled in here." Once more Dean leaned in close. "Do you think they're a couple?"

Lacey glanced in Miss Ketty's direction to make sure she couldn't hear but she was deep in conversation with her three neighbours. Something about a change in council rates.

"I don't know. They're old friends."

"Well, good on them, I say. You're never too old for love."

Lacey fiddled with her bracelet, unable to meet the soft look in his deep brown eyes.

"Anyway, if Carlos does stay around I might be in for more of Judith's fussing," Dean said. "She's very kind-hearted but some-times it's as if she's my mother and I've already got one of those."

He straightened up as Judith bustled back around the table clearing the last of the clutter ready for mains. Lacey watched her from below lowered lids. Judith was nice to everyone at work, even to

Lacey some days, but with no warning she could say something unkind. It was as if she were two people.

"How do you like working at Ketty Clift Couture?" Dean asked. "You're a lot younger than the rest of them."

Lacey lifted her head as Judith strode away. "Birgit's always good fun. She's only a few years older than me. Tien's a fan of reality TV and often has us giggling over whatever she's watched the night before. I think of Ning as a mother hen. She's a bit like Miss Ketty, calm and wise. Everyone brings something different to the mix. I truly love it here." She glanced over her shoulder to the glass double doors. The curtains were drawn but beyond was the workshop where magic was created. "We're a team. I don't think about the differences." Except for Judith, but she wasn't brave enough to admit that to Dean.

"It's funny you call her Miss Ketty."

"I called her Miss Clift when I started. She insisted I call her Ketty but it didn't seem respectful. We agreed Miss Ketty was a compromise."

"You're a special individual, Lacey."

Once more she looked away and fiddled with the bracelet. Then something inside her softened and she blurted, "I think you are too."

They stared at each other a moment, then Dean's face lit up in a grin. "That's what my mum always says but she can be a bit biased where I'm concerned." He crossed his eyes and poked out his tongue.

Lacey laughed.

thirteen

Day One – Travelling South

"What a couple of cute guys." Birgit slid back into the seat opposite.

Her sudden appearance brought Lacey back to the present.

Birgit winked. "I think we're both in with a chance there."

"They seem nice."

"Nice! That Rhys was hanging on your every word. Not that you said much. Rory and I had a real good chat." Birgit swallowed the contents of her water glass. "I'd better sober up before we go on this excursion. Shite but that word makes me feel like I'm back at school."

"It's called an off-train experience, not an excursion."

"Experience, excursion, whatever."

A waiter refilled their water glasses and Birgit put up a hand to stop him leaving while she downed the contents and put her glass out for another refill.

"Thanks very much," she said when he obliged.

"I hope you don't think I'm prying, Birgit, but…well, I thought you'd moved in with—"

Birgit's hand shot up again, stopping just short of Lacey's nose. "Don't mention his name. I'm not spoiling this holiday thinking about that gobshite. We're here to enjoy ourselves. Luckily we've found possibly the only two male passengers under thirty-five on board to help us with that."

Birgit had seemed so in love and had been over-the-top excited about moving in with her partner. It was a shame the relationship had broken up but she was obviously putting it behind her if today's flirting was anything to go by. Lacey wished she could be as carefree. She wasn't sure how to take the two Irish chaps though. They'd been good company but there was something about them, or Rory, at least, that wasn't quite right and she couldn't put her finger on it. She hoped Birgit wasn't in for more disappointment.

Judith was glad she'd seated Tien close to the window with her back to Birgit and Lacey's table. She would not have approved of either young woman's behaviour. They'd got quite noisy at times, and from the snatches she'd caught of Birgit's voice she had a few drinks under her belt. Judith was glad the young men had gone and Birgit was sculling water.

The dining car was almost empty. Judith didn't look back but she had when Ketty and Carlos had first come through. They'd been given a table at the far end of the carriage and Tien had announced that the kind man called Warren and his wife had been seated with them.

Judith was reluctant to move after their big lunch and neither Ning beside her nor Tien opposite appeared to be in a hurry. After her sharp words earlier she'd smoothed the waters with both of them and they'd had a pleasant meal together. Beyond the glass the view was constantly changing and it was easier to pick out more details now that the train didn't seem to be going quite so fast. The landscape was predominantly long grasses and trees with glimpses of red dirt and the odd smaller bush bright with flowers, giving the appearance of a big mauve lollipop.

"Cows." Tien tapped the window.

Cattle of various colours were dotted among the trees and then gone from sight.

"No kangaroos," she sighed. Tien had been watching all through lunch hoping to see one.

"I doubt you'd see a kangaroo," Judith said. "They're smaller and we're moving too fast."

"Maybe we will see some in Katherine." Ning gave Tien an encouraging smile.

"Speaking of which, we should be there soon," Judith said. "Time to go back to our cabins and get organised. I think we'll be away from the train for quite a while by the sound of it."

"I hope it's not too hot," Ning said.

"We'll need our hats and sunscreen and water." As Judith stood she glanced back. Ketty and Carlos were deep in conversation with Warren and his wife but most of the other diners had left. Ahead of them Lacey and Birgit were exiting the dining car.

"Should we remind Miss Clift it's soon time to get off?" Tien said as she got to her feet.

"I think she'll manage." Judith put a gentle hand at Tien's back to guide her forward.

Since Ketty had broken her wrist back in February Tien had fussed over her a lot more. Ketty was too polite to say but it was obvious to Judith she didn't appreciate the overzealous attention.

Back in their cabin, Ning and Judith were both ready in quick time and they sat on their couch just as the train passed over a water course with sandy banks and the taller forms of scattered gums throwing dappled shade. The commentary coming from the speaker in the wall mentioned the Katherine River.

"The train is going slow now." Ning slipped her lanyard around her neck. Caryn had left them one each while they'd been out at lunch. Judith checked the ticket on the end of hers again. The Nitmiluk Gorge rock art cruise they'd chosen had been ticked and they were both allocated to coach four.

She pressed her face to the window. "We must be almost there. I can see the train curving around a bend ahead."

Behind her Ning's phone began to beep. Judith sat back, trying to keep her expression neutral.

"We must have signal again." Ning gave her a nervous glance and dug the phone out of her bag. "There's been nothing since we left Darwin."

Judith hadn't even checked her phone. There was no-one to message her. The only reason she had it in her backpack was so she could take the odd photo. Ning's phone beeped again.

"Goodness, you're popular."

"My family. Excuse me." Ning turned slightly away and hunched over her phone.

Judith swallowed the niggle of envy that Ning was obviously missed and looked back to the window. They were hardly moving now. The land close to the track was bare of vegetation and they passed some outbuildings and idle rail trucks. This must be the Katherine rail station.

fourteen

Day One – Katherine, NT

Ketty sat beside Ning on the bus, Tien and Judith were together further back, and Carlos had taken a front seat and was chatting to the driver. Ning was in the window seat, but instead of taking in the sights she was tapping on her phone.

"My family," she'd said apologetically. Her phone had beeped several times and each time she tapped more furiously than the last.

"Is everything all right?"

"Yes, yes." Ning nodded. "They just want to know why I didn't answer earlier and what's happening now."

"Didn't you speak to your son this morning?"

"Yes." Ning nodded distractedly. "He wants to know about the train and my other son is messaging, and my daughter-in-law."

The phone beeped again.

"Why don't you turn it off?" Ketty suggested.

Ning gaped at her. "There would be many more messages when I turn it back on."

Another beep drew her gaze back to the phone.

Ketty had always turned her phone off when she cruised but of course these days a phone was many more things than something to speak on or send messages. Her own was in her bag in case she wanted to take a photo but nonetheless a small burst of frustration niggled in her chest. Not only was Ning missing the sights along the way but Ketty had hoped to take the opportunity to talk a little more about Ning's retirement while they were sitting together.

It had only been a couple of weeks earlier Ning had stayed on after work and told Ketty what she'd planned. It had come as a complete surprise. When Ketty had realised that was the reason for Ning's reticence to join the holiday she'd focused on that, urging her long-serving seamstress to come along as a retirement gift. Since then, with orders to finish and trip planning, there'd been no time for chatting. Ketty thought back to the afternoon Ning had announced she was retiring, trying to see what she may have missed. She'd been waiting for a client and thinking about the cocktail dress they were making for her when Ning had said she'd wanted to chat and she'd handed Ketty a small gift, wrapped in tissue.

"That's kind but—"

"I made it for you." She'd insisted.

Ketty unfolded the pale pink tissue to reveal a white handkerchief with the letter K embroidered in a swirl of pretty blue stitching. She rubbed the fine cotton between her fingers and peered closer at the embroidery. "It's beautiful, Ning."

"I know you prefer handkerchiefs to tissues."

"There's nothing nicer than a good-quality handkerchief." Ketty wrapped it back in the paper. "Thank you."

"There's something I need to tell you."

Ketty faltered at Ning's troubled expression. "What is it?"

"Ketty, you've been so good to me, I feel terribly bad." Tears brimmed in Ning's eyes. "I'm sorry, I don't know how to tell you but…" The tears overflowed.

"What is it?" Ketty's mind whirled wildly.

"I have decided…" Ning swallowed. "I have decided it's time to retire."

"Oh." The sound puffed over Ketty's lips like the last pop of a deflating balloon. Of all the things she'd thought Ning might be upset to tell her that had not been one of them. "Is there something wrong?" Ning had worked for Ketty since she'd first opened her shop. She was only fifty-eight and usually in good health and spirits. "Are you unwell?"

"No, nothing wrong." Ning shook her head vigorously. "But with the baby coming…"

"Not long now." Ketty smiled encouragingly. They'd been getting weekly updates on the stages of Ning's daughter-in-law's pregnancy for several months.

"That's why I must retire. I want to spend more time…with family." She was getting more distressed.

Ketty reached an arm around her shoulders. Ning trembled beneath her touch. It had only been five years since Ning's husband had died. It had been a shock, of course. Their two sons had still been at university. One was working now and the other had nearly finished his degree.

"Can we talk about this?"

Ning shook her head. "No, no. It's decided. But I will stay as long as I can…until you have someone else."

"Are you sure, Ning? You could take a holiday when the baby comes. Stay home for a while. We can rearrange—"

"No." Ning wiped the tears from her face. "I am sure and no, I won't change. I feel bad telling you now. I haven't been able to say anything earlier, we've been so busy. I don't want you to be short-staffed."

"Oh, Ning." Ketty hugged her. "You're a wonderful seamstress and a dear friend and I shall miss you but I'd never stop you from doing what you thought was best."

Ning hesitated, doubt in her eyes, then hugged Ketty back.

"Thank you, Ketty. I always thought you'd retire before me. Things change. Perhaps you won't need to replace me if you sell."

Ketty had stepped back. "I'm not selling."

Ning's look had changed to puzzlement. "Oh, no." She'd flapped a hand in the air between them. "It was just something Tien said. It doesn't matter."

Ketty frowned as she remembered the end of the conversation. Her after-hours client had arrived and she'd not had the chance to ask Ning exactly what Tien had said. Now they were pulling into the gorge parking area with barely a word spoken between them and Ning was still peering at her phone, only raising her head as the other passengers began to move.

Ketty stepped off the bus and after its almost-too-cold air conditioning the moist heat hit her like a wet towel. Carlos was already off and waiting for them, patting at the perspiration on his neck. Ning unfurled a small fan that she waved in front of her face with one hand, still clutching her phone with the other.

"It's hotter here than at the train station," Tien wailed as she and Judith joined them.

"I can't imagine how hot Lacey is in those thumping boots," Judith said.

"Oh!" Ning stopped fanning for a minute. "I meant to remind her about sunscreen for her legs."

They'd all paused earlier at the sight of Lacey stepping from the train wearing frayed denim shorts that barely covered her bottom, her long pale legs reflecting the bright sunlight.

"She has an amazing eye for putting things together," Ketty said. "That soft cotton shirt was perfect and at least her arms are covered."

"But not her legs," Ning said. "She needs sunscreen."

"She's an adult," Judith snapped. "None of us need to be reminded to apply sunscreen."

"Her boots are sensible in case of snakes." Tien's eyes had been wide since they'd first got off the train to be greeted by a sandwich board that said *Beware of Snakes*. It had taken their collective persuasion to prevent her from bolting back onto the train.

"We'll be out on the water soon." Ketty changed the subject, dragging their attention towards the gorge where a boat full of passengers was moving serenely away from the bank, the small ripples behind it the only disturbance on the mirror-like surface of the water.

"Might not mean cooler." Ning waved her fan harder. Even she had lost her positive outlook since this morning. Ketty wondered about the messages she'd been reading on her phone and hoped everything was all right at home.

"And what about crocodiles?" Tien said. "They can be in the gorge."

"We won't be in the water," Ketty said.

"They can jump."

"Remember what Caryn said." Ning patted Tien's arm. "The boat is very safe."

"People take these tours every day. I'm sure we'll be fine," Ketty soothed. "And the scenery will be amazing."

"Gosh, I'm dry." Judith drained the last of her water bottle.

Ketty spied a table set up in the shade. It was laid with a white cloth and set out with jugs of juice and water. On the ground beside it were eskies full of bottled water.

"Let's top up before we get on our boat," Ketty said. "Come on, everyone, chins up." She used her best upbeat voice and led the group forward, trying hard to stifle the niggle of doubt.

Lacey and Birgit were seated in the middle of their boat as it moved slowly away from the bank and out into the gorge. It was warm under the canopy but being on the water gave an illusion of coolness. Their guide was a cheery Jawoyn man who delivered an upbeat safety talk then explained a little about the trip ahead, telling them about the traditional owners, the Jawoyn people, and the name they had for the gorge, Nitmiluk, which meant cicada's place.

Lacey repeated *Nit me look* in her head, determined to remember how to say it correctly.

"...the cicada being very significant in the traditional stories from this region," the guide continued. "You'll hear them soon."

Lacey stared at the rock formations and the trees growing from narrow ledges, trying to imagine what it would have been like for someone living here thousands of years ago.

"I'm glad it's just us."

Birgit voiced Lacey's thoughts. They'd chosen to go on a different tour to Miss Ketty and the others. It would take them on to the second gorge. Not that Lacey minded being with her work-mates in general but it was a relief to be away from Judith. Their argument played over and over in her mind and Lacey still couldn't believe she'd found the strength to speak up. Tien's fears were real to her, and Ning was so kind-hearted that Lacey couldn't bear to hear harsh words about her. It was also easier to enjoy the tour away from Tien's anxieties and if the truth be told she was a little intimidated by Carlos's presence.

When Lacey had stepped off the train that morning they'd all been waiting for her. She'd made a last-minute dash back to her cabin to change from the skirt she'd been wearing to the cut-off denim shorts she'd found in an op shop in Darwin. She'd thought shorts a better option for climbing in and out of boats but the way Judith had stared her up and down, she'd felt like jumping back on the train and hiding.

A helicopter sounded above the drone of the boat motor.

"A pity Rory and Rhys aren't with us," Birgit said.

Lacey looked skywards, her heart soaring with the helicopter as it swept across the sky above the gorge. "If I'd had some spare money I'd have taken that helicopter flight."

"Would you?"

Lacey hadn't thought about it until Rhys and Rory had explained the possibility of their flight over lunch and then their excitement when they'd got tickets. Their enthusiasm had been infectious and had fired her imagination.

"Flying up there and getting a bird's-eye view. How amazing would that be?" Lacey's gaze followed the fast-moving helicopter until it became a pinprick and blended with the vibrant blue sky.

Birgit screwed up her nose. "I don't like heights."

Lacey glanced at her friend. "Really?"

"I get a nosebleed on a balcony."

"I suppose I would be nervous," Lacey admitted. "But I'd like to give it a try."

"You should have booked a ticket."

Lacey's already warm cheeks felt warmer. "I...not on my budget this month."

"But Ketty's picking up the tab for this holiday. There's nothing much but souvenirs to buy. You should treat yourself to something special. Put it on credit and pay it off when you get back. You'll probably never do this again."

"Mmm," Lacey said vaguely. "There might be something else later." Which was a lie. The credit card she kept for emergencies was scarily almost maxed out and the council rates notice awaited her return home.

"Would you look at that," Birgit exclaimed.

Lacey followed the direction of her pointing finger. Their boat was approaching a bend in the gorge and towering above them was a huge sandstone cliff made up of strands and blocks of varying creams, reds and browns. Their guide began to explain some of the rock formations and their significance.

Lacey was glad of the distraction. She shut out her thoughts of the bills waiting for her at home, her lack of money and worry for her dad. Instead she got out her phone and began to take photos. There was not a breath of wind and it was hot on the water but where the sunlight hit the cliffs it highlighted the beautiful colours of the sandstone. Lacey's mind raced as she imagined it as fabric and what she could create from it.

fifteen

Day One – Nitmiluk

The tour group picked their way across the rock-strewn path. They were all being careful about where they put their feet. Judith wished she'd worn sneakers instead of her sandals. Even though they were flat, the open toes weren't very practical for this kind of thing. Sand was getting under her heels and she'd slipped on a rock earlier and taken a bit of skin off her ankle. No-one else had noticed, thank goodness. And then of course Tien had asked their tour guide about snakes and crocodiles and he'd delighted in regaling the group with all kinds of stories. Judith thought he was exaggerating for the sake of overseas tourists – next he'd be talking about drop bears. All the same it had been enough for her to watch every step.

She was towards the rear of the group as they made their way back to the boat. She wasn't looking forward to getting back on board. It was cooler there in the shade of the giant cliffs than out on the water, where the mid-afternoon sun beat ferociously on the scant cover over the boat. Their tour guide's talk about the

114

creation and importance of the gorge for the Jawoyn people had been interesting and distracting but now the heat pressed in on Judith again.

Ketty and Carlos were several strides ahead and Judith studied Carlos's back as he walked. He was taller than Ketty and every so often he stooped a little to tell her something or listen to her reply. It was obviously an intimate conversation because Judith had gone close during one of their pauses for another brief story from the guide and they'd both clammed up immediately.

Judith had hoped there'd be time on this holiday for her and Ketty to have a good chat, like they used to on Friday evenings after work. That had stopped once Carlos had settled in with Ketty. Judith had stayed on a couple of times on a Friday if Ketty had been home but the conversations had been general with Carlos there. She'd been glad when he'd gone off to spend time with his interstate cousin and family in late January. And Judith had stayed for a short time in February when Ketty broke her wrist, but dealing with that had been their focus and then once more Carlos had turned up to help Ketty and Judith had returned home. Even when his mother had died and he'd returned to Spain, they'd not resumed their Friday drinks. Either Ketty or more rarely Judith had had other commitments and somehow they'd not got back to their routine of debriefing the week.

Judith had used those opportunities to bring any staff issues she noticed to Ketty's attention. She wondered now if Ketty even realised how fractured the once-firm relationships between her staff had become. Since Carlos had flitted in, then out, then back in to her life Ketty had become distracted.

It had been a long time ago but Ketty had been her rock when Judith had been flailing under the pressure of living with a useless and sometimes violent husband and caring for her terminally ill mother-in-law. When her poor mother-in-law had died, Ketty had helped Judith leave her husband.

Judith was proud of her achievements since those terrible times. She enjoyed her job at Ketty Clift Couture, a place she felt as much at home as she did in the apartment she rented in a building with a few other long-term residents she called friends, but that too was to change soon. It had taken her by surprise. Like a rug being whipped from under her. She longed to talk to Ketty about it, to confide in her like she had many times over the years.

Judith stopped abruptly, the brim of Carlos's Panama hat only centimetres from her face. The guide was talking again and she hadn't realised the group ahead of her had paused to listen.

She took a step back as Carlos twisted to look at her. He smiled. She gave a tight smile in return. He tipped his hat slightly and turned back to listen. He could pour out his smarm as much as he liked but it had no effect on Judith.

Their guide moved on, leading them back to the boat. Ketty and Carlos fell into step beside Warren and his wife but Tien and Ning waited for her. Judith placed her foot on a large rock. It was flat but sloped and had been sprinkled with sand by many people walking over it. Her sandal slipped sideways. She adjusted her balance and quickly pulled herself up straight. How embarrassing it would be to fall.

"Are you okay?" Tien rushed back and grabbed her sore elbow, making Judith wobble more. She withdrew carefully from Tien's clasp.

"Fine, thank you," she replied stiffly.

"Did you hurt yourself?" Ning asked.

"You must be more careful and watch where you put your feet," Tien said.

"I'm fine." Judith raised her chin. Lately Tien's overly solicitous sphere had been widened from Ketty to take in Judith, and she didn't like it.

"You should have worn shoes and socks." Ning lifted one foot encased in a beige canvas slip-on shoe.

"Socks and closed shoes are needed for these expeditions." Tien put her dark blue sneaker forward.

Then they all looked down at Judith's sandals.

"I didn't realise it would be like this," she said. "I thought boat travel and a short walk on a prepared path."

"Oh, look, you're bleeding." Tien waggled a finger at Judith's feet.

Blood was oozing from the scrape on her ankle that the recent slip had made bigger.

"I have bandages in my bag." Tien slid the handle of her bag from her shoulder.

"It's all right." Judith dabbed at the graze with a tissue. It must be deeper than she thought because it throbbed. "I don't need a bandage."

"Are you sure?"

"Yes. It's not that bad." Judith held the tissue to her ankle and gritted her teeth. It was actually stinging ferociously.

"I think we're going back to the visitor centre now." Ning's fan came out again and Judith enjoyed the puff of air that reached her.

Ketty sat on the deck of the information centre gazing back out across the gorge. She was alone for a moment. Carlos had gone to buy them a coffee and most of the passengers were perusing the souvenirs, buying snacks or using the bathroom facilities. Ketty had wanted one last look at the beauty of the gorge before her. The colours were magnificent. She felt a little dismayed that she'd never thought to visit the region before.

"What did you think, Ketty?" Warren pulled up a chair beside her and offered her a jube from an almost-empty bag.

"Beautiful," she said as she shook her head to decline the sweet.

"Agreed." He nodded emphatically, pushing two jubes into his mouth and chewing steadily as he looked out across the water. "I hadn't realised how big the whole system of gorges was and we only visited the first."

"I loved the changing colours of the rock in the cliffs and then the contrast of the vegetation."

"I tried to capture some of those beautiful shots the guide lined up for us where the cliffs were perfectly reflected on the water but I'm not much of a photographer. Val's the one to capture the essence of a place." He took out his phone and began to scroll.

That may be because Val had her phone up to her face for most of the tour. Ketty wondered if she'd actually taken in the amazing vista with her own eyes or only from the screen of her phone.

"That's not a bad photo of the rock art." Warren held out his phone.

"That's a great shot," Ketty said. "So clear."

"New phone. I thought our old ones were still pretty good but Val wanted to get new ones before we came away. Probably worth the money now that I look at these."

"I told you so." Val appeared from behind them, two bags of souvenirs dangling from her hand. "I've got something for each of the grandkids," she said, handing him the bags.

Ketty had taken a brief look in the shop. She'd wanted to purchase something for her two great-nieces but hadn't been sure what to pick from the large assortment of toys and trinkets. She'd found the choices overwhelming and they already had so many toys. Hopefully she'd find something unique and useful along the journey somewhere.

Warren pulled out a chair for his wife.

"Can I have one of the jubes?" she said as she sat and took out her phone.

Warren plucked the empty packet from the table. "All gone, sorry," he said cheerily. "I thought you said you didn't want any more."

"I asked you to save me some."

"Did you? Sorry, seniors moment."

Val was focused on her phone. "I got some lovely photos."

Ketty did her best to show interest as Val proceeded to scroll through a swag of photos. She stopped regularly and insisted Ketty look at images from the trip she'd just seen with her own eyes.

"I find it hard to comprehend that rock art has been there for thousands of years," Ketty said as she handed back the phone yet again. "Some of them longer than Stonehenge or Machu Picchu or even the pyramids of Giza, all those places people are in awe of."

"That American chap beside us was commenting to his friend how special it was." Warren nudged his wife. "Wasn't he, Val? We kind of take Aboriginal art for granted, don't we?"

"Rock paintings are hardly in the same league as the wonders of the ancient world." Val sniffed and kept scrolling through her photos.

Ketty felt the sting of her dismissive words. "I feel guilty that I know so little about the early history of my own country," she said.

Val glanced up, a puzzled look on her face.

"Gosh, you've got a bit of stuff in these bags, pet." Warren pulled out a fluffy black bird with a red tail.

"That's a red-tailed black cockatoo," Val said.

Next he held up a kookaburra with blue wings.

"The guide pointed out that blue-winged kookaburra in the tree by the boat landing, remember," Val said. "I thought the girls would like one each."

"How many grandchildren do you have?" Ketty asked.

"Six," Warren said.

"Seven," Val corrected. "Five girls and two boys."

"Surely you didn't buy one for the new baby." Warren dug deeper.

"Don't pull them all out," Val plucked the cockatoo from the table. "It's not too clean here."

Warren peered into the other bag. "Books and pens as well. We have to fit all this stuff in our cabin, pet. This is only our second stop." He glanced at Ketty. "Val already bought them all T-shirts in Darwin and—"

"I like to take home little gifts for them, Warren." Val's face scrunched and her eyes brimmed with tears. "It gives them and me so much pleasure."

Warren pulled his wife into a hug. Her scowl turned to a smile and she tucked her head against his broad shoulder, her face hidden from Ketty's view while Warren's crumpled with remorse.

There was an undercurrent between them that Ketty couldn't quite put her finger on. Warren was big and loud and brash and Val more demure and quiet. At first Ketty had thought she was overshadowed by her husband but in that smile Ketty had thought she'd seen something manipulative. There was definitely something amiss with Val and Warren and she was determined to find out what.

Ning stepped through a door further along the deck. She was alone but rather than taking in the view of the gorge she was busy on her phone again.

Ketty rose to her feet. "My work colleagues and I have organised to sit as a group for dinner tonight."

Val lifted her head, her face blotchy from pressing against Warren's shoulder.

Ketty smiled. "Perhaps we can catch up again in the lounge car for pre-dinner drinks? That's if you're free."

"We'll see you there," Warren said.

Ketty waved as she walked away but her mind was already moving on to Ning, who'd crossed to the other end of the deck and was talking on her phone.

Judith wandered between the rows of souvenirs, heading for the counter. She hadn't planned to buy anything but found herself with a couple of items to pay for. She'd picked out a cloth shopping bag that had been decorated with an indigenous design. The colours reminded her of the sandstone colours in the gorge and *Nitmiluk* was printed across one corner. It would be useful, something she'd keep for herself, but the stubby holder in her other hand was to take home for her neighbour Dean.

Ahead of her at the counter, Carlos was leaning in. He appeared to be fiddling with his card and the EFT machine. She hung back. She'd passed him earlier looking at the hand-painted silk scarves and he'd asked her what colours she'd thought Ketty might like. Judith had waved to one in vibrant pinks and blues and it was now neatly folded on the counter. Lucky Ketty. Judith had been attracted to the unique scarves herself but they were very expensive.

"I'm sorry, it's not working." The young woman glanced at Carlos like she couldn't care less.

He waved the hat he held at his face to create a breeze, even though Judith thought the aircon was working quite well. She hung back, not wanting to get involved yet pleased to see Carlos squirm.

"Can you put it through again please," he asked in his smooth tone.

The young woman almost rolled her eyes as she ripped the paper from the EFT machine. She shifted her weight to her other side and punched some buttons on her keyboard.

"Try again." She sighed.

Carlos did and seconds later she plucked up the machine again and ripped off another piece of paper. "It didn't work. Would you like to try another card or pay cash?"

Carlos opened his wallet but Judith couldn't see what he was doing from where she stood.

"No, I'll leave it." Carlos shoved his wallet into his back pocket and spun away without noticing her.

She stepped forward and placed her items on the counter as the young woman picked up the scarf.

"Can I see that, please?" Judith asked.

The attendant handed it over.

The silk slipped softly over Judith's wrist as she held it out. She recognised the quality of the fabric immediately.

"It's authentic," the young woman said with an air of boredom. "It comes with a box and a card about the artist."

"It's certainly beautiful." Judith knew Ketty would love it. And for some reason Carlos was out of pocket. She'd often wondered about his financial situation. He liked to make a show of paying for things but the whole time he'd been in Sydney he'd stayed at Ketty's, rent-free Judith assumed, and he'd driven a car borrowed from an interstate relative when he'd returned in the new year. It was still in Ketty's garage. Judith placed the scarf back on the counter and took out her credit card. "I'll take this as well, thank you."

Ketty slowed as she got closer to Ning, who had her phone pressed to her ear and was speaking rapidly in Cantonese.

Ning had explained to Ketty when they'd first met that her name meant tranquillity. It was the perfect name for her. In the many years since, Ketty had rarely seen Ning act in anything but a serene manner. Even when her husband had died she'd been a calm beacon of resigned strength, at least in Ketty's presence, but now her fingers tapped on the top of the deck railing, her forehead was lined with creases, her lips twisted in a grimace.

She caught sight of Ketty and stiffened. "Four more days." She spoke English now. "I have to go. I'll call again tomorrow." She flipped the cover back over her phone and dropped it into her bag as if it were too hot to touch.

"A call from home?" Ketty asked.

"My oldest son, Peter."

"How is he?"

"Very well." Ning still looked worried.

Ketty nodded. "Is everything okay?"

"Yes."

Ning had two sons, Peter and Henry. They'd been babies when Ning first started working for Ketty and she'd watched them grow. During their school years Ketty had always made sure they were welcome to come with Ning on student-free days or during school holidays. They'd take their books and games into the back room, which was set up with beanbags and a TV, or Ning sometimes worked from home. They'd been quiet boys, well-mannered and very studious. Once they'd gone to university Ketty had rarely seen them, in fact the last time had probably been at Peter's wedding a few years prior.

"Are you sure, Ning? They seem to be in touch a lot. They don't do that when you're at work so why…."

Ning's look turned to horror and she ducked her head and rummaged in her bag.

"Ning?" Ketty was worried but when Ning turned back, her face was composed and she held out a small book.

"I bought a souvenir. It's a Dreamtime story about the rainbow serpent," she said quickly. "I will read it to my grandchild, so they learn about this beautiful place and its history."

"That's a good idea."

Ning slipped the book back into her bag. "They are planning a nursery in my back room."

"Who is?"

"Peter and his wife."

"But that's your sewing room?" Ning's husband had created the special space for her. Ning had cherished it, especially when her family were small. She'd had a place she could keep her sewing and it also made it easier for her to work from home when she needed to.

Ning looked up, battling to hide the sorrow on her face. "I can sew on the dining table if I need."

"But the baby won't be there all the time. I know you still have Henry at home but what about Peter's old room? Can't they put the baby there when they visit?"

"He and his wife are moving in with me. They want to save money to buy their own house."

"But—"

"Sorry I took so long." Carlos joined their group.

Perplexed that her conversation with Ning had been interrupted Ketty sighed then glanced at his empty hands. "No coffee?"

Judith and Tien stepped out after him, carrying a small souvenir bag each.

"Sorry," Carlos said. "I got sidetracked and then the queue was so long. I think we have to return to the bus soon."

Ketty glanced at her watch. "So we do."

"I'll get you a coffee when we're back on the train."

"Aren't we lucky all the on-train costs are covered." Judith stared at Carlos a moment before turning her gaze to Ketty and pulling her lips up in a smile. "With thanks for your generosity, Ketty."

Behind Judith, Carlos stiffened and once more Ketty had the sense that something was going on and she was missing it.

"They are calling us for the bus." Tien beckoned them wildly.

"It's okay, Tien," Ketty said as they all began to stroll in that direction. "They won't go without us." The two women went ahead and she waited for Carlos, who'd stopped to look at his phone.

"Is everything all right?" she asked.

"Yes." He tucked the phone back in his pocket. "I'm expecting a call…hoping to hear about my case."

"I meant between you and Judith. I'm sorry she seems a bit gruff at times."

"I don't think she likes me very much."

"She's a reserved person, that's all. She takes a while to get to know people." Ketty was quick to defend her friend but deep down she'd got the same vibe.

"And I'm afraid Tien thinks I'm the devil for sharing your cabin."

"Has she said something?"

"No. It's just that horrified look she keeps giving me."

"Don't take it personally. Tien gives lots of people that look. Including me sometimes. She takes a while to process things but she'll come round."

"She almost knocked over a display stand trying to move away from me when I joined the group in the shop. I know we're still meant to keep our distance in crowds but she bolted."

"Oh dear." Ketty laughed. "I'm sure it must have been something else that startled her, not you. Anyway, you're not usually one to take things to heart. Look at all the cruise passengers you've dealt with over the years. You usually ended up having any disgruntled customers eating from your hand."

"This is different, Ketty. These women are your friends and I don't want to damage that relationship."

They'd reached the bus, the last of the stragglers. Ketty climbed the steps. The front seat was vacant. Warren gave her a wave and a hearty smile from the seat behind. Val was looking at her phone. Ketty took a window seat then realised Carlos was still outside. He was peering at his phone. Ketty despaired. Phones everywhere – even Carlos was checking his regularly.

He joined her and immediately struck up a conversation with the chap opposite. Ketty was left to gaze out the window. Behind her she heard Warren and Val speaking in low tones but their volume increased when the bus started up. The noise of the motor was loud. Ketty moved her ear closer to the gap between the seats but she only caught snatches of their conversation.

"It'll be a week be…we get back," Val said.

"They can…"

"It's not…them."

"I'm not doing it, Val." Warren's voice was louder and Ketty straightened away from the gap. "I've promised the t…"

She eased back as she lost his words in the engine noise again.

"You're so selfish!" Val's response was loud and clear.

The driver turned on the music and Ketty was left to wonder what that had been about. She was looking forward to pre-dinner drinks.

Carlos sat back and rested his head against the seat. A shaft of sunlight crossed his face and highlighted the dark shadows beneath his eyes.

"Are you all right?" Ketty asked. "You're not still worrying about Judith and Tien, are you?"

"No. I'm suddenly very tired. I didn't sleep much last night."

"You've been travelling for days, you poor thing. Why don't you shut your eyes? A fifteen-minute catnap might help you get through till bedtime."

"Once upon a time I'd power through the jet lag but now…"

She patted his arm. "Sleep for a few minutes. I'll wake you when we're nearly back to the train."

Carlos closed his eyes and it was barely a minute before his face relaxed and his mouth sagged open a little. A short time later he was deep in sleep, the snuffles and burbles of his breathing swallowed by the noise of the bus. She wondered if he was a snorer. No doubt she'd find out tonight. A little flutter of concern rippled inside her.

She'd been gung-ho insisting he share her cabin. When he'd arrived they'd had to organise his tours so Caryn could book his choices. He'd had a quick look at their cabin and they'd got talking then realised it was lunchtime. He hadn't even unpacked before they'd gone to the lounge car and then on to dine. Then they'd only had time to grab their hats and bags before they'd left for the tour buses.

Carlos's head slipped sideways and the weight of it flopped to her shoulder at an almost ninety-degree angle. This close she could smell the spicy scent of his deodorant mingled with that of perspiration. She wrapped her scarf around her handbag and wedged it between her shoulder and his head, hoping he'd be more comfortable. From his relaxed pose and deep breathing she was sure he was out for the count.

She relaxed too, imagining for a moment what it would be like to have a husband and for this small piece of intimacy to be an everyday occurrence. Not an experience she was familiar with. There'd been men in her life since the disaster that had been Leo in her late twenties but there'd never been enough of a spark for her to want to make it permanent, even though one of them had asked her to marry him.

Ketty wasn't looking for that kind of relationship but she was happy if it found others. And even better if she could encourage people in the right direction. Her Christmas lunch had partly been planned with that in mind. She'd been delighted when Lacey and Dean had hit it off. She'd thought them well suited. Judith was a hard nut to crack but Klaus was obviously interested so Ketty hadn't given up. It had been such a happy day, made better by having Carlos there. He'd charmed her guests and overall her lunch had been a success, she was sure of it.

sixteen

The previous December — Paddington, Sydney

Christmas morning had been busy with the last of the food preparation, but once it was done Carlos turned his hand to cocktails while Ketty and Judith changed. They'd set up the staff kitchen downstairs as the bar and Carlos was ready with his festive drinks by the time the first guests, Maurice and Lee, arrived.

"The green one looks refreshing," Lee said.

"It's fruity," Ketty said, having already tasted both the green and the red drinks and decided her few sips were enough for the moment if she was to last until lunch.

Carlos handed Lee a glass of his vibrant green cocktail. "It's melon liqueur, clear rum and fizzy lemon-lime soda, sweet but not overly."

"What's in the red one?" Maurice boomed.

"My usual sangria but with the addition of brandy and a dash of sweet syrup and cinnamon. I think you'll like it."

"Good for Ketty to have a man about doing this sort of thing for her." Maurice took the glass of fizzing red liquid. "Lee always

129

puts me in charge of drinks when we entertain. One less thing for her to worry about."

Lee smiled but Ketty noticed the slight raise of her eyebrows.

Dean arrived at that moment, closely followed by Lacey who was wearing an elegant black chiffon dress with silver embroidery at the halter-style neckline and the vintage hat Ketty had given her for Christmas a few days before.

"Have you two met?" Ketty asked.

"We introduced ourselves on the way in," Dean said.

Judith was offering appetisers and had stopped beside Maurice. The two of them were eyeing Lacey's outfit.

"You look exquisite, Lacey," Ketty said. "You're so clever to have turned that remnant into a dress. The trapeze cut suits you."

"And I love the flowers on your boots," Lee said. "Different to your usual lace-ups."

"I had a lucky find of this pair in the op shop." Lacey twisted her foot to show the vibrant red flowers on the elastic inset. "Ning showed me how to do the embroidery."

"So you did it yourself?" Lee enthused. "How clever."

"Boots with flowers. Whatever next," Maurice muttered.

Judith smirked behind her hand.

Lacey's cheeks flushed pink and she turned away to remove her hat.

Heat rose inside Ketty too but it was from annoyance. Maurice was getting under her skin today and she didn't like Judith encouraging his pomposity. She took a deep breath. Klaus arrived at that moment and pressed a roughly wrapped bundle into her hands.

"I told you not to bring anything," she chided as she peeled back the paper to reveal a Stollen loaf. She brushed his stubbly cheek with a kiss and encountered a waft of something spicy. He'd obviously given himself a liberal splash of aftershave. Klaus was several years younger than her but his buttoned-to-the-neck shirt and well-worn cord trousers made him seem older. "You know how much I love this. Is it from your favourite shop?"

He nodded. "They make the most authentic." Once a week Klaus travelled several suburbs to a German butchery and deli that stocked many of his favourite foods.

She put the fruity German Christmas bread on the bench. It was sealed inside a special wrapper so it would keep for the week or so it would take her to work her way through it a slice at a time.

Ketty drew her arm through Klaus's and led him forward. "This is my friend Carlos. You must try his holiday sangria. It's almost like having mulled wine but chilled."

Klaus accepted the glass, took a sip and smiled.

"I don't think you've met Lacey."

"I've seen you coming and going from the shop," Klaus said as he nodded at Lacey.

"And you know everyone else."

Judith approached with a plate of hors d'oeuvres.

"Do taste one of these blinis with smoked salmon," Ketty said. "Judith made them and they're divine."

"It's not that special," Judith murmured.

"I'd like to try one."

Klaus smiled warmly and Ketty was pleased to see his focus was on Judith. She let go of his arm. "Take two," she insisted, wishing Judith would loosen up a bit. She and Klaus would be good company for each other.

Klaus took one in each hand, still smiling at Judith, and Ketty stepped away. "We need music." She picked up her phone to find the playlist she'd created for the day. In her rush she fumbled.

"Give it to one of the young ones." Maurice chuckled. "They'll make it work."

Thankfully Michael Bublé started singing 'Holly Jolly Christmas' or Ketty may well have snarled at Maurice.

"Please sit down, everyone." She waved a hand towards the table. "There are place names at each setting."

"This looks lovely," Lee said. "What have you done for us this year?"

She lifted her name plate from where it was propped against the gold linen napkin tied in the shape of a pudding with a sprig of holly through the top.

"Very festive," Carlos said as he pulled out a chair for Ketty and then for Lacey on his other side.

Klaus did the same for Judith, who was sitting at the opposite end of the table to Ketty.

"Did you make these, Miss Ketty?" Lacey had undone the knot at the top of the napkin pudding and pulled out a dainty bow tie.

"I did."

Lacey immediately wrapped the straps around her wrist and asked Dean to tie it for her. Ketty was so glad she'd chosen red taffeta and silver trim for Lacey's bow. It went perfectly with the silver at her neck and of course the red flowers on her boots.

"Is that what you do with them?" Lee said and immediately turned to Maurice to tie her green and silver bow to her wrist.

"They can go in your hair, on your ankle, the strap of a handbag – you can wear them wherever you like. I'm guessing the men will prefer the neck," Ketty said. All the men bar Dean had tied their sparkling bow ties at their neck. He held his left hand to Judith.

"Wrist for me, thanks. Can't have all the blokes the same."

Ketty grinned at Dean and tied hers in her hair like a headband so it held her chin-length bob back from her forehead. "Vive la différence!"

"Much better idea than those ridiculous paper hats." Maurice nodded approvingly.

"You've all got a silly thing in your swags as well," Ketty said. "There's something to wear, something to eat, something useful and something silly."

They all set aside the small individually wrapped Christmas truffles, except for Dean who popped his straight in his mouth. "I know I won't have room for it later." He laughed.

"You should have taken it home," Judith rebuked. "There's so much food to come."

Dean wiped his chocolate-smudged lips with the napkin.

"The napkin is the useful." Ketty chuckled.

"And I'm guessing this is the silly." Carlos waggled a slip of paper between his fingers.

"You have to have the Christmas jokes."

Carlos cleared his throat. "What do you get if you eat Christmas decorations?"

"Tinsilitus," Dean quipped. Everyone else groaned but then took turns to read out their jokes.

Ketty glanced around her table, decorated simply with holly woven between the sparkling crystal glasses and her mother's silver cutlery, polished to a shine the day before by Carlos. To the background sounds of her Christmas jazz playlist, her guests chatted and joked. Ketty let herself relax. Her Christmas luncheon was going well.

seventeen

Night One – On board the Ghan

Ketty's eyes sprung open and her head pressed back against the seat. She focused on her surroundings and realised the bus was almost back to the train, which stretched out along the platform a short distance ahead.

"Carlos." She shook him gently but he didn't rouse. An odd buzzing sound came from somewhere nearby. She looked around and realised it was coming from his pocket. "Carlos." She tapped his cheek softly and his eyes fluttered.

He groaned and looked around blankly as if he didn't recognise her or where he was.

The bus stopped and people began to fill the aisle.

"You went into a deep sleep," Ketty said. "I should have woken you earlier but I was drifting off myself. I think your phone was ringing."

He leaned away, tugged it from his pocket and peered at the screen. "Mierda!"

Ketty was surprised. She so rarely heard Carlos lose control. "Was it someone about your case?"

"No." He moved his head from side to side and rubbed at his neck. There was a deep crease in his cheek where it had rested on her bag. "I had hoped to sort something before we lose signal again. It's not important."

He sat forward as if to get to his feet then flopped back against the seat.

"Are you feeling all right?"

"Like I've been hit by this bus instead of riding in it." He gave her one of his trademark smiles. "I'll have a shower when we get back on board. That should wake me up."

"Let's wait till everyone's off the bus. Then we can take our time."

"Was the tour too exciting for you, old mate?" Warren grinned at them as he ushered Val ahead of him towards the door.

"Jet lag." Carlos rubbed a cheek with his hand.

"You still up for drinks later?"

"We'll be there, won't we, Carlos." Ketty smiled.

He nodded. "See you there."

Several more people filed past and then Tien was peering at them, worry all over her face.

"Is everything all right?"

"Yes." Ketty nodded. "We were a bit slow getting up so we're waiting till everyone's off."

"I can help." Tien glanced from Carlos to Ketty, no doubt calculating how she could assist Ketty without touching Carlos in the aisle seat.

"We're perfectly fine to get ourselves off," Ketty said firmly. "We're just waiting for the rush to subside."

"What's the hold-up?" someone called from behind. "I've got a drink at the bar with my name on it."

Tien shot forward.

Judith was next, her gaze on Ketty. "Would you like us to wait for you?"

"No, no. You go ahead. We'll see you in the lounge car before dinner. Our booking is for seven o'clock."

Ning followed, smiling as she passed. No sooner was she off the bus she was back looking at her phone and would have wobbled off the path if Tien hadn't put a hand out to guide her.

The last passenger stepped down and Carlos rose to his feet. He swayed and gripped the handrail beside the steps.

"You okay, mate?" the driver asked.

"Jet lag," Carlos said swiftly then stamped from foot to foot. "My leg is sleeping."

"Do you need help getting off." The driver was half out of his seat.

"No, no." Carlos put up a hand.

Ketty could see he was embarrassed. "Thank you," she said to the driver. "We'll be fine."

She slipped her arm through Carlos's. "Are you sure you're all right?" she murmured as they navigated around the last of the stragglers and set off for the train.

"I hate to admit it but the fatigue has caught up with me. I've always powered through in the past."

"That was the beauty of cruising." Ketty gave his arm a squeeze. "No jet lag."

They reached the bitumen path beside the train. A vehicle resembling an oversized golf cart slowly overtook them with several passengers on board.

Warren leaned out and waved. "Don't take too long, you two," he called. "Drinks await."

They laughed and waved back, then Ketty noticed Mr Visser facing them from the rear seat. She smiled and nodded. He gave a brief nod in response as the cart rumbled away.

"Do you know that man?" Carlos asked.

"We met briefly – why?"

"I'm embarrassed to say I entered his cabin thinking it was ours. Must have been the jet lag."

"Oh, no. I think it's easily done. The carriages are identical but for their letters."

"I was sure I was in the right place but there he was—"

"Mr Visser is his name."

"I apologised and left quickly. Very embarrassing. We must remember to keep our door locked when we're inside. Anyone could walk in."

"Yes." Ketty gazed after the cart. "I could hail you one of those," she said.

"There's no rush." Carlos shook his head. "Walking is the best thing right now."

The long string of carriages stretched off into the distance and Ketty stared a little enviously at the cart-load of people being ferried towards them. She was feeling a little weary herself but she wasn't going to admit it.

"Tell me, Ketty, what are you thinking about our cabin sharing now?"

She glanced at him, the hint of a smile twitching at the corners of his mouth.

"We'll manage admirably, like friends do."

"Siblings."

Ketty frowned.

"We're brother and sister, remember."

"Oh, yes." She laughed and enjoyed the warm sound of Carlos joining in.

Judith stood in the corridor looking out the window. She'd offered to give Ning a moment's privacy and had planned to sit in the lounge car but the pair strolling past on the path outside caught her eye. It was Ketty and Carlos looking like the perfect couple. They were deep in conversation. Carlos leaned in and Ketty laughed. They acted for all the world like a pair of love-birds. At her age!

Judith glanced up and down the corridor. Thank goodness no-one else was around to witness their embarrassing behaviour. And as much as Ketty said it was none of anyone else's business that they shared a cabin, Judith was sure people would make it their business, especially a couple of Carlos and Ketty's age. People loved to gossip.

She could hear the two of them now, chatting to Caryn as they climbed back on board. Judith stepped back into her cabin so they wouldn't see her. The bathroom door was shut and she could hear the shower was still running.

Judith paced the tiny cabin until the sound of the water stopped then she let herself out into the corridor again. She looked left then froze as she turned right. Carlos was walking away from her, a towel over his shoulder, a toiletries bag in one hand and his phone pressed to his ear with the other.

He rounded the corner. Judith followed cautiously. He was obviously headed to the single-cabin bathrooms in the next carriage. If he was out of the way, she'd slip back and talk to Ketty.

When she came to the dogleg at the end of the corridor she halted. Carlos was in the kitchenette, but thankfully his back was to her.

"You've got to help me out, please."

His desperate tone stopped Judith mid-backward step. Help him with what?

"It shouldn't be for long." He moved slightly and she saw the phone still pressed to his ear.

A door opened further down the corridor behind her. Her knees went to jelly. Carlos took a step further into the kitchenette and, holding her breath, Judith eased open the door of the toilet opposite and went in, closing it carefully behind her. She locked it then leaned against it, pressing her ear to the thin panel.

"I know. I thought it was all sorted." Carlos's voice carried clearly. "I don't want Ketty to know about it."

Judith pressed her ear closer as a long silence followed. Perhaps he'd walked away.

"Mierda!" He spoke rapidly in what Judith assumed was Spanish.

She huffed, not understanding a word, then started as his voice sounded right outside her door.

"Okay, okay, English." There was a pause. "Yes, yes, I get it but I'm making some headway and I don't want to frighten her off."

Judith clamped a hand over her mouth to stifle the gasp that escaped. Whatever he was up to she didn't like the sound of it.

"Ketty's not a fool," he continued. "She'll soon catch on if I don't..."

The door to the next carriage opened. Someone walked through and then silence. Once more Judith wondered if Carlos had left. Then he spoke again, his voice further away.

"All right, as long as you can do it soon. She'll be none the wiser."

Judith sucked in a breath to swallow the anger that threatened to erupt.

"We're moving. I've got to go."

Judith felt the gentle vibration under her feet and it continued up through her hand and cheek pressed against the door.

"I know what I'm doing. You just—" Once more his words were lost to her as the door opened and shut again.

"Hi, Carlos." Birgit's voice carried through the flimsy door. "Are you heading to the shower?"

"Yes. I'm giving Ketty some space." Carlos was all charm again. "We're going to meet for drinks in the lounge car later."

"That's where I'm off to. See you there."

Doors continued to open and close and several different voices sounded outside until finally it was quiet again but for the sounds of the train picking up speed. Judith's anger gathered pace with that of the train. She'd known Carlos was up to something. She'd heard of women being duped by men who took all their money and left them and Judith wasn't going to allow that to happen to Ketty.

She eased the toilet door open a crack and peered out. The kitchenette was empty. Judith emerged from her hiding place and began to pace the long corridor just as Ning opened their cabin door.

"I'm finished in here now. I'll meet you in the lounge car."

Judith let herself in and began to fling off her clothes. She didn't have time to shower, she'd simply put on a fresh outfit. She wasn't sure how she was going to broach the subject of Carlos but she needed to warn Ketty.

Lacey glanced around the cabin that was identical to hers and yet looked somehow more stylish. The table was clear of clutter unlike the one in Lacey's room, which was covered with drink bottles, sun and hand cream tubes, and Tien's huge stack of travel brochures. They were neat, of course – Tien straightened everything regularly as she did her spare shoes tucked under the seat and all the items they'd stowed in the tiny shelves behind the door.

You'd barely know two people shared Miss Ketty's cabin. A handbag was the only item tucked in the corner under the table where Lacey and Tien had stashed their toiletry and cosmetic bags. The shelves were neatly arranged with drink bottles, travel brochures and a scarf patterned in deep green and silver that was hooked over the rail and draped along the shelf. And Miss Ketty herself sat at the opposite end of the couch, fresh in the elegant moss-green linen dress she'd made for the previous Christmas. It was a sleeveless V-neck midi-length dress with a broad belt in the same fabric tied in a loose bow at the waist. Lacey had swapped her shorts for a long floaty skirt and her top for a plain black turtleneck T-shirt. She'd added a long gold chain that had been her gran's in the hope it looked smart enough – Miss Ketty had warned them to come prepared to dress for dinner.

"You look lovely. Please do a spin for me."

Lacey turned on the spot and Ketty reached over to pluck at the fabric of her skirt.

"It's mesh."

"Yes, so I made it double-layered."

"The salmon pink is perfect beneath the black floral." Ketty eyed her up and down. "And an elastic waist, simple yet elegant with the black top."

"Not in the same class as your gorgeous dress. That colour and style is perfect."

"I think I'll be overdressed but I do love to change for dinner. It's not something many do any more. Please sit down." Ketty patted the seat beside her. "I'm glad I saw you in the corridor. I wanted to check that you've settled in all right. I'm sorry about all the shifting around."

"I haven't had to move."

"I know, but as much as I love Tien I'm sure you would have enjoyed sharing a cabin with Birgit."

Lacey lowered her eyes to avoid Ketty's piercing gaze. "Tien and I get along fine."

"Of course, but it's good of you to be so accommodating – thank you. How was your tour?"

"It was great. The gorge was amazing and the colours..." Lacey looked up and paused, recalling the sandstone cliffs and her desire to replicate them in fabric.

"I know what you mean. I could imagine a range of garments coming out of what I saw today."

"Oh, me too."

"I thought you might."

"Wide linen pants or long floaty skirts in creams and ochres worn with silk shirts, the fabric in patched blocks like the rock wall and..." Lacey had a sudden recollection of Judith lashing out at her in the kitchenette, her harsh words. *Miss Clift shows some indulgence for your crazes.*

"Don't stop. You've such a great eye for design."

"They're just crazy ideas." Lacey looked down, thinking about the sketches she'd started the moment she got back to her cabin but recalling Judith's words made her clam up. Miss Ketty was probably planning retirement soon and she didn't need the distraction of Lacey's fanciful ideas, as Judith had put it.

"Your ideas are never crazy." Ketty's smile was warm, genuine, and she leaned forward and pressed her soft hand to Lacey's. "You've so much talent, Lacey. I sometimes fear you're wasted working for me."

"Oh, no." Lacey shook her head. "I love working at Ketty Clift Couture. The staff are all so talented each in their own way and with you overseeing...I've learned so much."

"I'm glad you feel that way but if you ever saw an opportunity to extend your career somewhere else don't feel you can't and please let's discuss it."

"That's very generous of you."

"My staff are my family." Ketty patted her hand again then nestled back in her seat. "I want what's best for each of you. I've sensed there's been some unrest lately. I hope you'd feel you could talk to me if there was anything..."

"You're not retiring, are you?" Lacey blurted. "Selling to Judith."

"No, I'm not. Where on earth would you get that idea?"

"It was something Tien said." Lacey grimaced. "Only I couldn't stay on if Judith owned the business."

"Oh? Why is that?"

Lacey wished she could talk honestly. Ketty was so kind but she was also very close to Judith, and besides, what was there to say? Judith didn't like Lacey and the feeling was mutual. How could they get past that?

"We're two very different people," she said carefully.

"It's what makes the world go round but difference doesn't mean one is right and the other wrong."

Once more Ketty was studying her with such kindness the walls around Lacey's resolve slipped.

"I'm really not sure why…Judith and I have never been close but lately her antagonism towards me has got worse." She took a breath then blurted, "I'd go as far as to say she hates me."

Ketty gasped. "Hate is a very strong word."

"I don't know how else to put it." Lacey wrung her hands in her lap. "And lately it's got worse."

"In what way?"

Nausea churned in the pit of Lacey's stomach but Ketty spoke so gently and she'd come this far. "Well, there was just the other day when Judith had brought cake. You were due back from the hairdresser and she cut it up for afternoon tea. She put a piece on everyone's desk and when she came to mine she had none left. She said she was sorry, she'd miscalculated, but the look on her face said otherwi—"

Lacey jumped at a sharp rap on Ketty's door. It cracked open.

"Ketty?" Judith called gently from the other side then stuck her head in. "Oh. I thought…I didn't realise you had someone here."

"Carlos has gone off to shower and change in the singles bathroom and he's meeting us later in the lounge car. Lacey and I were making the most of some quiet time."

"Oh." Judith stared so hard Lacey was sure she could read her mind.

"I should go." Lacey leaped to her feet.

"You don't have to," Ketty said.

"There is something I need to discuss with you, Ketty." Judith looked pointedly at Lacey. "In private."

"I need to go anyway." Lacey stepped past her. Out in the corridor the door clicked shut behind her and Lacey put her hands to the wall to steady her trembling knees.

Ketty smiled at Judith to hide her annoyance. It was the first time in a long time that she'd had such a revealing conversation with Lacey and she'd been keen to hear her side of things. Ketty often enough heard Judith's point of view when they had their Friday drinks, not that she said a lot about Lacey. In fact, now that she thought about it, Judith often talked about the others but said little about the quality of Lacey's skills or her tenacious work ethic.

Somehow she'd pin down Lacey later but for now she was curious about whatever it was Judith seemed worked up about. She was pacing the tiny floor space in a fresh set of clothes but she looked dishevelled, which was unusual for Judith.

"Please sit down." Ketty patted the seat beside her with a small sense of deja vu. It felt like her cabin had a revolving door. "Would you like some water? I must admit I'm looking forward to the lounge car and a sip of something stronger soon."

"I don't need anything, thank you." She studied Ketty. "What were you and Lacey talking about? She looked quite upset."

"Just chatting." Ketty waved at the seat again. "Do sit down and tell me what you're so bothered about."

Judith sat but sprung up again as if she'd been poked with a pin.

"What is it?" Ketty smoothed her hand over the cushion to check.

Judith turned, her face creased with concern. "I'm worried for you, Ketty, and I don't know how to start."

"Goodness." Once more Ketty patted the seat beside her. "You don't need to worry about me. I'm perfectly fine. Why would you think otherwise?"

Judith sagged to the seat again. "You're my friend, and you've worked so hard to build your business, prepare a comfortable retirement—"

"Why do people keep mentioning that?"

"Perhaps they've noticed you haven't been as…present as you used to be?"

Ketty frowned. "Are you suggesting I'm losing touch?"

"Not at all." Judith winced. "But you have been away often over the last few months and—"

"And you've ably filled in."

"Thank you. You know I'm happy to but when you're not there it's not the same and I wonder if the others think you're slowing down."

"Good grief, I've taken a few days off to spend with Carlos."

Judith raised an eyebrow.

Ketty huffed. "Several days perhaps," she conceded. "And then I broke my wrist, but I was still able to be at work. I don't believe any of that equates to slowing down, as you put it, and whatever they think, I'm not planning to retire any time soon."

"I know. When I said your retirement I was thinking about the distant future…for when you do—"

Ketty glared at her.

Judith gripped her hands together and went on. "You don't want to end up with no money like one of those women who lose their life savings."

"Good grief." Ketty frowned. Ketty Clift Couture was doing very well. The pandemic had provided a silver lining for her business thanks to a few clever changes, some of which Lacey had suggested. Ketty had spent a lot of money on this holiday – there'd be no Christmas bonus for her staff this year, and she'd taken some of the money from her personal nest egg but that was still healthy enough. "I've no intention of being one of those women."

"This is so hard." Judith groaned.

Unease fluttered in Ketty's chest. Was there something about the business that she'd missed? "I really don't know what you're trying to—"

"I have concerns about...about Carlos," Judith blurted.

"Carlos!"

"Something's wrong with—"

"What's happened to him?" Ketty half rose.

"Nothing but he's acting a bit odd."

"Oh, no, he's fine." Relief blew away the unease. Judith's tangled way of talking had Ketty jumping to the wrong conclusions. "He's suffering from jet lag but—"

"No, I mean I'm worried Carlos is...not who you think he is."

"I know perfectly well who Carlos is. You're not making sense, Judith. Are you sure you wouldn't like some water?"

"You think you've known him a long time but how well can you really know someone you only meet up with every few years for a week or so?"

On occasion Ketty had thought the same thing. "I'll admit we have a unique friendship but it works for us."

"Do you know his financial situation?"

"It's none of my business. Just as my finances are no concern of his. We act independently of each other in that regard. I really don't know why you're even bringing it up." Ketty straightened. "It's none of your business either." Then in an attempt to lighten the moment she said, "Surely you're not going to ask his intentions."

Judith put her hands in the air. "I know he's an old friend but—"

"Stop right there." Ketty wagged a finger at Judith. "I will not have you cast aspersions on Carlos's character."

"Please, Ketty, hear me out. I don't think he has money or at least not much of it."

"He's flown back and forth to Spain. That's probably put a dent in his finances, not that it's any of my...*our* business."

"You don't know he's paid for those flights himself," Judith muttered. "It could have been someone else. He's lived rent-free at your place while he was in Sydney and probably with his cousin in Brisbane."

"You have no knowledge of that." Ketty glared at Judith, who had the good sense to look away. Carlos had tried to pay her for his accommodation but she hadn't allowed it. When I visit you in Spain you can put me up, she'd said.

"He didn't have a working phone when he first came to stay and he borrowed a car from his cousin."

"His phone died and it took a while to get a new one." It had been Ketty who'd convinced him there was no rush. They'd used her phone while he'd stayed with her and when he came back from his cousins he'd had a phone again. "And the car he borrowed was idle. It was his cousin's mother-in-law's and she's no longer allowed to drive."

"He's not paying for this holiday."

"Ridiculous! He gave me money towards my train ticket and bought a ticket for himself."

"Which has conveniently been double-booked so he's actually travelling on your ticket."

Ketty gaped at Judith. She'd obviously been thinking on this for some time and there was no changing her mind.

"And today at the shop his credit card wouldn't work," Judith continued, obviously taking Ketty's silence to mean she was listening.

"Hardly a hanging offence. Credit cards and EFTPOS machines are often trouble. You know that from our work."

"Today I heard him speaking on his phone." Judith sucked in a breath. "I couldn't hear exactly what he said but it was something he didn't want you to know. Whatever it was he thought it would frighten you off."

"Frighten me off what?"

Judith's shoulders sagged. "I don't know. I was in the spare toilet. I couldn't hear properly."

"So Carlos was having this, I'm assuming what he thought was a *private* conversation?"

"He was in the train corridor." Judith huffed. "Not very private. I just couldn't hear every…"

Ketty's eyebrows shot up. "I can't believe you're taking a partly heard conversation, one you had no right to listen to, I might add, and now you're turning it against him. This is not like you, Judith."

Judith opened her mouth and closed it again then stood up, took a step towards the door and turned back. "Ketty, you are my dearest friend. I had to warn you. Be careful is all I'm saying." She turned on her heel and let herself out.

Ketty sagged back against the seat, her heart racing. She was angry at Judith for creating doubt about Carlos, upset that she'd not been able to change her mind and sad that her beautiful friendship with Carlos had been cast in a shadow.

eighteen

Night One – Travelling South

Once she'd stopped shaking after leaving Ketty's cabin, Lacey had sought the safety of her own. Tien was in the shower so Lacey sat and gave her jelly legs a chance to return to normal. The light was dull in the cabin. She reached across and opened the blind, staring out at the vast landscape sweeping by but not really seeing it. Instead she was replaying her conversation with Ketty over and over and her stomach continued to churn. She should never have said anything. Judith and Ketty were close. It had been ridiculous of Lacey to think she could unburden to Ketty. No doubt Judith told Ketty her version of things anyway.

The bathroom door opened. Tien stepped out wrapped in a towel and followed by a cloud of steam.

"The blind," she squeaked and reached for the handle then quickly grabbed at her towel again.

"I'll do it." Lacey gave a last fleeting look at the empty vista whizzing past before the blades of the blind shut it out. When she glanced back, Tien was standing rigidly in the middle of the

150

cabin, her hands gripping the towel wrapped around her. "I'll go to the lounge car now."

"Thank you."

They edged past each other and for a moment their eyes met across the small space between them then Tien took a small step back towards the bathroom, eyeing her warily. "Your cheeks are flushed again."

"I might be a bit sunburned."

Tien smiled at Lacey. "You look nice."

Surprised at the sudden change of subject Lacey glanced down at her skirt. "Not as glam as Miss Ketty. I've just been talking to her and she's wearing that fab green linen dress she made herself for last Christmas."

"She always looks so good for a woman of her age."

Lacey tipped her head to the side. "I never think about her age but...well, retirement came up and she said she wasn't even considering it." Lacey had been so relieved to hear that. "Didn't you say Miss Ketty was selling her business to Judith?"

Tien frowned.

"It was a few weeks ago. We were sitting out in the courtyard eating our lunch and you said something about it, I'm sure."

"Oh, yes. It was the day Miss Clift had gone to get her plaster off. She's had one fall. At her age she should be taking it easy. And she has started to. She doesn't do as much as she used to. I can't see how she can continue much longer and Judith would be the obvious choice to take over the business."

Lacey chewed her lip. The way Tien had spoken about it Lacey had thought it was a plan in progress. "Miss Ketty doesn't seem keen on the idea."

"Judith has the most experience and..." Tien leaned closer. "Ning is retiring."

"Really?" Lacey didn't know how much of what Tien said to believe now.

"Don't say anything. She only told me a couple of weeks ago. It was one of the reasons she didn't want to come on this trip. She didn't think it fair Miss Clift spend the extra money on her but I made her speak up. I knew Miss Clift would insist Ning come."

"Did she say why she's retiring?"

"Her family need her and she's not getting any younger."

"She's only in her fifties, isn't she?" Lacey sighed. "She'll be missed. None of us can do the hand embroidery as quickly and neatly as she can. And she's always so calm and kind." Ning was a wonderful counterbalance to Judith as far as Lacey was concerned and if she was truthful she'd also thought of Ning as a sort of mother figure. Something she lacked in her personal life.

Tien dragged her long straight hair back from her face, untangling it with her fingers. "I must dry my hair."

"I'll head down to the lounge car while you get ready." Lacey stood. "Would you like me to come back in a while so we can walk together?"

"You're very kind." Tien straightened her shoulders. "But I think I can manage it now. I close my eyes and don't look as I cross the gangway between the carriages."

Lacey wasn't sure how safe that was. She hoped Tien didn't meet someone coming the other way.

The carriage jiggled a little harder and Tien hooked a corner of the blind with her finger and peered out.

"You could probably leave the blind open, you know," Lacey said. "There's not likely to be anyone out there, and if there was the train's moving too fast for them to see in."

Tien shuddered and turned back, leaving the blind closed. "I'll be with you soon," she said.

Lacey smiled and let herself out. It was going to take a bit more time to get Tien to relax completely.

She moved off in the direction of the lounge car then stopped. Ahead of her at the other end of the carriage Judith was walking briskly away, her conversation with Ketty obviously over. Lacey glanced back. Was Ketty still inside or had she been ahead of Judith on her way to the lounge car? Lacey continued on slowly. She hoped Birgit was already there and had saved her a seat.

Judith held her breath as she entered the lounge car. Now that she'd expressed her concerns to Ketty she wasn't sure how she was going to make conversation with Carlos. To her relief there was no sign of him nor of Lacey or Tien but Birgit was tucked up at one of the tables with those two young men she was extra chummy with already, and to Judith's surprise Ning was there too.

"Are you looking for Ketty?"

Judith glanced sideways. The couple Ketty had eaten lunch with were both smiling up at her.

"No, she'll be along in a minute."

"Would you like to sit here?" Val patted the seat beside her. "It'll get busy soon so we're saving some seats."

"Thanks."

"Carlos is just getting us a drink," Warren said.

"Oh." Judith glanced towards the bar. The people being served had moved along and there he was. "Oh," she said again and snuck into the space between Val and the end of the couch. At least Carlos couldn't sit beside her.

"Would you like a drink?" Warren asked. "I'll go and add to his order. He hasn't been served yet. Val's having a cocktail."

"Not for me. Perhaps a white wine." And before she could elaborate, he was gone.

"You're on a staff holiday," Val said. "Ketty was telling us about it on the gorge tour."

"Yes. There are six of us. Ketty owns the business, of course, but we all work there."

"I think that's lovely. I can't imagine many employers who'd do that. And you obviously all get along so well and with Ketty's brother."

"Brother?"

"Carlos."

"Oh." Judith laughed, perhaps a little too forcefully.

Val startled.

"Carlos isn't her brother. They're old friends." Judith swallowed her laughter at the pained look on Val's face.

"We seem to have misunderstood."

"What's that, pet?" Warren asked as he sat.

"Nothing. It doesn't matter."

"I forgot to ask which white wine you'd like, Judith, but Carlos seemed to know."

"Thank you." She smiled but beside her Val sat ramrod straight and Judith got the distinct impression she'd just put her foot in something.

Warren chatted away about the train journey so far. Judith smiled and responded but Val remained silent.

"Here we are." Carlos arrived with a tray of drinks. He sat a glass of wine in front of Judith. "Pinot grigio for you, a margarita for Val, and martinis for you and me, Warren. I expect Ketty should be along very soon so I got her a gin and tonic." He put the last glass on the table. "I'll just return the tray."

Tien arrived at Judith's side, her customary mask in place. "That's a nice colour," Judith said, taking in Tien's midnight-blue sheath dress. From the corner of her eye she saw Val lean towards Warren and put up her hand as if to whisper in his ear but he lurched forward, a grin on his face.

"Hello, Ten," he boomed. "You look very nice this evening."

"Thank you." Tien's eyes crinkled in a smile.

"Your group makes us look rather dowdy, doesn't it, Val?" He gave his wife a nudge. "Although that shimmery black top looks lovely on you."

"Miss Clift asked us to dress for dinner," Tien said. "I suppose it's something people of her age did back in the day."

"I've put on my best polo top." Warren chortled.

Judith had noticed he'd changed his blue striped shirt for a plain black one in an identical style. She glanced down at the black velvet pants and black lace top that were her nod to Ketty's request for them to dress up. She wasn't one for a lot of fuss either.

"I see you're doing the carriage changes on your own now," Warren said.

"Yes." Tien stood tall. "I close my eyes and move quickly."

Once more Warren laughed loudly. "An interesting strategy."

Carlos returned. "Hello, Tien. Can I get you a drink?"

"No, thank you. I'm okay for now. I've drunk lots of water." She glanced around the group. "You must do that more often when you're in the outback."

There was a moment's pause and then a call from Birgit.

"Tien?" She pointed at a seat beside Ning. "We've saved you a spot here."

Tien walked away just as the carriage door opened once more. Judith inhaled quickly as Ketty entered then paused inside the door to look for them. She smiled and made her way to where they sat. Judith slowly released the breath.

"Well, well, well, Ketty," Warren said. "Don't you look a million dollars."

"That's very kind. I do like to dress for dinner."

Warren got up so Ketty could slide onto the seat beside Val, who edged a little closer to Judith. "That's what Ten said. She reckons it's something us old fogies like to do."

Ketty flinched. It was almost imperceptible but Judith noticed.

"You and I can take these club chairs, Carlos." Warren lowered himself to one and patted the arm. "They're quite comfortable for aging bones, aren't they?"

"Indeed they are,' Carlos said as he sat in the other. "Ketty, this is yours." He leaned across and slid the tumbler towards her then lifted his martini in the air. "A toast to our first day."

"It's certainly been interesting,' Ketty said, tapping her glass to his. She glanced at Judith but her gaze didn't linger.

"To friends and family." Val looked pointedly from Ketty to Carlos.

Surely she hadn't really thought they were siblings. Judith sunk a little lower in her seat.

"To leaving family behind and making new friends," Warren said and took a swig from his glass.

"Something you're good at," Val muttered.

Ketty heard Val's comment but she was still reeling from her conversation with Judith and uncomfortable with the cloud of doubt that now hung between them. As much as Ketty tried to ignore it, she couldn't help but look at Carlos with a different eye. Judith's concerns could all be explained away but Ketty had been almost burned before with Leo.

After Judith had left the cabin, Ketty's thoughts had strayed back to her last South Pacific cruise several years ago, when she'd met up with Leo again. She'd been blinded to his flaws to begin with, been tempted – flattered if the truth be known; he was a handsome man and knew all the right things to say. However, she'd realised he was as interested in her money as he was in her. Not that she was a wealthy woman, in fact business had been slow back then, but she'd had some money and Leo had been stony broke. She'd found him out and walked away without a backward glance.

She shivered. There was no way she could even begin to compare Carlos to Leo. She glanced at him and discovered he was studying her expectantly. Then she realised Warren and Val were too. Judith was looking the other way.

"You weren't with us there for a moment," Carlos said.

"I hope you didn't get a touch of the sun today." Warren reached forward as if he was going to put a hand on her forehead.

"Oh, no, I'm sorry. My mind was elsewhere. What were you saying?"

"Just that I couldn't imagine sharing a cabin with my sister. You're very good friends. Have either of you married?"

"Warren," Val chided.

Warren's face fell. "Sorry, I suppose it's a bit personal but I did wonder, if you had partners, why they wouldn't come with…" He faltered. "I'm guessing there could be a lot of reasons why they're not here…if you had partners, that is."

Judith looked down the length of her nose at Ketty then glanced away. This was getting all too complicated.

"Actually, Warren," Carlos said in a low tone. "Can you keep a secret?"

"Of course." Warren nudged Val. "Our lips will be sealed, won't they, pet?"

Val sniffed and raised her eyebrows and Ketty had the distinct feeling she'd missed something important.

"I'm afraid I wasn't truthful when we first met," Carlos said. "You see, I very nearly missed out on this journey. There was a mix-up with my cabin booking."

Carlos smiled at Ketty. The warmth of it filled her heart and dispersed the doubt Judith's words had sown.

"Ketty and I aren't siblings. We're old friends," Carlos continued. "And because she's such a kind person she offered me the spare bunk in her cabin."

"I see," Warren said.

"Why would you lie about it?" Val huffed.

"It was a joke between Ketty and I."

Val raised her chin and glared at Carlos. "You were laughing at us."

"Not at all." Carlos was quick to reassure her. "Ketty is an independent woman who can do with her own life whatever she wishes but not everyone thinks like her. I'm already imposing on her kindness and...perhaps I'm being old-fashioned but I wanted to protect her reputation. Just before you arrived at our table Ketty had assured me we would manage our arrangement very well, in fact 'like brother and sister', she said."

"I did." Ketty nodded.

"And so I blurted that out when we met." Carlos looked from Warren to Val. "Then it was hard to unsay without causing a fuss. I apologise for misleading you."

"I see." Warren nodded sagely. "No harm done then, old mate, is there, Val?"

Val hesitated and Carlos smiled benignly. "Of course not," she agreed.

Judith let out a large sigh, reminding Ketty of her censorial presence. The angst returned and Ketty wondered how she was going to get through dinner.

As it turned out she didn't have to worry. Lacey and Tien sat with Ketty and Carlos, while across the aisle Ning, Birgit and Judith shared the opposite table. Judith and Ketty both had window seats and were as far apart as they could be in that setting. It was difficult to engage the other table in conversation with the waitstaff continually moving between them so Ketty had to be content to find out more about Tien and Lacey's day. Lacey was rather quiet, not unusual for her but Ketty was sure their interrupted chat earlier was playing on her mind, as it was Ketty's.

They were served by Simon and Belinda, who were as attentive as cruise ship staff. Ketty couldn't help but notice Carlos watching them carefully. She didn't think he'd find them wanting.

The entrees arrived quickly, giving them something else to focus on. Ketty's vegetable terrine melted in her mouth, Carlos inhaled his smoked duck and both Tien and Lacey raved over their prawn and crab dumplings. With the first course under their belts and another drink each the conversation flowed more easily.

Tien surprised them all by ordering a glass of red wine to go with her main course of braised beef cheeks and then had an in-depth conversation with Carlos about the merits of shiraz, which he was drinking, compared to the grenache she had chosen. Ketty had never seen her drink wine before. There was always something new to learn about people, even those you thought you knew well.

With the other two occupied she took the opportunity to speak to Lacey. "I'd like to continue our earlier conversation."

Lacey reached for her glass, almost knocking it over in her haste.

"Not here and now, of course, but perhaps later this evening." Ketty kept her voice low. "Carlos would give us some time alone if you came to my cabin."

"I shouldn't have said anything."

"Yes, you should, and a long time ago, I suspect. I'm sorry to think you've been unhappy."

"Oh, but I haven't." Lacey's emphatic tone drew Carlos's and Tien's attention.

"What haven't you?" Tien asked.

"Travelled on a train before." Ketty gave Lacey a reassuring smile.

"None of us have," Tien said.

"Except Carlos, who has travelled in Europe via train."

"It was nothing like the Ghan," Carlos said. "Although many years ago I did travel from Paris to Barcelona on a sleeper train."

"I can't imagine how I'll get any sleep," Tien groaned. "The train rumbles so much."

"I think we'll all be so tired we'll soon be asleep." Ketty reassured her as much for her own benefit as Tien's. The younger woman had been quite lively tonight and Ketty didn't want to see a return of the angst she'd displayed earlier.

The waitstaff arrived with their desserts and Tien groaned. "Chocolate pudding seemed a good idea when I ordered it."

"Luckily they're not big serves." Lacey lifted a spoon of ice cream to her mouth.

"And ice cream slips down easily," Carlos said as he dipped a spoon into his.

Ketty had ordered the cheese platter and was glad she had as more wine arrived.

"My goodness," Tien said. "What's this?"

"I ordered you and me a late-harvest riesling for our desserts," Carlos said. "And another white for you, Ketty, and champagne for Lacey."

"I don't usually drink very much," Lacey said, her eyes wide.

"That was kind of you, Carlos," Ketty said.

"And you don't have to drink it if you don't want to," he said but Ketty noticed both women taking sips between mouthfuls of dessert.

They were still chatting when Birgit got up from her table. "I'm meeting the double Rs in the lounge for a nightcap."

"We might see you there," Ketty said.

"Not us." Ning stifled a yawn. "Judith and I are off to test out the beds."

"Sleep well." Ketty waved her fingers. Judith avoided eye contact.

"I'll go too," Tien said.

Lacey took her barely touched champagne glass from the table. "I'll sit in the lounge for a while, give you a head start."

When Ketty entered the lounge car there were groups of people enjoying a nightcap and a chat but no sign of Birgit or the Irish cousins. Lacey sat on a couch by herself.

"I'd like to have a little chat with Lacey before bed," Ketty murmured in Carlos's ear.

He nodded. "I'll go back to the cabin. That meal and the wine were magnificent but I'm very fatigued now."

Ketty sat beside Lacey. "I'm giving Carlos some time to prepare for bed. He's been travelling on and off for three days, poor man is very tired."

The carriage door opened and Lacey glanced that way expectantly. A man entered, smiled and joined a group near the bar.

"Perhaps Birgit's having an early night," Ketty said.

"Maybe." Lacey looked to the door again as if waiting for it to save her.

"While we're passing the time I was hoping you and I could have another talk...if you feel up to it?"

Ketty was relieved when Lacey gave an almost imperceptible nod.

nineteen

Night One – Travelling South

Lacey perched on the edge of the seat and took another sip of her champagne. They sat either side of a small table, their club chairs turned so that their backs were angled towards the carriage behind them. It gave the illusion of privacy. Now that she'd come this far she was resolved that she would tell Ketty about her experience with Judith. The third glass of champagne had given her courage but she wasn't sure how or where to begin.

"When we were interrupted earlier you were telling me how Judith omitted you when sharing the cake," Ketty said. "Does that happen often?"

"Not exactly that. She's only ever done that once. It's just that she's always..." Lacey paused – 'always' wasn't quite true. "*Sometimes* she says unkind things."

"I see." Ketty frowned. "It must make work unhappy for you."

"Oh, no, I love my work and you, Miss Ketty. You're...inspirational." Lacey paused, trying to think. "I've never found Judith easy to be with, not like Ning and Tien and Birgit but...perhaps in the last year or so she's been quick to find fault with my work, especially if you've praised me for it, and it's more recent that her...unkindness has escalated. Judith is your friend and I know it sounds like I'm making it up—"

Ketty pressed a hand to hers. "I want to assure you that I believe you, Lacey."

Lacey took another sip of champagne.

"I know it's not easy for you to tell me," Ketty said. "And you're right, Judith and I are friends, but that doesn't mean I can't put that aside and wear my non-prejudicial employer's hat. We're speaking in confidence, of course."

Lacey tipped the champagne glass and drained the last mouthful. "Judith told me I was putting too much pressure on your business."

A puzzled look crossed Ketty's face. "In what way?"

"She said some of my ideas, like the online shop, were good for your business but that my other suggestions were crazes and that you...indulged me. She said most of my suggestions were fanciful and would ruin your reputation for fine couture garments."

"Oh dear." Ketty tutted and then they both fell silent. The chatter of the other travellers was muffled by the rumble of the train, which vibrated under their feet.

Lacey pushed back against the seat. She wished it could open up and swallow her. Now that she'd aired her concerns about Judith there could be no going back. She wondered what Ketty would do. Would this be the end of Lacey's dream job? The job she'd taken straight from school while she'd studied dressmaking and design part-time. The job where Ketty had encouraged her creativity and given her the space to flourish, but had that all been pretence?

"You must miss your gran. How is everything at home...your father?"

Lacey blinked. Ketty's question was not what she'd been expecting.

"He's fine."

"It can't be easy now without your grandmother. Forgive me if I'm wrong but I got the impression she was the glue for your family."

Lacey felt a fresh stab of the loss that had been blunted a little with time. Her gran had died over a year ago. "She was."

"And your sister moved away, didn't she?"

"To New Zealand." It was as far away as Freya's job would take her. "She loves it there and she and Dad weren't getting on so well."

"Oh, that's a shame. You must miss her."

Lacey thought about the last phone call she'd had with her sister. It had ended in an argument about the house again but Freya meant well. "I do."

"So it must be quiet with just you and your dad? Does he get on with Dean?"

Lacey sucked in a breath. Their difficult talk about Judith had morphed into something else entirely. "I haven't seen Dean for a while." She pressed her fingers to her trembling lips.

Ketty's face fell. "I'm sorry, Lacey. Your personal life is none of my business. I don't mean to pry." She reached out a hand. "Unless you'd like someone to talk to. You know I'm a good listener."

Lacey swiped a tear from her cheek. "I'm on my own...at home, I mean...Dad left."

Ketty didn't speak but squeezed her hand gently and waited.

"He told me he was going one morning after we'd done our weekly shopping. He was acting a bit jittery, more than usual." Lacey pictured her father in the driver's seat, the keys jiggling up and down in his hand. "He said he wished he'd taught me to drive and when I asked why he said it was a good life skill to have if he wasn't there." Lacey sniffed. "As if I could afford a car let alone the cost of running one. Anyway, that's when he told me he had a new job, that he was going back to what he loved."

She paused and looked at Ketty, who was studying her with nothing but kindness in her eyes. Once more Lacey bit her lip to hold back the tears.

"His friend Watto had heard about a farm worker job in the country not far from where we used to live."

"That would be very different to what he'd been doing – factory work, wasn't it?"

Lacey nodded. "He never liked it. He only moved to the city because Gran offered us a place to live and to help with Freya and me after Mum died. He and Gran never really got on and then when she left me the house..."

"My goodness, I didn't realise she'd done that."

"It was a surprise to us all. My sister got her life insurance and savings. Dad wasn't happy – he drank more and gambled his spare cash. The work was patchy. He was going downhill fast. He was excited about this job but he'd been excited about other jobs and nothing had come of them. This time was different. Two days after he told me about it he was gone. He sent a text to say he'd arrived then called to say he was definitely taking the job. He sounded so excited. He said he'd come back in a few weeks to visit and collect the rest of his things. Dean and I were still seeing each other then so I suppose I didn't miss Dad so much to begin with but..."

"You're living all alone." Ketty let go of her hand and sat back.

Lacey nodded. "I'm not bothered by that so much as...before Dad left he borrowed money from me to service his car. He promised to pay me back when he got his first pay. I know he got there safely but this last two weeks he's not been in touch, or replied to my messages..." Lacey dashed another tear from her cheek. She was determined not to cry there in the middle of the lounge car.

"Oh, Lacey, what a torrid time you've had. This discord with Judith, things not working out with Dean, worrying about your father and now you're dealing with the house and the bills...on your own, I assume?"

"Yes." Lacey took a tissue from her purse and dabbed at her eyes. "I'm pretty good at budgeting. Dad's not...well, he hasn't given much towards the household expenses since he found out the house was mine." Lacey heard Ketty's sharp intake of breath but she didn't look up. "I manage but there were a couple of big bills and Dad borrowed that money and now...it's all...overwhelming."

"Of course it is." Lacey sensed Ketty lean in closer. "I can give you a loan or an advance on your pay if—"

Lacey gasped. "Oh, no, Miss Ketty. I didn't tell you so that you would offer money...I...I just..."

"You needed someone to talk to. I understand. I'm so sorry, Lacey – I feel as if I've failed you."

"None of it's your fault."

"But I can see I've lost touch, not only with you but with the other women as well." Ketty put a hand to her forehead. "I'm just realising how much."

"Miss Ketty, you are the best employer."

"Technically I'm probably your only employer."

Her smile eased Lacey's distress just a little.

"I pride myself on open communication with my staff but I've realised since the pandemic I haven't got back into the routine of meeting with each of you regularly to discuss your goals and any highs and lows. I had that awful chest infection and I was just getting over that when Carlos came and it was Christmas and then in February I broke my wrist and…I knew things have been going a little awry but I hadn't realised how bad they were, at least in your case. I'm sorry."

"You don't need to apologise for something someone else has done."

"You're a mature young woman, Lacey. I can't change your home life but I want to reassure you that I do not think your suggestions at work are fanciful. We've discussed many changes over the years. And if you remember I've asked you to implement some and not others for reasons I stated at the time, so I want you to be clear that I am certainly not indulging you."

"Thank you, Miss Ketty." Lacey drew in a breath, wondering how far she could push this conversation. "I know you're definite that you're not retiring but I've noticed there are a few things you don't do any more and I wondered…"

Ketty studied her expectantly.

"I wondered why you don't write the notes for the eboutique sales any more. I know you couldn't when you broke your wrist but…"

"I hadn't given it a thought. Judith took it on and…" Ketty's expression was puzzled. "I suppose I've not bothered to take it up again."

"You've always said how it's important to make the customer feel special and we worked out ways to embrace that in our online business."

"It was your idea to include the handwritten note with each purchase and you were right. Customers appreciate it."

Lacey scratched at her cheek. "Your notes were written so beautifully with the purchaser's name and you always added the little sketch of the outfit."

"I know Judith's writing is a bolder style."

"And she doesn't include the buyer's name or any little embellishments like you did."

Ketty frowned. "I don't think I've ever seen one of her notes."

"It's my job to wrap the parcels so I see each one. I don't mean to be unkind to Judith but her notes lack the extra personal touch. It's such a little thing but..."

"It's important."

Lacey blew out a breath. "Yes."

"And from what you've told me you'd be in no position to mention it to her."

"No."

"I see."

"And," Lacey continued, "I think the important thing is that customers get a handwritten note from you, the owner of the business."

Ketty tapped a finger on her glass. "Thank you for being so frank, Lacey. I'm glad you've been brave enough to confide in me. Not just about work but your personal life as well. You've given me some things to think about."

"I hope you don't think I'm complaining. I love my job."

"I know you do. It shows in the many things you accomplish and I appreciate them all but a trouble shared is a trouble halved."

Lacey smiled. "Gran used to say that."

The carriage door burst open and Birgit strode in and made a beeline for Lacey, followed by Rory and Rhys.

"We've been busy gasbagging," Birgit said. "I've been hearing all about the boyos' helicopter flight. You'd have loved it, Lacey. Looks like you need another drink." Birgit waved at Lacey's empty glass. "Can I get you something, Ketty?"

"No, thanks. I'm heading off to bed."

"On my way to the bar." Birgit strode off after the two men.

Lacey dabbed at her eyes again.

"Your make-up is fine," Ketty said. "Maybe reapply your lipstick and no-one will notice you've been teary."

"I'll probably be a bit of a wet blanket if I stay."

"Nonsense! I'm glad we got to chat but you should stay a bit longer. Try to forget about your troubles tonight and have some fun." Ketty stood. "Nothing will be gained by worrying about something you can't fix for the moment. Enjoy yourself." Ketty patted her shoulder and moved off down the carriage.

Lacey wasn't so sure that she wanted to stay on to party with Birgit and the fellas but Ketty had been right. The weight of her worries didn't feel quite so heavy now that she'd shared it.

Ketty paused in the empty passage. She'd had her head buried firmly in the sand and it was time to pull it out. She'd always known Judith and Lacey had their differences but she hadn't realised it had grown to dislike. Judith had hinted at it once or twice, but Ketty had always changed the subject, not wanting to encourage tattling.

It broke her heart to have two women working for her who didn't get on. Both were talented in their own way. She knew that and had hoped they'd work it out and she'd be able to let it slide. But if Lacey was to be believed, and Ketty had no reason to doubt her, instead of building bridges it sounded as if they were being blown up. It was hard to imagine the sensible, kind Judith that Ketty knew would purposefully omit Lacey from sharing cake. Such a spiteful and foolish thing to do. And yet she had all those hurtful things to say about Carlos.

And then there was Lacey's home life falling apart as well. The poor girl had more than enough to deal with. Ketty was sure there was something she could do to help but she would have to work out what. Lacey would not accept charity.

The door Ketty had just come through opened and a man stepped in behind her juggling a full cup and saucer in each hand.

"You're loaded up. Are you going far?" She smiled then realised he was the man who'd been with the stick-wielding woman she'd noticed earlier. She hadn't seen either of them since before lunch. Up close she realised he was a lot younger than she'd first thought.

"Next carriage," he said, concentrating on his delicate cargo.

The train wobbled and a few drops of tea slopped from the cups.

"I'm going that way. Let me get the doors for you."

He nodded, and each time she glanced back his gaze was firmly on the cups, concentrating on not spilling more, no doubt. Once they were into the next carriage he indicated the first door. Ketty opened it for him and stepped out of the way.

"You've taken your time." The woman's plaintive voice carried.

He gave Ketty the lightest of smiles and stepped inside.

"They were busy at the bar. But they had some of your favourite camomile, honey and vanilla."

"I thought you must have stopped for another drink. I've been trying to get myself propped up comfortably."

Ketty hovered just back from the door, which was still open.

"Do you want me to get the steward?" he said.

"Good heavens, that won't be necessary. Surely you can reach down a pillow."

"I thought you wanted something firmer for your knee."

The train lurched and Ketty wobbled forward a small step, putting her in sight of the open door. The woman looked up from where she was propped on the edge of the bunk. She wore ivory silk pyjamas not unlike the blush silk pair awaiting Ketty, and their eyes met briefly. There was something in that determined gaze that Ketty found familiar.

"Shut the door, Beau, for goodness sake. There's so little privacy on this train."

Ketty stepped back as the door shut firmly in front of her. She berated herself. She'd been caught eavesdropping and she didn't blame the woman for being snippy. Her interest had overruled her common sense. Not a customer. Ketty knew them all well. Perhaps they'd met on a cruise but Ketty couldn't place her.

She turned and retraced her steps. She'd planned to make her own cup of tea in the little kitchen at the end of the carriage, plain camomile for her, but perhaps it would be better to get it at the bar as the man, Beau, had done.

Lacey and Birgit smiled as she passed them on her way as did a few other people whose faces were becoming familiar after the tour today. More passengers stood at the bar, chatting in merry and high tones that suggested they were well past several drinks under their belts.

She moved into a space created as a couple left and ordered her tea. A uniformed man stepped in beside her, nodded to the attendant behind the bar and put one arm on the counter. It was Matt, who'd helped her earlier in the day.

He smiled. "Enjoying your journey, Ketty?"

"I am, thank you, Matt, and thank you for your help earlier with the cabin."

"Not a problem. There's usually someone who picks the wrong carriage or the wrong cabin door."

"They do all look the same."

"Everything else is all right? You're being well looked after?" he asked as the bar attendant placed a mug beside him.

"Most certainly. I'm travelling with six companions and we're all having a wonderful experience."

Behind her there was a loud chortle and Ketty recognised Birgit's laugh.

She nodded in that direction. "Those two young women are part of my group and they chummed up with a couple of Irish cousins right at the start of the journey."

"It's good to know you're all enjoying yourselves." His arm shot out to steady the elbow of a passing woman who veered sideways with the motion of the train.

"Thank you," she said as she gripped the back of a chair with one hand and lifted her glass with the other. "Didn't spill a drop."

Ketty sensed Matt keeping one eye on the woman as she moved on to join her friends. There was an air of confident authority behind his genial exterior.

"What's your role on board?" she asked.

"You might say I'm police officer, medico, counsellor, statesman, sorter of wrong cabins." His moustache twitched with his good-natured grin. "And everything in between. But my official label is train manager."

"That must be an interesting job."

"It certainly is," he said as the man behind them loudly pondered their arrival time in Alice Springs the next morning. "We should be set up at the terminal by nine," Matt said.

"Thanks, mate."

Matt nodded and turned back to Ketty.

"I must say your staff have all been very helpful," she said. "We had a few problems at the start – nothing to do with the train, more the chopping and changing of my party. Jade was a big help."

"Were you the group where a booking was mucked up?"

"Yes. My friend's cabin was rebooked for someone else, but the issue was caused by his travel agent not the train."

"Normally we'd have a spare cabin or two but we're at capacity this trip."

"We don't mind sharing."

"I'm glad it worked out."

"Excuse me." Jade approached from the dining car. She glanced at Ketty and smiled. "Sorry to interrupt but would you mind checking something for me, please, Matt?"

"No worries."

"I'll leave you to it." Ketty looked at her cup, which she'd left on the bar, and realised she'd drunk the tea while they'd been talking. She waved at the girls again as she left. Birgit appeared to be full of energy but Lacey was a little pale. "Don't stay up too late. Big day tomorrow," she joked.

"We won't." Birgit waved an empty glass. "Last drinks."

"Don't worry, Granny, we'll have them home before midnight." Rory smiled smugly.

Lacey and Birgit both gasped and Rhys looked down at his hands.

Ketty took a breath then pinned Rory with her most steadfast look. "Sadly, Rory, I'm not anyone's granny. I would prefer you to call me by my name, Ketty."

"It was just a…" His smirk dropped away. "Sorry, yes, okay… Ketty."

"Goodnight then." Ketty smiled and as she turned away she caught Lacey's eye and winked.

She took care as she walked, sure they were watching her still. She'd discovered the trick to not looking like a swaggering drunk was to keep in rhythm with the sway of the train.

Safely in the next carriage, Ketty paused and leaned against the wall to catch her breath. She often let ageist remarks slip but in Rory's case she hadn't been able to. Carlos was the one to suggest she speak up when such comments bothered her. It had been after she'd broken her wrist and she'd been feeling down. He'd arrived back from his visit with his cousin the week after it happened and had lifted her from her doldrums.

The break hadn't been a bad one but had required a plaster that covered her hand from the base of her fingers and stopped just short of her elbow. Of course she'd told Carlos about it on the phone. He'd been coming back her way anyway so he'd returned a few days earlier than planned.

"Tell me again what happened?" he'd asked as soon as he'd settled back in.

"Nothing exciting. Tien thought she was helping but she knocked me off balance. I put a hand out to stop myself and…" Ketty had raised the plastered arm a little. "This is the result."

"Bad luck."

"That's what I said. It was early evening. I went to hospital reluctantly. I already felt like I was wasting their time. Judith was with me and when we first got to the ED there were some desperate cases waiting to be seen. I wanted to leave but Judith insisted we stay and it turned out I had a scaphoid fracture."

"We saw a lot of broken wrists at sea."

"It was a simple break but the doctor praised Judith for insisting I go in. He said it was best I hadn't left it overnight. Evidently it mends easier when it's treated early. I was glad of her company through it all."

"Is the arm bothering you?"

"No." Ketty raised it up and down again.

"But something else is?"

"It was for the best that Judith insisted I have the wrist seen to..."

"I sense a 'but'."

"She's an employee and we've become friends over the years, good friends. She's my right hand with the business." Ketty felt her annoyance build. "Here's the but. The doctor who assessed my arm spoke with Judith as if I wasn't there."

"That was rude."

"It was more him taking the lead than her, and normally I would have interjected but I think by then I was so tired and my arm was aching...I just let them talk. What really irked me was Judith telling the doctor I'd had a fall. I felt it was more of a push but anyway it brought his attention back to me. He asked me so many questions about my general health I thought he'd forgotten about my arm." Ketty drew in a deep breath. "Before that, while they were talking over me...it's silly but...just for a moment, I felt like an invisible old woman."

"You, my dear Ketty, will never be invisible and age should have nothing to do with it. You were off your stride, that's all. Quite understandable."

"I've had a bit of reflecting time since. I should have spoken up."

"You were probably in shock. Judith as your support person should have redirected the doctor's initial questions to you."

"Later one of the nurses came to take my obs and said something like 'What have you been doing to break a wrist, young lady?'" Ketty's shoulders sagged. "I was already feeling vulnerable and she spoke to me in a patronising tone as if I was a child who'd been up to no good. It was humiliating."

"I'm so sorry."

"Why should you be sorry? You wouldn't be so unkind. I think it happens more with women."

"Not at all. I saw that kind of response with my parents from time to time, both of them. And there was a job I went for where I was told they were looking for someone younger."

"Are they allowed to say that?"

"Probably not but I was too surprised to take it up with them. I left feeling rather useless and yet the job description fitted my skills perfectly. I should have spoken up. I think we both should from now on. Life is for everyone, not just those under sixty."

"I don't like to make people feel bad about what they've said."

"But they make you feel bad about yourself and that's not right either. Give it some thought. I'd be guessing neither that doctor or the nurse realised how undermining their comments were. I'm sure with your diplomacy you could respond in a way that lets them know how you feel. In case it were to happen again. I've certainly been thinking on it since the job rejection."

"Was it back in Spain? I didn't realise you were looking for work."

Carlos had cleared his throat. "I…" He'd shrugged. "It doesn't matter. Now what can I do to cheer you up? Do you feel like a meal at Felix and Anna's cafe?"

Ketty's spirits had lifted at the thought. "Yes, please," she'd said.

The door to the carriage opened behind her and Ketty was suddenly back in the present. She hurried forward, moving silently along the carpeted floor and letting herself quietly into the cabin. From behind she heard a distant tap. She peered back around the doorframe. Matt was standing at the far end of the corridor. The cabin door in front of him opened and he stepped inside. She wondered what the stick woman in that cabin had requested at ten o'clock at night. Ketty shook her head. She really must find out the woman's name and stop thinking of her as 'stick woman'.

She shut her own door, sliding the lock just in case Mr Visser got lost in the night and ended up in the wrong cabin again. She slipped off her shoes and enjoyed the soft feel of the carpet beneath her feet. Carlos had left a reading lamp on over her bunk and it gave the cabin a cosy glow. He was a dark shape on the bottom bunk, his face to the wall, snoring softly. They'd agreed she'd take the top, and she rested her foot on the first step of the ladder, testing its stability. It seemed firm enough.

She used the bathroom then slipped out of her clothes and into her pyjamas, all the while listening to the steady sound of Carlos's deep breathing. It was strange, sharing this tiny space with Carlos, and yet not so. He had been her house guest on and off over the previous Christmas and summer. Her apartment had two bedrooms but it wasn't huge. She only had one bathroom, although he often used the staff bathroom downstairs out of business hours. They'd made it work as friends did.

Ketty gripped the ladder and carefully made her way up to the top bunk. She slipped between the sheets and turned out the light. Lying there in the dark she was more aware of the sounds and movement of the train. The vibrations, rattles and bumps had more urgency to them. It seemed to her that it was travelling faster than it had during the day.

She knew she shouldn't compare this train journey to cruising. It was a totally different experience, but she couldn't help but wish for the gentler movement and hush of a cabin in a ship on the water.

Ketty nestled further into the bunk; the sheets were soft, the pillow just right and the mattress comfortable and yet she knew sleep would elude her. For that she could hardly blame the train. It was more than the first night in a new bed, when she was often restless. Her head swirled with all the revelations she'd heard today. The discord between Judith and Lacey was far worse than she'd realised and there was something going on with Ning. Ketty wondered about Birgit and Tien and if she'd missed vital clues concerning their lives as well. And then there was Carlos. Despite Ketty's bravado, Judith's outburst left a small niggle of doubt. Was there some truth to what she'd said?

Ketty rolled to her side. The cabin was dark but not pitch black. She stared at the panelling in front of her. She'd known Carlos a long time. He was a good friend, delightful company, a decent man. And yet... She closed her eyes and rolled to her other side, settled into the bunk again and took long slow breaths. Her thoughts drifted to the new people she'd met today. A train journey certainly gave plenty of opportunity for that. There'd been lots of incidental chats with various individuals and she'd found Val and Warren good company. Then there was the couple from the cabin at the other end of her carriage, something about them intrigued her. The woman in particular, but she couldn't quite put her finger on it.

She rolled to her back and sighed. Her brain ached with the constant round of thoughts. She needed to distract herself. She thought about the book she'd brought but it was still in her case, which was too difficult to get down without disturbing Carlos. She was glad at least he appeared to be deep in sleep. He'd travelled for a long time and the first day on the train and off had been so busy. They'd had little chance to talk privately since the train left Darwin. Judith's words ricocheted around her brain again. Ketty rubbed her face with her hands. She'd come full circle and was thinking of him once more. Beyond her cabin she heard the occasional sound of a door closing and muffled voices. She wasn't the only one still awake.

twenty

Night One – Travelling South

Judith lay on her back staring up into the dark, the vibrations of the train keeping her awake rather than rocking her off to sleep. There was so much going on and she wasn't handling any of it very well. She'd been snappy with Ning and Tien and rude to Lacey, who rubbed her up the wrong way, especially now. She'd never been close to Lacey, had found her too forward when it came to knowing her place but after what happened with Dean... Judith huffed out a breath. She should be thankful. He could do so much better than Lacey.

And then the worst thing of all – Judith had tried to warn Ketty about Carlos. It hadn't gone well and she hated to think she'd ruined her longstanding friendship with Ketty in the process. How was she going to get through the next few days? It was impossible to avoid each other in the confined spaces of the train.

She had hoped this holiday would give her some respite from her troubles but so far it had only compounded them. She'd also planned to talk to Ketty about her personal dilemma. Trouble was there didn't seem like there'd be time for heart-to-heart conversations, especially now that she'd blathered on about Carlos.

Judith rolled to her side and her elbow, still sore, knocked the wall beside her. "Blast!" she hissed.

"Judith?" Ning's tentative voice came from the bunk below.

"Sorry, just bumped the wall. Did I wake you?"

"I can't sleep."

"Me neither."

"Shall I go down to that little kitchen and make us a cup of tea? I've brought my peppermint tea from home."

"Perhaps—" Before Judith could say any more, Ning's light flicked on and she was out of bed, sliding her robe over her shoulders and her feet into her slippers.

She waved a packet of tea bags at Judith. "It won't take long."

Judith sat up and flicked on the reading light as Ning let herself quietly out the door. She'd been worried about sharing and yet so far it had been the easiest part of the trip. Ning was certainly an agreeable roommate. And she was well prepared. Judith hadn't worried about packing a dressing-gown. She wasn't planning on anyone but Ning seeing her in her night attire of an oversized T-shirt and loose pants.

The cabin had a cosy glow in the low light from their bed lamps. She took it in for a moment then climbed carefully down the ladder. Even though the rungs felt solid beneath her feet she took extra care. Her ankle, like her elbow, was a bit tender from the scrapes she'd had at the gorge. She looked around the small space wondering where they'd sit – the couch had been transformed into a sleeper for the night. There was a gentle thud on the door. She opened it to find Ning, elbow extended – no doubt it had caused the thud – and a mug in each hand.

Ning handed one over. "I thought mugs easier than cups and saucers."

They shimmied around each other and Ning put her mug on the little table and crawled back into her bed. She patted the end of it. "Can you fit under here?"

Judith climbed onto the other end and slid down a little. She sat with her legs crossed, nursing the hot mug in her hands. Ning took a sip of her tea. Judith blew gently on hers then took a tentative sip. She was surprised by the spicy peppery flavour.

Ning leaned forward, studying her. "I didn't ask if you like peppermint tea."

"I've never had it before."

"Haven't you?" Ning's eyes widened. "I drink it most evenings before bed. It's good for your digestion as well as sleep."

Judith took another sip. The taste was growing on her. She eased back against the spare pillow propped behind her, and even though she was sure it was mind over matter, she felt some of the weight of her day begin to slip away. She smiled at Ning. "I like it."

The low glow of the reading lamp illuminated Ning's wide smile and there was a sparkle in her eyes Judith realised she hadn't seen much of lately.

"I feel like I'm back in my childhood," Ning said. "Sometimes when my parents worked late my sisters and I would take our tea and huddle together in the lamplight."

"Are any of your sisters in Australia?"

Ning shook her head. "They're both in America. They keep promising to visit. We stayed with them before my boys started high school."

"Of course. I remember that now. You were away for over a month." Judith sipped more tea. "It doesn't seem that long ago and yet your boys are grown and Peter's going to be a dad."

"Yes." Ning's eyes shone and then her face fell. She looked down quickly.

Judith thought of all the phone calls. "Everything's all right with the baby, isn't it?"

"Yes, yes. My daughter-in-law has kept very well and all the tests they have these days tell us the baby is good too…"

Her voice trailed off. Judith waited.

"They're going to move in with me."

"Peter and his wife and the baby?"

Ning nodded. "They want to save money to buy their own house."

Judith leaned forward. In the low light it was hard to read the look on the other woman's face.

"How are you feeling about that?"

"I know you don't have children," Ning said softly. "But for me, being a grandmother…it's very special."

"I'm sure it is." Judith could only imagine. Having lived with a husband who was regularly drunk and sometimes violent with it, she'd been glad she'd had no children. She'd never dwelled on it. Ning's marriage had been a happy one and she adored her children but Judith wondered how well it would work for Ning with them all living in her house. "Henry still lives at home too, doesn't he?"

"Yes." Ning nodded slowly. "We'll all be together again. And I'll be able to look after the baby once it's older, so my daughter-in-law can go back to work."

"Is that why you're retiring?"

Once more Ning nodded.

Judith thought it a shame. "You're such a good seamstress and your embroidery is exquisite. Won't you miss it?" Even though

Judith had struggled to see Ning's expression clearly there was no missing the flash of despair that crossed her face in that moment.

Ning lowered her head quickly and took a sip of her tea. Judith did the same and thought about all the messages and calls Ning had been receiving.

"Your personal life is none of my business, Ning, but I...well, Ketty and I are sorry you're leaving. It's not just your sewing talents but you're a well-respected member of our team. Are you sure it's what you want?"

Ning continued to stare into her cup. "I do love working for Ketty but...I'm excited for the baby." Her voice was so low Judith could barely hear it above the background noise of the train.

"Of course you are but do your son and daughter-in-law realise what they're asking you to give up?"

"They're both very...focused."

Judith thought that an unusual choice of word. To her it sounded as if Peter and his wife were being selfish but then she didn't have children. "I'm not prying, Ning, but while you're helping them to save, what about your income? You're young to retire."

"My husband's life insurance covered the house, so Peter doesn't need to pay board and I don't need much to live on."

"Neither do I, but you still have one son at university and now the other is coming home with a wife and baby. Your expenses will go up."

"Peter has it all worked out." Ning nodded emphatically but just as quickly her shoulders drooped.

Judith imagined he did but she wondered if it was mutually beneficial. Free rent and potential childcare might help him but what about Ning's future? "I'm sure Ketty would always find a place for you if you decided to come back to us."

"As Peter reminds me, no-one is irreplaceable."

Judith opened her mouth then closed it again. She had no idea what to say to that but she was fast becoming annoyed with Peter.

"Ketty will find someone else," Ning said. "And she has a strong team with you right behind her, plus Birgit and Tien and Lacey, of course. That young woman has something extra." Ning leaned a little closer and held Judith's gaze. "Don't you think?"

"I…yes…she's definitely good with computers."

"She's very creative but I think maybe her home life is sad. Work is her happy place."

"I wouldn't know about that." A prickle ran down Judith's spine and she shivered even though the air was comfortably warm.

"She doesn't say much but I think maybe her father is not a good man."

Judith knew little about Lacey's home life except that her mother had died many years ago and her gran more recently.

"She had a boyfriend," Ning said. "But she's gone quiet about him."

Judith bristled at that. "That was my neighbour, Dean, and they're not together any longer."

"Oh, that's sad."

Judith swallowed the remains of her tea. It was very sad but none of Judith's sympathy was for Lacey.

"I'm getting sleepy now," Ning said. "Shall we try again?"

"Of course." Judith shuffled off the bunk. She used the bathroom, but when she came out Ning was peering at her phone instead of being tucked up in bed.

"Have you got signal?"

"Yes." Ning barely glanced at her before she began furiously tapping on her phone.

Judith made her way carefully up the ladder, eased between the sheets and turned out her light. She'd enjoyed the peppermint tea but she felt no closer to sleep than she had before her chat with Ning. And now she could see the glow from Ning's phone so she obviously wasn't sleeping any time soon either.

Judith didn't get many text messages so typing on that tiny keyboard was a skill she lacked. Dean teased her about her sometimes strange responses. She smiled as she recalled the worst of her muddled texts. It had been a few days after their lovely Christmas lunch at Ketty's. Ketty and Carlos had gone away to their separate families for New Year and Judith had called in to feed Ketty's cat. She'd been about to head home when she got a text from Dean inviting her to share fish and chips with him. It had been good timing. There was a lovely shop near the bus stop on Oxford Street that made delicious ready-prepared meals. She'd messaged Dean to say she'd pick up a salad. When his response had been several laughing faces, she'd re-read her text. The jolly phone had changed it and she'd sent *I'll sick up a salad*.

That had been the evening he'd quizzed her about Lacey.

twenty-one

The previous December – Randwick, Sydney

The remains of the takeaway fish and chips were spread across the table. Replete, Judith sipped her wine. Outside the evening was hot and muggy. Dean's air conditioner was making quite a racket but not lowering the temperature in the apartment all that well. The warmth was making them both lazy.

Dean popped a chip into his mouth. "Not quite the calibre of Ketty's Christmas lunch but that was nice fish." The corner of his mouth quirked up. "Even the salad wasn't bad for one that you sicked up."

"Stop," she said as he laughed again.

"Ketty's food was pretty good," he said.

"She loves to feed people."

"And Carlos is good on the drinks. They make the perfect couple."

"Oh no, they're just good friends."

"You're never too old for love." Dean grinned and Judith's cheeks warmed even more.

"They've known each other for years, that's all," she said sharply. "Besides, Carlos is only here on a visa, he has to go back to Spain eventually."

"They looked pretty comfortable together to me."

"That's as may be but they're simply friends." She sniffed. "Ketty has many friends."

"She's a generous lady. Lacey likes her. She sang Ketty's praises."

"You two seemed to have your heads together an awful lot over lunch."

"No offence," he pulled a cheesy grin, "but it was good to have someone around my age at the table."

"She's only in her mid-twenties."

"And I'm only thirty."

Judith took a measured sip of her wine. She had to concede he was right. The rest of Ketty's luncheon guests were much older than Dean. They all had quite a few years on Judith for that matter. Except for Klaus.

"Klaus and I aren't ancient yet," she said.

"Tell me about Klaus. He certainly had his eye on you."

"There's nothing to tell." She pulled herself up straight. "He can do what he likes. I'm not in need of a man in my life." Klaus had tried to engage her in conversation but she'd kept busy helping with the food and washing dishes. He was a nice man, kind and interesting, but that was as much as she would admit.

"Jude, Jude, Jude." Dean shook his head. "What am I going to do with you?"

Dean was the only one she tolerated shortening her name. Her ex-husband had always called her Jude and she'd hated it, but somehow when Dean called her Jude it was fun and she allowed it. She reached for the wine bottle he'd put in a bucket of ice and refilled her glass, wanting to divert the conversation. The sudden extra loud rattle of the air conditioner gave it to her.

"Have you heard any more about when they're going to replace your air conditioner? The old one's hardly working." She put the replenished glass against her cheek, enjoying the brief chill before taking a sip.

"Old grumble-guts down the back doesn't reckon it will happen."

The man in the apartment at the very back of the building had been there even longer than Judith. He wasn't the easiest person to get along with but Judith was always civil to him and usually got a decent response. "Why not?"

"He reckons the owner is up to something, perhaps going to sell the building."

That gave Judith a moment's fright before she thought it through. "In that case it would be in his best interest to have the place in good repair."

She sipped the chilled wine and glanced around Dean's apartment. It had been painted before he'd moved in a few years earlier. Her place had been painted once since she'd moved in over twenty years ago. It needed doing again. Her aircon was only eight years old but the carpets were worn, a couple of her windows were jamming and the cupboard under her laundry trough was more rust than metal. Some updates wouldn't go astray.

"She didn't mention a partner," Dean said.

Judith dragged her gaze back to him. "Who?"

"Lacey. She didn't say anything about anyone special in her life."

"I wouldn't have any idea. We don't discuss our personal lives at work." That wasn't true, of course. Judith heard plenty about Birgit's boyfriend – too much detail; it was a fiery relationship.

Ning was always talking about her family and the upcoming grandchild got an almost daily mention. Tien regaled them constantly with the latest reality TV show updates.

"We've organised to catch up."

"Pardon?"

"We're meeting up again in a few days."

"Who is?"

He frowned. "Have you had a brain fade, Jude? Lacey and me."

"Do you think that's wise?"

"Is there something about her I don't know that I should?"

"I don't know anything about her."

"Someone you've worked with for several years? You must have some inside goss. She's not a smoker, is she? I didn't see evidence of that. No weird habits I should know about?"

He studied her intently with eyes that sparkled and that cheeky look on his face.

"Would it change your mind if I did?"

"No."

"Then I guess you can find out for yourself."

She took a gulp of wine. She'd never say as much to him but Dean was the closest to a son that she'd get. She cared for him very much. She didn't think Lacey was right for him but it wasn't her place to tell him.

twenty-two

Day Two – On board the Ghan

"Ketty." The voice calling her was gentle but insistent. She pulled away from an image of Judith dressed as Mother Christmas sitting on Carlos's knee, both of them grinning knowingly at her.

"Ketty?" The voice called again. The dream faded as she opened her eyes. Carlos stood a short distance away, peering at her, his head at the same height as hers.

"I'm on the train." She blinked and looked around.

"Yes, you are." Carlos smiled. "Were you dreaming of somewhere else?"

She nodded, the fantasy of her sleep world being replaced by the reality of the cabin, which was light despite the blinds being closed.

"What time is it?"

"Nearly eight o'clock. I've brought you a cup of tea."

"That's kind of you." She propped herself up, pushing away the nightmarish memory of a deceptive Carlos.

He handed the cup up to her. "Do you mind if I go to breakfast without you? I've woken up feeling extremely hungry."

"No, you go. I took ages to go to sleep and then I must have slept deeply. I'll be a while getting organised."

Once he'd gone she settled back against the pillows and sipped her tea. She'd lain awake for a long time thinking about Carlos and Judith and then the things Lacey had told her about her home life and about Judith. There was a common denominator – Judith – and Ketty had pondered how she was going to tackle her good friend about her behaviour. Not reaching any conclusion that was palatable and with her empty mug in one hand, Ketty eased her way carefully down the ladder. It made her think of Maurice. He'd turn her descent into some derogatory reference to aging, no doubt. She frowned as she remembered he'd been in her dream too, wearing a huge paper Christmas hat and shouting "you're too old, Ketty".

She rolled her shoulders to dispel the image and opened the blind to be greeted by a flat landscape stretching as far as she could see. Grey knee-high grass was scattered across the ever-present vibrant red earth and the odd stunted tree reached gnarled limbs towards the brilliant blue sky. The view made her think of Lacey, whose creativity was flourishing in this strange new terrain. She was important to Ketty Clift Couture but Judith was obviously making her unhappy.

Ketty pondered Judith's comments about Carlos. It was problematic but not as urgent as the clash with Lacey. Like Lacey, Judith had been timid and unsure of her strengths when Ketty had first employed her. Since then she'd proved Ketty was right to have that faith in her over and over again. Judith was forthright, well-organised, a capable seamstress and an excellent pattern maker, who also managed the paperwork with efficiency. Both women were important to the future of Ketty Clift Couture. There had to be a way forward. Ketty simply needed to work out what it was.

By the time she got to the lounge car it was almost empty but she was pleased to see Val and Warren just in front of her heading in to breakfast.

"Are you on your own?" Warren asked.

"Yes, I slept in."

"So did we," Val said. "Join us if you'd like."

Ketty was delighted to be seated with them – the perfect opportunity to find out a little more. On the way to their table they passed Carlos and Tien seated with two women, and Lacey and Birgit with Rory and Rhys at another table. They all said good morning, Rory's "Good morning, Ketty" the loudest of all. Of Judith and Ning there was no sign.

Their waiter was Simon again. He remembered Ketty's name, his smile was warm and genuine and his waiting skills were perfect, even when the train wobbled a little as it did from time to time. He poured water into their glasses with expertise and not a drop spilled.

"Thank you, Simon." Ketty glanced out at the sparse landscape topped by a cloudless blue sky. "It looks like a beautiful day out there."

"Perfect weather for your daytrip, Ketty." He glanced around their group. "What have you chosen for your off-train experience?"

"I've never been to Alice Springs before," Ketty said. "So I decided on the Alice Explorer tour."

"Great choice. You'll get to see quite a bit."

"I wanted to do that one," Val said, "but Warren wants to see birds and animals so we're going to Alice Springs Desert Park."

"You'll enjoy that too," Simon said.

"I hope so." Val gave Warren a sharp look.

"We've been to Alice Springs before," Warren said.

"That was years ago and only for a couple of days." Val straightened her cutlery. "I can hardly remember it."

"I'm sure you'll all enjoy your day," Simon said diplomatically. "I'll be back in a moment to take your order."

Ketty glanced over the menu. It had several choices including quandong and hazelnut pancakes, which sounded very tempting.

"I'll be having a full breakfast," Warren declared and Val immediately suggested he have the fruit and yoghurt parfait instead.

"You overdid it last night," she said and nodded at Ketty. "He was up at two am looking for his indigestion tablets."

Warren cut in. "There was something spicy in the beef cheeks, that's all."

"Nothing to do with all the red wine you drank," Val said.

Ketty tipped her head to the menu again and observed them through lowered lashes. Warren was getting quite defensive and Val seemed to enjoy pressing his buttons.

"We're on holiday," Warren said.

Val sniffed. "Every day's a holiday for you."

"Except when you line me up for childminding."

"Listen to him." Val turned her attention to Ketty who looked up. "Anyone would think he didn't like his grandchildren. Do you have any, Ketty?"

"No."

"Oh, that's such a shame – they're a delight."

There was a soft grunt from Warren but Simon arrived back to take their orders. Ketty avoided eye contact with Val as Warren ordered the full breakfast.

"I've never married, never had children," Ketty said once Simon had left.

"Warren and I couldn't have children of our own so we fostered. We've welcomed ten children into our home over the years but only five of them have remained close and we ended up officially adopting them."

Warren gave a snort.

Val poked him.

"I do love them and their kids but—"

"You don't want to look after them." Val huffed. "I know."

"It's not that, it's just...I'm getting too old to manage..." He petered out as Simon arrived with their teas and coffee.

Val added a juice to her order and then asked Ketty about her business. The food came and when Ketty saw Val's plate of pancakes she was glad she'd gone with the fruit and yoghurt parfait. Like Warren, Ketty had overindulged the night before. Perhaps one of the reasons for her crazy dream that still hung at the edge of her consciousness.

No sooner had Warren finished his large plate of eggs and bacon and all the trimmings he rose, patted his lips with his serviette and eased out from behind the table. "Nature calls."

"I was planning on a coffee," Val said.

"I'll have another with you." Ketty smiled.

"All right," Val said to Warren. "I'll meet you back in the cabin in a while."

He gave a mock salute and hurried away.

Val shook her head. "Too much food and drink does it to him every time but he won't be told."

"Everything is so tempting and delicious," Ketty said. "It's hard to refuse."

"You must have a wonderful business. I've never visited a dressmaker before. I'm over seventy, a bit old for anything fancy."

"You don't need a dressmaker to dress with style. It's all about how you put it together."

"You're right. Our two daughters are clever like that. They always look stylish but neither of them have a big budget. They love op shops."

"So do I. You can pick up some gems."

"Warren can take the credit for setting the girls on that path," Val said.

"A man of many talents."

"He was so patient with them," Val said wistfully. "Our budget was tight when they were all living at home. One rainy weekend the girls were bickering over what they were going to wear to a family wedding. They were lamenting their lack of funds for new outfits. I was ready to bang their heads together but Warren sat them down and asked them what they thought they'd like to wear. Of course they had no idea so he suggested they look in magazines at styles they liked and said once they had a good idea about what they wanted he'd help fund it. The girls were so excited." Val tsked and shook her head.

"I just walked away. I knew they'd pick things way beyond our means to buy and I was sure Warren would be out of his depth. They all surprised me. The girls were selective about what they wanted but the items were still beyond our budget. Warren said he'd take them shopping. They were gone for hours and came back happy as larks. He'd taken them and their ideas to op shops and they got the basics. We dug out the sewing machine." Val winced. "I can mend things but I'm not a sewer. The girls' enthusiasm and my little bit of sewing knowledge went a long way. They looked gorgeous on the day. I was so proud of them… and Warren. He'd given them a budget and they'd worked out if they pooled it they'd do better and they helped each other with their outfits."

"Sounds like Warren killed two birds with one stone." Ketty was impressed with his smart thinking as well. "How clever to set them a task where they could work as a team and end up with the outfits they wanted."

"We gave them both sewing machines for their twenty-firsts. Not quite a fancy dressmaker like you but they've become quite adept at sewing and remodelling."

"I like it when clothes get a second or even third adaptation. I upcycle clothing and some of my staff do too."

"I think it's so wonderful of you to bring them on this holi-day," Val said.

"I'm very proud of my business but it wouldn't be what it is today without my ladies."

"I haven't had a chance to speak with them all yet but I've had a chat with Judith and…Stacey, is it?"

"Lacey."

"Oh. Lacey's a perfect name for a dressmaker. She's such a pretty young thing and wears…" Val leaned in. "I hope it's not being offensive but her clothes are…" Val screwed up her nose. "Rather unusual but somehow on her they all come together with flair."

"I know what you mean. Lacey's one that upcycles and she thinks outside the box, that's what I love about her. It's impor-tant to have someone like that in a dressmaking business or we could get stuck in our ways. She's been instrumental in creating a few new lines and she's a whiz with social media, anything to do with IT really. I resisted having a decent web presence for years. I couldn't see how we could keep the personal touch but under Lacey's guidance it's added another dimension to our enterprise. I've learned a lot about that from her."

"I suppose each of your staff bring something different to the mix."

"Oh, yes. Ning can do just about anything with a needle and thread. Her embroidery, both with machine and by hand, is exquisite. The brides love her work." Ketty felt another pang of sorrow for the imminent loss not just of Ning's skills but her calm presence in the workshop. "Tien and Birgit are excellent seamstresses. I think of them as my soldiers, cutting and sewing. And Judith, well, she's my right hand. What she doesn't know about pattern construction isn't worth knowing, and she keeps her finger on the pulse with paperwork, which is of great assistance to me and..." Ketty stopped. Ning, Tien and Birgit each had a role that was clear and defined. Lacey and Judith had areas of expertise that were broader and sometimes overlapped, such as sharing front-of-house duty with Ketty. From Ketty's point of view she enjoyed the fluidity of it but perhaps someone like Judith needed more structure. Ketty thought about Warren's clever way of getting his daughters to work as a team.

"Is something wrong?" Val cut into her thoughts.

"No, not at all. There was a work issue I'd been thinking about this morning and I've just had an idea about how to manage it. It actually sprung from your recount of Warren getting your daughters to work together." At least it was the start of an idea. Ketty would need to work on it a bit more but she felt a little surge of optimism. She smiled as Simon appeared to take their drinks order.

"A cappuccino for Val and a latte for Ketty," he repeated. "Can I get you anything else to go with it?"

"No, thank you," Val and Ketty spoke together and then laughed.

"He's a genial young man." Ketty watched him walk away, wondering if he had a partner and if he would suit Lacey.

"It's nice how they remember your name after such a short time."

"One of the perks of this kind of travel, I suppose."

"I do like it but I'd be happy to drive places, stop when and where we wanted and stay in cabins," Val said. "I cook for us then and we don't eat out as much but Warren loves the train journeys."

"I love to cruise. It gets in your blood and you keep wanting to go again."

"We haven't done a cruise." Val glanced wistfully out the window. "I nearly had Warren convinced a few years back but he hasn't been keen since the pandemic. Now he says he's too old for it."

"Good heavens! I can't imagine anyone being too old to cruise. I'm looking forward to going again one day but in the meantime this train journey has been wonderful so far."

"How's the cabin sharing working out?"

"With Carlos?" Ketty smiled. "He's very easy to get along with and really we've hardly been in the cabin together except for when we're sleeping. By the time I got in last night he was already fast asleep. Poor man travelled for days to get here. And then this morning he was up well before me."

"I never sleep well the first night on the train. And we had a message from one of our sons while we were in Katherine. His youngest has been in hospital for a small op and now she has an infection. Poor little lamb will need some extra recovery time. If Warren and I were home we'd be able to help."

"You help out quite a lot, by the sound of it."

"I do. And don't listen to Warren's grumbling. He adores our grandies. I just wish he'd help out with them more, help keep them entertained when we have them. He was always so good at it with our children. Even though work took him away a lot in the early days he was hands-on when he was home. He was a travelling salesman until his dad expanded the shop and needed his help, and then of course we took it over fully. Since he's retired he's become a different man."

Simon placed their coffees on the table. Val stirred sugar into hers in sluggish circles. Ketty was reminded of Maurice. "My neighbour has recently retired from a high-powered office job. He's nearly driving his poor wife, Lee, mad getting under her feet, wanting to help her with things she's done on her own for years."

Val snorted. "Warren's the opposite. Since he's retired he occupies himself well. He's extended our back patio and taken up orchid gardening and he enjoys golf. Of course I took up some sport and hobbies once our children had all left home, but they need our help now they have children of their own and Warren's quite reluctant."

"Hello, ladies." Carlos stood beside their table. "May I join you?"

"Of course," Val gushed and Ketty heard the smoothness of his words as someone new would.

Carlos lavished them with his smile and slid in beside Ketty. "Once more a delicious meal," he said.

"Oh yes," Val said.

"I think I'll get another coffee too since you've only just started."

"Of course." Val nodded profusely.

Ketty wanted to roll her eyes. Last night Val was ready to crucify Carlos for lying to them and now she was fawning all over him. Ketty was also a little disappointed. Val had been quite forthcoming and Carlos's arrival had interrupted them.

twenty-three

Day Two – On board the Ghan

Judith glanced out the cabin window. The flat landscape had been replaced by low hills and the vegetation had changed to thicker bush and bigger trees.

"Are we going slower?" Ning asked from the other end of the couch.

"It seems so, yes." Judith picked up her book again and Ning went back to her tour booklet. They'd both been awake in time to watch the sun come up this morning, then had got themselves ready and gone for an early breakfast. There'd been no sign of the rest of their party, except Judith had seen Carlos disappearing around the end of the corridor in the opposite direction when she'd been returning from breakfast.

Now she and Ning were organised and ready to depart once they arrived in Alice Springs but that was still a while away. She put her book on the table – it wasn't holding her interest. She kept going over things in her mind and couldn't concentrate on the story. It was crime fiction and needed her full attention.

She stood and paced the small floor space. Their attendant had folded the top bunk away and restored Ning's sleeper to a seat while they'd been at breakfast so the space didn't feel quite so small, but it was still only a few steps from one end to the other. Beneath her sock the plaster she'd put over the gouge on her ankle wasn't doing much of a job to stop the chafing.

"Is something wrong?" Ning asked.

Judith stopped pacing and sat again. She hadn't mentioned her foot to Ning – she'd only fuss and besides there were bigger hurts to worry about. "No...I..." She twisted on the seat to look directly at Ning. "Do you think I'm too forthright?"

Ning's face fell. She opened her mouth but no words came out.

"I'm worried about Ketty," Judith blurted.

"Why? Isn't she well?"

"Perfectly. It's not her health, it's her...it's Carlos."

"Oh." Ning shook her head. "It's not right for them to share a cabin but it's not my place to say."

"I'm not so much bothered by them sharing a cabin as..." Judith winced, trying to form the words. "I'm worried he's targeting Ketty for her money as his ticket to stay in Australia."

"Ticket?"

"You know, visa."

"Ohh," Ning said again, drawing the sound out. Then she shook her head. "I don't think so."

"You don't?"

"Carlos is a nice man from a nice family."

"You don't know his family."

"No, but I've heard about them from Ketty. She's very fond of Carlos and she is a good judge of character."

Judith sighed. Ning hadn't seen the version of Carlos she had. "I tried to warn Ketty last night."

"What do you mean by 'warn'?"

Once more Judith winced. "I told her what I told you. That I think he's after her money and a visa to stay in Australia."

Ning gasped.

"Not quite like that but…we didn't part on good terms."

"Oh, that's not right." Ning shook her head. "You and Ketty are old friends. You mustn't let this come between you. You must apologise."

"Apologise?"

"Yes." Ning waved her hands at Judith as if she were shooing a chicken. "You must fix this."

"Ketty might not want to listen to me."

"Of course she will. She is a good woman." Ning clicked her tongue. "And so are you. You must sort this out or you won't enjoy this holiday and neither will Ketty. Let's go and sit in the lounge car." Ning shooed her again. "I'd like another cup of tea and we can watch for the right moment for you to speak to Ketty."

"You go on," Judith said. "I'll be there shortly. I need to change my socks."

They both glanced down at the thin anklets she was wearing. Ning had nodded her approval when she'd seen Judith putting on her sneakers earlier.

"Don't be long," she said.

"I won't." Judith shut the door after her and sat down. She wasn't ready to talk to Ketty, let alone try to apologise for something she'd said out of care for her friend, and on top of that her foot was bothering her. She took off the shoes and socks and the plaster fell away revealing the graze, which was now quite red. It hadn't looked too bad after her shower.

"Damn," she muttered and rummaged in her toiletries bag. She applied her last two plasters, and put on a thicker pair of socks and then her sneakers. She tested the injured foot and could hardly feel the graze. All she had to do now was make a quick getaway. She picked up her bag and hat and waited for the train to stop.

They were moving very slowly now. Lacey leaned closer to the window and looked out. A road stretched along parallel to the track and then a group of sheds came into view. Their arrival in Alice Springs was announced via the intercom.

Lacey was wearing her op-shop shorts again, a loose shirt and a hat, and had lathered herself in sunscreen. She and Birgit had opted to go on the Simpsons Gap tour and she wanted to make sure she'd be well covered up. Her legs had turned a little pink yesterday even though she'd managed to be in the shade most of the time. It might not be so easy today.

"Lacey?" The call was accompanied by a tap on her door.

"I'm here." She smiled as Birgit stuck her head in. "I'm ready."

Birgit came right in and shut the door behind her. "Change of plan."

"Oh."

"Rory and Rhys have booked the camel ride tour and there's room for two more. I'm keen and I thought you would be too."

Lacey's stomach sunk. She'd read about the tour in the brochure. It did sound like something she'd like but she'd noticed there was an extra cost for it.

"No, thanks," she said quickly. "I'll stick with the hike at the gap."

"Oh, no, please," Birgit pleaded. "It was craic with the boyos last night, wasn't it? Except for Rory calling Ketty 'Granny'."

"I thought Miss Ketty wonderful to speak up. My dad used to call my gran 'the old woman'. She hated it but ignored him to keep the peace." Lacey smiled. "Apart from that, it was a great night." Lacey had been tired but staying up with Birgit and the two fellas had been fun in the end.

"Rhys especially said he hoped you could come." Birgit smiled brightly then grabbed her hand. "Pleeease!"

Lacey shook her head, wishing she could but there was no wriggle room in her finances. "Camels terrify me."

"Pfft." Birgit batted a hand at her.

"It's a fear, like you and heights."

"Oh."

Lacey tried to smile. She wasn't good at lying. "I'm sure you'll have fun and we can compare our day over drinks later. It'll be like getting to do both trips because we'll hear all about each other's firsthand."

"I'm sorry to desert you." Birgit's shoulders drooped. "I promised we'd do the hike together."

"I won't be on my own. There'll be plenty of other people."

"If you're sure?"

"I am."

"Are you coming to wait in the lounge car? We'll be arriving soon."

"I'll be there in just a tick." Lacey picked up the tube of sunscreen she'd been using. "I've got to finish lathering and then I'll catch you up."

"Okay." Birgit gave her one last wistful look then let herself out.

Lacey put the tube back on the table and picked up her phone. Once more she checked the balance in her account and once more she was disappointed. Her dad still hadn't sent through the money he'd promised. Her recent texts remained unanswered and her calls rang out. Her sister, Freya, always said he wasn't to be trusted but Lacey's view of him had been different. She'd stubbornly clung to the ideal dad she imagined him to be.

Her phone pinged. Freya's name appeared on the screen.

How's it going? What's the train like? Met any cute guys yet? Send photos xx

Lacey smiled and scrolled through the photos she'd taken. Hers were all images of scenery. She found the group shot Birgit had forwarded from yesterday and a selfie with Birgit from the night before and sent them to her sister with a brief message to say all was well and the trip great with good company.

She pictured Rory and Rhys. Were they good company? She'd describe them both as cute and they were fun to be with but that was all. She got the impression that was what Rhys thought too but Birgit appeared besotted by Rory and he was certainly paying her plenty of attention. For Lacey it was still too soon. Her heart belonged to Dean even though it wasn't reciprocated.

Her finger hovered over her phone and before she knew it she was looking at the few photos she had of her and Dean together. There was one in particular she loved. They'd been out for a meal and it had been taken afterwards back at Dean's apartment. He'd snapped a selfie of them. She was wearing his hot pink T-shirt and they were cuddled together beaming at the phone.

It was the night when she'd known he was more to her than a casual acquaintance.

twenty-four

The previous February – Randwick, Sydney

"I'd better get going soon," Lacey said when for the first time that evening there was a lull in the conversation between her and Dean.

He smiled at her across his kitchen table. "Going to turn into a pumpkin?"

"I hope not." She grinned. "But I've got a few things to do tonight and you're heading off early tomorrow."

"Fair enough. You can keep the T-shirt."

"Oh, no. I'll wash it and return it."

"I don't think my sister wants it back."

Lacey glanced down at the vibrant pink T-shirt Dean had loaned her. It was a breast cancer awareness shirt and *Do it for the girls* was printed across the front. It hung in folds even though she'd tied a knot in one side and tucked the other into her skirt. "Not my usual style."

He laughed. It was a hearty sound and one that she'd discovered, from their now regular catch-ups, came easily.

"I still can't believe how useless that waiter was when he splashed sauce all over you," Dean said.

"My T-shirt came clean." Thankfully they'd finished their meal before the waiter had accidentally splattered tomato sauce down her back. None of it had reached her linen skirt but her white shirt had been sprayed. The waiter had apologised and dabbed uselessly at her shirt with serviettes. He was only young and very embarrassed. "It was an accident. Thanks for letting me rinse my shirt here before I head home."

"Lucky my place wasn't far away. And you're lucky it's tidy at least." He waved a hand around. "I did a quick clean-up and clear-out ready to get away tomorrow."

Lacey liked Dean's apartment nearly as much as she liked him. It was run-down like her house but it had a comfortable vibe and it didn't reek of cigarette smoke. And in the background his favourite country playlist was something she was getting used to. Her dad liked country music but he was a fan of the older tunes from singers like Slim Dusty, John Williamson and Smoky Dawson. Dean's playlist was a mix of modern musicians.

"Your family will be pleased to see you."

"It will be a crazy weekend. Weddings in my family are big and boisterous."

Lacey glanced down. He'd been invited before Christmas, before he and Lacey had become, how would she describe it, close? He'd suggested he ask his cousin to add her as his plus one but Lacey had said no. Their relationship was still new and fresh and she kind of liked keeping it to themselves. They hadn't got to the point of meeting each other's families.

"Mum will be happy," Dean said. "I haven't seen her since the new year. She'd like me to go home more often."

"She must miss you." Lacey nearly said she envied him but swallowed her words and smiled instead. He'd talked a lot about his big extended family. Lacey said little about hers.

"I think it's a mixture of that and guilt."

She tipped her head to the side. "Guilt?"

"Mum blames herself for this." He tapped his legs.

"Oh." Lacey had been surprised when he'd got out of his wheelchair once they were inside his flat and used sticks to support himself to move around. He'd only ever used the chair when they were together. "Do you mind me asking what your disability is?"

He looked surprised. "Haven't I told you? It's usually one of my opening lines. If we're going to be friends you should have all the gory details."

Lacey studied him, anxious she was going to hear about some terrible accident.

"Don't look so worried. It's not contagious. I have cerebral palsy."

"Oh." She'd heard of it, of course. "I don't know much about that."

"It can vary but for me it mostly affects my legs. I prefer to use a chair when I'm out and about. It's easier. But at home it gets in the way and I can manage better with the sticks."

Lacey hesitated. "So why does your mum feel guilty?"

"She thinks I'm like this because of something she might have done while I was in utero. And for not realising sooner there was something wrong when I was young. We've been through it with the medicos. In my case there's no one thing that CP can be pinpointed to. It's what it is. My dad's way of dealing with it is to ignore it so I wasn't cut any slack growing up as the middle child of five kids and because of that Mum overcompensated and felt guilty. I've grown up surrounded by love and learning not to feel sorry for myself." He grinned and opened his arms wide. "And look what a great guy I've turned into."

"You're amazing." Lacey grinned back.

"You picked up on that." He got to his feet. "Do you mind if we get a photo? Mum will ask."

"In this T-shirt?" she wailed.

"Just head and shoulders."

She stood beside him. He leaned one shoulder against hers, held his phone out for a selfie then showed her.

"That's not too bad," she said.

"I'm not totally useless."

"I'd never think of you as any kind of useless."

His deep brown eyes, only a short distance away, studied her carefully. "I don't believe you would." He leaned closer. "May I kiss you?"

She nodded, her throat suddenly dry. His lips brushed hers then gently pressed, the kiss deepening. A tingling sensation rippled through her. He wrapped one arm around her, pulling her against him. She felt at ease, alive, excited, all those things in one embrace, then he suddenly let her go, wobbled slightly and adjusted his stance.

"Sorry, lost my balance." His look was sheepish. "You almost knocked me off my feet."

"I'm sorry." She flapped a hand at him, appalled at the thought of him falling.

"I'm teasing." Once more that easy laugh of his relaxed her immediately.

"Now that I'm up I'd better go," she said.

"I'll see you next week?"

She nodded and he leaned in for another quick kiss.

Flustered by her body's enthusiastic response, Lacey quickly gathered her bag and her own T-shirt that was a wet lump on the kitchen sink.

"Let me get you a plastic bag for that," Dean said.

They fumbled over it, the T-shirt almost missing the opening, and laughed together as they both tried to catch it and push the soggy fabric into the bag.

Dean opened the door and she tumbled through it, pulling up quickly as she nearly bumped into a woman in the outer entry.

"Miss Carslake?" Judith dropped the hand that had been poised to knock and looked her up and down.

Lacey couldn't help but glance down at the oversized T-shirt that had obviously caught Judith's attention.

"Hi, Jude." Dean's welcome was bright as usual.

"I was coming to see if you needed anything done while you were away." Once more her gaze went back to Lacey.

"I was just leaving." Lacey smiled at Dean and took the plastic bag he was holding. "Thanks for a lovely dinner."

"You actually cooked dinner?" Judith gaped at Dean.

"Well, thanks for casting nasturtiums on my cooking prowess in front of Lacey." He laughed. "We did eat out though, Jude." He grimaced at Lacey. "Something you'd better know about me is I rarely cook unless it comes out of a jar or a packet."

Lacey smiled but didn't speak, aware of Judith's close scrutiny.

"I'll see you Monday, Miss Carslake," Judith said.

"Crikey, Jude. What's with all this Miss Carslake business? You're work colleagues, aren't you?"

"I must go," Lacey said. She smiled again at Dean, gave Judith a quick nod and set off.

"I'll ring you," Dean called after her.

Lacey thought about Dean and his kiss all the way home.

twenty-five

Day Two – Alice Springs

Voices sounded outside Lacey's door. She slipped her phone into her pocket and glanced out the window. The train was barely moving now. She picked up her bag and hat. She was going to be among the first to get off so she could avoid Birgit and merge with the crowd. Hopefully there'd be lots of buses and people milling about like there had been at Katherine the day before.

Lacey opened her door and peered out. She could hear people talking in the distance but there was no-one in the corridor so she strode down to the carriage door where she came to a sudden stop. There was a woman in front of her carefully making her way down the steps and a man hovering on the platform holding an ornate walking stick. He reached for the woman's hand but she batted him away.

"Don't fuss, Beau. I'm best to do it myself."

Once she reached the platform Lacey followed her down. One of the golf-cart style buggies waited alongside the train. Lacey turned away to set off on foot down the platform but the woman called to her.

"Young lady, would you like a ride?"

"I'm fine, thank you."

"It's a long way to the buses. Please do sit next to me." The woman indicated the seat beside her. "Beau and I enjoy company when it's fresh and bright like you."

"Don't embarrass her, Mum." He smiled apologetically at Lacey.

She smiled back and looked along the platform. Their carriage was a long way from the buses. She did want to get there quickly and the day was already hot.

"Thank you, I'd love a ride," she said and climbed on beside the woman. Beau took a seat behind.

"I'm Virginia," the woman said. She wore little make-up over her softly creping skin but her elegant features needed no enhancement and her silvery hair sat gently around her face in a silky cloud. It was hard to guess her age.

"I'm Lacey."

"It's nice to see some younger people on this rattling antique." Virginia waved a hand at the train as the buggy set off along the platform.

"I'm travelling with my work colleagues. There are six of us including our employer. She's treating us to a staff holiday."

Virginia gave her a haughty look. "She must be a very rich woman."

Lacey had a sudden pang of guilt. She'd been so worried about her own finances she hadn't considered at all how much Ketty had spent on this trip. She must have thought Lacey so ungrateful, bleating on about her money troubles the previous night. "She's very generous."

"What kind of place do you work?"

"It's a dressmaking business in Sydney. Ketty Clift Couture."

"That sounds intriguing, doesn't it, Beau?"

The buggy had reached the bus area and Beau had already stepped off. He appeared at Virginia's side.

"Yes." He nodded. "Sounds right up your alley, Mum."

"I was a model once, you know," Virginia said. "Not that you'd know it to look at me now."

"This is just a small setback." Beau handed over her stick.

"A knee replacement isn't a small setback." Virginia shook her head then turned back to Lacey. "Don't let anyone tell you it's a simple thing. Almost three months and I'm still hobbling. Once upon a time I strode down a catwalk in six-inch heels. I modelled for several of the well-known Australian designers." She paused then said, "Virginia Dupont."

She spoke the name with a French accent, giving it some extra pizzazz.

"I'm sorry...I don't..." Lacey fumbled, not sure how to tell this rather imperious woman she'd never heard of her.

"Don't worry." Beau came to her rescue. "It was a long time ago."

Virginia glared at him. "My son doesn't appreciate what it took to achieve what I did."

"Of course I do." He gave his mother a wide smile.

Lacey hopped off the buggy. "I'd better go and find my bus."

"Which tour are you taking?" Beau asked.

"The Simpsons Gap walk."

"I'd have chosen that if I was able," Virginia said. "Touring the town in a bus doesn't appeal."

Beau smiled indulgently at his mother. "We've never been here before. You might be surprised."

He offered his hand. Virginia sighed then accepted the support and stepped down.

"I hope you both have a great day." Lacey eased away. There were steady queues of people boarding the buses.

"We might see you in the lounge car later." Virginia smiled hopefully.

"Yes, perhaps." Lacy nodded and set off to find her bus. It was already half full when she reached it but at least she'd avoided Birgit and being pressed again to take a camel ride she couldn't afford.

Ketty peered at herself in the bathroom mirror. She didn't look too bad for someone who'd had little sleep. She put her toothbrush away, patted her lips dry, reapplied her lipstick then ran a comb through her straight chin-length hair.

The train had stopped at the Alice Springs terminal and she'd already heard the voices of passengers alighting for the buses. Carlos was waiting for her in the cabin. A couple of times she'd thought she'd heard him talking beyond the thin veneer of the bathroom door.

She was looking forward to her first view of Alice Springs. She hadn't had a chance to ask what the others had chosen, except for Birgit who she'd almost run into in the lounge car, and who'd told her excitedly about the camel ride she was taking. Ketty could see Birgit was enjoying herself. She could only hope the rest of her staff were.

She opened the door.

"That's good news, Felix." Carlos had his back to her. He spun, his phone to his ear. "That's fine," he said into the phone. "I'm sorry, I have to go. I'll call when I'm back in Sydney."

"You don't need to stop your call because of me," Ketty said as he slipped his phone in his pocket. "Was that Felix from the cafe?"

Carlos gave a slight shake of his head, then held out his hands, palms up. "You look ready to tackle the day. How did your chat with Val go?"

"Very productive. I think their problem might be not managing the change from Warren working to retirement. Like my neighbour Maurice, but it sounds like Warren is better at occupying himself. Maurice is constantly checking on Lee to see what she's doing."

Ketty settled on the couch by the window and Carlos took the other end.

"How are your Paddington friends?" Carlos asked. "I'm looking forward to seeing them again. I enjoyed our get-togethers when I stayed with you in Sydney. You don't have to travel to gather an interesting group around your table, Ketty. Your friends are a fascinating mix. Not at all lame geese, as Maurice described them."

Ketty laughed. "The expression is lame ducks and no, none of them could be described as that, tempted as I am to brand Maurice with his own label. Nothing much has changed since you saw him last. He's still opinionated and tries to dominate the conversation."

"He is a bit fond of the sound of his own voice but he's an interesting character. And what a varied life Klaus has led. An engineer turned architect turned wood carver."

"He's such a nice man. So sad he's got no family in Australia now but he says he doesn't want to go back to Germany. I've tried a couple of times to have him over when Judith is at my place. We had dinner together, just the three of us, after I broke my wrist. He seems to enjoy her company but she doesn't say much."

Carlos raised his eyebrows.

"Don't give me that look, Carlos. Judith would never admit it but she's a lonely woman."

"And yet when I returned the week after you broke your wrist I seem to remember you hurrying her away."

"I didn't hurry her away. It was a help to have Judith there for the first few days after it happened but then I was ready for her to leave. I'm used to living on my own, having my own space. Sometimes her attention can make me feel crowded."

"Then I came back to stay for a while and now here I am again, crowding your space."

"You're not at all. It's different with you, Carlos."

He held her gaze a moment as if he was trying to read her thoughts. Ketty glanced down, avoiding his piercing look and trying not to think of Judith's concerns.

"I suspect that's one of the reasons she's not so fond of me perhaps," he said. "I take up some of your time. Especially now I've come on this holiday."

"I see Judith nearly every day," Ketty said. "But you and I don't…won't get the chance to catch up often…I want to make the most of it." She looked up at him. "You're welcome here, and to stay with me when you're in Sydney any time, Carlos…truly."

He turned one of his enigmatic smiles on her. Sometimes he was hard to read.

"I don't want to monopolise your time though." Ketty suddenly felt selfish, remembering his phone call. "You've got family and other friends to catch up with."

"But for now we have this wonderful journey to experience, for which I'm most grateful to you for including me."

"It was your idea and your generous gift of the voucher that convinced me to book."

"And always so magnanimous. You're one of a kind, Ketty."

His fine words and slight accent still had the ability to make her feel special, as they always had. She looked down and flicked an imaginary speck from her trousers.

"How's that other chap getting on?" Carlos asked. "Judith's neighbour?"

"Dean? He's fine, I assume."

"He was the life of the party at Christmas. Do you know him well?"

"Not very. He lives in the apartment below Judith and she's kind of adopted him when it comes to social events. I always enjoy his company." Ketty tapped a finger to her chin. "He and Lacey started dating after that Christmas luncheon. I was pleased. They seemed so well suited but something's happened and they're not seeing each other any more. Such a shame."

This time Carlos tutted as well as raising his eyebrows. "You can't help yourself, can you?"

"I've no idea what you mean."

He simply shook his head and she laughed.

"This is fun. It is good to have you here, Carlos."

A call came over the intercom announcing the tours were ready to start.

"Our coach awaits," he said.

Judith had been one of the first to get off the train. She put her head down and strode along the concourse, making for the line of buses. When she'd found hers, she'd waited close to the front door hoping Ketty hadn't chosen this tour.

"You're keen," the smiling driver had said and let her aboard, where she'd made her way towards the back of the bus, slumped low onto a seat and kept her head down. She was still there, tucked away as people slowly filled up the bus, but thankfully so far no-one had asked to sit next to her. She was happy to keep to herself.

Through the window she could see people boarding the next bus. None of them were familiar. She was looking forward to taking a tour by herself. She pulled out her phone and turned it on in case she wanted to take photos. To her surprise a text message appeared on the screen. It was from Dean.

Hey Jude, she read then smiled. The text was brief. *Hope train good. No luck yet with new digs*. And that was it. Not even the smiley face that he usually added to his texts.

He'd lost his spark lately, no doubt worrying about accommodation or perhaps his break-up with Lacey. Judith tried not to think about that. She'd been secretly happy it hadn't worked out – Dean could do better. But she felt for him. Lacey had been the first girl he'd been a bit serious about in a long time. It was just another reason for Judith to dislike Lacey, who was far too fickle to see how important the relationship had been to Dean.

The lack of new accommodation was of bigger concern. She thought about the letter she carried in her handbag. Silly to have brought it. It was like a smouldering fire needing only a little bit of oxygen to ignite it. She recalled the evening she'd received it, just a few short weeks ago. She'd read it in the fading light at the front entrance to her apartment block and her first impulse had been to screw it into a ball and toss it in the bin. Then she'd read it again, convincing herself it wasn't as bad as she'd first thought and that her landlord only wanted her out temporarily while renovations were done. She'd even thought perhaps she'd be able to stay with Ketty for a while.

Despite its dilapidated state, Judith loved her apartment. It was in Randwick and as the crow flies it was straight across Centennial

Park from Ketty's place. Most days she walked to work. The forty minutes it took was good exercise and she caught the bus home in the afternoon, but that particular Friday night she'd had some errands to run along Oxford Street. She'd eaten a quick meal at the RSL and caught a taxi home. She'd been about to head upstairs to her apartment when she'd run into Dean.

twenty-six

The previous March – Randwick, Sydney

Dean's apartment door opened and he rolled forward in his wheelchair.

"Hello, Jude. You're late home. Been on a hot date?" He winked.

Judith ignored his teasing. "Where are you going at this time of night?"

"I'm heading out with some mates. Party's just getting started."

"At this hour you shouldn't..." Her voice dwindled at his raised eyebrow. Who was she to tell him what to do?

"I can take care of myself, Jude."

"I know I..." Judith flinched. "I didn't mean you weren't capable."

"I know, you just worry about me."

Dean smiled, but his eyes lacked their usual sparkle. His thick curls were unbrushed and he wore the same shirt and trousers she'd seen him in the day before. If only he'd tidy himself up he'd be positively handsome. It was only then she realised this was the first time in a long time she'd noticed him lacking in personal grooming.

"You often have dinner with Lacey on a Friday night, don't you?"

His smile dissolved. "Not always." He nodded at the envelope in her hand. "Hey, did you get one of those eviction notices too?"

Judith frowned. "Yes, but not renewing a lease isn't quite the same as evicting."

"I can't see the difference." He waved a hand at the door behind him. "Took me ages to find this place. It suits me fine and it's close to work and transport. Don't know what I'll do for new digs."

"I was hoping we'd only have to move out temporarily. There'd be a refurbishment and then an offer of renewal."

"Nope. Grumble-guts asked the owners. Evidently they're knocking the place down, building a bigger, fancier, new apartment block. We're being evicted. And even if I had somewhere else to go in between I sure as hell wouldn't be able to afford whatever they're building to replace this. I've started looking for another place already."

"My lease isn't up for three months."

"They'll be pressuring you to get out before that. Evidently they've got a builder ready to go."

Judith glanced around the foyer of the building that had been her home for more than twenty years – since she'd left her husband. Ketty had helped her find it, supported her emotionally and even financially in the early days. Judith had long since paid her back but the apartment was the only home she'd ever felt truly at peace in.

The building only housed five residences, three down and two up. Other tenants had come and gone over the years – the place opposite hers was currently empty. The dear lady who'd lived there had taken ill two months ago and gone into residential care. Judith had often shopped for her in the last year, helped get her to appointments, had regular cuppas and chats.

Judith drew herself up. Until she'd got that notice she'd assumed a new tenant hadn't been found but when she read the letter she realised there would never be one.

"Maybe we could find a place together, Jude." Dean's grin was back.

It was something Judith might consider but she knew he was joking. He was very protective of his personal space and independence. Judith was too, but sharing with the right person in the right apartment or even a small house could work.

"We should keep in touch with any possibilities we see at least," he said.

"Good idea."

A taxi pulled up and he wheeled towards it.

"Night, Jude – don't wait up," he called.

She watched him manoeuvre out of his chair and fold it so it could fit easily in the back of the taxi. She wanted to tell him not to drink too much tonight. The last time he'd gone out with his mates he'd been so drunk he'd fallen out of his chair. That had been before Christmas, before he met Lacey. Once more Judith swallowed her thoughts and her words. She knew she'd be wasting her breath.

twenty-seven

Day Two – Alice Springs

The driver began to explain about the trip ahead, bringing Judith back to the present. She only half listened, recalling she'd run into Dean looking very much worse for wear late the next afternoon and over a shared coffee she'd found out he wasn't going out with Lacey any more. He'd been the saddest she'd seen him and Lacey was to blame.

The bus moved off and she typed a quick reply to Dean and made sure her phone was on silent. She didn't expect any calls or texts but she didn't want to be one of those people. Ning's phone was going every five minutes. It was so annoying.

The ride out took about twenty minutes with the driver commentating on the sights and what to expect once they got there. Judith relaxed and by the time the bus came to a stop she was looking forward to the hike ahead. The brochure had said it was a moderate walk and Judith enjoyed walking.

People at the front of the bus moved off and those closer to Judith stood to gather their things. One of them was very familiar.

Judith slouched back in her seat. Lacey had been sitting a few seats
in front of her and she hadn't realised. Judith hung back, urging
the couple beside her to go ahead. She just hoped there'd be several different groups and she wouldn't be put with Lacey. That
would really spoil her day.

Ketty stepped out from the Royal Flying Doctor Service Museum
into the bright sunlight of the courtyard garden. Carlos was having a good look inside the aircraft on display. Ketty had peered
in but as his large frame almost filled the small space already
crammed with medical paraphernalia, she'd left him to it. Ning
was still wandering through the souvenir shop where Ketty had
purchased a teaspoon and a tea towel. Both items would be useful
and it was some small way of showing support to such a marvellous organisation. She'd had no idea how big the service was and
the work it did.

She squinted and slipped on her sunglasses. The woman with
the stick hadn't been on their bus but she was sitting across the
other side of the garden, her back to Ketty and on her own. It was
too good an opportunity to miss.

Ketty had only taken two steps when Tien called to her. She
was beckoning from her seat under a market umbrella, a hedge of
plants with brilliant purple flowers behind her.

"Do come and sit, Miss Clift."

Ketty gave a quick glance towards the woman with the stick,
still sitting alone, then crossed the outdoor cafe area to join Tien.

"You should stay in the shade," Tien said as Ketty sat. "Your
skin gets thinner as you get older, you know, and you burn more
easily."

"I've applied sunscreen," Ketty said, surprised to hear the curtness in her own voice. Why was it that conversations with Tien often left her feeling as if she'd suddenly lost the ability to take care of herself?

"Although on the other hand you do need some sunshine to make sure you have enough Vitamin D—"

"Aren't the flowers pretty?" Ketty waved a hand at the wall of green and purple beside them. She was quite sure if Tien kept on down this path she'd have her wrapped in a blanket and using a wheeled walker.

"Yes. And the tour has been very interesting. I didn't know about the School of the Air. And the Flying Doctor museum was so interesting. The hologram was amazing but a little creepy. That founder man seemed almost real."

"John Flynn? It was clever, wasn't it?"

"It was like he was really there talking to us."

"A great way to share the history."

"Yes." Tien took a swig from her water bottle then took her time placing it back in the pocket of her bag.

"You're enjoying the train so far?"

"I am. I'm sorry about the fuss I made about the cabin."

"It's all settled now."

Tien lowered her voice. "But you have to share...with a... a man."

"Carlos is not just any man. He's a very old friend...almost like a brother." Ketty fought the urge to laugh.

"I would not share one of those cabins with my brother."

"It's all right, Tien, truly. We've hardly spent any time in the jolly cabin."

"Are you on the top bunk?"

Ketty nodded.

"Oh, please be careful. Lacey has taken our top bunk but I tested the stairs and—"

"The ladder is quite solid."

"But so steep for the elderly."

Ketty bristled. She was older than Tien, of course, but the way she said "elderly" made it sound like some kind of disease. Tien, like her neighbour Maurice, was pushing her too far. She'd been able to redirect Rory's poor choice of name the previous night but she still wasn't sure how to tackle Tien's ageist remarks without hurting her feelings. She decided to change the subject.

"Tien, I've heard a little rumour among the staff."

"Really?" Tien leaned closer.

"There seems to be a story that I'm going to retire."

"Yes." Tien nodded.

"It's not true."

Tien nodded again. "But you've been cutting back so…" She shrugged.

"No, I haven't."

Tien shrugged again.

"If you hear it mentioned please say it's not true. It's unsettling for everyone."

"But at your age—"

"My age has nothing to do with it." Ketty smiled but her voice was stern.

"You had that fall."

"If you remember it was more of a trip." That was Ketty's recollection. She'd picked up one of the mannequins to put it in the dressing area for the mother of the bride who'd had an appointment early the next morning. It had been one of Ketty's old dummies and much heavier than the newer versions. She'd been surprised by a gasp from Tien and her sudden grab at the mannequin. It had seesawed between them until Tien finally had the firmer hold, snatching away the weight and off-centring Ketty. She shoved out her arm to steady herself but the wall was further away than she thought and she'd hit it at an angle with a thud. "It was an accident. Something that could have happened to anyone."

"But elderly bones break more easily. My grandmother—"

"Really, Tien, I could have managed shifting the mannequin on my own and all would have been perfectly fine if you hadn't interfered." Ketty paused. That had come out more forcefully than she'd intended.

Tien gaped at her. "You're saying your broken wrist was my fault."

"Not at all. I'm saying it was an accident. They happen, no matter your age."

"But if it wasn't for me you wouldn't have broken your wrist." Tien pressed her fingers to her mouth. "I'm so sorry."

"I'm not blaming you. I'm just trying to explain—"

Tien shot to her feet. "Excuse me, Miss Clift. I need to find the bathroom."

Before Ketty could stop her, Tien strode away. Ketty tapped her fingers on the table. How had the conversation gone from her refuting her retirement to Tien thinking she was being accused of breaking Ketty's wrist? Ketty would have to smooth those waters quickly. When Tien became fixated on something it was hard to budge her. Hopefully Ketty could seek her out again in a while when she'd calmed a little. Ketty turned to search the other side of the courtyard. The woman with the stick was gone. "Bother."

"Is something wrong?" Ning sat on the seat Tien had just vacated.

"No." Ketty took out her water bottle. "The heat here makes me extra thirsty. Did you enjoy the museum?"

"Yes, so very interesting, and look." Ning pulled a small fluffy toy from her bag. "It's a pilot koala."

Ketty smiled. "For the baby?"

Ning nodded and tucked it away.

"You're not leaving work because you're unhappy, are you, Ning?" If there were issues between Judith and Lacey she hadn't known about maybe there were others.

"Of course not." Ning looked startled. "I told you it's to help with the baby."

"So things at work are okay?"

Ning nodded, a perplexed look on her face.

"You've been with me a long time, a part of Ketty Clift Couture – you don't think I'm...well, that I'm losing my touch, do you?"

"Oh, Ketty, no, no, no!" Ning shook her head fiercely then paused, her head to one side. "Are you worried about those two customers we lost?"

"Not specifically. People are free to choose."

"They'd both been with us a long time."

"Hmm."

"Have you seen Judith today?"

"No." Ketty shook her head and if the truth be told she was glad. Apart from Tien's upset she'd been enjoying herself. Sadly, being with Judith would put a cloud over everything.

Ning leaned in. "I think she's embarrassed and doesn't know how to fix things between you."

"Fix things?"

"She told me she'd said some things about Carlos."

Just at that moment Carlos appeared from the museum exit.

Ketty snapped up straight. "I really don't think Carlos nor I need to be the subject of gossip." Carlos saw her and began to walk in her direction.

"Of course, I only said she—"

"I'm sorry, Ning, but I'd rather we didn't discuss this any further."

Ning pursed her lips and her shoulders sagged. "I'm sorry, I—"

"Here you are." Carlos arrived at the table. "Those RFDS planes are maravilloso."

"You were certainly taken with them."

"So amazing. They're like flying hospitals. Better than what we had on cruise ships."

"There's Tien." Ning jumped up. "Please take my seat, Carlos. I'll go and show her my purchase."

Carlos lowered himself to the chair. "Sorry, did I interrupt something?"

"I'm losing my touch." Ketty pressed a hand to her cheek. "Perhaps they're right, I'm getting older."

"My dear Ketty, every one of us is getting older."

"Maybe too old then."

"Too old for what?"

"Managing my business, my staff."

Carlos pushed back against his seat, a frown creasing his handsome face. "Who told you such nonsense?"

"I seem to have upset nearly all of my staff and those I haven't... well, they have their own issues."

"What's going on?"

"I believe they all, well, some of them, think I'm almost in my dotage."

Carlos puffed a breath of disbelief over his lips. "Then they are wrong. You have a wonderful business and I've had the chance to observe firsthand your talents, and those of your somewhat ungrateful staff."

"Ungrateful?"

"If they think you're in your dotage they don't appreciate all you do for them."

"I'm being silly, I know. Perhaps distracted is a better word for how I've been at work lately. That's how Judith described me." She fanned her face with her hand. "I knew there were little rumblings. That's why I booked this holiday. Now here we are, almost halfway through our trip and I'm no closer to sorting them out."

"I don't like seeing you so bothered." Carlos shuffled closer and took her hand in his. His grip was warm, firm, reassuring. "You have a magical way with people, Ketty, but there are some people who don't want to take a different path or make changes in their lives, no matter how unhappy they are."

"That's kind of you to say but—"

"I'm not simply being kind, I'm being truthful. I've seen you transform many a cruise passenger over the years." He squeezed her hand briefly and let it go. "But you know there were some even you couldn't help."

Ketty sighed. He was right. "But I can't neglect my staff." She thought about the relationship – or lack of one – between Judith and Lacey, Judith's misplaced concern for Ketty and then the recent mismanaged conversations with Tien and Ning. She couldn't not try to fix them all.

"There are people who like to wallow in their own misery or disappointments or those who are simply too afraid to try something different. Even you can't change that."

"Oh, I'm quite sure none of my staff fit that category."

"Look around, Ketty. Are any of them here looking out for you?"

"Probably because I've scared them off, and to be fair they're not all here on this particular tour."

"You've given them this wonderful holiday; it's up to them to make of it what they will. Why don't you stop worrying about them and think about yourself for a change? Enjoy this holiday with me." He picked up her hand again and pressed it to his lips. His deep brown eyes regarded her closely. Full of concern or was it something more?

Ketty pulled her hand back.

"I'm sorry." A small smile played on his lips. "That probably wasn't very brotherly, was it?"

"Probably not."

His smile dropped away. "Ketty, there's something—"

"Oh, look, they're calling us to the bus." Ketty rose. "I think our next stop is lunch at the desert park. I'm feeling rather hungry." She collected her bag and water bottle, quite sure she'd heard enough outpourings for today. Whatever Carlos had been going to say could wait. She didn't want to risk upsetting him too.

twenty-eight

Day Two – Alice Springs

The sun pounded down from a clear blue sky as Lacey took in the view before her. The contingent on the bus had been divided into smaller groups and hers had been the last to reach the viewpoint on their second walk for the day. The first walk had been a circuit, not as rugged as this Cassia Hill route, and dotted with majestic ghost gums, plenty of other flora and the odd bit of fauna. Their guide had pointed out several lizards that made Lacey think about Tien and her reptile fear. She wouldn't have enjoyed this walk.

"Not a bad view, is it?" Gregor and his partner, Vance, came to a stop beside her.

"Certainly worth the walk," Lacey said.

"It wasn't that strenuous," Vance said as he mopped his brow and cheeks with a large handkerchief. "But hiking in the full sun slows you down."

"As it should," Gregor said. "No need to rush."

Gregor and Vance had been quick to introduce themselves to the group when they'd gathered at the start of the first walk.

They'd fallen into step with Lacey. They were good fun and had included her in their conversation.

"Make sure you have plenty of water." Gregor offered Vance a bottle from his backpack. "Do you have some, Lacey?"

Lacey loved that they were so thoughtful of each other but also included her when there was something to look at or discuss. While she guessed they were more than double her age, they'd outpaced her along the creek beds and up the hill that gave them this view out across the rugged valley and the ranges beyond.

During their walk they'd shared the basics about their lives. They were both pharmacists and since the pandemic had decided to do as many Australian walking trails as they could. They'd spent the week before catching the train taking various hikes at Kakadu. Lacey had filled them in on her work and why she was on this holiday.

The two men had sung her employer's praises, saying the most they'd ever given their staff was a free Christmas party and a holiday bonus. She didn't say Miss Ketty did that and more. She felt guilty about the cost of the trip all over again.

"I'm looking forward to tonight." Gregor offered Vance a mint and then Lacey, who declined. "We've got to get glammed up for the dinner under the stars."

Vance clapped his hands. "Won't it be great. People we know who've done this trip say it's a highlight."

"Just being here together is a highlight." Gregor put an arm around Vance's shoulders and hugged him close. "We're so lucky."

Seeing Vance and Gregor so affectionate and enjoying each other's company made her ache for Dean. The guide began to explain the features of the scenery before them, which included the rugged ridges of the West MacDonnell Ranges. Lacey took some photos to distract herself but then once more found herself scrolling back. She stopped at the most recent photos of her and Dean together.

They'd been to a movie. Dean had let her choose and she'd picked a romantic action-adventure film, thinking it would be something they'd both enjoy. They had, she thought, and then he'd wanted to go on for drinks and a late dinner at a wine bar afterwards. Lacey had said she was tired and needed an early night. It had been an excuse but she had no money for anything extra.

Dean had tried to change her mind but she couldn't. It had ended awkwardly. That had been about a month ago. Then a week later had come his call to say he was going home to see his family and not sure when he'd be back and he'd get in touch. When he hadn't, she'd sent him a message and the reply had been short. *Cooling things for a while*, he'd sent. She'd been devastated. She'd enjoyed his company so much and she'd thought he felt the same. They weren't rushing anything but Lacey had truly believed they had a strong connection. Then he'd called it off.

She tried to remember exactly what she'd said that night after the movie. Had there been something in her words or the way she'd spoken that had upset him? She'd been over it before and there was nothing, except that she'd turned down his suggestion of dinner.

"Ready to go?" The guide interrupted her torturing herself further. She put the phone away, falling into step behind Vance and Gregor as they made their way down the hill and along the other part of the loop. To add to her mood, her boots were beginning to feel like lead weights.

Judith sat alone on a bench near the start of the path to Simpsons Gap. The solicitous tour guide had left her only after she'd reassured him she was fine but had a sore ankle she'd decided to rest. She was off to one side of the track in the shade of a tree and most people hadn't noticed her sitting there. The few who had stopped to check on her she'd waved on with a cheery smile and an assurance she was fine. In reality she was miserable.

She undid the lace of her sneaker and eased her foot out. Immediately the pain in and around her ankle eased but she could see the sock was stuck to her skin. She tipped a little of her drinking water on it then slowly peeled the fabric away. The plasters went with it and she was left with an angry weeping graze covering her puffy ankle and the skin around it. She poured a little more of her water over it. It stung briefly and then settled to a dull ache.

She propped her heel on her shoe and let out a long sigh. She should have chosen a tour without so much walking, but when she'd left the train that morning she hadn't expected the graze would rub and flare up so badly. Of course, trying to avoid Lacey had only added to her discomfort.

When the bus had pulled into the car park at Simpsons Gap, Judith had stayed where she was and watched as people had been directed to form into three groups for the walks. Once she saw Lacey join the last group, Judith had scurried from the bus and merged with the first. She'd only said a few words to the other people in her own party. They were all friends or couples, friendly enough but she'd not got involved. The walks had been interesting but she'd spent a lot of time looking over her shoulder and the consequence had been a couple of missed steps that had aggravated her sore ankle.

She wondered what tour Ketty had taken and how much more enjoyable it would have been to be together, but Carlos had put an end to that. Forlornly sitting alone with an aching foot, Judith's misery grew. She'd be happy to see Ning's friendly face about now or Tien's or Birgit, who seemed to be off away from their group most of the time. Or even Lacey. Judith knew she'd been silly trying to avoid the girl. After all, they saw each other every day at work – what would it have mattered if they'd been in the same tour group?

She bent to shoo some flies from her ankle and tipped a bit more of her water over it. She wasn't sure how she was going to get her sock back on, let alone her sneaker.

By the time Lacey's group reached the drinks station near the bus, most of the first two groups had finished and already set off for the third and final event of the tour, the walk to Simpsons Gap.

Lacey was glad to get a fresh bottle of water. Hers was all but empty. She looked longingly at the locked bus. Her Docs were usually so comfortable but they'd become stiffer and tighter during the last part of the hike and her feet were hurting. She'd gladly give up the last trek for a soft seat and air conditioning.

"Ready, Lacey?" Gregor asked.

"We're the last." Vance waved a hand towards the path. "Don't want to miss out."

Lacey's feet began to feel like they were being squeezed by a vice with every step she took. The two men set off at their usual pace and she could tell she'd have trouble keeping up.

"Hello." Gregor spoke to someone as they passed a seat in the shade just off the track. "Are you all right?"

"Yes, thank you. Just resting."

Lacey recognised the voice. She slowed her pace further as she rounded the bush that was blocking her view. Judith sat on a bench in the shade, one shoe and sock off.

"That looks nasty." Vance waggled a finger towards the exposed foot.

"What happened?" Lacey said.

Judith looked up, open-mouthed, as if she'd just conjured up a ghost. "Lacey?"

"I didn't know you were on this tour."

"Is this your wonderful boss?" Gregor asked. "We've heard lots about you."

Lacey shook her head. "We...this is..."

"Judith Pettigrew," Judith said firmly. "Lacey and I work together."

"Well, you're both very lucky," Vance said.

"What have you done to your foot?" Gregor crouched down beside Judith.

"I scraped it yesterday. It wasn't that bad but after that last trek up the hill it's flared up and I've run out of plasters."

"I can't believe the tour guide left you alone."

"Oh, he didn't. At least, I simply said my ankle was a bit sore and I'd wait here until they got back. I didn't mention the scrape."

"We've got plenty of first-aid supplies." Vance patted the pack on Gregor's back.

"It's fine really," Judith said. "I've rinsed it with water and I'll give it some fresh air while everyone's off looking at the gap."

"That's probably the best option but it's a pity you're missing the main attraction," Vance said.

"I've got some non-stick dressing you can put on it." Gregor stood up.

Vance glanced from Judith to Gregor. "We don't want to miss seeing the gap."

"I'm fine, really. You should keep going." Judith waved them on. "I'm happy sitting here."

"If you're sure?" Gregor raised his eyebrows at Lacey, who was feeling like she couldn't continue on.

"I'll wait with you," she said.

"There's no need," Judith protested.

"That's good of you, Lacey." Vance smiled. "Are you sure?"

Lacey nodded.

Judith sniffed. "I don't need—"

"We won't be gone long," Gregor said. "I don't think it's very far."

"We'll take photos." Vance waved his phone at them and the two men set off.

"I don't need anyone to wait with me," Judith muttered.

"I know." Lacey sat on the other end of the bench. The relief for her feet was instant.

In the silence that followed a magpie warbled from somewhere nearby.

"It's good of—"

"Mrs Pettigrew, how—"

They spoke at once and Judith shook her head.

"You should call me Judith. We've worked together for a long time, and out here..." She cast her arm to indicate the empty landscape around them. "It seems out of place to be so formal."

Lacey nodded. "How are you finding the train?" She couldn't bring herself to say "Judith".

"It's...interesting."

Lacey nodded again.

"I don't usually go far for holidays," Judith said. "And I haven't ever had one quite like this."

"Me either."

Judith glanced along the track in the direction everyone else had gone. "We'll have to look at other people's photos of the gap."

"I'm pretty sure Gregor and Vance will have plenty."

They lapsed into silence again. Judith was the first to break it.

"You and those boots." Judith shook her head. "I always thought they were too heavy."

"They're the most comfortable footwear I own." Lacey's old sneakers had a hole in the sole and she'd had no money to buy a new pair before they left.

Judith raised her eyebrows.

"They weren't very forgiving during that last hike up the hill," Lacey admitted.

"Why don't you take them off?"

Lacey stared at her boots. "We've still got lunch and some sightseeing to go before we're back at the train." Her other shoes were cork platform sandals and a pair of thongs. Neither were any good for tramping around on a tour, and no use anyway given they were back on the train.

"I didn't want to take my sneaker off," Judith said. "I was worried I wouldn't be able to put it on again."

Lacey chewed her bottom lip. "Same," she admitted.

"The fresh air is a relief."

Lacey hesitated for another heartbeat then bent, undid her laces and worked them loose with her fingers. Immediately the pain eased.

"What a pair we are," Judith said and her lips twitched upward in the smallest of smiles.

Lacey smiled back. Judith shifted her gaze to the track and once more they lapsed into silence with only the sound of the magpies to fill it.

"Did you enjoy the walk...the scenery?" Judith pointed at Lacey's boots. "I suppose the walking part wasn't that good."

"My feet only started to hurt as we got back from that second walk so I did enjoy it. The colours and lines are inspiring."

"Hmm! Not sure I'd use the word inspiring but I did enjoy the views."

And that was one of their big differences. Lacey took in a view and saw colour and design. She imagined Judith saw the colour but only the features of the landscape and not what the landscape could become.

"Gregor and Vance were good company." Lacey steered the conversation away from a topic that might cause friction. She was happy to be having this casual chat with Judith. And she wondered, if they did continue, whether Judith might tell her something about Dean. Lacey was eager to hear he was all right at least.

Judith nodded.

"I think they kind of adopted me because I was on my own. They're a couple of pharmacists and they've done a lot of travel. They love to hike though. After today I think my preferred style of sightseeing will be from a bus."

"You didn't want to go on the camel ride with Birgit? That would have been easier on your feet."

Lacey shook her head.

"I enjoy walking. But walking on paths in Sydney is a bit different to here." Judith sighed. "I should have had my sneakers on yesterday, then this graze wouldn't have happened."

She lifted her foot a little and peered at it. Her often stern features were replaced by a pained look.

"Is it hurting you badly?" Lacey asked.

"Hardly at all while I'm sitting here like this."

Each time Lacey moved her feet several pressure points stung. She had no idea how she was going to do her laces up again. A dragonfly hovered in the air just in front of her foot. Lacey took it as a sign.

"Do you..." The words stuck in the back of her throat and she gave a little cough. "Do you see much of Dean?"

When there was no reply she glanced up. Judith was staring into the distance. Warmth spread over Lacey's cheeks. Why had she been so silly as to ask?

Judith turned her head slowly. Her eyes were hidden by her sunglasses but Lacey felt the intensity of her look nonetheless.

"Why would you care?"

The venom in her response made Lacey gasp. "I...I care very much."

"Not enough."

"What do you mean?"

"You say you care but you hurt him bad—"

"How?" Lacey shook her head. "I didn't—" She stopped and looked Judith squarely in the face. "I wouldn't intentionally do anything to hurt Dean."

Judith sniffed. "The damage is done now."

"What damage? What's happened?"

"You broke his heart."

"I..." Lacey gaped at Judith. "How?"

"Oh, for goodness sake. Leading him along, letting him think you'd have a relationship and then calling it off."

"I didn't!"

The vehemence in Lacey's response silenced Judith a moment then she slowly shook her head. "Well, something went wrong," she muttered.

Lacey's heart broke all over again. "It did but I don't know what," she murmured.

A puzzled look crossed Judith's face then she turned away.

Lacey studied the ground around her feet. Several ants travelled back and forth moving a tiny crumb; a large, flat brown-and-white striped beetle scuttled from under a rock into the shade of another; and a small moth flitted from plant to plant. She watched each tiny movement. How much easier to be an insect. No money troubles, broken hearts or lonely days for them.

A cricket chirruped and voices carried in the distance.

"I don't want a fuss." Judith bent down and pulled her sock back on and Lacey was left to wonder what she meant.

Judith stood. "I'm going back to the bus."

Lacey pulled her left lace tight and bit back the urge to scream, from her annoyance at Judith's frustrating lack of empathy and from the burning pain in her feet. By the time she'd done up the right laces she was in agony. She rose slowly to her feet and the pain ratcheted up another notch forcing her to sit again immediately.

"What's the matter?" Judith asked.

"My feet...I think I'll wait here for Gregor and Vance. I might be the one needing their help."

The first of the walkers went past and waved. Judith turned back to Lacey. The stern look on her face made Lacey's heart hammer a little harder.

"If it's that bad you should take those boots right off," Judith said. "We'll wait for the two men to come back. They might be able to patch you up enough to get you back to the bus."

Judith stood guard, literally, warding off anyone showing the slightest hint of good Samaritan intentions.

"We don't want a fuss, do we?" she'd muttered after she'd reassured the tour guide they were waiting for friends with fresh plasters and then they'd make their way back.

Gregor and Vance returned and removed Lacey's boots and socks to reveal a blister on each heel, one on the ball of her left foot and one each on her middle and small right toes. They'd tutted, cleaned and patched and then insisted on doing the same with Judith's foot. By the time they'd finished Judith and Lacey were able to ease their footwear back on and walk gingerly back to the bus. The rest of the passengers were already aboard and the tour guide was at the door waiting for them.

Judith was first up the steps and took an empty single seat part way along. Lacey felt the eyes of the rest of the travellers follow her as she walked along the aisle nearly to the back before she came to the next vacant seat. The two men sat opposite her.

"Okay?" Gregor asked as the bus set off.

"Yes, thank you." Lacey nodded and turned to the window, worried they'd see the tears in her eyes.

twenty-nine

Day Two – Alice Springs

Ketty had to admit Carlos had been right to encourage her to put her staff issues aside for the moment. Lunch at the desert park had been a convivial affair with good food and good company.

She'd pulled up sharp when they'd first arrived. The tables were arranged in the shade of the sails on one side of the building with a view to the rugged ridges beyond. They were set with white cloths, proper serviettes, gleaming glassware and sparkling silver cutlery. That had been a pleasant surprise but it was the tables themselves that had made her pause. They were round and set to seat at least eight people. If only her group had been on the same tour she could have had them all at her table as she'd been longing for. Not that Tien and Ning, who had been part of her group, had joined them. Ketty and Carlos had sat with Warren and Val and the two women Carlos had met at breakfast. She'd pretended not to notice Tien and Ning stride past to a table several metres away.

She and Carlos had talked about what they'd done during the morning and Val and Warren and the two women had filled them in on the desert park tour. The women were travel companions from Germany on a two-month Australian holiday and raved about what they'd seen so far. Like everyone else they were enjoying the train and daytime tours. They went with Val to look for souvenirs and Carlos excused himself to the bathroom, which left Ketty with Warren.

"Val put up a fuss about the park tour." Warren shook his head as he watched his wife walk away, chatting animatedly to the other two women. "She's made some new friends and she loved the bird show."

"I wish we could do all the tours," Ketty said. "They all sound interesting. And what a wonderful taste of Australia this whole journey is for the two overseas tourists."

Warren kept gazing in the direction the three women had gone. "I hope Val doesn't buy too many more souvenirs. Our cabin's not big enough to take much more."

"She obviously enjoys buying things for your grandchildren."

"She indulges them." Once more Warren shook his head. "She managed our children so well. Foster kids sometimes come with challenging baggage. I was on the road a lot and then working long hours taking on the business but Val had everything in hand."

"She was telling me how wonderful you were with your children too."

"Was she? Must have been a seniors moment." He quirked his lips. "She's lost her common sense when it comes to the next generation. All I hear these days is how much I'm not doing."

Ketty tipped her head to the side. "I'm sure you both do what you can for your grandchildren."

"It's never enough for Val." He let out a long sigh. "We had a good succession plan for our business. Things went smoothly, although our son still needs my help in the shop from time to time. I was looking forward to retirement. To travels like this with Val, improving my golf game, catching up with mates, learning some new skills. We went to Thailand once years ago. I enjoyed the food. I've always thought I might do a cooking class but…"

Ketty thought of her neighbour Maurice, how he drifted around home rudderless, driving Lee crazy. The way Val had spoken over breakfast, Warren sounded the opposite and yet…

"Sounds like you have lots to keep you busy," she said.

"I try but Val has other ideas."

Ketty's tour leader announced their departure would be in five minutes and they should head to the bus soon and Carlos was making his way back towards her.

"Bother," she muttered.

"Not ready to go?"

"Oh, yes, it's just— I'd better go to the bathroom first." She'd really rather have been talking to Warren a little longer. She wanted to hear more about why he and Val were paddling in opposite directions.

"Where to next for you?" Warren asked as she stood up.

"The reptile park, I think."

"We're heading up to Anzac Hill."

Carlos arrived back at the table.

"I'll meet you on the bus," she said. As she hurried to the bathroom she saw Val leaving the souvenir shop, another bag in her hand.

Instead of taking in the 360-degree view from the top of Anzac Hill, Judith was off to one side in the shade of a tree staring fixedly at the mountain range that edged Alice Springs. She was keeping away from Lacey, the concerned tour guide and the two pharmacists. Lacey because she didn't want to talk to her if she could help it and the other three because she didn't want any more embarrassing fuss about her foot.

"Excuse me."

Judith started and glanced sideways at the man who'd come up beside her. She'd noticed him earlier among the group from her bus. Tufts of hair stuck out from under his cap and his accent had reminded her of Klaus.

"Would you mind taking a photo for me, please?" He held a battered phone towards her.

"I'm not much of a photographer," she blustered.

"It's not difficult. Just point and click." He continued to hold the phone out.

"All right."

He handed it over then stepped away. "Me at the side with the ranges beyond, please."

Holding the phone out in front of her, she lined up the photo as he'd asked and tapped the button. "Shall I take another?"

"Thank you."

She shifted to a slightly different angle and pressed the button again. "I hope they'll be what you want."

He took the phone from her and peered at the screen. "Very good, thank you." He looked up and smiled. "I'm Erik."

"Judith."

"Can I take a photo for you, Judith?"

"Oh, no, I don't need…" Judith glanced around at all the people snapping photos in every direction. She could get one to send to Dean, she supposed. "All right, yes, thank you." She handed him her phone.

Erik looked at the view, asked her to shift a little to the right then lined up the photo.

"I took several," he said as he handed it back. "How are your feet?"

"My feet?" Judith glanced down, wondering if the plasters were showing.

"Our tour guide said you and the young lady had both hurt your feet back at the gap...when we were waiting for you on the bus."

"Oh." Judith was mortified. That's why all eyes had been focused on her when she'd stepped onto the bus. She'd sunk into the first empty seat she'd seen. "It's not that bad, really, just a scrape that began to rub along with a bit of a sore ankle. I'm fine."

"And the young lady?"

Judith followed his gaze. Lacey was sitting on a seat and one of the pharmacists was chatting to her.

"She ended up with several blisters. I suspect walking is quite painful even with plasters covering them."

"That's bad luck. It's a shame to spoil this journey. But then life often gives us surprises." He glanced back to the view they'd both just photographed.

Judith thought she'd move on but his look had been full of despair and she found herself stuck to the spot, not sure whether to stay or go.

"The train has been interesting, hasn't it? The train itself then all these tours," she blurted. "I've never been to the middle of Australia before – have you?"

She watched his shoulders rise and fall as if he'd blown out a breath then he turned back. "Not here but I've spent a lot of time in remote South Australia. We...my wife and I lived in Coober Pedy for over twenty years."

"I don't suppose you'll want to sightsee tomorrow then." She smiled. "You'll have seen it all."

"It's several years since I left." He shrugged. "Maybe there is change."

"Is your wife with you?"

He shook his head. "No longer."

Judith winced. His wife's death was still raw, judging by the sorrowful look on his face, and she would guess he wasn't yet sixty despite his weathered appearance. "I'm sorry for your loss."

He shrugged. "Thank you. Life is what it is."

Judith tried to think of something less fraught to talk about. "Where do you live now?"

"Near Adelaide, a small place called Freeling."

Judith shook her head. "I've not heard of it."

"It's a small rural area in South Australia. Not a long way from Adelaide though."

"I'm from Sydney."

"Ahh." Erik nodded sagely as if that was the answer to everything. "They say they're taking us to the town centre next. Maybe the young lady needs to purchase some different footwear."

Judith turned. Lacey was making her way towards the bus. She cut a forlorn figure, moving painstakingly slowly. Judith was torn between hanging on to the anger she felt for Lacey and empathising with her. There was only a small spot now on one of Judith's feet that rubbed but Lacey's had been covered in blisters.

Erik stepped forward. "Perhaps I could offer an arm—"

"No...thank you." Judith pursed her lips. "I'll go." She'd only taken two steps when there was a yell and Birgit ran across the open space, grabbed Lacey and began to talk animatedly. Another bus had pulled in, obviously with the group from the camel ride as the two young Irish men were there as well, dawdling along behind Birgit. Honestly, that girl was a flirt. Judith hadn't ever realised it before.

Lacey was shaking her head vigorously but Birgit was waving her arms about and next thing the two men had Lacey in a fireman's lift and were carting her towards the bus. Judith was sure Lacey would not like the attention but at least her feet would thank her for it.

It seemed to Ketty that most of the tour groups were spending the last part of the day in and around the centre of Alice Springs. Their bus had stopped in a side street just behind another bus and she could see a third pulling away up ahead. People looking decidedly like tourists from the Ghan wandered in small clusters in every direction. They'd been given the choice of an hour's stroll around the town or going back to the train. She and Carlos had opted to go back to the train so were waiting on the bus, but most people were staying in the town centre.

Ning and Tien had been waiting when the bus pulled up. Tien had refused point blank to enter the reptile park so the two women had walked to the town centre instead. Ketty had felt rather on edge herself as they'd viewed the collection of Australia's most deadly snakes. Tien would most definitely not have been able to set one foot inside. She pushed her concerns for her staff from her mind and turned to Carlos.

"You know, I've been thinking…"

Carlos smiled. "I never know whether to be excited or alarmed when you start a sentence like that."

"I hope excited."

"Go on."

"I think we should stay on in Adelaide for a bit longer after Celia and Jim's celebration. I haven't been back to South Australia in years. I'd like to visit some old haunts again, show you some of the sights."

"I'd like that. And hopefully my case will have been found and caught up with me by then."

"If not, Adelaide has plenty of shops."

"Looks like there are a few shops here." Carlos leaned over Ketty and peered out the window.

"I suppose there are if it's the town centre," Ketty said. "And it seems Ning and Tien have bought some things. They've both got more shopping bags than they had before."

He leaped to his feet. "I think I'll stay in town then, if you don't mind."

"Of course not, do you want me to come—"

"No, no." He waved her back, the gold of his watch glinting in the sunlight. "I need to get a couple of things to make do until they find my case."

"I thought you were managing without it."

"I thought so too but I'm running low on some essentials. It's a good chance to pick up some things."

"Are you sure?"

"I am, I'll see you in a while." He took his phone from his pocket as he strode forward and off the bus.

Ketty was relieved. She'd done enough walking for today and was keen to get back and relax before they went out for dinner tonight. Then she recalled Judith's mention of Carlos's failed card and lurched forward. She wondered if he'd take hers to get his essentials. She searched the people moving along the path below but he'd already disappeared from view.

"Have you been shopping?" Ketty asked as Tien and Ning drew level with her.

They both nodded, Ning with the added extra of a smile, but instead of taking the seat opposite they moved further down the bus.

Ketty definitely had some fences to mend. She was pinning her hopes on tonight's dinner. She'd heard a few rumours about what was involved from other passengers and she hoped to confirm with the steward on the train. Another reason to get back there as soon as possible.

Judith kept a discreet distance as she followed the man with the phone pressed to his ear. There were enough people about and Carlos was tall enough that she could keep him in view without him being aware. Not that he was taking in his surroundings. He appeared to be caught up in the call, occasionally waving a hand in the air, then stopping abruptly, forcing the groups of people behind him to walk around him.

Judith stopped too, turning to study the window of the shop beside her. It was a bank. She read posters about home loans and credit cards while keeping a watch on Carlos. His call had ended because he was holding his phone in front of him now, studying it closely. He looked up and down the street. Judith sucked in a breath but he didn't appear to have noticed her. She froze as he began walking quickly towards her but thankfully he was staring at his phone. Then he stopped abruptly, turned back the way he'd come and continued on around the corner.

Judith walked to the corner where she paused then took a small step forward, nearly colliding with a woman coming the other way.

"Sorry," they both said, sidestepping together and finally in different directions.

When Judith looked down the smaller side street there was no sign of Carlos. A few parked cars, a man and a child sitting on a bench in the shade but little else happening. She moved on cautiously. If Carlos suddenly appeared she'd have nowhere to hide.

She gasped as a door opened beside her, then moved on quickly as the man who'd stepped out of the workwear shop looked at her quizzically. A few steps along she glanced at the huge sign that covered most of the window in the next shop. At the top it said *Pawnbrokers* and below that a list in bold letters: *Only Way to Buy and Sell or Loan, Quality Goods Bought and Sold, Buying Gold Today.* Beyond the signs, through the glass she saw the tall figure of Carlos, his back to her. She moved on quickly.

She made her way around the next corner, paused to get her bearings then set off again pondering what he was up to. She assumed selling something. He must be desperate for money. She wondered why he wouldn't just ask Ketty for a loan if he had nothing to hide. Judith paused again as she reached the next street and the foot traffic became busier. Carlos didn't fool her with his smokescreen of charm but he had Ketty firmly under his spell. There was no point trying to warn her though. Judith had tried that and failed. She'd just have to hope there'd be another way to uncover Carlos's plan, whatever that was.

The ride back to the train didn't take long and Ketty was one of the first off the bus. She moved to one side to wait for Ning and Tien, sure their good manners would force them to be part of any conversation she initiated on the stroll back along the platform

to their carriage. Ahead of her people were having photos taken
with the train in the background, or beside the statue of the camel
complete with cameleer. Helping one group with their photos
was the familiar figure of Matt. He would be able to answer her
questions about tonight.

Ketty ambled in his direction, waiting for him to finish. She
caught sight of Ning and Tien setting off along the platform ahead
of her. Perhaps it was just as well she give them a bit more space.
If all went to plan after her talk with Matt, she'd have her staff
sorted by the end of the evening and if not, well, perhaps Carlos
was right and they could sort themselves.

It didn't take any time at all to walk back to her carriage. Matt
had strolled along beside her as she'd plied him with questions and
when things were organised to her satisfaction he'd been waylaid
by some other passengers.

Ketty stepped up into her carriage and gave a small sigh. She
was growing quite fond of the train. She felt like she could sink
into the comfortable furnishings and kick off her shoes as she
would at home. And she was getting used to the sounds it made,
the clicks and sighs when they were stationary, as if it was gently
resting, and the louder noises and swaying motion when they were
underway. The whole experience was very different to cruising
but she was glad now. "Vive la différence," she murmured as she
reached her cabin door.

She turned the handle and almost bumped her nose on the
door when it remained firmly shut. She jiggled the handle again
and glanced at the number. It was definitely cabin two. Then she
recalled the mix-up with Mr Visser on the previous day. Had she
come aboard the wrong carriage?

She hastily retraced her steps and climbed down to the platform where Matt stood chatting to another passenger.

"Everything all right, Ketty?" he asked.

"I'm just checking I'm on the right carriage." She looked up at the gleaming Q by the door. "And I am."

Matt nodded.

"But I couldn't open my door. They can only be locked from the inside, can't they?"

"That's right," Matt said. "Is Carlos back?"

"No." Ketty's heart beat a little faster. "I left him in town. He's coming back later."

Matt stepped up into the carriage and Ketty followed.

"Which cabin?" he asked.

"Two."

Ahead of them Ning and Tien poked their heads out of their cabins then ducked back in again, like a pair of alarmed meerkats.

Matt stopped at the door and knocked. "Anyone in?"

Ketty stood beside him and listened. There was no answer. Matt tried the door and to her amazement, it opened. She stepped in and looked around. Everything was just as she'd left it.

"Perhaps you tried the wrong door."

Ketty spun back. "I checked the number. That handle wouldn't budge."

Matt tested the handle, which sprung back and forth. "I'm sorry you had trouble. It seems to be okay now."

"It's so strange." Ketty took a deep breath and wrinkled her nose.

Beyond Matt out in the corridor, Ning peered in. "Is everything all right?" she asked.

"Yes," Ketty said. "I had trouble with my door but it's fine now."

Matt stepped around Ning. "I'll leave you to it but please let a staff member know if it happens again."

"Thank you." Ketty smiled but inside she cringed, doubting herself and imagining Matt thought her a bit silly.

"You're all right then?" Ning said.

"Yes." Ketty nodded. "It was good of you to go with Tien after lunch. Did you enjoy the afternoon?"

"We did, and truthfully I didn't mind missing those snakes. We saw some interesting buildings, an art gallery and called in at some shops."

"Something more for the baby?"

Ning smiled. "Yes, and a wonderful hand-woven bag for my daughter-in-law. She will love it for her shopping."

"What does she think about moving in with you?"

Ning's smile fell away. "We get on very well."

"I know you do." Ketty had heard about all the caring things the younger woman had done for Ning after her husband had died. "I just wondered how she was feeling about moving."

"She's fine with it," Ning said firmly but her look was more uncertain.

"Ning, I—"

"I must—"

They spoke over each other and stopped.

"I'm going to rest for a while before Judith returns," Ning said.

"I'm going to put my feet up too." Ketty smiled. "It's dress-up night again tonight for a beautiful dinner under the stars."

"I'm looking forward to it."

"I'm going early. I have a surprise for everyone. Do you think you could all come on the same bus so that you arrive together?"

"Of course. You're so kind, Ketty." Ning looked as if she were about to cry. She grabbed the door handle. "I'll see you later."

The door shut and Ketty was left alone in her cabin. She sniffed the air again. There it was, the odd smell she'd noticed when she'd entered a few minutes ago. The scent of…maleness, perspiration mingled with a scent, deodorant or aftershave. She hadn't noticed it on Matt and it was certainly not Ning or Carlos.

She sat and her feet tapped against something. She bent forward. The corner of the ladder was sticking out a little. Usually it was tucked right away under the couch. She pushed it into place then sat back, sweeping her gaze over the cabin. She stopped at the jumble of extra pillows in the overhead compartment. They hadn't needed the extra pillows and they'd remained neatly stacked, until now. Someone had been in her cabin, she was sure of it.

thirty

Night Two – Alice Springs

Lacey walked carefully up and back in the small cabin space, Birgit and Tien watching her every move.

"How are they?"

All three women looked at Lacey's feet, smothered in plasters and encased in a pair of flat shoes. The black leather was soft and decorated with sparkling beads in starburst patterns.

Lacey raised her gaze to Birgit's. "They're very comfortable but I don't feel right wearing your special shoes."

"You're fine. I've got another pair with me."

"They're perfect for your dress," Tien said. "Better than your boots, I think."

Lacey glanced down again. They'd all dressed up for tonight's dinner. She was wearing the black chiffon dress with silver embroidery that she'd made for Christmas lunch at Miss Ketty's. She loved the way it flowed, and her boots went…had gone perfectly with it.

"I'm just glad they fit," Birgit said. "Your foot's a bit smaller than mine."

"The layer of plasters helps. Vance gave me a whole packet full before we got off the bus."

"You shouldn't have let the blisters get so bad," Tien tutted. "Do you have other shoes for tomorrow?"

Lacey chewed her lip and shook her head.

"You should have got something at the shops this afternoon," Tien said.

"I didn't think of it then." When they'd got back on the bus after the lookout, Lacey had taken off her boots and then walked barefoot around the town centre. She'd met up with Birgit, Rory and Rhys there. They'd wandered the mall and surrounding streets and if they had to cross a road Rhys had insisted on piggybacking her. He'd done it in a good-humoured, teasing way and she'd been both grateful and embarrassed. They'd passed a shoe shop at one stage and Rhys had asked if she needed to get anything. She'd said no.

Now Birgit was studying her closely. "Is everything all right with you, Lacey?"

Lacey met her look and glanced away as tears began to form in her eyes.

"I knew you weren't well." Tien drew back to a corner of the couch.

"I'm not sick." Lacey spoke firmly. "My feet hurt, that's all, but these shoes are comfortable and if you don't mind, Birgit, I'll wear them to the dinner tonight. I'm just worried they'll be covered in dust by the time we get back."

"It'll brush off." Birgit waved a hand at her. "But what about tomorrow in Coober Pedy? Sounds like we'll be in and out of mines and walking on rough terrain."

Tien sat bolt upright. "Ning has nearly the same size feet as you. Remember when she tried your other boots after you embroidered them?"

"Yes, but—"

"She has a pair of sneakers and a pair of slip-on canvas shoes. I'm sure she'd lend them to you."

Before Lacey could protest Tien had leaped up, sidestepped her and opened the door. "I'll be back," she called.

There was a moment's silence and then Birgit looked Lacey in the eye. "Now, what's up?" She waved at the empty seat beside her. "Come on, girlfriend, spill your guts."

Lacey studied Birgit a moment then sat. "I'll tell you my troubles if you tell me yours."

"I don't have any."

"It wasn't that long ago you were moving in with your boyfriend and—"

Birgit's deep brown eyes flashed and she folded her arms. "Don't mention that gobshite of a sleeveen. May the cat eat him and the devil eat his cat."

Lacey frowned, trying to make sense of the garble that had just come out of Birgit's mouth. When she was excited or tipsy or angry like she was now, her Irish ancestry took over her tongue.

"You were together for a long time."

"Two years of my life I won't get back."

"What happened? Was it the house sharing that didn't work?"

"Evidently I wasn't invested enough in our relationship. Translated, it meant I enjoyed my work and being social too much and wasn't the housemaid he'd thought I'd be once we moved in together."

Lacey remembered Birgit's excitement when the gobshite, as she'd called him, had asked her to move into his place. She'd been living in a tiny two-bedroom apartment with two of her cousins and had been ecstatic to not only move in with the love of her life, as she'd called him then, but also to have a much bigger place that he'd encouraged her to decorate.

"That was just before Christmas, wasn't it?"

Birgit nodded. "All over by March."

"I'm sorry it didn't work out. And you made all those fabulous cushions and curtains and things." Birgit had been beside herself when he'd given her free rein. She'd never made anything like that before but she'd thrown her heart and soul into it. Lacey hadn't been to their apartment but she'd seen the photos of Birgit's handiwork.

"Which are his now."

"You're entitled to something, surely?"

"Bit hard to take the specially fitted curtains, and I've nowhere to put the cushions and the couch I re-covered even if he would let me have them. Anyway, it's ancient history now and I don't want to waste any more breath on it. Luckily my cousins fitted me in again. It's better than sleeping in my car." Birgit's piercing gaze met Lacey's. "Tell me what's bothering you."

Lacey took a breath and gave Birgit a potted version of what she'd told Ketty the night before.

"So your dad's run off and not sent the money he promised," Birgit exclaimed when Lacey told her about him leaving.

"I'm sure he will," Lacey said.

"Yeah and pigs might fly." Birgit shook her head, and when Lacey got to the part about Dean cooling their relationship, Birgit let fly with a string of expletives. "More fool that Dean if he's broken up with such a grand person as yourself."

"It could hardly be called a break-up," Lacey said. "It was a fizzle-out of something that had barely begun rather than the break-up of a relationship."

"We've both had problems with men." Birgit threw her arms around Lacey, hugged her then sat back. "My family excluded, I could say all men are gobshites but then there's Rory and Rhys."

"You've spent more time with them than me. They seem nice enough."

"More than nice." Birgit grinned. "Rory's been wonderful. You know he's saying he thinks he'll apply for a working visa to come back to Australia now that he's met me. This could be more than a holiday fling, you know."

"What does he do?"

"Hospitality – he'd get work, no worries." Birgit pouted. "I wish you'd been with us more. Poor Rhys is a bit of a third wheel sometimes. Anyway, now I understand why you didn't want to do the camel ride but I wish you'd said. I paid for Rory, I'd have happily paid for your ride."

"I can't have people paying for me every time I get stuck." But Lacey wondered why Birgit had paid for Rory's ride.

"We're friends. You'd pay me back."

"It's kind of you but I have to sort myself out." Lacey smiled to cover her concern. Birgit was so generous but Lacey couldn't afford any kind of extra debt, not even if it was her friend she owed.

"Rory wanted to know what the job scene was like in Sydney and if I'd help him find somewhere to stay. If he did come back, I said we could get a place together and he seemed keen. He and Rhys will be there in a few weeks. It will be their last stop before they head home. We can catch up again then." Birgit clasped her hands together and grinned. "I'm so glad I've got my own cabin. Rory and I had a good old snog last night." She wriggled her eyebrows. "Who knows what will happen tonight."

This was all moving a bit fast for Lacey, but Birgit was older and hopefully wiser. "Don't do anything I wouldn't do."

"I'd like to say that leaves the door wide open but if you and Dean had only got as far as kissing after a couple of months, well…"

Lacey ignored Birgit's teasing. It didn't bother her. She was glad now that the relationship hadn't been more than kisses and a few exploring hands but she was worried about Birgit. Lacey still had her doubts about Rory but it was something she couldn't put her finger on and she didn't want to be a spoilsport.

Ketty relaxed and took another sip of her gin and tonic. She'd managed to shake off her earlier concerns about someone being in her room, and had locked her door, had a short doze and dressed for dinner before Carlos had returned. Now it was his turn to freshen up so she'd decided to enjoy the benefits of the lounge carriage.

Through the window she could see the last of the stragglers making their way back to the train. She glanced at her watch. In thirty minutes the first of the buses would depart for the dinner at the telegraph station and she intended to be on it. Matt had told her she needed to be early to secure her table and she was ready to go. She was excited about the dinner but also about the idea that had come to her regarding Judith and Lacey. She'd drifted off to sleep thinking about them and about Warren and the task he'd set his daughters, and when she'd woken it had come to her.

The carriage door opened and, as if she'd conjured him up, Warren came in followed by Val.

"Would you like company?" Val asked.

"Yes, of course. I'm glad I saw you. I wondered if you two would like to sit with us at the dinner tonight."

"We'd enjoy that, wouldn't we, Warren?"

"Fine by me. I'll get some drinks." Warren quirked an eyebrow at Ketty. "Can I get you another?"

"No, I'm still going with this one, thank you." Ketty turned to Val. "Did the rest of your day go well?"

"Yes, except for a call from our son wondering when we'd be home."

"Is your grandchild still sick?"

"On the mend but things are busy with the business. Even though it's his now, Warren still goes in sometimes and they're in need of our help. But Warren wants to stay an extra week in South Australia. We drove to Adelaide, left our car there and flew to Darwin to catch the train. We'd planned to sightsee on our return but now...well, the kids need us and I want to get back. Warren's being so selfish. He wants to visit Clare Valley before we travel home via Coonawarra. He's into his wines and then there's a golf game he's promised to play the weekend we get back. We won't be much help with the children or at the shop for at least another week." Val crossed her arms over her chest and glared in Warren's direction. "Family should come before holidays and bloody golf."

"I suppose it's hard when you're part of a team," Ketty said gently.

"That's what Warren says but he can let the golfers know they need to find someone else."

The two German ladies arrived and made a beeline for Val and Ketty, full of excitement about their trip to the reptile park. Warren came back and regaled them with over-the-top stories about his encounters with snakes as thick as his arm and a goanna as big as a crocodile. Val took several gulps of the cocktail he brought her and lost her grumpy disposition. Ketty listened while she finished her own drink then excused herself.

"I'll save you a seat at the dinner. See you there," she said and let herself into the next carriage.

Ahead of her a door opened. A man stepped out clutching a small box. He glanced in her direction, then his eyes widened and he shot back into his room. By the time she drew level with cabin two the door was firmly shut with Mr Visser on the other side. There was something very odd about his behaviour but Ketty didn't have time to dwell on it. She moved on to her carriage. The door to the first cabin was open and stick woman, as Ketty thought of her, was complaining again.

"They should have had a buggy ready for me," she muttered. "My knee will be like a balloon after all that walking."

"Jade said she wouldn't be long." Beau stood in the open door with his back to Ketty but turned as she approached.

"Oh, hello," he said. "We're waiting for some assistance."

"Anything I can do?" Ketty peered past him but all she could see was the distinctive stick on the floor and a set of trousered legs on the couch. The rest of the woman was hidden by the open door.

"No, but thanks. Jade's getting us an icepack." He leaned closer. "The knee is playing up." He spoke in a lowered voice and a tone that suggested he wasn't sure it was the case.

"Who are you talking to, Beau? Shut the door. The waitress can knock if she ever comes back."

Beau gave Ketty a rueful look and stepped into the cabin, closing the door behind him.

Ketty felt a little sorry for them both. Neither of them appeared to be having the enjoyable time that she was. She'd only taken several more steps when another door opened and she almost collided with Tien as she rushed out, a pair of shoes clutched to her chest.

"Hello." Ketty glanced at the door. Tien had just left Ning and Judith's room. The room she shared with Lacey was the one Ketty had just passed. "Everything all right?"

"Yes." Tien nodded. "It will be. Lacey has bad blisters on her feet and Ning is lending her shoes for tomorrow."

"Oh, I'm sorry to hear that. Has she had some medical attention?" Ketty half turned back.

"Yes." Tien drew herself up importantly. "She's been patched up. Some men from her tour group helped her out and Birgit has loaned her some slip-on shoes for tonight." Tien leaned in closer. "Lacey hasn't anything else but a pair of flip-flops and some useless platform sandals."

"I see. That's kind of both Ning and Birgit, and lucky for Lacey she can fit their shoes."

"They both have bigger feet but with all the plasters it seems to work."

"Oh dear, poor Lacey." Once more Ketty half turned to the door.

"We're looking after her." Tien drew herself up importantly again.

"Of course you would be." Ketty smiled. "Tien, I hope you're not bothered by our conversation earlier. I would never blame you for my broken wrist. I hope you know that."

She nodded and her face softened. "I'm sorry I got so silly over it. Ning has set me straight."

"Good, because you know how much I value you as a friend as well as an employee."

"Of course, Miss Clift."

A door opened behind Ketty and a couple left the next cabin on from Lacey's. They headed off in the direction of the lounge car.

"That's lucky," Ketty said. "There's not much room for passing in the corridor, is there?"

"Goodness, no," Tien agreed. "I nearly got knocked over by a man earlier. It was just after we got back. Lacey was in our bathroom so I went down to the kitchen to fill up my water bottle. I was nearly back to our room when a man came from behind and tried to squeeze past me, and we collided." She rubbed her shoulder. "He was carrying a shoe box. It dug into me and he dropped it. The lid was held on by a fat rubber band and we both scrambled to pick it up. Goodness knows what he had in it – it was quite heavy and made of strong cardboard. He snatched it from me and almost ran off along the corridor to the next carriage."

Ketty recalled her earlier sighting of Mr Visser. He'd been carrying a small box. "What did he look like?"

"His hair was sticking up and he was jumpy, on edge." Tien leaned in. "I thought perhaps he was a little strange, you know, like someone who takes drugs or something."

Ketty didn't know about Mr Visser's personal habits but Tien's description fitted him, and Ketty was sure her door had been locked when she'd first got back to the train.

"Did you see which cabin he came from?" she asked.

Tien shook her head. "The passage was empty when I left the kitchen and made my way back and then suddenly he was pushing past from behind me."

"Could he have come from my cabin?"

Tien gasped. "Why would he be in your cabin?"

"The door was locked when I got back from the tour and then by the time I came back with Matt it was open again." Ketty didn't mention the scent that also lingered in her room.

"Goodness, he could have come out of your cabin." Tien gaped at her. "The box, was it yours? Has he stolen something?"

"No, it's not my box and anything important is secured in the safe. It might just explain the locked door, that's all."

"But why would he be in your room?" Tien gasped. "He could have been through all our rooms. Maybe he had stolen things and put them in the box. I must go and check."

"I don't think—" Ketty's words were lost as Tien squeezed past and into her cabin, gabbling about checking their belongings before the door shut behind her.

Ketty sighed. She really didn't think Mr Visser a thief but there was certainly something going on. She glanced at her watch. She had no time to follow it up now. She hoped Carlos was ready to go. She had to collect her things and make sure they were on the first bus to the old telegraph station for dinner.

Behind Judith the bathroom door opened. She stepped back quickly from the cabin door, through which she'd easily been able to hear Ketty and Tien's conversation.

"What's wrong?" Ning asked.

"I'm not sure but there may have been a man in our cabin."

"A man!" Ning clutched at her neck and glanced around as if he was about to spring out.

"He's gone but I heard Tien say he pushed past her in the corridor and Ketty seems to think her door was locked when she came back from the bus so perhaps he was inside then."

Ning's hand dropped to her side. "Oh yes. She couldn't get in. She asked the steward to come and check but the door opened then."

Judith nodded. She'd heard that conversation through the thin door panelling as well.

Ning snatched up the little bag she kept a small selection of jewellery in. Judith was wearing the few items she'd brought with her so she wasn't worried about that but she didn't like the idea of someone snooping in their room.

"It's all here," Ning said then reached for her case. "My souvenirs."

"I don't think—"

Ning's case crashed to the floor and she got to her knees and checked inside. "Everything is still here."

"Of course it would be." Judith shook her head. Ning had only had the case down a few minutes earlier to get out her spare shoes for Tien to give to Lacey. "We don't know anyone was in here."

"Oh, I hope nothing is missing from Tien and Lacey's cabin, or Ketty's." Ning hoisted her case back up. The fabric of her emerald-green and pink floral silk dress swirled and glittered with the motion. "I'll go and check on the girls." She glanced back at Judith. "Goodness, you need to change. Ketty has asked us to make sure we get on the bus together to go to the dinner."

"I'll have a quick shower now. It won't take me long."

"Have you spoken with Ketty yet?" Ning asked. "Apologised?"

Judith shook her head.

"Dinner under the stars will be far less constrictive than being on the train. Perhaps there will be time tonight but you must get ready quickly."

Ning made a shooing motion then hurried out the door.

Judith sighed and took out the dress shirt she was planning to wear over her black pants for the dinner. It had a collar, buttoned all the way down and finished just above her knee. She'd made it from teal-blue taffeta that had a laser-cut eyelet pattern creating a swirling chevron effect. She'd chosen the fabric and made it herself, knowing how important dressing up for this dinner was to Ketty. It had been a thrill to work on something so special for herself, a rare occurrence, and she'd been so sure Ketty would love it. Judith removed her clothes and stepped into the bathroom to freshen up. Now she had no idea if Ketty would even look twice at her outfit, let alone be prepared to speak with her.

Carlos was still in the bathroom when Ketty re-entered the cabin. She immediately got down on her knees and checked the safe in the bottom of the small wardrobe. He'd put a gold watch in there along with a set of gold cufflinks and she her pearls and a bag containing a bracelet and some rings. She was relieved to see the pearls nestled in the case when she opened it. They'd been her mother's. She left them out. She'd forgotten to put them on earlier and they'd be perfect with her dress. Next she opened the little case that contained Carlos's items.

"Oh no." The cufflinks were still there but not his gold watch. He'd said it had been his father's. Like her pearls, of sentimental as well as monetary value.

She snatched up the small drawstring bag containing her other jewellery as Carlos stepped out of the bathroom looking very suave in chinos and a long-sleeved shirt. His missing case contained his only evening attire.

He pulled up short when he saw her. "What are you doing down there?"

"I thought your watch was missing but then I remembered you were wearing it today."

A strange look crossed his face and Ketty felt a little chill. Ever so briefly he'd looked furtive, almost afraid, then he'd smiled.

"It's in my bag." He waved in the direction of his hand luggage stowed above them. "It stopped...needs a new battery. I've put my other one on." He tapped the smart watch on his wrist.

Ketty blew out a small sigh and placed the jewellery bag back in the safe. She could tell from its weight everything was still inside it. "Thank goodness." She shut the small door, locked it and picked up the box containing the pearls. "I'd forgotten to get out my pearls and I wanted to check everything was still there."

Carlos gave her a wary look. "Why?"

"Do you recall last night? We were in the lounge car. You came back to use the bathroom and you opened the door and there was a man in the cabin and you thought you had the wrong cabin."

"Oh, yes, I flung open the door and there was poor Mr Visser."

"Are you sure?"

"Yes. Once you pointed him out to me I'm certain it was Mr Visser."

"No, I mean are you sure you had the wrong cabin?"

Carlos frowned. "I was jet lagged, in a rush and embarrassed. To be honest, I don't really recall. I assumed I'd only gone along one carriage and not into the second. Why?"

Ketty told him about the locked door that was no longer locked when she'd come back with Matt and Tien being mowed down by Mr Visser out in the corridor.

"She said he'd come out of nowhere. It was while I was off finding Matt so it's possible he was in our cabin. This cabin." She stabbed a finger towards the floor. "And that was the reason the door was locked."

"Why would he be in here?"

"I don't know but Tien said he was clutching a small box to his chest."

Carlos glanced around. "Surely he's not taken anything?"

"No." Ketty shook her head. "I checked the safe to be sure. The only valuables we have are in there or on us."

"I suppose I could have been in the right place when I opened the cabin door but as I said I was in a hurry. I went on to the bathroom at the end of the carriage." Carlos stroked his neatly trimmed beard. "I didn't ponder it much at the time but now... when I think about it, I did return through two carriages before I got back to you in the lounge car. Perhaps I had the right cabin after all. It all seems a bit odd."

"I know but I wonder..."

Carlos tipped his head to one side, studying her intently. "What's going on in that brilliant brain of yours?"

"Well, Mr Visser was in my cabin when I first boarded in Darwin."

"How?"

"He'd mistaken the carriage. Matt says it happens sometimes. People have the right cabin but the wrong carriage."

"So Mr Visser was in here?" Carlos held out his hands.

"Yes. He was a bit put-out, but when Matt explained he moved on to his own cabin quickly enough. Now I wonder if he left something behind. Something he's been trying to recover."

"Like a small box?"

Ketty nodded.

"Surely you would have found it when you put your things in here."

"Not if he stowed it up there." Ketty pointed at the case storage area. "We haven't used the spare pillows and I noticed they were disturbed when I returned this afternoon."

"After the door had appeared to be locked and after Tien ran into Mr Visser in the corridor."

"Exactly." Ketty nodded. "Perhaps he'd stowed it up there and forgot it momentarily when he moved on."

"Why wouldn't he simply have said he'd left something behind?"

"I've no idea." Ketty smiled at Carlos. "But I intend to find out."

"Of course you do."

"Now, will you help me put on these pearls, please?" Ketty lifted the strand from its box and held them around her neck. "The clasp is tricky."

Carlos did as she asked then she turned back to him. They were close. So close she could easily have brushed a kiss across his cheek but she stepped back and said "Thank you" instead.

"The pearls are perfect," Carlos said. "You look so glamorous in that..." He frowned. "What colour would you call that?"

Ketty glanced down at the shantung dress she'd made specially for this dinner. "Chocolate truffle."

His eyebrows raised then he shook his head. "I'm sorry, I look rather underdressed to be your escort."

"Don't worry about that. Your case is missing — it can't be helped."

"It's very annoying."

"And still no word on its location?"

"No."

"Carlos, if you needed, I could lend you some money...to tide you o—"

"Why would you think I needed money?"

Ketty's discomfort grew. She didn't want him to know Judith had mentioned his card not working. "You didn't have any parcels when you returned from the town."

"Ah." He looked down and brushed at his shirt. "I'd thought perhaps a tie might add a little pizzazz to my simple outfit but they were all of the tourist variety. Not really what I was looking for."

"This might help." Ketty reached into the bag she'd placed on the couch and took out the small gift she'd wrapped for Carlos. "I've got one for everyone at our table but perhaps you'd appreciate yours before we leave."

He ripped open the paper and smiled. "You've been sewing again. I still have the bow tie you made me for Christmas…" he sighed, "in my case at some unknown destination."

"It would have been the wrong colour anyway." Ketty reached for the bow tie that she'd made from the same fabric as her dress. "Let me do it up for you." She smoothed his collar down over the band and he turned back. "I hope you don't think it presumptuous of me," she said as she tweaked the bow a little. "But I liked the idea of your bow tie matching my dress."

He reached for her hand. "I like the idea too." He studied her closely, his deep brown eyes only a short distance from hers, his lips plump above his beard.

She pulled away and picked up the gift bag, her purse and pashmina. "We'd better go. I've got a bit of organising to do when we get there."

thirty-one

Night Two – Alice Springs

The team from Ketty Clift Couture walked in an orderly group along the platform. Judith had lost all enthusiasm for organising but to her surprise Ning had been the one to step up and make sure they left together to catch the bus. It had been like rounding up the proverbial cats again. Tien and Lacey had taken forever to finish dressing and Birgit had wanted to leave when Rory and Rhys did. To Judith's surprise, Ning had insisted they travel on the same bus so that they could arrive together and Birgit had agreed.

Heads turned as the group of women moved along the platform. Not everyone had dressed for dinner and certainly not to the level of the style that the women from Ketty Clift Couture had managed. Although Judith wasn't sure about Birgit's dress, which was too flashy for Judith's taste. It was black with vibrant red roses. Birgit had cut the roses from a different fabric and appliquéd them on. The dress itself clung to her rounded curves and showed a generous amount of her bust. At least she was wearing a pair of the flat beaded shoes she was fond of making rather than high heels that wouldn't have suited the terrain. Luckily she had two pairs of the flats with her and the other had fitted Lacey.

Judith was bringing up the rear of their group. Lacey was walking carefully but she appeared to be doing all right. The sparkling black and silver shoes looked pretty with her dress, so much better than those blasted boots. Perhaps after today they'd be consigned to the bin.

Judith had been surprised by Lacey's outburst while they'd been waiting for their tour group at Simpsons Gap. She'd been emphatic in her belief that she'd not been the cause of the break-up with Dean. On the morning he'd told Judith he was no longer seeing Lacey, he'd been maudlin and had clammed up about what actually happened. Judith had been outraged on his behalf. It had been easy to add another black mark to Lacey's copybook and she hadn't held back on her disparaging remarks about how self-centred she thought Lacey to be. Dean had been in a low state and easily accepting of Judith's version of Lacey.

Now Judith was feeling a bit sorry about that. She'd been quick to dismiss Lacey from Dean's life but since they'd been on this trip Judith had seen another side of her. There'd been her calm reassurance of Tien about sharing a cabin when Judith was sure she'd have preferred to bunk with Birgit, she'd leaped to Ning and Tien's defence the previous day when Judith had been cross, and today at Simpsons Gap she'd waited behind with Judith, although as it had turned out, her own feet were sore so it had probably been self-serving. Nonetheless Judith wondered if there was a side of Lacey she'd kept hidden and that had caused Judith to misjudge her.

Ahead of her Lacey stopped and lifted one foot.

"Are you all right?" Judith asked. The others had kept walking unaware.

"I think I've managed to get a stone in my shoe."

"The path is a bit gravelly. Can you get it out?"

Lacey wobbled as she reached down to remove the shoe. "I don't want to disturb the plasters."

"Put one hand on my arm." Judith kept her arm steady as Lacey gripped it and removed her shoe carefully with her other hand.

"Everything all right here?"

Judith glanced over her shoulder as a man strode towards them. She smiled. "Yes, thank you, Erik."

"Just a stone in my shoe," Lacey said.

"You two ladies seem to have a lot of trouble with shoes."

Lacey glanced from Erik to Judith, her look puzzled.

"I met Erik up at the lookout today. He'd heard about our poor feet and was coming to your assistance when you were walking to the bus but Rory and Rhys reached you first."

"Much nicer for a young lady to have them to help her." Erik smiled then bent down to peer at Lacey's foot as she tried to slip her shoe back on. "May I?"

Before they knew it he was down on one knee and easing the back of Lacey's shoe over her heel. "You've caught the back on one of the bandages."

Lacey's eyes widened as Erik fiddled with her shoe.

"That's fixed it," he said and rose nimbly to his feet. "How does it feel?"

"Much better thank you, Mr—"

"Please call me Erik."

"Thank you, Erik." Lacey ducked her head but Judith had already noticed the red glow of her cheeks.

"I don't think either of us realised our feet were going to give us so much trouble," Judith said.

"All I wore was boots or thongs when I lived in the bush. Now I like my Dunlop Volleys."

They all looked down at his shoes – they were canvas that had once been white and was now a grubby beige.

"They look comfortable," Judith said.

A whistle pierced the air. Ahead of them Birgit was beckoning wildly.

"That's our group," Lacey said and began walking again.

Erik fell into step beside Judith. "You look very fine in that colour, Judith."

"Thank you." She glanced down at the teal that seemed to shimmer as she walked. "I mostly wear black or navy but my…my friend was keen for us all to dress up tonight."

"It's very…elegant."

Judith took in Erik's brown trousers, crumpled shirt and cor-duroy jacket. They were rather old-fashioned in cut and style but he wore a vibrant tie with slanting stripes of purple, blue, yellow and orange that gave his outfit a modern touch. "Thank you," she said. "You're looking rather smart yourself."

"That's good of you to say but I've never been one to worry about clothes. When I realised there was a dinner as part of this trip I got all this from an op shop, apart from my underwear and shoes." He looked a little lost. Judith wondered how long ago his wife had died. Perhaps he wasn't ready to go alone to big social functions like the one they were headed to.

"Come on, Judith." Birgit was waving as they approached. "We all have to get on the same bus."

"Sorry," Erik said. "Didn't mean to hold you up."

"You could come on our bus," she said.

Erik's hangdog look lifted. "All right."

They'd only moved a couple of steps when he stopped.

"I forgot. I'm meeting someone," he blurted. "Might see you there." And without even looking at her he spun on his heel and disappeared around the back of the bus.

Judith stared after him as if he'd suddenly return.

"Judith!"

She turned back to the bus. Tien was waving at her. "The bus is ready to go."

Judith followed Tien and climbed the steps, feeling just a little disappointed.

Ketty fiddled with the bow at her waist as Carlos walked back through the tables towards her. "Can you see them yet?" she asked.

"They were on that bus that just pulled in. They're getting their welcome drinks. I caught Ning's attention and pointed this way."

"Thank you."

Ketty glanced once more around the beautifully set table with seating for ten. She'd been delighted when she'd heard that the dinner under the stars meant there would be large round tables and her group could all sit together. She'd confirmed it with Matt, but he'd said the only reserved seating was for platinum guests and everyone else sat where they liked. He'd told Ketty if she got to the dinner early she could save a table for her group and that's what she'd done.

Now she checked the seating carefully. She planned that they'd swap around between courses. Another thing she'd checked with Matt, who'd explained the staff would bring entree and sweets but the main meal was self-serve so there was no need to remain in the same seats. To begin, Ketty had placed Judith and Lacey on either side of her. She had a proposal for them and she wanted to discuss it early. After that she hoped she could sit with each of her staff and even Warren and Val if there was time. Tonight she planned to find out as much as she could so that by the time they all returned to Ketty Clift Couture the following week she would be well on track to setting her staff back to rights.

Ketty's gaze reached Carlos, who was standing on the opposite side of the table. "I hope you don't mind we're not seated together to begin with."

He shook his head, a wry smile on his lips. "I'm quite used to your games, Ketty."

"It's not a game. These women are my most important priority."

"Perhaps 'game' is not quite the right word but—"

"Here they are." Ketty waved to Ning, who was leading the group between the other tables towards her. Ketty had purposefully picked a table on the edge of the dining area against the backdrop of a beautifully restored stone shed and a large gum tree towering high into the sky, and now in the golden light of the end of the day there was a dreamy appeal to the setting.

"It's perfect," Ketty murmured as she cast one last look over the table. The candles flickered brightly inside the lanterns, the cutlery and glassware sparkled and at each place setting sat Ketty's small gift. The tenth seat was empty at this stage but she'd brought an extra gift just in case.

"Doesn't this look wonderful," Ning said.

"I didn't expect this." Tien turned in a slow circle taking in the whole scene. "And you can even have a camel ride."

"No, thank you." Birgit rubbed her hands up and down over her behind. "My butt's had enough camel riding for one day and this dress is much tighter than it was at Christmas."

"Did you enjoy it though?" Ketty asked.

"It was great."

"Please take your places everyone. There are names on the gifts." Ketty pointed to the setting on her left. "Yours is here, Judith."

Judith had been the last to arrive at the table and she hung back, not meeting Ketty's gaze.

"Lacey, you're here." Ketty tapped the back of the chair on her right. "I know I'm being a bit bossy but I thought we could change seats after each course. That way we'll all have a chance to talk with everyone. Warren and Val are joining us as well so we need to keep a watch out for them."

Everyone found their places.

"Oh, wait." Ketty put up a hand. "Please, before you sit down I want to say thank you for making the effort to dress up tonight. You all look splendid. I'd love to have a group photo before we begin. Perhaps in front of the stone wall?"

They followed Ketty's lead and Carlos offered to take the photo with Ketty's phone. Then she asked a waiter to take a shot that included Carlos and finally she asked them all to take their places.

"What are these, Ketty?" Ning sat and took up the small gift-wrapped parcel in front of her.

"Open them." Ketty clapped her hands in excitement. "You two will know," she murmured to Lacey and Judith.

Everyone unwrapped at the same time and took out the bow ties she had modelled in the style of those she'd made for Christmas. This time she'd used the same chocolate truffle-coloured fabric as her dress so they were all nearly identical.

"It's lovely but what do I do with it?" Ning asked.

"Wear it," Lacey said and lifted her wrist towards Ketty. "Would you tie mine, please?"

"They can go anywhere." Ketty glanced around as she fastened the bow for Lacey. "In your hair." Ketty tapped the bow she'd secured like a headband to hold back her bob. "Or on your bag or at your neck like Carlos."

He twiddled his between his fingers to show it off.

"Wherever you'd like." Ketty sat back. Beside her Judith was staring at the bow in her hands. "Can I tie it for you?"

Judith glanced up and Ketty almost gasped at the pain etched in her face.

"Is everything all right?" she asked.

"Not at all," Judith murmured back. "I feel so terrible that I've caused an upset between us."

"Let's put it behind us." Ketty smiled. "We've been friends too long to be bothered by a few discordant words. Please let me help you with this. What if we slip it through a buttonhole and tie it on your beautiful shirt?"

"Thank you." Judith's lips twitched up in the smallest of smiles and she turned in her chair so that Ketty could add the bow to her shirt.

"There we are." Ketty patted it in place.

A waiter arrived and more drinks were accepted. Once everyone had a glass, Ketty raised hers and proposed a toast to the fabulous team that was Ketty Clift Couture.

"And to our mascot, Carlos," Birgit added with a giggle.

Val and Warren arrived. There were more bow tie explanations and toasts. Val chatted with Warren and Carlos while Birgit regaled her side of the table with stories about the camel ride, which just left Judith and Ketty.

They spoke as if they were mere acquaintances, asking each other their thoughts of the tours, Ketty concerned over Lacey's and Judith's feet problems and Judith wanting to know what Ketty had eaten for lunch at the desert park. Ketty was relieved they'd broken the ice at least.

"How are you and Ning managing in the cabin?"

"We're very comfortable. In fact last night we settled on Ning's bunk and had a cup of tea and a chat; it was…pleasant."

Ketty pressed her lips firmly together. Judith wasn't ever effusive and Ketty took pleasant to mean she was enjoying herself. "I don't suppose Ning mentioned her retirement?"

"We did talk about that." Judith glanced across the table in Ning's direction then leaned a little closer. "Did you know Peter and his wife are moving in with her?"

"She told me, yes."

"She keeps getting messages and phone calls from her family. Mostly it's Peter, I think." Judith leaned even closer. "I think he's forcing her to retire. He told her she wasn't irreplaceable."

"Oh, dear." Ketty's heart broke for Ning. She risked a quick look across the table. Ning was studiously listening to Carlos. Ketty had known something was not right with her sudden retirement plans.

She turned back to Judith, who was distracted by something behind her.

"Sorry, Ketty." Judith stood abruptly. "I want to catch someone I met earlier and I see them over there."

Ketty looked in the direction Judith indicated but as there were a number of people milling about the blacksmith shop watching the men in action at the forge and more people wandering the grounds, she wasn't sure who Judith meant. She took a sip of her wine and pondered what Judith had said. It reminded her of their Friday night drinks when they'd often nip any staff issues in the bud over a glass or two of wine. They hadn't done that in such a long time.

"Judith's found the nice man who helped me with my shoe earlier." Lacey was peering over Ketty's shoulder. "Although I was a little embarrassed when he got down on one knee." Lacey giggled. "I felt like Cinderella."

Ketty twisted in her seat. She could see Judith but from her position the man was partly obscured behind the huge trunk of the gum tree.

"His name's Erik and his accent's a bit like your neighbour, Klaus," Lacey said. "I think he must be in one of the carriages close to us but I haven't noticed him in our lounge or dining car."

As Ketty continued to watch, the man moved a little. His back was to her but his tall lean frame and tufts of grey hair were very familiar. "The man she's talking to now?"

"Yes, that's him."

"Mr Visser?"

"I didn't find out his last name. He asked me to call him Erik." Lacey lowered her voice. "I think Judith likes him."

"Excuse me, Lacey." Ketty rose to her feet and moved swiftly towards the couple beside the tree, not taking her eyes from the back of the man's head. Perhaps he sensed her scrutiny because he turned when she was still a few steps away. His eyes widened. He swung back to Judith and said something. She looked up and in two more strides Ketty had arrived beside them.

"Hello, Mr Visser." She beamed widely and he blinked like a rabbit caught in the headlight of her stare. "It's lovely that you two know each other. Judith is at my table and there's a spare seat. Won't you join us?"

"I was just asking the same thing. Erik hasn't found a seat yet but he declined." Judith glanced warily between Ketty and Erik. "Do you two know each other already?"

"Nee." Erik shook his head firmly at the same time Ketty said, "Yes."

"We almost do, just not officially," Ketty said. "There was a mix-up with our cabins when we first boarded the train." Ketty held out her hand. "I'm Ketty Clift, Mr Visser. Or may I call you Erik now?"

Erik stared at her hand, his look guarded and a few tufts of hair jutted at odd angles as if missed by his brush. Ketty had to clamp her lips together to stop the laugh that burbled in her throat. She understood why Tien had thought he'd looked a little odd. His glance darted beyond her in the direction of their table.

"I believe you ran into Tien in the corridor today...after you retrieved your box from my cabin."

Erik's gaze came back to Ketty.

"Was that you?" Judith said.

There was a moment's hesitation then Erik nodded. Just once.

"Why?" Judith mumbled.

"I wish you'd just told me you'd left something behind, Erik. I would happily have given you access." Ketty took a gamble she'd uncovered the truth behind the locked door to her cabin and Erik's erratic behaviour.

His face flushed. "I...I'm sorry. I wasn't thinking straight."

"Please don't worry about it." Ketty patted his arm.

"You've tied yourself in knots over a box?" Judith frowned.

"The contents are of sentimental value," he said quickly.

Very heavy items if Tien was to be believed, but Ketty didn't mention that.

"Tien wasn't hurt," she said instead. "Don't let that stop you from joining us."

"Tien can be a bit..." Judith paused, searching for a word.

"Highly strung?" Ketty offered.

"Yes. Do come with us, Erik," Judith said. "You can sit next to me."

He hesitated, glanced from one to the other then gave a slight nod.

"I'll go ahead and arrange it." Ketty smiled and strode back to the table, to give them a moment to chat alone.

She asked Val, Warren and Carlos if they'd shuffle along one space so that Erik could sit beside Judith, and while they were moving Ketty spoke quietly with Tien. She hadn't had the chance to explain fully when Tien must have caught Erik's approach.

"The box man," she hissed.

"Please don't call him that," Ketty said.

"But he was in our rooms."

"Only mine and I think that was a misunderstanding. Please make him welcome, Tien."

Judith and Erik arrived at that moment and introductions were made. Ketty didn't put out the extra gift. Erik might be a bit overwhelmed by it and he was already wearing the most vibrant tie. She waited beside Tien, who managed a perfunctory hello.

Ketty was just back to her seat when Birgit bounced up from hers. It seemed they were going to be a party of continuous musical chairs.

"There's Rhys and Rory," Birgit said. "Let's go and have a chat, Lacey. You don't mind, do you, Ketty?"

"Don't be too long." Ketty tapped her side plate. "It looks like some people are being served entrees already."

"You go," Lacey said to Birgit. "I'll see them later."

"You sure?"

Lacey nodded and Birgit wiggled off as fast as her figure-hugging dress would allow.

"You could have gone," Ketty said as Lacey continued to stare after Birgit. "It'll be a while before the waiters get to us."

"No. I'm okay." Lacey broke a piece from the bread roll on her plate but didn't eat it.

"Are you still concerned about your dad?"

"A little." Lacey glanced in Birgit's direction again then back at Ketty. "But more about Birgit. She's broken up with her boyfriend and I'm worried…she might be making a bigger mistake with Rory."

"Oh, dear. Do you mind saying why?"

"I can't put my finger on it but there's something about him that's too…" Lacey wrinkled her nose and flapped her hands. "Too…"

"Too good to be true?"

"Maybe. He's filling her head with all kinds of ideas."

"Such as?" Ketty was concerned. Birgit had been a bit off her game the last few months. It had been the final straw for one of their customers when the cuff of a fine silk shirt had frayed because it hadn't been finished properly. Birgit had made the shirt, so she'd been the one to fix it and she'd been very apologetic, but the woman had said she wouldn't be back. Ketty wasn't sorry. She'd only had a few garments made prior to the shirt and had become increasingly difficult to please. Ketty had, however, been surprised by Birgit's poor sewing. Breaking up with her long-time boyfriend might explain it. Ketty wouldn't like to see her hurt more.

"Rory told her he might come back to Australia to work and perhaps they could share a place."

"Surely that's just talk."

"She paid for his camel ride and goodness knows what else."

"One thing about the train, at least she doesn't have to pay for anything on board." Ketty made light of it but she planned to find out a bit more about Rory. Apart from his cheekiness there was something about him that didn't gel with her either.

thirty-two

Night Two – Alice Springs

Judith was pleased Erik had agreed to join them. She'd been on edge about spending time with Ketty before they'd had a chance to reconcile, and her anxiety had ratcheted up several notches as soon as she'd arrived at the historical telegraph station. She'd eagerly taken the glass of white wine offered by the waitstaff as they entered the dining compound. And then across the sea of white-clothed tables and chairs there was Ketty with Carlos. They'd been standing either side of the table Ketty had saved, looking for all the world like a couple ready to receive their guests for dinner, and all Judith's misgivings about Carlos had flooded back.

With Erik at her table she had someone totally different to focus on and she was pleased for the distraction.

"Your friend keeps glaring at me," Erik murmured as he sat back from his empty entree plate.

Judith glanced across the table but Tien was talking to Ning, who was looking at her phone again. "Ignore her. She'll get used to you."

"I did bump into her rather hard today."

"She's not hurt and you've apologised. Please don't worry about it."

Erik glanced around the table. "I'm glad Carlos and Warren aren't as dressed up as you ladies. I don't feel quite so underdressed. I thought they might be in dinner suits."

"Carlos has only just flown in from Spain and his case was lost. I believe he only has his carry-on baggage with him, and I suspect Warren has a polo shirt for every occasion."

"Thanks for letting me join your table. I wasn't sure where I was going to sit."

Judith smiled and relaxed a little. On her other side she was conscious of Ketty chatting with Lacey. She was glad she'd had the chance to break the ice with Ketty but there was still more to say, she hoped maybe later in the night. In the meantime Erik obviously needed company and Judith was glad to be able to fill that role.

"This is an interesting place," Erik said. "Did you enjoy the tour today?"

"Yes. Alice Springs was much bigger than I'd imagined. Will Coober Pedy be similar?"

"Nee." He shook his head. "Very different. There is so much you can't see because it's underground."

"What did you do there?"

"I was a miner."

"For opal?"

He nodded. Judith wasn't sure it was polite to ask if he'd been successful.

"For many years we only scraped by. A lot of opal found is potch. Little value. Then we had better luck with the opal but... my wife..." He shook his head, his lips pressed together, his look haunted.

"It must have been an awful time for you."

"Terrible." His face hardened and his voice dropped to little more than a mutter. "I have a plan for closure." He stared across the table, appearing lost in some dark place.

Judith had a sudden urge to reach out and lay a hand on his but instead she shifted the topic from his dead wife. "Have you decided what you'll do there tomorrow?"

There was a pause before he replied. "Yes," he said finally. "I've asked if I can go in on the bus and then do my own thing. Because I lived there, Jade said it would be all right."

"I see." Judith's anticipation ebbed. For a brief moment she'd imagined one of the bus tours with Erik as company.

"I'll meet the bus at the end of the day to come back."

"You won't walk?" Some people had done that in Alice Springs. Not that Judith planned to do much more walking on this trip.

"Nee." He shook his head vigorously and smiled. It softened his angular features. "The rail track doesn't pass through Coober Pedy. There's a siding at Manguri. It's over forty kilometres away."

"Oh?"

"We'll be stopping in the middle of nowhere."

Judith found it hard to imagine. Val asked Erik his suggestion for the best tour to take and Judith sat back in her chair. She hadn't asked anyone else what their choices were for the next day's tour. In her current frame of mind she wasn't sure if she wanted to avoid them all or travel with them.

The people two tables away were moving off to get their main meals and Ketty knew her table would soon be asked to take their turn. Erik was in conversation with Val on his other side so Judith was free, as was Lacey. Ketty decided to seize the opportunity.

"Would you both come with me a moment please? There's something I'd like to chat with you about. It's to do with work. Just the three of us."

Judith stiffened and glanced from Ketty to Lacey, her look grim.

Lacey got to her feet. "Of course."

"Bring your drinks." Ketty plucked hers from the table and led the way past the stone buildings to a lawn area out of sight of their workmates. "I'll get right to the point as I don't want to keep you from dinner. We still haven't decided on the styles and colours for next year's autumn/winter ready-made range." Mainly because they hadn't been able to agree on which direction to take. Now that she'd heard Lacey's side of things Ketty had realised their discussions were probably being hampered by the lack of cohesion between her two key workers, Lacey and Judith. "We're running out of time and I think this trip is the perfect place to draw inspiration." Judith retained her poker face but Lacey's eyes sparkled with interest. "I know you've already been thinking about some fabric designs and garment styles, Lacey, and Judith, you have a wonderful knowledge when it comes to sourcing fabric—"

"So do you." Judith's look was full of suspicion. "What's this about? Are you taking another step back?"

"Not at all." Ketty swallowed her annoyance at Judith's response. "I'm thinking ahead. We've been creating two collections of ready-made garments a year for a while now. The colours of the gorge at Katherine started me thinking about possibilities for next winter and I know Lacey has drawn some inspiration from the landscapes we've seen. If she were to design the fabric we could get it printed."

Lacey gasped, masking Judith's censorial sniff.

"Really, Miss Ketty? You want me to design the fabric and the garments?"

Ketty nodded. "We'd work on the garments together. I'd like your input on the designs too, Judith, but I'd also like you to find the right linens, cottons, silks, whatever we need and somewhere to have Lacey's designs printed."

"We've never printed our own fabric before," Judith said.

"I know," Ketty agreed. "It wasn't an easy thing to do in the past but now—"

"And the cost of all this?" Judith retorted.

Lacey glanced warily at her. Once more Ketty fought to keep her composure. She took a sip of her wine.

"Naturally this would be fully costed and we'd have to approve them before we committed," she said. "I'm planning to stay on in Adelaide for a week after this trip finishes."

"A week?" Judith's response was sharp.

"Yes. There's Jim and Celia's wedding celebration and then Carlos and I will do some sightseeing. It's a long time since I've been back to South Australia so I thought we'd make the most of it. Carlos was keen when I suggested it." Ketty ignored Judith's soft snort and continued. "I was hoping by the time I get back you might have some rough ideas for the three of us to discuss. I wanted to mention it now while we're still in the midst of this inspirational landscape." She smiled at Lacey. "Immerse yourself in the possibilities."

"Oh, Miss Ketty, that would be wonderful."

"And really, Lacey, we are a close team. I must insist on you calling me Ketty."

Lacey opened her mouth to protest.

"Please," Ketty said.

"I'll try, Mi…Ketty."

"There you are." Tien hurried around the corner of the old shed. "It's our turn for dinner."

"We're coming." Ketty waved to Tien then looked from Lacey to Judith. "This is something to think about. It might not come to anything but I'd like us to try or we might not have a collection for next year's winter."

"It's a fabulous idea," Lacey said.

Ketty held her glass up. Lacey tapped it and smiled. Judith's tap was slow in coming and there was no smile.

"Now our dinner awaits." Ketty began to walk.

Lacey almost bounded ahead, her sore feet forgotten in her excitement.

"You indulge her too much," Judith muttered.

Ketty stopped, drew in a breath and turned to Judith. "I don't think encouraging her creativity is an indulgence and I hope you'd never say something like that to Lacey."

Judith's eyes narrowed. "What's this really about, Ketty?"

"You know if we don't get the basics done soon we'll be too late. It's about giving two of my most-valued employees the opportunity to work as a team."

"Ketty Clift Couture is a team."

"Not always."

Judith glanced in the direction Lacey had gone. "Has she said something about me?"

"Why would you think that?"

"You were having that cosy chat yesterday in your cabin."

"Lacey had some personal issues we were discussing. This has nothing to do with that." Ketty hoped her face didn't give away her lie. This had everything to do with getting Lacey and Judith working together in the hope that Judith might soften towards the younger woman, see her as Ketty did – a bright, creative spark in their enterprise. "She's brought some fresh ideas to the business but she still has a lot to learn. She could benefit from your experience in the fabric sourcing and buying department."

"As she could from yours, but you're taking another week off."

"Good heavens, I can't believe you'd begrudge me that." Ketty tried not to be annoyed. "Or is this more about me spending time with Carlos? He is not the monster you're making him out to be."

Judith's steady gaze met Ketty's then she let out a sigh so long her shoulders sunk with it like a deflating balloon. "It's your business, Ketty. I'll do whatever you need of me." She turned away and strode back to the table, leaving Ketty floundering in a pool of despondency. She'd thought her idea had merit and Lacey was keen but Judith was proving difficult and obviously still harbouring doubts about Carlos. What was it he'd said? There were people who wallowed in their own misery or disappointments and those who were simply too afraid to try something different. Did Judith fit one of those categories or was she simply punishing Ketty for living her own life?

Lacey had a selection of beautiful meats and vegetables on her plate. It was far too big a serve but it was all so hard to resist, and it was already paid for. Since she'd come on this holiday, she'd probably eaten double the amount that she normally would. She told herself it would be rude of her not to make the most of Miss Ketty's— she pulled herself up, Ketty's generosity.

"Hello, Lacey."

"Virginia, hello." She nodded at Beau, who was seated beside his mother. "The food looks wonderful, doesn't it?"

"My meat was a bit chewy but Beau said his was perfect."

Lacey glanced at Beau. He raised his eyebrows. "Perhaps Mum got a sinewy piece. I'm sure you'll enjoy it."

"Do come back and see us once you've finished eating." Virginia leaned closer. "Beau will enjoy some younger company."

Lacey glanced at Beau but he'd gone back to his meal and didn't appear to have heard his mother's last words. "I might see you later," she said and went on to her own table. No sooner had she sat than Ketty tapped her on the arm.

"Who was that woman you were talking to?"

Lacey glanced back. She could just see the soft grey fluff of Virginia's hair. "Her name's Virginia. I met her this morning before the tour began."

"Do you know her last name?"

"Something French sounding." Lacey screwed up her nose. "Dumond...no, Dupont."

"Do you know anything else about her?"

"She's travelling with her son, Beau. She's pretty hard on him but I think her knee's bothering her. She was pleasant enough to me. Oh, and she said she was a model but her knee must have caused her a lot of trouble because she's had a replacement and..." Lacey stopped talking. Ketty had sunk back against her seat, staring in the direction of Virginia.

"M..." Lacey swallowed the word. "Ketty?"

Ketty blinked and turned to Lacey.

"Do you know her?" Lacey asked.

"I've noticed her a few times on the train." Ketty tapped a finger to her lips. "There's something about her but I can't...Her cabin is in our carriage. I thought perhaps Beau might be her husband."

"Oh no, he's much younger than her, although I do agree he looks older at first and..." Heat flooded Lacey's cheeks. "Not that it matters about age, I suppose."

Ketty picked up her cutlery. "We should eat before this food goes cold."

Lacey ate several mouthfuls and there was certainly nothing chewy about the meat, which melted in her mouth, but it churned in her stomach with a mix of excitement and nerves as she thought over Ketty's proposal.

When she'd first mentioned the idea of a new winter collection with some of the fabric designed by Lacey, Lacey had been excited by the possibilities but as she'd stood in the serving area the cold chill of reality had set in. It sounded like Ketty wanted her to work closely with Judith. That was odd, given Lacey's revelations to Ketty about their rocky working relationship. And Judith's sharp reaction to the idea had left Lacey in no doubt she wasn't happy either. Even worse, Ketty wasn't going to be back at work for another week and Judith would be in charge.

A waiter came with another tray of drinks. Lacey accepted some more champagne and took a large gulp hoping the bubbles might dissolve the mire of worry in her stomach. A band was playing and Tien asked if she knew the song. She listened so she could catch the melody over the hum of voices and chink of cutlery against china. It was country music, a song Dean had on his playlist.

Lacey took another gulp of champagne. "It's a Lady A song. 'What If I Never Get Over You'."

Ketty picked at her food. On one side of her Lacey chatted with Tien and Ning was tapping on her phone. And since they'd come back with their food it was Erik who was now on Ketty's other side. She assumed Judith had put him between them so she could avoid talking to Ketty. Across the table Carlos was obviously enjoying the conversation around him. The table was too wide and the background noise of the band and people talking made it difficult to converse with anyone more than two seats away.

Not that Ketty was taking in anything at her table anyway. Her thoughts were on Virginia. Now she knew why she'd seemed familiar. They'd known each other forty years ago. They'd met under the worst of circumstances, had only spent a few days in each other's company and not kept in touch, but they'd bonded.

Gasps and exclamations brought her back to the group at her table. They were looking up at something beyond her.

"Here comes the moon," Erik murmured.

Ketty turned. The light was fading and the three-quarter moon had risen, a single brilliant glow in the cloudless sky. Phones were brought out for photos but something else had caught Ketty's eye and she slipped away from the table. Virginia was making her way towards the toilets and Ketty wanted to catch her alone.

Ketty wandered along the verandah of one of the stone buildings, looking in windows and studying the architecture and the restoration work while keeping an eye out for Virginia exiting the toilet block. Finally she stepped out, leaning on her stick across the uneven ground. She moved slowly and Ketty intercepted her easily.

"Hello, Virginia."

Virginia paused, peering at Ketty in the fading light. "Who are...oh, it's you from our carriage. The snooping woman."

Ketty forced her lips up into a smile. "I've only just realised who you are. We met a long time ago." She lowered her voice as two women walked past. "In the hospital. I'm Ket...Kathy Clift."

Virginia's eyes widened. "Kathy Clift?" She leaned closer. "It is you." She dropped her stick and wrapped Ketty in her arms.

"Yes, it's me," Ketty murmured into Virginia's shoulder as they hugged. In that moment Ketty was transported back forty years to the desolate young woman she'd been when they'd last met. The delicious meal roiled in her stomach at the powerful memories.

Virginia let her go. "I can't believe it, after all these years. I have glasses but I'm too vain to wear them. Beau tells me I often miss the small details."

Ketty picked up the stick and offered it back.

"Oh, damn thing," Virginia said. "It's been with me far longer than I'd thought."

"It's rather a statement piece though. Like a fine fur or a smart hat."

"Trust you, Kathy."

"I'm Ketty these days. I wanted a fresh start and Ketty sounded better than Kathy for a couture dressmaker. And you used to be Virginia Pontifex. Did you marry?"

"Good god, no! But Virginia Dupont had a better ring for a modelling career."

They both laughed.

"And did it work? Did you break into the big time as you dreamed?"

The smile left Virginia's face. "I did, although it's all in the past now. I injured my knee badly several years ago and finally I've had a replacement."

"And...you have a son, I see."

Virginia's features hardened but there was sorrow in her eyes. "Strange how life is. You so badly wanted a child and had all hope removed. I never wanted a baby and I ended up with Beau."

"And you never cease to remind me how tough that was for you."

Ketty startled at Beau's words, though they carried no malice. Neither woman had noticed his approach.

"Too right it was," Virginia said. "Single parenting isn't for the faint-hearted."

"Lucky you ended up with the perfect son then."

"As I often tell you, my dear Beau," Virginia quipped then turned to Ketty. "This is an old friend of mine, Ketty Clift."

"Miss Clift." He held out his hand. "We've run into each other a few times already."

"We have." Ketty accepted his firm shake. "Please call me Ketty."

"I'm glad Mum's found you, Ketty. She's been a bit down in the dumps."

"I have not." Virginia drew herself up haughtily.

Beau smiled. "They're serving dessert when you're ready."

The two women watched him walk away.

"He's good to me. Better than I deserve." Virginia sighed.

"I don't understand. You lost your baby after...while I was recuperating from my surgery. You were adamant you'd never—"

"'Make the mistake of getting pregnant again' were probably the words I used." Virginia tapped her stick up and down. "God, I haven't smoked for years but I feel like one now." She glanced around. "Let's sit on that bench a moment. I need to explain to you what happened."

Ketty followed her and they sat.

Virginia set her stick against the wrought-iron armrest, smoothed her hands over her skirt then twisted to look at Ketty. "When we were in the hospital you were inconsolable. To lose your baby and then your womb, to have no chance of future babies…"

Ketty swallowed. It was all so long ago and yet seeing Virginia took her back to those terrible days when her life had been tipped upside down, as if it had been months instead of forty years. She'd been so in love with Leo, had been imagining a future with him. Then all in one day she'd discovered she was pregnant, miscarried and had an emergency hysterectomy, and then discovered the man she'd pinned her future to was married. "You were wonderful to me back then," she said. "Holding my hand, telling me jokes, when you'd lost your own baby."

"That I didn't want." Virginia glanced in the direction of the diners. "It turns out they thought I had vanishing twin syndrome. I probably had two babies and one didn't survive, which explained the cramping and bleeding I had. The technology wasn't so good back then so it took a few days for them to work out I was still pregnant."

"You didn't tell me."

"I didn't know how. Anyway, you'd been discharged by the time I knew for sure. We'd promised to keep in touch but I couldn't. Not knowing I was going to end up with a baby, the very thing you wanted."

Ketty shook her head. "I was so lost in misery it was a while before I realised I hadn't heard from you."

"After I had Beau I did try to visit. I left him with a friend and thought I'd see how you were, whether you were strong enough to take my news, but you were no longer at the address you'd given me."

"I moved to Sydney. New beginnings."

"And it worked?"

"Yes." Ketty smiled then. "It's so good to see you after all these years."

Virginia smiled too and Ketty caught a glimpse of the beautiful, tenacious young woman who'd been determined to take the modelling world by storm.

"There's so much to catch up on." Virginia reached for her walking stick. "But I can see your friend is coming to get you."

Ketty caught sight of Carlos heading in their direction.

"Shall we meet after we've eaten?" Virginia said. "Perhaps back here where it's a bit quieter?"

Ketty hesitated, thinking of the chats she'd planned to have with the rest of her staff.

"Oh, but you're with your friend," Virginia said. "I don't want to take up your time."

"I do want to catch up but I'm also travelling with my staff and I have a few fences to mend. If it doesn't work out tonight, let's make a date for breakfast together in the morning. I can tap on your door as I pass. Eight o'clock?"

Virginia winced. "Eight thirty?"

"Fine." Ketty leaned in and they hugged again. "It really is so good to see you after all this time. I'm sorry I didn't recognise you sooner."

"Here you are." Carlos held out his hands as he walked towards her. "Dessert is being served. I didn't want you to miss out."

"Sorry I've been gone a while but I ran into an old friend. This is Virginia." Ketty smiled at her. "Carlos and I have known each other longer than you and I."

"How good to meet another friend of Ketty's." Carlos gripped Virginia's hand.

"Oh, what a divine accent."

"Carlos is visiting from Spain," Ketty said as they made their way back to the dining area.

"I loved the time I spent in Spain," Virginia said. "The men were…passionate." She leaned closer to Ketty and winked. "See you again soon."

"So you've worked out who your mystery woman is," Carlos said as they made their way back to their table. "And you've worked out where Erik fits. You're crossing a few mysteries off your list."

Ketty nodded. There was still so much to find out about both Virginia and Erik.

"I'd hoped to sit next to you for dessert but it seems the others aren't moving." Carlos waved a hand towards their table, where everyone else had kept the same seats.

"Perhaps you and I could swap at least and then after dessert we can have a shuffle," Ketty said.

His brief look of disappointment was swept away by his charming smile. "This is your special night, Ketty."

"Special for all of us, I'd hoped, but I'm not sure how special the others are finding it."

He slipped an arm around her shoulder and gave her a brief hug. "Don't forget to enjoy yourself."

Ketty gave a little shrug and took her seat. Carlos didn't understand how much she still had to sort out and they were already halfway through their train holiday.

thirty-three

All around people were leaning back in their seats, faces tilted to the amazing star display provided by Mother Nature in the night sky overhead. Even Judith was impressed as she followed the green light of the laser pointer the speaker was using to indicate the constellations. No fireworks or city light show was a match for the spectacle above. It probably helped that she was a little more relaxed after their delicious meal, several glasses of wine and Erik's company.

"I suppose you're used to this array if you've lived at Coober Pedy," she said as the lights on the buildings were turned back on.

"We should never take it for granted."

Judith glanced at Erik. His head was still tilted skywards but somehow she felt he meant more than the star show above.

"So true," she said, thinking of her own predicament with Ketty's new plan to force Judith and Lacey together.

Erik dropped his eyes to hers. She drew a quick breath at the deep sorrow she saw in them.

"You think when you marry someone it's forever," he said.

"I...I suppose...yes," she stammered, feeling awkward under his intense gaze. "My marriage ended in divorce though so..." She shrugged, not sure what to say.

His face lost its colour. "I'm sorry."

"Don't be. My husband was abusive. My life has been better since."

"I didn't realise," he muttered.

A waiter came with fresh glasses of wine and Judith took one even though she knew she shouldn't. The last thing she wanted to do was compare her failed marriage to someone who was obviously grieving for his wife. She took a quick sip. The music started up again. Country wasn't her thing but it suited the setting. Carlos, who had seated himself on Erik's other side, asked him about the place he lived. She was grateful for the distraction, and she couldn't really join in. It was difficult to hear what they were saying with the music playing again.

Val and Warren got up to dance. "Let's show these young ones how to do it," he announced.

Judith pretended to search for something in her bag, aware that the two empty seats meant Ketty was the next person along. She needn't have worried – when she risked a glance Ketty and Ning were huddled close. No doubt the music was making it hard for them to hear each other too and they were so deep in conversation Judith doubted they would notice anyone else.

She studied Ketty surreptitiously, searching for clues. From this angle she looked the same as ever but it was as if the Ketty Judith had known for so many years had changed into a different woman. There was nothing to show from the outside but...Judith flicked her gaze in Carlos's direction and gasped as sudden anger, as fierce as molten lava, surged inside her. She took a quick sip of her recently replenished wine. He was the reason for Ketty changing and losing interest in the business. This sudden idea of Ketty's for Judith to work closely with Lacey was just another sign that, no matter how much she protested, Ketty was stepping back. Dear god, what if Tien's theory that she was selling was actually true? Judith could never afford to buy the business – what if no-one could?

She was already losing her home, she couldn't lose her job too. She reached for her wine again but instead bumped her glass, snatching it up before it tipped. A quick glance around revealed no-one was paying her any attention. She took another sip of wine. Just above the music Judith heard a familiar ringtone. Ning plucked her phone from the table and moved away. Before Ketty could turn in Judith's direction she pushed up from her chair, deciding now was a good time to take a toilet break.

Ketty took a sip of wine and sat back. Swapping with Carlos had allowed her to sit next to Ning and then when Val and Warren had got up to dance Ketty had thought it the perfect opportunity to broach the subject of Ning's retirement. Judith's concerns that Ning was being coerced into retirement matched Ketty's but before she could broach the subject Ning had spoken enthusiastically about the wonderful star talk they'd just had. Then her phone had rung and she'd excused herself and taken the call. Ketty had watched her walk away, the phone pressed tightly to one ear and a hand over her other.

She took another sip of wine. Across the table she'd been aware of Judith slipping away at the same time Ning had. Ketty was almost ready to believe Carlos was right and that she should stop worrying about them all and think about herself. Enjoy this

holiday with me, he'd said, but there'd been something in his look
that had disconcerted her.

Ketty jumped as Ning's phone clunked to the table, closely followed by Ning thudding onto her chair. There was a disgruntled
air about her, so unusual for Ning.

"Was that Peter again?" Ketty asked gently.

"Yes, and I've told him not to call me any more. I'll be home
again on Saturday."

"Is this to do with them moving into your house?"

"Yes." Ning's dark brown eyes flashed and then her face fell.

"Have all your calls and messages been from Peter?"

"Sometimes Henry." A little smile curled at the edges of Ning's
lips. "He can't find a special T-shirt or his favourite meal I left in
the freezer." Ning chuckled. "Clearly marked."

"You're too good to him, Ning."

"My daughter-in-law has also sent texts. The last was about
measuring the sewing room so that she could get new floor covering. Peter wants carpet in there." Once more Ning's face fell.

"Oh, Ning." Ketty leaned in a little closer. "Is there anything
I can do? You seem so caught up in Peter's plans but is it really
what you want?"

"Yes...no." Ning shrugged. "Yes, I don't mind them moving
in. I'm happy to help them..."

"And the no?"

"I don't want to let you down."

"If retiring is what you truly want you're not letting me down.
But if it's not what you want...well, again you're not letting *me*
down...it's you who's being let down."

Ning blew out a breath and with it her agitation. "I don't
want..." Her words were lost in a sudden loud voice that blared
from the microphone encouraging people up to dance.

"I'm sorry." Ketty edged a little closer to Ning. "Did you say you didn't want to retire?"

Ning nodded. "Peter is the head of our family now. He is doing what's best."

Once more this evening Ketty was forced to swallow her annoyance. "But surely you can make this important decision for yourself."

"We discussed it and Peter and Henry both agreed."

"What does Peter's wife think?"

"She doesn't say too much at family meetings." Ning's face lit up. "She's very excited about the baby."

"Of course. I know you all are but does she want you as full-time carer?"

"She'll have to go back to work. She loves her job."

"And you're giving up the job you love," Ketty said gently.

Ning's shoulders sagged.

"You're only fifty-eight. I don't know what your finances are but it's young to retire."

"Peter and Henry will look after me."

"I'm sure they will but won't that be a little…" Ketty searched for the right word. She'd always supported herself financially but she understood families worked in different ways. "Limiting? What if you need money for something extra? A visit to your sisters in America, for instance? Do you want to have to ask your sons for that kind of money?"

Ning frowned.

"You've been with me since the beginning. My business has grown, endured difficult times and now it's blooming again. A journey you've been…you *are* an integral part of."

"You're very kind, Ketty."

"I'm not saying it just to be kind. I'm saying it as your friend and as your employer. Your embroidery skills are sought after. I will have trouble finding someone with your talent and expertise. I'm not trying to pressure you into staying, I simply want to be sure you're making the decision to retire yourself, that you're not being...coerced into leaving."

Ning slumped further into her chair.

"We've been friends a long time, Ning. Please feel you can tell me the truth. Is retirement what you want?"

Ning's head drooped. She shook it almost imperceptibly.

"Oh, Ning." Ketty gripped one of her hands. "If it's not what you want you must speak up."

Ning lifted her head, deep sorrow etched her face. "Peter already has everything organised." She spoke so softly Ketty could barely hear her.

"There must be another way. A compromise."

A small glimmer of hope sparked in Ning's eyes.

"You could work part-time, work from home like you did when your boys were babies."

"I would have no space."

"Then don't give up your sewing room. You could agree to help with childminding as long as you keep your sewing space. Peter and his family should share the bedroom. Babies don't take up too much space when they're little."

"I suppose I could talk to him."

"Look, Ning, they have peppermint tea at the hot-drinks station." Tien placed a cup in front of Ning. "Can I get you something, Miss Clift?"

"No, thank you. I've still got some wine." Ketty leaned closer to Ning. "Let's think on it and chat again tomorrow."

Ning nodded. "Thank you," she mouthed as Tien began to tell them about the man she'd just seen.

"I'm sure he's been on *Amazing Race*." Tien gasped. "What if this was one of their challenges? Maybe Mr Visser is a part of it? He's acting very strangely. Although he doesn't appear to have a partner. Unless they're incognito." Tien scanned the area around them. "That box Mr Visser had might be something he has to retrieve or—" Once more she gasped. "Maybe he has to place the contents somewhere."

Ketty tuned out and left Ning to try to talk Tien down from the dizzying heights of the story she was making more fanciful by the minute.

Rory turned up at Birgit's side. "Let's dance." He drew her up from her chair, one hand on hers and the other beckoning her to the dance floor. Rhys asked Lacey with less fanfare, and they all wove their way between the tables to join those already dancing. A small ripple of unease prickled Ketty's chest as Rory spun Birgit in his arms. She'd suddenly remembered what it was about him that bothered her. Her night was only getting busier.

Lacey had accepted Rhys's offer to dance but the band started playing 'Little Less Lonely'. The Adam Brand song had been another of Dean's favourites and a sudden wave of sadness swept her.

"Sorry." She almost bumped into Rhys as she turned away. "I can't...it's just...I'm not much of a dancer...and my feet are a bit..."

"You're okay," he said kindly. "I forgot about your poor sore feet. Another drink instead?"

She nodded. It wasn't totally a lie. She'd been sitting a lot of the night and her feet hadn't bothered her but her little toe was beginning to feel sore again. They moved to a quieter space and Rhys waved down a passing waiter. Lacey took another glass of champagne. She'd lost count of how many she'd had tonight.

"Hello, you two." Ketty walked towards them, a glass of wine in hand. "Not dancing after all?"

"Bit crowded out there," Rhys said. "And I didn't want to tread on Lacey's toes."

"I'm sorry, Lacey," Ketty said. "I heard about your blisters and I've forgotten to ask how you are."

"Not too bad with plasters all over my feet and these nice soft shoes." Lacey looked down and was dismayed to see Birgit's pretty shoes coated in red dust.

"And you're enjoying the train, Rhys?" Ketty said. "You're getting to see a big stretch of Australia."

"It's been grand. Trip of a lifetime. We landed in Perth and went up the coast to Ningaloo and swam with the whale sharks, went on to Broome then across to Darwin. I'm looking forward to visiting the wine regions in South Australia. My family owns a couple of wine bars back home in Dublin and we sell a lot of Australian wine. After that we've only got quick stops in Melbourne and Sydney and it'll be time to fly home."

"That's an amazing holiday," Ketty said and Lacey nodded. She'd heard bits and pieces about their travels but hadn't realised how much they'd done and still planned to do.

"We've been saving and planning it for years. Then just when we were ready to set off covid hit." He threw out one arm and tipped his head to the sky. "But here we are at last."

"What's your role in the family business?" Ketty asked.

"I'm the wine buyer."

"A big responsibility."

"My da has us all in charge of various parts of the business but we collaborate a lot."

"What's Rory's role?"

"He's not in my family's business. He helps us out sometimes behind the bar nights and weekends but his day job is at Arnotts."

"The department store?" Ketty said.

"Yes." Rhys grinned. "Usually when we say that here in Australia people think he works in a biscuit factory."

Ketty nodded. "That's what Arnotts is famous for in Australia."

"So we've discovered, but Rory's a furniture salesman at our Arnotts."

Lacey was surprised that Rhys was totally engaged in the conversation. But then Ketty had a way of speaking to people that drew them in and had them fessing up their inner secrets. Lacey was well aware of that.

"And are you both married, Rhys? Do you have children?"

Lacey blinked. Ketty had slipped that in so seamlessly she could almost believe it hadn't been said at all but Rhys was suddenly studying his feet.

"I only ask because when we first met, your cousin was wearing a ring on his left hand and it's not there any more. There could be several reasons for a young man away from home on holidays to remove a ring from his wedding finger but I'm wondering why Rory might?"

Lacey pressed her fingers to her lips as Rhys looked up, the freckles across his face accentuated by the pink glow beneath them.

"I'm divorced." He met Lacey's gaze. "Married young. It was a mistake."

"You don't have to explain." Lacey glanced desperately at Ketty. "It's not our business."

"No. It's Rory I was asking about." Ketty was still piercing Rhys with her sharp stare.

"I told him it wasn't the right thing to do, but I'm his cousin, not his keeper." Rhys glanced towards the dance floor. "They're both adults."

Lacey followed his gaze and felt sick. Rory and Birgit had stopped dancing. They were locked in each other's arms, kissing like there was no tomorrow.

"Yes, they are," Ketty said. "And I'm not Birgit's keeper either but I would like her to have all the facts. I wonder if Rory's told her he's married?"

Lacey pictured Birgit's beaming smile when she'd been saying Rory might come back and look for work in Australia. He'd even suggested they might live together. She shook her head slowly. "I don't think he has."

"They're only dancing," Rhys grumbled.

All three of them glanced in the direction of the dance floor where Rory and Birgit were so entwined they were almost one.

"I've known Birgit for twelve years," Ketty said. "The woman I know loves to have a good time but not at the expense of some-one else."

"His wife's having a baby," Rhys blurted. "Rory wanted one last fling before he settles down. His wife won't know."

Lacey gasped and Ketty's expression changed to one of incredulity.

Once more Rory's face turned pink. "I've tried to tell him."

A bubble of anger burst in Lacey's chest. "You've been with us for two days, a lot of that time with Birgit. You didn't think you could somehow slip it into the conversation, warn her?"

They glared at each other and then Lacey jumped as Birgit's arm went around her shoulder and Rory stepped in beside Rhys.

"We've worked up a thirst." Rory glanced around. "Where's that drink waiter?"

"What are you lot being so serious about? Don't tell me they've run out of champagne." Birgit laughed.

"No, we've just been chatting about family," Ketty said.

"I need to go to the toilet." Lacey grabbed Birgit by the hand. "Come with me."

"Oh, me too, then champagne." Birgit waved at Rory. "See you in a bit."

"Don't be too long, we're getting the next bus back to the train, remember." He winked.

Lacey's anger at his deceit almost exploded as she drew her friend away. Birgit chatted happily as they wove their way between the tables, telling Lacey what a good dancer and kisser Rory was. And how the night was young and there was more to come. Once they were out of sight and alone Lacey stopped. She hated that she was going to burst her friend's bubble.

"I need to tell you something."

"Ohh. This sounds serious. I wondered what you three were talking about. Rory's such a joker. I know he shouldn't have called Ketty 'Granny' but he's changed it to 'the boss lady' now and—"

"He's married, Birgit."

"Rhys? Not any more. Rory said he's divorced."

"Not Rhys." Lacey gripped Birgit's hand. "Rory."

Birgit laughed. "Bollocks. Where did you get that idea? He's footloose and fancy free." Birgit pulled away, did a little twirl then grabbed Lacey's arm as she wobbled. "Did Ketty tell you that? She's probably annoyed I'm not spending enough time with the team. You know I love her but she's getting a bit out of touch."

Lacey was offended on Ketty's behalf. "Ketty suspected and Rhys told us the truth. Rory's not only married but his wife is pregnant."

The silly grin dropped from Birgit's face. She tipped forward, her face only centimetres from Lacey's. "You're being serious."

"Very. I'm sorry, Birgit. Rory hasn't been honest with you."

Sparks glinted in Birgit's eyes and her lips pursed. Lacey braced herself, but to her alarm Birgit's face crumpled.

"That fecker," she whispered and sank to the ground, accompanied by the discordant sound of fabric tearing.

thirty-four

Night Two – Travelling South

The group from Ketty Clift Couture were silent on the bus journey back to the train. Ketty stared out the window into the blackness of the night and felt the bitter taste of defeat. She'd had such high hopes for this holiday and especially tonight's dinner and it was all in ruins.

After Lacey had dragged Birgit away, Rory and Rhys had started to argue. Ketty had left them to it and had set off to look for the girls. She'd found them as they were inspecting the ruined seam at the back of Birgit's dress. Birgit was sobbing and Lacey solemn. Ketty had returned to the table to fetch her pashmina to wrap around Birgit and discovered there'd been the Ketty Clift Couture version of whispers around the table – it appeared everyone had already got wind of what had happened. Ketty had told them she was accompanying Birgit and Lacey back to the train and the rest of her group, including Val, Warren and Erik, had all decided to call it a night too.

"Don't be too despondent, Ketty."

She turned back from the window. Carlos was beside her. She could be thankful for that at least. "I'm sorry we left early."

"Not that early. Quite a few people are heading back. The bus is almost full."

She nodded. It had been a busy day and the added emotion of tonight's events had drained her energy. "It was such a beautiful setting and a lovely dinner."

Carlos leaned in a little closer and lowered his voice. "Did you get a chance to talk to Erik?"

"Not much, why?"

"There's something about him. I don't know, it's hard to put my finger on."

"He seems to be a loner."

"Or he might be one of those lame ducks your friend Maurice talks about."

"Not mine, he's all Judith's – I've got enough on my plate with my staff."

"And when we get back to the train we're putting everyone to bed and you and I are having a quiet nightcap, just the two of us."

She smiled. "That would be lovely."

When the bus pulled into the train station Ketty and Carlos waited for Birgit and Lacey, who'd stayed on till everyone else was off.

"Will you be all right?" Ketty asked as soon as they'd left the bus behind.

Birgit managed a smile. "As long as I can avoid that gobshite and his fecker of a cousin, sure, I'll be fine."

Ketty winced. "I'm sorry, Birgit."

"It's not your fault all men are feckers." She grinned at Carlos. "Present company excepted."

"Thank you." Carlos put out his arm. "Can I escort you to your carriage?"

"Oh, Carlos." Birgit made a poor attempt at batting her soggy eyelashes. "As tempting as that sounds I'm sworn off men."

Lacey put an arm around Birgit's shoulders. "We'll stick together."

They were a forlorn sight, walking arm in arm, Ketty's pashmina wrapped around Birgit's waist to cover the ripped skirt and Lacey limping at her side.

"Hello, you two." Warren waved as he and Val appeared behind them.

"Is she okay?" Val asked as they followed Birgit and Lacey's slow progress along the platform.

"She will be," Ketty said. "Lacey's going to stay with her."

"I didn't take to that chap she was hanging around with," Warren said. "He pushed in front of Val in the bus line on the way to dinner tonight and when I asked him to watch his manners he said 'okay boomer'. We had no idea what he meant but he made it sound derogatory. Val had to google it."

"And what did it mean?" Ketty hadn't heard the term before.

"That Warren's dismissive and out of touch with the younger generation." Val smiled.

"Hang on, pet. You found much more than that about where it came from and what it means. Something about young people lumping anyone over fifty as a baby boomer and has—"

"Wrecked the world for them," Val said.

"Stupid generalisation," Warren huffed.

"Perhaps the modern-day equivalent of 'okay grandad'," Carlos suggested.

Val nodded.

"I still don't see what it has to do with Rory's bad manners," Warren said.

"I think he may have taken offence to you calling him 'young pup'." Val nudged her husband.

"A kind of generational verbal stoush," Ketty said.

"That's it." Val grinned.

"Why are we standing out here?" Warren threw up his hands. "Fancy a drink before we turn in?"

"We haven't had a chance to chat tonight, Ketty," Val said. "You seem to have been busy all evening. I hope you got time to eat your dinner."

"I did."

The four of them began walking.

"And a drink and a chat would be lovely, wouldn't it, Carlos? We were only just saying it was too early to end the night."

"We were."

Ketty sensed his irritation. She slipped her hand into his and gave it a gentle squeeze.

By the time they reached the lounge car it was already half full. Val and Ketty commandeered an empty couch and Warren and Carlos went to get drinks. To Ketty's surprise Erik and Judith came in together, and to her bigger surprise Judith slipped onto the couch beside her while Erik went on to the bar.

"We've had a shuffle around in our cabins," Judith said. "We were all worried it might be difficult for Birgit being in the same carriage as Rory. I'm going to sleep in her cabin tonight, Tien has taken my place and Birgit is sharing with Lacey."

"That's so good of everyone." Ketty berated herself for not thinking about the possibility of Birgit bumping into Rory in the corridors, although it was still a possibility, even with a cabin swap.

"I just wanted to let you know…in case you were looking for any of us."

"Thank you, Judith." Ketty had barely said the words when the men arrived back with the drinks and Judith rose and joined Erik a little further along the carriage.

Carlos and Warren drew some vacant club chairs closer but before Carlos could sit he patted his pocket then drew out his phone.

"I think it's the airline," he said and rushed out of the carriage to take the call.

"They still haven't found his case?" Warren asked.

"No, but maybe they have now and that's what the call's about." Ketty hoped so. "It's been a worry for him."

"Little things worry us more as we get older." Val raised her eyebrows at Warren.

"That's a dig at me, I assume," he retorted.

"You got so hot under the collar about a simple rearrangement of travel plans."

"You mean us dancing to our kids' tune again."

Val glanced at Ketty then leaned closer to Warren, lowering her voice. "The shop's busy and the grandkids are sick."

"It's only legwork he wants help with and he can employ a junior for that."

"That will cost him money."

Warren flopped out his hands, palms up. "You see, Ketty, this is where Val and I don't see eye to eye. I don't mind helping out our children—"

Val hmphed.

Warren ignored her and tapped one finger to another. "Gopher at the shop; childminder, gardener and Mr Fix-it at their homes. I've done it all but do I get any thanks? No. I'm only the 'old man', as they call me. They treat me like a servant."

"Oh, Warren," Val grumbled.

"And at least a servant gets paid."

Ketty remained silent as he took a sip of his drink and Val gave her an awkward glance. "We don't need the money."

"I know we don't but maybe they'd be more grateful if they had to pay me."

"They are grateful, Warren."

"To you maybe. I've worked in the electrical business in one capacity or another most of my life but it's as if that means nothing. I've simply retired, not lost my marbles."

"I think you're overreacting."

Warren lurched forward. "The last time I was there, Val, a younger couple came in about a new television. Everyone was busy so I asked what they were looking for, narrowed it down to a few choices, was giving them the ins and outs, and then our son interrupted me, corrected me about some minor difference between models and took over. As I walked away he made a joke about me and the older generation not keeping up with the technology."

Val gasped. "But you do."

"Of course I do. Just because it's not my shop any more doesn't mean I don't keep my eye on the latest products. I'm fed up with being called the 'old man'."

They both fell silent. From the corner of her eye Ketty saw Carlos come back. Val and Warren were focused on each other and not anything around them. Ketty made a quick series of face and hand signals to stop Carlos interrupting, then she felt bad when he turned and left the lounge.

"'Old man' is a term of endearment," Val said softly.

"Not when our children say it. I'm the butt of their jokes."

"Oh my goodness, surely not."

"And when you sign me up for childminding duties and go out I feel overwhelmed."

"With your own grandchildren?"

"I travelled a lot when the kids were young, you did the hard yards then. I'm out of touch. When I had the baby and the two toddlers last week and you went off—"

"I only went to the shops."

"You were gone for three hours, Val."

She flopped back.

"Their parents have so many rules," Warren continued. "No screen time, no sweets, sleep at a certain time. And they all needed nappy changes or toileting, they were hungry."

"I left snacks."

"And lately you've agreed to babysit several times then gone off to do something and I'm left holding the baby, literally. I'm out of my depth with one little person on my own, let alone three."

Val shook her head. "You've never said any of this before."

"I've been feeling it for a long time." Warren took a slug of his drink.

Once more Val shot Ketty an embarrassed look.

"It sounds like you've got a lot to talk about," Ketty said. "Would you prefer I left you to it?"

"No, let's have another drink." Warren plucked up his empty glass. Both Val's and Ketty's were almost full and Carlos's remained untouched.

Val opened her mouth but Ketty placed a restraining hand on Val's, resting on the couch between them. "I'm sick of wine. Would you get me a scotch on the rocks, please, Warren?"

"With pleasure." He stood and looked at his wife. "Val?"

"I'll stick with this."

As soon as he'd walked away Val shook her head. "I'm sorry we aired our personal business in front of you."

"Please don't worry." It seemed to be the night for revealing conversations but Ketty didn't want to dwell on her staff issues. "Poor Warren, he must have been harbouring his feelings for a while now."

"I thought he was just being selfish. I had no idea he was feeling so, so..."

"Diminished?"

Val sighed.

"I've had a little taste of that myself." Ketty glanced down at her wrist. "I had an experience where I was spoken to and treated in such a way I doubted myself and my abilities. More recently I talked the experience over with...with a friend and we came to the conclusion that the people who were making me feel that way probably didn't even realise they were."

"The family call me Gran. I think it's special."

"Of course it is but I don't think it's quite the same. I assume Warren is Grandpa or—"

"Pop they all call him and the littlest ones say Poppy." Val smiled, her eyes watery. "He adores them. I just don't understand where all this is coming from."

"You've brought up several children almost single-handed at times, by the sound of it. I take my hat off to you. It's beyond my experience. I've got one nephew and two great-nieces but I only used to have Greg stay when he was older. And his girls are still young – I've never looked after them on my own. I can empathise with Warren just a little."

"I kind of pushed him into it, thinking he'd enjoy looking after them once he got the hang of it. And I'd no idea he felt as he did about our kids. I've heard them say things but they're only teasing."

"I wonder if it would help for you to talk as a family?"

"I can't imagine Warren doing that."

"Warren doing what?" He placed a drink in front of Ketty and took a sip of his own before he sat and looked from her to his wife. "What are you signing me up for now?"

"I was suggesting it might be a good idea to talk with your family about how you're feeling."

"As if they'd be interested," he scoffed.

"Perhaps one at a time then. It might be your son in the business who needs to know how you're feeling. As Val said, 'old man' is often a term of endearment but it depends on the relationship and the context. And I think you definitely need to explain how you feel about your son embarrassing you at the shop. He thinks he's making a joke but if it's hurtful to you then it's not very funny, is it?"

Warren took another sip of his drink. "He'll say I'm being too sensitive."

"I assume you have customers of all ages?"

Warren nodded.

"I think sometimes we're our own worst enemies when it comes to ageism. People make jokes about it and we go along with them. My neighbour Maurice is a case in point. He says things to me like 'give the technology to a young person who can make it work'. Yet he's perfectly capable of managing every aspect of his mobile phone and I am too. And if there's something I don't know I ask."

Val waggled a finger at her husband. "You make those kind of jokes."

"No, I don't."

"What about the last birthday card you bought me? That dreadful frumpy-looking woman on the front holding a bottle of wine in the air saying something like 'don't worry about getting older, drink up and roll with the paunches'."

He chuckled. "It was a joke, pet."

Val raised her eyebrows. "If you don't like being called 'old man' by our son, imagine how I felt when my husband gave me a birthday card portraying me as a fat, wrinkled drunk."

Warren gaped at her. "I never…"

"I know you didn't, love, but a more positive birthday message would have been nicer."

Warren took another gulp of his drink.

"This is just an idea," Ketty said. "Perhaps you could tackle how you feel with your son by projecting it further afield. You could say someone you met on your travels felt intimidated by a salesperson who spoke down to them, or supposed they didn't understand the technology. How you'd hate for that to be one of his customers. Instead of assuming someone doesn't understand we should assume they do and encourage them to ask questions if they need. It might get you talking enough that you could mention your concerns about how he speaks to you."

Warren sighed. "He sees me as old."

Ketty smiled. "Old is just another word for experienced."

"And our children do value that, even if you don't think so," Val said.

The floor vibrated beneath Ketty's feet followed by the familiar gentle sway of the carriage. "We're moving." She glanced at her watch. "It's late and Carlos hasn't come back." He had tried but not since she'd waved him away. "We've hardly spoken tonight.

I'd better find out how he got on with the call from the airline. I'll see you tomorrow."

"Goodnight," Val said and as Ketty left her seat Warren slipped in beside her. Ketty glanced along the carriage but there was no sign of Erik and Judith – they must have left as well. She hoped poor Carlos was still awake.

thirty-five

Night Two – Travelling South

Lacey tapped tentatively on the door to the single cabin then peered back and forth checking the curves of the corridor. She was alone.

When they'd first got back to the train Lacey had expressed concern about Birgit being on her own. Judith had been the one to suggest the changes to their sleeping arrangements. "If Rory tries anything stupid, he can deal with me," she'd said.

Now Lacey wondered if she was in the cabin or perhaps in the bathroom. She tapped again.

"Yes," Judith snapped brusquely from the other side.

"It's me, Lacey."

The door opened part way. Judith stuck her head out and they both looked from side to side.

"Birgit forgot her toiletry bag," Lacey said.

"Right." Judith glanced behind her. "It's here on the basin."

There was little space in the cabin with the bed made up. Judith stepped away into the small area in front of the basin. Lacey leaned forward. From further along the passage behind her there was a loud bang.

Judith stepped back to the door and they both froze at the sound of raised male voices, young voices with Irish accents.

"Inside, quick," Judith hissed.

Lacey squeezed in. Judith shut the door behind her and turned the lock. Lacey jumped and Judith flinched at a loud thump on the door.

"Birgit, I want to talk." Rory's voice was slurred but as clear as if there was no door.

There was another thump.

"Will ya leave it out," Rhys said. "Let's get to our cabins."

Judith sat on the bed and indicated Lacey should do the same. She was relieved to take the weight from her trembling knees. She sunk into the soft bedding and realised she and Judith were both jiggling slightly from side to side. The train was moving again.

She glanced at Judith. "Do you think they've—"

Judith put her finger to her lips just as there was another thump on the door.

Further away Rhys called out to Rory.

The two women waited.

"I think they've gone now," Judith whispered. "But perhaps you'd better stay here a little longer...just in case."

"You don't think they'd do anything? Try to hurt you...us?"

"No. But they've had a skinful and drunks can turn nasty."

Lacey thought of her dad then. She wondered where he was and what he was doing.

Judith gave her a searching look. "Don't worry, we'll be fine."

"I was thinking of my dad. He drinks too much sometimes but usually he just goes to sleep. Trouble is it could be anywhere. Last time he was at the kitchen table with a lit cigarette in his hand."

Judith's eyes flashed. "You don't want to be putting up with that."

"He's moved out now anyway. Got a job in the country."

"You're on your own at home?"

Lacey nodded and they both fell silent.

"It must be hard to meet the rent."

"My gran left the house to me."

Judith's eyes widened. "You're very fortunate to own your own property at your age."

"It's not as easy as it sounds. The place needs repairs and there are more bills when a house belongs to you." Something Lacey was still discovering.

"You could rent out a room." Judith tugged at the cuff of one sleeve. "Plenty of people are desperate these days."

"So desperate they'd even live with someone like me."

"That's not what I meant."

Lacey plucked up the toiletry bag. "I better get this back to Birgit."

"Please, Lacey, don't get hot under the collar. I was simply trying to be helpful."

Lacey shrugged. Judith's kind of help she could do without.

"Before you go…what you said about you and Dean…" Judith gripped her hands together then stood in front of the basin again. "I know you can tell me it's none of my business but…are you sure you didn't do or say anything to make him think you weren't interested?"

"No." Lacey hugged the bag to her chest. "I didn't."

Muffled voices sounded in the corridor and Judith put her finger to her lips again but the murmurs quickly faded and they were left with the noise of the train gradually picking up speed.

"I'm worried about him." Judith's voice was soft but the concern in it made Lacey's heart beat faster.

"Why, what's happened?"

"Our apartment block is being renovated and we've all been given notice. We've…he's had no luck finding another place yet and on top of that you broke…he's heartbroken and I'm sure it's because of you."

"Because of me!" Lacey leaped up into the small space between the bed, the door and Judith.

Judith waved her hand. "Keep your voice down."

"I told you I didn't break it off with him," Lacey hissed. "We'd been to a movie. Had a good time, I thought, then a week later he rang to say he was going home for a visit and he'd call me when he got back. When I didn't hear from him I sent a message. His reply was short. *Cooling things for a while.*" Lacey sagged back to the bed. The anger that burned in her chest was quickly enveloped by the hurt. "I didn't know what to reply. I waited but I've heard nothing more." She lifted her teary gaze to Judith. "He's the one who called it off."

Judith sat beside Lacey and turned to face her. "When I said he's heartbroken because of you, I meant because I think he still… I think he likes you very much."

"He's got a funny way of showing it."

"He's got an overactive defence mechanism."

Lacey frowned.

"Before he sent that message you said you'd been to the movies. What did you see?"

"He wanted me to pick. It was a romantic adventure comedy. We both enjoyed it," Lacey said defensively.

"And afterwards?"

Lacey's cheeks warmed as she recalled Dean badly wanting to go on for drinks and dinner and she being quite firm in her refusal.

"I'm not asking for every detail," Judith said. "But I wondered if something had happened."

"Nothing happened, maybe that's what put him off me."

Judith pursed her lips. "Dean's not like the Rorys of this world."

"He wanted to go on for a meal. I couldn't go." Lacey shrugged. "He was disappointed at the time but I didn't think he was that upset."

"Did you tell him why you couldn't go?"

The warmth built in Lacey's cheeks. "I was tired, I wanted an early night."

"That's it? You didn't argue? Say something in the heat of the moment you regretted later?"

"No."

Judith sighed.

"I just assumed he's lost interest," Lacey murmured.

Judith stared at the door, a small frown on her brow.

Lacey stood up. "I'd better go. Birgit will wonder what's happened to me."

"Let me." Judith squeezed in front of her, turned the lock and eased the door open just a little. She poked her head out and looked both ways. "All clear," she whispered.

Lacey stepped around her. "Goodnight." She moved off, following the curving waves of the corridor, thinking about Judith's questions, never imagining they'd have such a detailed talk about Lacey's love life, or lack of it.

Ahead of her a door clunked shut. Lacey paused and listened. It had been a heavy sound, like that made by the door between carriages. She hoped she wasn't about to run into Rory or Rhys.

There was no sound but the carpet could muffle careful footsteps. Then she recalled Rory had sounded rather drunk so she couldn't imagine him being careful. She moved on, and collided with two bodies hurrying from the other direction. A chorus of screams echoed in her ears. One of them was hers.

Ketty paused in the walkway between the two carriages, wondering what was going on. When she'd got back to her cabin, Carlos had been in bed and asleep. She'd been leaning against the door feeling sorry she'd been so long when she'd heard muffled voices in the corridor beyond. Curious, she'd stuck out her head and just caught sight of Ning and Tien in their pyjamas and dressing-gowns creeping along the passage in the direction of the single-cabin carriage. As they'd rounded the corner, she'd stepped out and followed. By the time she let herself out of one carriage and into the next, they'd already gone through the other door and disappeared from sight.

Ketty reached for the next handle as a series of shrieks sounded above the noise of the train. She yanked open the door and barrelled around the dogleg corner, running into Ning and setting off another round of piercing screams.

"Shh!" Lacey hissed from beyond Ning and Tien.

The cabin door beside Ketty opened a crack.

"It's all right, we're fine. Sorry to bother you," she reassured the worried man peering out.

The door shut and Ketty turned to the three women huddled in front of her. She beckoned them back through the doors into their carriage, where they stopped beside the small kitchenette.

"What were you doing?" she said.

The three of them looked at her with the frightened faces of naughty schoolgirls caught smoking behind the toilets.

"I've been down to Birgit's room to get her toiletries." Lacey lifted a small bag into the air.

"Tien and I were waiting with Birgit," Ning said.

"But Lacey was gone a long time." Tien's eyes were still wide with fright. "We decided to go and check on her."

Ketty looked the three of them up and down. "And what were you going to do with the mug of tea and the umbrella?"

"If that nasty Rory was giving her trouble, Ning was going to throw the tea in his face and I was going to hit him over the head." Tien brandished the umbrella in the air.

Ketty shook her head.

"The tea's not hot," Ning assured her.

"Everything all right here, ladies?" Matt came round the corner, making all four women jump.

Tien swung her umbrella and it sailed down through the air, narrowly missing Ketty's right arm. Ketty glared at Tien before turning around and forcing her lips up in a smile for the train manager.

"We're perfectly fine, thank you, Matt." She waved a hand at the others. "Bedtime, ladies," she said. "We've got another full day tomorrow."

They squeezed past Matt one at a time and moved on along the corridor. Ketty opened her door and stepped in, nodding a goodnight as each woman passed. The last was Tien, the umbrella tucked under her arm. She gave Ketty a rueful look and hurried on. Ketty shut her door, leaned back against it and pressed her lips firmly together to stop the laugh that burbled up inside her.

thirty-six

Judith opened her eyes to discover light filtering around her blind. She hadn't imagined she'd get much sleep, there'd been so many things going around in her head when she'd climbed into bed. But as soon as she turned out the light the bed had become a cosy cocoon. Instead of the noise and motion of the train keeping her awake, it must have put her to sleep.

She propped herself up and peered around the blind. The sun was a glow on the edge of a flat landscape stretching as far as she could see. Today they'd spend their time in and around Coober Pedy. Erik had been distracted when she'd asked about the best places to see. The poor man was obviously stressed about returning to the place where he'd lived and worked with his wife. Not that he mentioned her at all. In spite of his moments of distraction, Judith had enjoyed his company. It had been refreshing to chat about the events of the day with someone new. There was something about him that reminded her of Ketty's neighbour, Klaus. It might have been just his accent because they were not alike in

335

other ways. Klaus was a gentler man and not so rough around the edges, like Erik who occasionally got a fierce look in his eye when he talked about his mining days.

Judith shrugged. Today she had other things to think about and Lacey was at the top of her list.

The small scraps Lacey had revealed about her personal life had surprised Judith. Both out at Simpsons Gap and then during her visit the previous evening, Judith had seen a different side of Lacey, a vulnerability. Lacey usually acted very reserved in Judith's presence, revealing little about herself.

From the first day she'd started at Ketty Clift Couture she'd been an insular package, not needing help. She did ask questions when necessary but always of Ketty or one of the others, never Judith. And if she was being honest, Judith thought perhaps that's why she'd never truly taken to Lacey. She'd kept Judith at arm's length, not needing her or asking for her help as the others sometimes did. Then as time progressed Lacey had started to suggest business changes and Ketty listened to her. That had always been Judith's role.

The familiar niggle of annoyance returned. Judith plonked her hands firmly on top of the covers. She couldn't believe she was even bothering about Lacey but she was concerned for Dean and it seemed the two were still linked, albeit tenuously.

Judith had been quick to blame Lacey for the break-up, for hurting Dean when he'd suffered several rejections in the past, but there was obviously more to it if Lacey's story was to be believed. This last month Dean had lost his spark, had been going out drinking with his mates more, had put up the shield he was so good at. He made light of his disability but Judith suspected his well-honed defence mechanism had come from challenges he'd faced in the past. He was good at giving the impression to the world that all was okay but Judith knew the real Dean.

She'd seen this "I don't care" behaviour before and she hurt for him. It was always after a break-up with a girl and so Judith had been quick to blame Lacey. But if she still liked him and hadn't called it off and Judith knew Dean was still smitten with Lacey, what had gone wrong? She wished she could ring him but there was no signal out there and it was hardly the kind of conversation she could have with him over the phone. It'd have to be over drinks and home-cooked food, that was Judith's currency, and she'd have to wait until she got home to tackle him on it.

Now she wondered if Ketty knew that Lacey's father was a drinker and that he'd moved away. Perhaps that had been the conversation Judith had interrupted in Ketty's cabin. Once more Judith was sorry her relationship with Ketty was so fractured. This was something she might have talked over with her. If only Carlos wasn't on this trip.

Judith threw back the covers and sat up. She didn't want to think about Carlos and whatever he was planning. It was too early to go for breakfast. She'd go to the little kitchen in the next carriage and make herself a cup of tea. She might run into one of the others and perhaps go to their cabin instead of sitting alone.

Judith had just stepped through the gangway into the next carriage when Carlos came swiftly around the corner, a towel draped over his shoulder.

"Good morning," he said with his trademark smile.

Judith responded with a brusque nod.

"Is everything all right, Judith?"

"Of course. Why wouldn't it be?"

"You seem to be avoiding me and I wonder if I've offended you somehow."

"It's been very busy, hasn't it?" she said. "I've hardly seen Ketty either."

"I think she's a bit sad about that."

"Is she?" Judith studied him closely. There was no guile in his look but she was sure this was just another of his tricks to engage her and try to draw her in with the charming persona he inveigled other people with.

"She respects your opinion, values your friendship and your expertise."

Judith's chin went up. "I know that. It's mutual." Why was he telling her this? It was so awkward standing there in the small space in their sleeping apparel, the train occasionally rocking them on their bare feet and the likelihood of another passenger passing through at any moment.

"I'd hoped you and I could also be friends."

"We are, of course." She looked down, unable to meet his steady gaze.

"I hope so. I wouldn't like to think my friendship with Ketty was detrimental to that between you and her."

Was there a warning tone to his voice? Judith straightened. "You don't need to worry on that count. I'm very loyal and I look out for her." She lifted her chin. "I'm always here for Ketty when she needs me, whereas you're not here to stay, are you?"

He opened his mouth and closed it again, and Judith gained some small satisfaction from his moment of uncertainty. He always seemed so confident.

"I won't hold you up." She stepped sideways into the kitchenette and busied herself getting a cup and selecting a tea bag until she heard the heavy clunk of the carriage door closing behind her. Then she rested her hands on the bench and took slow deep breaths to calm her thudding heart. No matter how much she told herself she no longer cared what happened between Ketty and Carlos, she knew she couldn't bear for her friend to be hurt.

"Are you awake?"

Lacey was relieved to hear Birgit's whisper. She hadn't wanted to disturb her friend. She leaned over the bunk and was pleased to see Birgit smiling. "Yes."

"Sorry I chewed your ear for so long last night."

"Don't worry about it."

They'd talked late into the night. Mostly Birgit had done the talking, ranting about Rory and then moving on to unloading all the faults of her previous boyfriend and how having to move back with her cousins had been so hard after the space of his apartment. Lacey hadn't been able to keep her eyes open and had drifted off to sleep before Birgit had, she was sure, but she'd woken early this morning with an idea brewing.

"I wonder how Judith got on last night." Birgit yawned. "It was good of her to offer to take my cabin."

"It was." Lacey climbed down the ladder. She was totally bamboozled by Judith's hot-and-cold behaviour.

"Look at your face." Birgit laughed and sat up, making space for Lacey to climb onto the bed. "Judith's not such a bad person."

"The jury's still out on that but she did make me think about something."

"See, not all bad." Birgit pulled a face. "Unless it was something *bad* of course."

"No, I don't think so. It might be something good for both of us."

"Go on."

"Well, you know how I'm living on my own now—"

"Your dad might come back."

"Even if he did, I've got a spare bedroom. It's a two-bathroom house with a big living area."

"So what are you thinking?"

"Judith mentioned renting out a room and I was thinking that might work."

"It'd help you with your bills, that's for sure. You'd have to be careful though. You wouldn't want to end up with some weirdo."

"I've got someone in mind already, actually. A weirdo I quite like."

"You said you'd broken up with Dean. Has something happened?"

"Dean's not a weirdo."

"I'm just teasing. Go on then, who's this weirdo you're thinking could take your spare room?"

"You."

"Me?" Birgit's eyes were as round as dinner plates.

"If you'd like to—"

Birgit squealed and leaped forward, wrapping Lacey in a hug. "I'd love to." Then she sat back. "Hang on, you just called me a weirdo. I might take offence." She threw her arms around Lacey again. "But I'm not going to. Oh, Lacey, it would be wonderful."

"Don't get too excited yet." Lacey was glad Birgit liked her suggestion but she had no idea how to organise it. "I'll have to do some research and see what we'd need to do."

Once more Birgit sat back. "I had a proper agreement with my cousins the first time I moved in. It was easy to organise. We haven't renewed it 'cos I was hoping to find a better option." She clapped her hands. "Your place would be perfect."

"You haven't seen my house yet. It's a bit run-down. You might not like it."

"Are you kidding? I'm sleeping on a fold-out bed in a small decrepit apartment with dodgy plumbing and two other tenants. I'm going to love it."

"Last winter I had saucepans catching the drips from the leaky roof. It's been patched but I'm not sure how long it will last."

"Lucky I've got a set of saucepans in storage. I'll bring them."

Birgit laughed and her excitement was infectious. Lacey laughed too. It wasn't just the extra money that would be good but having someone else in the house again. She hadn't been sure Birgit would be interested and she still didn't want either of them to get their hopes up too much.

"Like I said, wait till you've had a look before you decide."

Lacey was trying to be sensible about it but already her thoughts raced ahead to how she might rearrange the bedrooms. She could take her gran's with the en suite and if her dad came back for visits he could have the middle bedroom, and she could give Birgit the front room. It had a nice view over the verandah and the street.

"It'll be grand." Birgit clapped her hands.

"I hope so," Lacey said and the weight of her worries lifted just a little.

The closing of the cabin door woke Ketty and she took a moment to orientate herself. Top bunk, train still moving — she opened her eyes wider — morning light. She assumed the door had been

Carlos heading to the bathroom. She lay still a moment, then leaned over the bunk. His nightwear was neatly folded on his bed beside his toiletry bag. She sat up. He must have showered already. She blinked and reached for her watch but the numbers blurred and her reading glasses were still in her purse.

"Bother."

The door opened and Carlos peered around. "You're awake." He came right in, a mug in his hand. "I made you tea."

He passed it up to her.

"Thank you. You're very good to me and I feel as if I've let you down."

"How?"

"We didn't get our quiet drink together. I got caught with Val and Warren and shooed you away. I didn't mean for you to stay away. You didn't even get a sip of your drink." She grimaced.

"They found my case."

"That's wonderful news."

"It's in Dubai."

"Oh, not such good news, by the look on your face."

"It might take a while to get to Adelaide, that's all."

"Well, that's all right, isn't it? We'd already decided to spend some extra time there and if worst comes to worst they'll have to send it on to Sydney. We can go shopping for any extras you need."

"I don't want to have to shop."

He looked rather disgruntled and once again Ketty wondered if it was the missing case or money problems or something else that bothered him. "Let's wait and see how things stand when we get to Adelaide."

"Such a nuisance."

"Thank you for the tea." Ketty took a sip, hoping to distract him. "I could get used to being waited on each morning."

His customary smile returned. "Once you're ready we can have breakfast. Perhaps just the two of us this morning."

"Oh, Carlos, I'm sorry. I've organised to have breakfast with Virginia. We haven't seen each other for forty years so there's a lot to catch up on."

"That's all right." His face said otherwise but Carlos was too polite to make demands.

"We'll be together on the tour today,' Ketty said. "And then it could be just us for dinner tonight. I've given up trying to organise my staff. Oh, and you'll never guess what they got up to last night." She filled him in on the cabin swaps and then Ning and Tien's attempt at being protection for Lacey. She was pleased he was laughing with her by the time she'd finished.

"I'll go for breakfast now then," he said. "Leave you to get ready."

"What time is it?"

He looked at his watch. "Seven forty-five."

"Oh dear. I'd better get a move on. I said I'd meet Virginia at eight thirty."

Ketty chose a pair of linen pants and a silk shirt from last summer's ready-made collection. Her thoughts strayed briefly to Judith and Lacey and her request that the next winter collection be based on their travels, then she quickly pushed them from her mind. She'd told Carlos she was giving up on her staff but it wasn't completely true. Seeing the way they'd all looked out for each other the previous night, comical as it was, reassured her that they were a good team. She just needed to smooth out a few kinks. What to do to help Ning was top of her list.

She glanced at her watch. That would have to wait though. It was time to meet with Virginia.

thirty-seven

Day Three – Travelling South

Ketty had barely tapped on the door when Virginia opened it and slipped out.

"It's still very chilly in my cabin," she said.

Ketty frowned. "I've found the temperature very comfortable."

"I'm referring to Beau. He gave me a bit of a telling-off last night after I complained about the food."

"Didn't you like it?"

"It was fine," Virginia huffed. "I've been a bit down over the slow return to normal with my knee. This holiday was supposed to be about revitalising and taking a fresh outlook. Beau doesn't think I've been trying hard enough."

"I see. Well, if it's any consolation this trip was supposed to be about building relationships with my staff and I've not been all that successful with that either."

Virginia was ahead of Ketty but she stopped suddenly. "Blast, I've left my stick. I'd better get it just in case."

Ketty stood aside as Virginia slipped back into her cabin. While she waited she heard a familiar Irish accent. Rory and Rhys were heading her way along the passage. She turned so that there was space for them to pass.

Rory's eyes narrowed when he saw her, just as Virginia stepped out with her stick.

"Good morning, Rory." Ketty nodded. "Rhys."

"Well, well, two old grannies for the price of one." Rory's smile was smug.

Ketty decided it best to ignore him but Virginia stepped closer, the handle of her walking stick resting on her shoulder.

"I'm curious, Rory," she said. "Is it your notion that you're going to be young all your life? You could be wrong about that, you know..." She leaned closer. "Or you could just be unfortunate and die young."

Rory gaped at her. Virginia strode on, tapping her stick as she walked but not appearing to lean on it as Ketty followed in her wake.

"You certainly put him in his place," Ketty said as soon as they reached the lounge car.

"I simply won't put up with the Rorys of this world any longer." Virginia's defiant look once more reminded Ketty of the young woman she'd known so briefly all those years ago.

Jade greeted them with her usual warm smile although Ketty thought there was a tiredness in her eyes. The staff worked long hours and keeping all these people happy wouldn't be easy. Jade sent them through to the dining car where they were seated at a table by themselves as requested. Ketty paused beside the table where Ning, Tien, Lacey and Birgit sat.

"Good morning," she said. "I hope you all managed to sleep well."

"We did," Lacey and Birgit chorused then laughed as if they'd said something funny.

"I thought I'd let you know I've just seen the two fellows. They're probably headed this way."

"They better not try to talk to us." Tien screwed her face up in a fierce frown.

"We'll be fine, won't we, girls?" Birgit said.

Lacey nodded emphatically and she and Birgit laughed again.

"That's the way." Ketty was pleased to see they were being positive but she did wonder if they'd both had champagne with their breakfast.

To Ketty's surprise, Carlos was at a table with Erik and Judith. He smiled as she passed and went on talking to Erik. Judith stared studiously out the window. Of Warren and Val Ketty had seen no sign but she hoped they'd found some common ground after she'd left them the previous night.

She joined Virginia a few tables further on. They sat opposite each other by the window. Simon wrote down their coffee orders and Ketty took out her glasses to check the menu.

Their food order had been taken and their coffees delivered when Ketty noticed Rory and Rhys enter the dining car. "Thankfully our young gentleman friends have been given seats near the entrance," she said.

"Are you worried?"

"No, but I'm not sure your response was quite the right way to tackle Rory. He strikes me as being the vindictive type and we've still got some time to go on this train."

Virginia snorted. "I've become intolerant of intolerance. Sometimes it just has to be called out. In my profession I've been running into it for years. I worked harder than younger models, I had chemicals injected into my skin, I dyed my hair, I constantly reinvented myself. Then I injured my knee and there was suddenly no work." She threw a hand in the air. "I felt...useless, like I'd been thrown on the scrap heap. I had to use a walking frame or a stick for years before I had my operation. A walking aid is like a homing beacon for jokes about aging. The last straw was just before my birthday. I treated myself to a manicure and this young woman passed me on her way out, patted my shoulder and said 'how wonderful to see an old lady getting her nails done'."

Ketty gasped.

"She beamed at me like an idiot. For once in my life I was speechless. It bothered me for days. I thought about it a lot and decided I might not be able to model any more but I wasn't totally useless and I'd no longer laugh or be silent when it came to put-downs about my age." She grinned. "I've developed quite a repertoire of comebacks."

They fell silent as they sipped their coffees.

"And there's not a lot of work for a sixty-five-year-old model with a limp so I've plenty of time to ponder it." She looked up. "If you ever needed a second career, Ketty, you could be a model. The way you enter a room, the fit and style of your clothes."

"You can keep that idea. Lacey has trotted me out a few times when we've been photographing new lines but I don't enjoy it at all."

"Is that outfit something you've made?"

Ketty glanced down. "We do a small range of ready-made for our online boutique. This is from last summer's collection."

"They look good on you."

"I'm very happy with the design and the fabric. They seem to flatter a variety of ages and shapes."

The door to the dining car opened and Beau was shown to a seat at the table across from Lacey and the others.

"Your son has arrived for breakfast," Ketty said.

Virginia didn't look around. "I thought he'd get moving once I was out of the way."

Ketty glanced down the carriage. Beau appeared to be chatting to Lacey.

"He's been a good son," Virginia said. "We have a few spats but he's very patient with me."

"It must have been a shock to discover you were still pregnant." Ketty spoke gently, being careful of her own tender memories as well as Virginia's.

"It was, and I'm not looking for sympathy but life was a struggle in Beau's early years. I got work but it was catalogue stuff, not regular and not paid well. And then I got my first big opportunity but it was in Sydney – Beau wasn't at school yet, I left him with a friend. I was only gone for a week but then more offers came and it became a regular thing. I moved us to Sydney and my hours were crazy. I was forever juggling childcare and work and then eventually he was old enough to stay home alone. Not when I was doing the overseas stints, of course. I had someone come and stay with him then. We moved around a lot – rental places, the first apartment I bought, then various houses. He didn't have a lot of close friends. By the time he went to uni I think we were both relieved. He got student digs and I could come and go without worrying about him."

Virginia paused as their food was delivered.

"The tropical salad for you, Virginia." Simon placed the dish in front of her. "And the eggs Florentine for you, Ketty."

Virginia took a small spoonful of her fruit then went on. "I've never felt that mother guilt people talk about. That was just how life was but..." She studied Ketty across the table. "Telling you now...I feel...sorry."

Ketty swallowed the delicious morsel she'd just put in her mouth with a gulp. "Why?"

"It should have been you. You'd have been a much better mother than me."

"How do you know that? If my baby had survived who's to know what choices I'd have made? I couldn't be with the father of my child so I'd have been raising him or her alone. Like you I've worked long hours, had to sacrifice a lot to build my business."

"Which is in Sydney?"

"Yes. After I'd recovered enough to work—"

"Dear god, they made a mess of you in that hospital, Ketty. It was as if they'd cut you in half and stitched you back together again."

"It was that or I died. Advanced sepsis due to an ectopic pregnancy wasn't easy to treat." Ketty put her hand to her stomach, where the scar snaked across her abdomen. "I thought my life was over for a while but I got a lucky break in Sydney and reinvented myself. I chose to live my life in a different way to the one I'd imagined. My scar is my daily reminder of how lucky I am. I've no regrets."

"I wish I could say the same. I'm proud of the modelling career I had." Virginia tossed a look over her shoulder. "Not so proud of my mothering."

Ketty pondered that and couldn't help but wonder what it would be like if she had a son sharing this journey with her.

"Don't misunderstand me," Virginia said. "I'm impressed by the man Beau's become. He's kind and intelligent, a much better human than me. He has a PhD in computer science and spends most of his time lecturing at university and working on his research, which is something about randomised algorithms and machine learning. Don't ask me any more than that – it's all too science fiction for me."

"And you're holidaying together?"

"His idea, not mine. As I said, he thought I'd benefit from a change of scene. I think he regrets it now."

"Surely not."

"I struggled for so long with this knee."

"What happened?"

"Simplest thing. I was at the local shops and a blasted dog tripped me up. I fell and landed awkwardly across a bike rack. I was pretty banged up, but my knee was the worst. And to add insult to injury it was assumed it was a fall."

"I can relate to that." Ketty held up her pale right arm. "Broke my wrist after a bit of a tussle with a shop mannequin. It was assumed I'd had a fall too. Why is there this sudden change from 'she fell over' to 'she had a fall'?"

"It's ridiculous, isn't it? And in my case the dog and its owner didn't even stop to help and no-one else saw it happen. Anyway, I've suffered with the knee ever since. Then Beau's marriage broke up. They'd drifted apart. She and I never got on, so I wasn't sorry to see her gone and I don't think Beau was terribly distressed in the end.

"When I finally decided to have a knee replacement he moved in to help me at home. It's taken longer than I'd thought to recover. He suggested a holiday might…" She put up her fingers to make air quotes. "'Get me out of myself', I think were his words. I thought a day lounge by a pool with a bar nearby would be the thing but he decided on this…" she flipped a hand out, "antiquated caravan on wheels."

"I must admit to being a sceptic when this trip was first suggested but I've discovered I love the train," Ketty said. "It's all about the journey, isn't it – the experience, the people you meet." Ketty smiled. "And the staff go out of their way to make it special.

There's something romantic about traversing our country in a train."

"But they keep making us get off." Virginia huffed. "I asked if I could stay aboard today instead of taking the tour but Jade said it wasn't possible."

"I suppose the staff need us out of the way so they can refresh our cabins et cetera. Anyway, I believe Coober Pedy will be very interesting."

Virginia gave an exasperated snort. While they'd been talking they'd finished their meal and Simon came to clear their plates. "Can I get you anything else, ladies?"

They both ordered more coffee.

Virginia studied the waiter as he walked away. "I do admit the food is rather good and the staff have been mostly helpful. I suppose there is a rustic elegance about it."

"There's always a bright side."

"You're sounding like Beau."

"Oh no."

"What is it?" Virginia twisted and tried to look back to where Ketty was watching.

"Rory's seen Birgit and he's heading towards her."

Virginia turned back. "There's always drama with young people."

"It's all right. Beau's stepped in. He's talking to Rory and now Rory's heading back to Rhys. They're leaving."

"Beau's calm in a crisis. Does your Lacey have a boyfriend?"

Ketty was surprised by Virginia's change of tack. "Oh…no…at least…I think she might be a bit young for Beau."

"One of the reasons I agreed to come was to address Beau's lack of female companionship." Virginia twisted her head to glance back again. "What was it all about anyway?"

Ketty filled her in on Birgit's brief holiday romance and Rory's lack of honesty about his marital status.

"Oh, I see." Virginia nodded. "Married men were a line I tried never to cross but some men…" She shrugged. "When I discovered their deceit I ended it and moved on. Like you with that man who fathered your child."

"You know I ran into him again a few years ago."

"I hope he was suffering from the pox." Virginia gave her a devilish look.

"No." Ketty pictured Leo as she'd seen him last on her cruise aboard the *Diamond Duchess*. "On the contrary, he's matured well as far as looks go. He was keen to rekindle our relationship."

"The bastard."

"He was no longer married and very charming. Thankfully I soon discovered that behind the sparkle and the eloquence nothing had changed. He was still a liar."

"So there hasn't been anyone else for you?"

"A few close calls." Ketty smiled.

"What about that Spanish man." Virginia wriggled her eyebrows. "The friend you're with?"

"Carlos? We're good friends and that's all." Ketty adjusted the glass of water in front of her. "There was a time years ago when I was tempted but our friendship was too important to mess it up with a holiday fling. And that's all it could ever have been. He sailed the world, and he's now based in Spain and I live in Sydney."

"If you're not interested I might be. I'm not averse to a holiday fling."

Ketty felt a sudden stab of jealousy but she pushed it away as ridiculous. "We're old friends, as I said. He was a maître d' with a cruise line and now that he's retired he's visiting Australia. He'll return to Spain eventually." Ketty didn't want to think about how she'd feel once he was gone.

"And sharing your cabin, I hear."

"There was a mix-up with Carlos's booking. Since he was the one to suggest this holiday in the first place and he also generously gave me a voucher towards it for Christmas, I couldn't leave him behind so I offered him a spare bunk. That's all there is to it."

"Does he know that?"

"Don't be silly."

Simon brought their coffees and Ketty fiddled with the cup. Virginia was very direct, probing a relationship Ketty didn't want disturbed but if she'd been the blushing type, her cheeks would have been glowing red.

Judith drank the last of her tea and set her cup neatly back on the table.

"Orange dirt as far as the eye can see but it seems to be more brittle, rockier than yesterday." Carlos turned back from the window to Erik. "How do you know where to look for opals?"

Over breakfast Erik had been explaining how he'd mined for opal. "It's more about luck than anything. You have to dig a hole and search. When you get closer to the town you will see the mullock heaps everywhere." His hands moved in an arc. "Mounds of loose stones, white and brown, dug out of the earth. I went on a flight over the area once. From above it looks like white ant holes erupting out of the flat red earth." His smile fell away. "In the scheme of things it's all we are…scurrying insects."

Carlos appeared to ignore Erik's bitter tone. "I'm looking forward to seeing it." Once more he turned to the window. "We're slowing now."

Erik lurched to his feet, bumping the table and making their water glasses wobble. "I must go. I have things to do before we get off." He rushed from the carriage, pushing past one of the stewards and almost crashing through the door when it didn't open with the same speed he was moving.

Judith folded her napkin. She didn't want to be left alone at the table with Carlos.

"Please stay a moment longer," he said as she started to rise. "There's something I need to talk with you about."

It was the last thing Judith wanted to do. She glanced around. The dining car was thinning out but all of the members of her party were still there.

Belinda came to clear their table. "Can I get you anything else?" she asked.

"I would enjoy a coffee, please," Carlos said. "Would you like another tea, Judith?"

She glanced from his expectant look to Belinda. "A cappuccino, please."

Once Belinda had moved away, Carlos settled back against the chair.

"Such a very different life Erik has led," he said. "I'm looking forward to seeing these opal mines. I find it hard to imagine even though I've seen photographs."

"Yes," Judith murmured.

"And he lives on his own?"

"He had a wife. I gather she died and that might be why he moved away."

"Too many memories perhaps?"

Judith gave another murmured response, wishing she'd left instead of agreeing to the coffee.

Once the drinks were delivered she took her time sprinkling sugar into her cup and stirring it slowly with her spoon.

"You've known Ketty for a long time," Carlos said.

Judith glanced up at his earnest expression. "Not as long as you have."

"But you've been more constant in her life – a friend, a confidante."

"I have." She met his gaze squarely now.

"Ketty is such a good person. She has many friends in her life. I've enjoyed meeting them."

Judith nodded and picked up her coffee. She took a small sip and placed it carefully back on the saucer. The train was moving slowly now but the occasional bump made the table vibrate.

"My case has been found."

She glanced up, surprised by his sudden change of topic.

"It's in Dubai so it still may be some time before I get it."

Judith waited, not sure why he was telling her this.

"I had something in it for Ketty. Something special. It was stupid of me to put it in my case. I'd meant to have it in my carry-on but in the frenzy of last-minute packing I made a mistake."

Judith took another sip of her coffee. Fancy Carlos making a mistake and admitting to it. She hadn't thought it his style.

"I'd planned to give it to Ketty on the train, perhaps over dinner, but as I don't have it, I wondered if you…I had a quick look in the shops yesterday but didn't see anything that seemed just right. Perhaps you might suggest something?"

Judith was momentarily speechless. Was that what he'd been doing in a pawnshop? Looking for something rather than selling something? She was surprised the all-knowing Carlos would ask her what Ketty might like, then felt guilty that she had the scarf he'd tried to purchase for her back in Katherine. If she admitted it she'd have to explain why she bought it. She could say she got it for Ketty to spite him. What would the saintly Carlos think of that?

"We're going to Coober Pedy," she said. "It's supposed to be the biggest producer of gem-quality opals in the world. Perhaps you could find her something there."

"I did do some research on that last night but we lost phone signal and we still don't have any. I wondered about a ring?"

Judith's eyebrows arched. "That's very personal. What about a brooch?"

"Would she like that?"

"She doesn't have many." Because she never wore them, but Judith wasn't going to tell him that.

"I don't have any idea if Ketty even likes opal."

"Why don't you ask her?"

"Ask me what?"

Carlos started and then composed his face quickly. Judith had seen Ketty and her breakfast companion approaching but with his back to them Carlos hadn't.

"Carlos wants to know if you're a fan of opal?" Judith slipped from her seat. "I'd better get ready. I think they want us to get off fairly soon."

She made her way out of the dining car without looking back. She knew what Carlos was up to. He thought by engaging her in conversation and playing on her friendship with Ketty that he could win her over under the pretence of buying something for Ketty. Judith wondered again about his trip to the pawnshop. Whatever it was that he was up to, she wasn't going to be fooled by Carlos.

thirty-eight

Day Three – Manguri Siding

Lacey, Birgit, Ning and Tien were all in the one cabin, waiting for the announcement to leave the train. Lacey was seated on the couch between Birgit and Ning while Tien paced up and back like a caged tiger.

"Why don't you sit?" Lacey said. "We can make room."

Tien shook her head. "I prefer to stand."

"The staff are quick to pack away the bunks and return the cabin to day use," Ning said, smoothing her hands across the couch.

"When we first came on board I thought working on the train seemed like a dream job." Birgit leaned across and pulled up the blind. "Now I'm not so sure."

Tien bent to the window then spun back, a look of horror on her face. "We are in the middle of nowhere. There's not even a waiting room or an office."

"Perhaps there's one further along," Ning suggested. "Remember our carriage is nearly at the end of the train."

Tien began to pace again. "It's like that TV show *The Tourist*. That man woke up in the outback with no memory and his friend got buried alive." Tien shuddered. "And there were scorpions!"

"I can put up with a few scorpions if your man Jamie Dornan comes with them," Birgit said.

"Was he in that?" Lacey asked.

"Every hunky bit of him." She winked and leaned forward to look out the window. "Hang on a minute. Isn't that your man there now?"

"Where?" Tien leaned beside her and pushed her face to the glass.

"Gotcha." Birgit laughed.

"Stop worrying, Tien," Ning said. "Come and sit down. We're all perfectly safe and I'm sure there won't be any scorpions."

Lacey moved along and both Birgit and Tien squeezed in beside her. They'd had lots of laughs this morning. The possibility of sharing her house had lifted the cloud of worry that had hung over Lacey. They'd told Ning and Tien about it over breakfast and, apart from Tien wanting them to make sure they did all the paperwork so they didn't end up in court like the tenants from hell program she'd seen on TV, the other two women thought it a good idea. There was still her dad to track down but with fresh hope she'd check her phone for messages and her bank balance as soon as she could find some signal.

A voice came through the speaker announcing it was time to head to the buses.

"Judith's not here," Tien said.

"She was ready when I saw her last." Ning stood. "She might be next door in our cabin. I'll check."

She let herself out while the others collected their things and was back quickly. "I think she's already gone. Her bag's not there. We should go. She'll probably meet us at the bus."

They stepped out into the corridor and followed other passengers heading forward along the train.

Jade greeted them in the lounge car and ushered them further. They walked on through the dining car and even the kitchen.

Tien, who was in the lead, stopped part way along the galley lined with stainless steel cupboards and benches. "Are you sure this is the right way?"

"Yes." Ning nodded. "Caryn said there's no platform here. We're almost at the end of the train and there's not a path so we have to walk some of the way inside." She shooed Tien forward and they kept going through several carriages like theirs before they reached a door that was open.

From there they climbed down onto a dirt track running parallel to the train. Overhead a brilliant blue cloudless sky stretched wide to infinity in every direction and the brightness of the sun had them all searching for their sunglasses, Tien adjusting hers while scrutinising the ground.

"It's a fair walk." Birgit pointed forward where several buses waited in the distance, looking like matchbox toys. "How're your feet?"

Everyone looked down at Lacey's feet safely covered by Ning's spare pair of canvas slip-on shoes.

"Fine so far." Lacey patted her bag. "And I've got extra socks, more plasters and my flip-flops if I'm desperate."

"I hope you don't need to wear them here." Tien was still scouring the ground for potential danger.

"Here's Judith," Ning said.

Lacey looked up. Judith was striding towards them from the direction of the buses.

"I thought I'd meet you at the coach but I didn't get far," she said. "I've forgotten my sunglasses. They must be in my other bag. Don't wait for me. I'll see you aboard."

"Let's go then," Birgit said, waving them all forward.

Ning had her phone out and was peering at the screen.

"No signal here," Lacey said. "I checked."

"See." Tien cast her arm in a wide sweeping motion. "Middle of nowhere, just like in *The Tourist*."

It made Lacey think of her dad and his lack of communication. He wasn't in the outback but what if something had happened to him? Like Ning she was keen to reach a place with signal and check her messages.

Judith rushed back along the corridors, occasionally having to squeeze to one side as she met passengers coming the other way. When she got to their dining car she almost ran into Val and Warren. She stepped into a space for them to pass.

"Hello, Judith." Warren beamed at her from under his broad hat. "You're going the wrong way."

"I forgot my sunglasses," she said.

"Oh, did I put mine in?" Val conducted a frantic search of her bag.

"I hope so, pet." Warren looked at Judith and shook his head. "We've already had to go back twice. I left my phone and then Val her hat."

"Got them!" Val waved a glasses case at them then slipped it back into her bag.

"Enjoy your day," Judith said and stepped into the aisle behind them.

The lounge car was empty but for one of the staff restocking a fridge. She was worried she might be the last and hurried along the corridor of the next carriage. She'd just passed the little kitchenette and had her hand out to open the door to the gangway leading to her carriage when movement to her left startled her.

"Erik," she gasped. "What are you doing?"

He looked just as surprised as her. His hands fell back from the outside exit door.

"You can't go out that way," Judith said. "They've opened a door further forward on the other side."

"I thought this might be easier."

"A million alarms would probably go off if you opened a door that wasn't meant to be." She smiled. "Everything's so secure and wrapped in red tape these days."

Erik smiled too but it didn't reach his eyes. "You're a very nice person, Judith. Thank you for taking the time to talk to me."

A little niggle of unease stirred inside her. "So are you. I hope you'll enjoy your time in Coober Pedy. Perhaps you'll see some old friends."

He gave a soft snort. "Perhaps." He shuffled a little to the left, revealing a small box at his feet. He bent to pick it up.

She took a step back.

"Are you still worrying over that box?" There he was, alone in their section of the train and all those unlocked doors. Perhaps Tien had been right about him after all.

"I told you. Sentimental stuff." He tipped his head sideways. "You may as well see. It will all be gone soon. Back to where it belongs." He gripped the bottom of the box with one hand

and slid the giant rubber band that wrapped around it to one side.

"You don't have to show me." Judith took another small shuffling step back.

He moved forward into a shaft of light from the little kitchen window and lifted the lid. The box looked like it was full of grey dirt but he ran his fingers through it and she realised the dirt was studded with opaque rocks, some of them with patches of colour.

"Years of my life in this box." He grinned. "Opals."

Judith blew out a breath. She'd been worried for a moment that perhaps he was lugging around his dead wife's ashes.

He poked his fingers into the box. "Some of it's not worth much but some of it, like this one—" He lifted a dirty white rock between his thumb and finger, licked it and held it towards her. Pink and green and blue flashed from a band in the middle of the rock. "Ten carats there, at about four hundred dollars a carat."

Judith gasped. Four thousand dollars for a rough-looking rock she would have ignored had she seen it.

"I have plenty more." Erik was rummaging again. "That's not the best one."

"That's a lot of money to be carrying around in a cardboard box," Judith said. "What are you doing with them, Erik?"

He stopped rummaging, looked up and frowned. "I've been trying to disperse them but..." He replaced the lid and shook his head. "I'm running out of opportunities."

"Opportunities?"

His eyes darted back and forth, and without his hat his hair stood out in every direction. He looked almost manic. He took a step forward and this time Judith took a bigger step back. She glanced along the corridor but it was empty.

"They'll be wondering where we are," she stammered. "The buses will be ready to leave."

There was a muffled clunk from the opposite direction and Erik glanced towards the joining door. Judith turned and broke into a fast walk back along the corridor.

"Judith!" he called after her. "Please don't…"

She didn't hesitate or look back as she pushed through the doors into the lounge. It was empty, no-one behind the bar either. She quickened her pace through the equally empty dining car. She was being silly but there'd been something about Erik that had felt menacing. By the time she burst through the door into the kitchen car she was almost running. The chef looked up from the pot he was scrubbing.

"Everything okay?" he asked.

"I was worried I might miss my bus." She steadied her pace.

"You'll be right. Too many forms to fill in if they leave someone behind." His loud chuckle followed her into the next carriage.

Outside Judith shielded her eyes from the bright glare of the full sun. "Damn." Erik's behaviour had been odd and she'd forgotten all about finding her sunglasses. In the distance a large plume of red dust followed the departure of a coach. She set off along the track towards the remaining buses. Up ahead there were other passengers walking that way and one of the stewards standing at another open door. Judith wondered if she should tell someone about Erik.

"Don't rush." The woman smiled as she approached. "They won't go without you."

Judith steadied her pace and moved on. What would she say? There's a man with a box of opals back on the train and he's acting strangely.

She berated herself for running away from Erik. Out there in the bright sunny day her response seemed ludicrous. He'd think she was crazy, but in that dark corner of the train, with just the two of them and him clutching that box, her mind had raced with fanciful ideas. Perhaps she'd been listening to Tien's stories too long.

thirty-nine

Day Three — Coober Pedy

Judith was able to relax once she heard the first stop on their tour was to be on the other side of Coober Pedy at a place called The Breakaways. Erik had said he was getting dropped off in the town so she didn't expect to see him out here. Not that she knew where 'here' was but they'd driven for over an hour since they left the train.

"Judith, over here. Photo."

The bus had pulled up on top of a large escarpment and Birgit and the other women were lined up on the edge with the amazing view behind them. Passengers wandered in every direction taking in the strange colourful rock formations erupting from the flat desert as far as the eye could see.

She joined the group, turned her back on the view and smiled as Birgit took another selfie.

"What about Miss Clift?" Tien said.

"She's too far away." Ning waved to a group of people standing further along the escarpment. "We can include her another time."

"One more." Birgit peered at her phone. "You had your eyes shut in that one, Judith, and you don't look happy."

Judith did her best to pull her lips up into a smile and keep her eyes open as Birgit snapped more photos.

"This landscape is totally freaky," Birgit said. "No wonder the film directors love it."

"It looks like someone's taken a giant paintbrush to it," Lacey exclaimed. "There's orange and tan and purple and maroon."

Birgit, Tien and Ning moved on to where their tour guide was explaining a different formation while Lacey was taking another photo of the landscape.

"How are your feet today?" Judith asked when she'd stepped back.

"Not too bad. What about you?"

"Fine. I've put a better layer of plasters on today."

"Tien has me so wrapped up my feet could end up mummified." They both looked down at her shoes.

"Judith, I wanted to say thank you."

"What for?"

"Your idea that I should rent out a room."

"Oh." Judith shrugged. "It just seemed obvious, but if you've never had to find rent yourself..." She still couldn't believe the good fortune of being Lacey's age and inheriting a house.

"I've mentioned it to Birgit and she's keen. We're going to look into how we should set it up when we get back...you know, make it official so there're no grey areas."

"That's very wise."

"I guess it gives us both some peace of mind, stability."

Judith hmphed. Thought of her own rental agreement. "As stable as renting can ever be, I suppose."

"You know I have a third bedroom…I just thought, if…well, you said something about your building being renovated and Dean having to move out. If you needed…"

Judith gaped at Lacey. Did she really think Judith would want to rent a room in her house?

"If you needed some temporary accommodation any time…" Once more Lacey's words petered out and she looked down at her feet again.

"Thank you, Lacey. That won't be necessary but it was kind of you to think of me." Judith had nowhere to go at this point but she was quite sure rooming with Lacey and Birgit was not in her future. She looked back at the view, desperate to change the subject. "I suppose this is what Ketty wants you to translate to the new collection."

"Us."

"Pfft! I'm just the organiser of materials and the assistant number cruncher."

"That's not true. Your translation of a design into a pattern is amazing. I wish I had your eye and your speed."

Judith studied Lacey's earnest face. It surprised her that she would admit such a thing.

"I can see the designs in my head," Lacey tapped her temple, "and sketch them but you and Ketty are the ones to bring them to fruition with a pattern. In fact, I've heard Ketty say she thinks you're better at it than she is."

Ketty had told Judith that many times over the years, more so in recent times when Judith had grumbled about the ready-made collection. It had been a lot of extra work. "I enjoy drafting patterns," Judith said. "It's straightforward."

"It takes me ages to do one sleeve let alone a whole blouse or dress."

Judith quirked her lips. "There has to be some advantage to years of practice."

"I wondered if a spin-off of Ketty's idea, that we work together more closely on this new collection, might be…" Lacey paused and gripped her hands in front of her. "Well…maybe…if we had time, that is…you might give me a few tips." Her cheeks glowed pink but she didn't look away from Judith's gaze. "Please…if you don't mind."

"I'm happy to show you any time," Judith blustered, although they both knew that probably wasn't true. "Let me take a photo of you with the colourful rock formation behind. It might be nice to have a picture of the creative in the environment for a future social media post."

Lacey looked at her strangely but stayed where she was as Judith backed away a little. Judith thought about the photo Erik had taken of her at the Alice Springs lookout. She'd been quite impressed by it. He'd seemed such a lost soul to begin with but then…on the carriage this morning clutching his box of opals he'd been acting strangely. Perhaps he was nervous about going back to the place that might have sad memories for him. She wondered how his revisit was going.

She turned her phone sideways and lined up Lacey in the corner of the shot. "That's great," Judith said. "Now perhaps one of you looking towards the view."

Lacey gave her another odd look but she complied. Judith snapped again.

The bus ride from The Breakaways to Coober Pedy didn't take long. Lacey studied what she could see of the town from her window. It was very different from anything she'd ever experienced. Somehow she felt far more isolated here than she had back at the train siding.

She glanced across the aisle at Judith, who wasn't looking out the window but at her phone. She was painstakingly typing something. It was odd. Lacey rarely saw Judith with her phone but she supposed even Judith Pettigrew had friends.

And that made Lacey think of Dean and the uncomfortable quizzing Judith had put her through, but the strangest part was when she'd told Lacey that Dean still liked her. That had played over and over in Lacey's head ever since but the stumbling block was always there – if Dean still liked her why didn't he get in touch? Lacey's head hurt from replaying her last date with Dean, from going over each little thing and still getting no answers to her questions.

The bus pulled into a large car park. Their second stop for the day was in the main street at a museum and opal mine display. They climbed down in front of a building facade abutting a hill. Inside was both a surprise and a relief. The museum was a series of wide tunnels and the air temperature a pleasant twenty degrees. According to their guide, even when the outside temperature climbed to over forty in the summer it was still cool underground. Lacey enjoyed the information about mining and the museum but when they reached the dugout house she was intrigued.

She stood in the middle of the bedroom and turned a slow three-sixty. "How good would it be to live here?" she exclaimed to Birgit as she took in the walls cut from rock, the shelves made simply by digging notches into the wall and the patterns and colours accentuated by the glow of a lamp. "You wouldn't need to worry about leaky roofs, paint peeling off walls, electricity to warm or cool it."

"Might be a bit of a long commute though," Birgit said.

"And just imagine the creatures that could get in here." Tien was right behind them and was on high alert, her eyes darting back and forth over every surface as they walked.

"I'm sure we're safe in here, Tien," Judith reassured her, and as the others moved on she said, "Let me get your photo by that lamp, Lacey. The colours it throws on the wall are lovely."

Lacey paused as Judith took another photo. She'd taken several with just Lacey in them, citing her interest in the colour or texture each time. She'd certainly changed her tune when it came to Ketty's idea for them to work together on a new collection.

At the end of the tour there was a shop, of course. Most people gravitated to the opals on display. Lacey drifted along, looking at the glass cases filled with opal jewellery, all beyond her price range. She wandered away to make more space for those actually wanting to purchase something and ended up in front of a large painting. It was a magnificent image with the colours of the landscape replicated well. Once more Lacey found herself dreaming about fabrics and styles.

"It's an amazing piece of art, isn't it?" Carlos said.

She glanced his way as he studied the painting. "The colours are perfect."

"I wonder if you might help me, Lacey." He turned to her, the power of his magnetic gaze hard to look away from.

"If I can."

"I've picked out a small gift for Ketty but I'd like it to be a surprise. I wonder if you'd buy it for me?"

"Oh, I don't..." Lacey's cheeks began to heat.

"The lady behind the counter with the red bandana has put it aside but Ketty will see me if I buy it. She's coming this way now."

Lacey looked down as he pushed something into her hand. She felt the crunch of the paper and saw the corner of a fifty-dollar note.

"I knew you'd like this painting," Ketty said as she joined them.

Lacey curled her hand around the money and looked back at the large canvas hoping Ketty wouldn't see the shock on her face.

"Lacey was just saying how perfect the colours were," Carlos said.

They discussed the painting for a while then made small talk about the tour. Lacey told herself she was imagining Ketty's piercing looks, which made the cash feel as if it was burning a hole in her hand. Finally she managed to edge away.

The woman Carlos had described was at the other end of the counter. Lacey quietly explained what she was after and the woman took a small gift-wrapped package from a shelf behind.

"All ready to go." She smiled. "The bloke said you'd have the money."

Lacey lifted her hand and as she uncurled her fingers she was surprised to see there were several notes.

"Two hundred dollars," the woman said and took the money from Lacey's outstretched hand. "Correct, thank you."

Lacey glanced around. Neither Carlos nor Ketty were in sight. She slipped the small parcel into her bag.

Birgit came up to the counter. "Did you buy yourself something?"

"Oh n—"

Birgit threw an arm around her shoulders. "Good on you for spoiling yourself at last. Now come on. Our tour leader has just said we're off to lunch next. Can you believe we're going to eat in a mine underground?"

Lacey let herself be led away, guessing there'd be an opportunity somewhere later to give Carlos his purchase.

The heat outside was intense after the pleasant cool of the underground facility. Judith blinked in the sunlight then moved to a small patch of garden that offered a seat in the scarce shade. She'd bought a pair of cheap sunglasses at the souvenir shop. They weren't great but helped with the glare. She glanced around but no-one was paying her any attention. She took out her phone. She'd become one of those people – checking it every few minutes.

On the trip from The Breakaways into town she'd spent her time carefully composing a text and selecting suitable photos, and once there'd been signal she'd pressed send. She'd been on tenterhooks ever since, wondering if she'd get any response. Dean would be at work so she wasn't sure when he'd check his phone. She'd never messaged him during work hours before, had never had the need.

She sighed. Her phone was stubbornly devoid of any recent texts. She checked again that it was on silent and slipped it into the pocket of her pants.

Beyond the bus she caught sight of Ning. She had her phone to her ear and appeared to be speaking excitedly. That family of hers hardly left her alone for a minute.

"This heat is certainly different to the tropics, isn't it?"

Judith moved along the seat as another couple from the tour joined her seeking the shade.

"Very dry," she said. "Like being in an oven. I hope we don't have to wait too much longer to get back on the coach."

The driver walked out of the museum as she spoke.

"Thank goodness," the woman said, fanning her face with a pamphlet.

They moved towards the bus and Judith paused at the sound of a siren. Coober Pedy had seemed almost sleepy. It wasn't a sound she'd expected. The sirens got louder and their tour group watched as a police car sped by, followed by a rescue truck and then an ambulance.

There were worried faces and concerned comments but the bus driver remained upbeat.

"Accidents happen from time to time in a mining community but we've got a good rescue team." As the sirens faded into the distance he encouraged everyone to climb aboard. "Don't want to be late for lunch," he said.

Ketty waited in the shade of the small verandah outside the entrance to the wildlife sanctuary. Their group had enjoyed another delicious lunch, this time in a tunnel that had once been part of an opal mine. She'd struck up a conversation with Belinda, who'd been serving their drinks. Belinda loved native animals and that had led Ketty to revealing Tien's wish to see a real kangaroo. Belinda had mentioned the possibility of visiting some kangaroos recuperating at the local native animal orphanage. Then, after lunch while the rest of the tour group were visiting an underground church, she'd directed Ketty, Ning and Tien across the road for a quick visit to the kangaroos.

There were two joeys in special man-made pouches and three kangaroos recuperating from various injuries, along with some birds and a goanna, most to do with being hit by vehicles. Ketty suggested to Ning they not mention the goanna to Tien who thankfully was totally distracted by the kangaroos.

She was overjoyed to the point of being speechless as she held a joey in her arms. Ning and Ketty looked on like a pair of doting aunts. But the facility was small and once she'd had a quick look and taken several photos for Tien, Ketty had opted to wait outside for the other two.

It was quiet and she relished some time to herself. On the surface things seemed to be better between her staff – perhaps Birgit's bad experience had been the catalyst to bring them together so there was a silver lining. And today at The Breakaways she'd noticed Judith and Lacey together, taking photos and appearing to be in conversation. She hoped it was a positive step and also that Ning would find the courage to talk to her family about continuing to work.

All hopeful signs for Ketty Clift Couture but that had highlighted something else. Judith had been right. Ketty had been missing in action quite a lot in the past few months. It was lots of small things, such as not meeting regularly to listen to her staff, heading off at short notice for long weekends with Carlos, handing some of her longstanding customers over to Lacey for the initial consult or to Judith for the final fit, not writing the personal notes for the eboutique orders and many more little things, but combined they'd meant her presence, her influence, the details that she added, the very essence that was the core of Ketty Clift Couture had been undermined.

And added to that Ketty wondered if Judith had been right about something else. What to do about Carlos was weighing heavily on her mind and, if she was honest, her heart.

Since Judith's accusations about him Ketty had been taking more notice and there were small things that didn't add up. Ketty had pushed them away but in the dark hours of this morning, in a patch of wakefulness, the seeds of doubt Judith had planted had appeared again. And today, after Ketty had seen Carlos press something into Lacey's hand then he'd denied it, the seeds had germinated.

She'd waited for Lacey to move away from the painting they'd all been studiously taking in at the opal shop, then Ketty had asked Carlos what he'd given her. From the distance it had looked like a bank note. Lacey had money troubles and Ketty had thought perhaps kind-hearted Carlos had got wind of it and loaned her some. Lacey was very independent and wouldn't accept it when Ketty offered but he'd looked insistent and Lacey startled, perhaps a little desperate. When Ketty had asked, he'd flatly denied giving Lacey anything, let alone money. If he could lie to her face about that, what else was he lying about?

And it was then Ketty had finally realised there could be some truth in Judith's fears. Ketty had scratched around trying to remember what Judith had thought she'd overheard, a plea about keeping something from Ketty and not wanting to frighten her off.

After Carlos's lie today, Ketty wondered about other things. She hadn't questioned any of them at the time. There was the other day when he was talking to Felix. He'd denied it was her friend he'd been talking to but Felix had texted asking her to pass his number on. Now she wondered how many Felixes he knew in Sydney and what it had been about. He'd said not about his visa, but if it had been why would he not simply tell her? He'd been strange about it once before.

It was when he'd come back to stay after she'd broken her wrist. She'd woken from an afternoon nap to find Carlos at her kitchen table, papers spread everywhere. He'd been quick to pack them up but not before she'd seen it was something to do with a visa. He'd deflected her questions that time too. He'd opened a rather nice bottle of wine, she recalled, an expensive one from her special stash. It wasn't true when Judith had suggested he was living off her. He'd given her the very generous travel voucher and he'd paid his own way when he'd stayed with her, but if Ketty looked harder there was probably an imbalance. She'd opened her home and her wallet without question.

Ketty had always had her own small doubts. How well did she really know Carlos when they'd not spent a lot of time together – but she'd always countered that with the ease with which their friendship resumed when they did meet up. It had always been like that but in the past Carlos had been working. Now he was retired and he no longer had strong family ties in Spain, and yet he'd been vague about what he saw for his future. In truth it was none of Ketty's business what he did with his life but since he'd retired and spent time with her in Australia she was curious. She'd joked about Judith asking his intentions but maybe it wasn't such a silly thing to do.

A distant siren drew her attention back to the street. Across the road people were coming out of the church so she assumed it was time to call Ning and Tien and join them. The siren grew louder and, as the other two women came out of the wildlife refuge, another police car raced along the street with siren and lights flashing. Coober Pedy was giving Paddington a run for its money in the siren stakes today.

forty

Day Three – Manguri Siding

Except that Judith had heard nothing from Dean, she'd enjoyed her day out and now she paused to take in the perfect evening. The bus had brought them back to the train and when they'd disembarked, instead of returning to their carriage they'd been greeted by stewards with trays of drinks and canapés. The sun was low in the sky and the heat of the day was ebbing with it. Fires crackled in strategically placed firepits and passengers stood nearby or grouped around picnic tables at bench seats, talking about their day.

Judith made her way to one of the tables where Ketty was seated with the woman she'd had breakfast with. They were alone and Ketty glanced up as Judith approached.

"Virginia, this is my friend and right hand in the business, Judith." Ketty smiled and Judith felt warmed both by her words and their sincerity. It was as if the old Ketty was back, the pre-Carlos Ketty.

Judith said hello then tilted her head to listen. Surely that wasn't a siren again, not way out there. Another bus rolled slowly into the parking area, its idling motor temporarily masking other sounds.

"Isn't this magnificent." Ketty waved her arm towards the setting sun.

"I suppose it has a kind of simple charm." Virginia quirked an eyebrow.

Beau slipped onto the bench beside her and gave her a gentle nudge. "Come on, Mum. This trip has been pretty amazing."

She sighed. "I suppose it has. And the bonus has been meeting Ketty again."

"A bonus for me too," Ketty said. "Oh, there's Erik Visser. I wonder how he enjoyed his visit to his old home town."

"Is that a siren?" Virginia said and they all listened.

"It is," Ketty said. "I hope no-one's unwell."

"So much for the ambience," Virginia snorted.

Beau stood. "I wonder what's going on?"

Other passengers had heard the siren too. People were looking towards the track the buses had traversed. Jovial conversation slowed and became low murmurs as a large plume of red dust with blue-and-red flashing lights at its base moved steadily closer across the flat plain.

From the corner of her eye Judith noticed movement. Erik was skirting the edge of the crowd, slipping off towards the train. The sip of wine she'd taken soured in her stomach.

The police car braked to a stop in the parking area and cut its siren, the sudden silence revealing another siren in the distance. Thankfully there was a slight breeze that carried the plume of red dirt created by its hasty arrival away from the passengers.

Matt spoke to the police while other crew members tried to distract people with more drinks and food.

Judith noticed Erik had reached the side of the train now. He glanced back, then moved quickly along the track past the carriages.

"If I could have your attention, everyone," Matt called and the crowd was instantly silent. He and the police constables moved closer to Judith's group and Matt climbed onto the end of the bench seat. "The police would like to speak with Erik Visser."

Judith felt as if her heart had stilled while around her there was an instant buzz of conversation. People looked around.

"If you know Mr Visser, can you let us know if you've seen him since you arrived back?"

"He just got off the bus," Ketty said.

"Where is he now?" the policewoman asked.

Ketty shook her head and turned to Judith. "Did you see where he went?"

Judith felt the full force of every pair of nearby eyes on her. "To the train."

Heads turned that way, including Judith's. The silver carriages stretched out along the track, reflecting the sun's golden rays, but of Erik Visser there was no sign.

Things happened quickly after that. The second police vehicle, a van with more police, arrived. Ketty gave them Erik's carriage and cabin number and Matt took another crew member and led the way. The remaining staff and passengers were asked to stay where they were.

"I wonder what on earth has happened?" Ketty said as the rest of her ladies came to join them.

"It's just like a TV show," Tien said excitedly. "I told you there was something odd about that man. And he's got a big head start on the police."

"It's a train parked in the middle of a desert," Virginia said. "Where's he going to go?"

"All those empty carriages and unlocked cabin doors," Tien said.

"If I'm staying out here I need another drink," Birgit said. "Anyone else?"

"Definitely," Beau said and hailed a passing steward with a loaded tray. Soon everyone had a drink, whether they wanted one or not.

A police radio crackled and the remaining policemen got back in the van and drove it slowly towards the end of the train.

"I wonder why they want him?" Ning said, and for some reason they all looked at Judith.

"I don't know," she said. "I haven't seen him since this morning."

"It's something to do with that box." Tien nodded emphatically.

"It was full of opals." Judith spoke quietly but she instantly had the attention of her group. She stared into her glass. "He said something about taking it back where it belonged but running out of opportunities."

"He stole the opal!" Tien said.

Judith faced the surprised or questioning looks from those around the table. Only Ketty's gaze was gentle, soft like an enveloping blanket.

"I got the feeling they were his opals but I really don't understand any of it."

"Poor Erik. I hope he's okay." Lacey's voice was only a notch louder than Judith's, her face creased in concern.

Lacey had liked Erik too.

"I think they've found him." Birgit nodded towards the end of the train where a man was being escorted to the waiting police van. Matt and the policewoman were making their way back towards the passengers.

They stopped when they reached a high point close by and the policewoman asked for anyone who'd had interaction with Erik Visser on the train to stay and make a statement to police. "No-one panic." She chuckled. "I have it on good authority the train's not leaving without you. We just want to hear from anyone who may have noticed anything or spoken with Mr Visser."

Matt said everyone else was free to return to their carriages. Not many people stayed – a couple who'd been on the return bus trip with Erik, and those from his section of the train who'd spoken with him. Turned out the only one who'd spent more than a few moments with him was Judith. By the time she'd finished speaking with the police it was almost dark. Everyone else had been asked to board the train and it was Matt who walked her back to her carriage. She felt so very sorry for Erik. He would have difficult times ahead.

Matt kept apologising that she'd been caught up in it all but she'd reassured him she was fine and that it was nobody's fault. A few people gave her an inquisitive look as she passed through the lounge car but none of her group were there. She assumed they'd all be getting ready for dinner. Judith was desperate for a shower. Her towel and toiletries were in Birgit's single cabin but she'd have to stop in at her own cabin for fresh clothes. She was almost to the door when it opened and Tien's head poked out.

"At last!" Tien beckoned her wildly. "We're all waiting."

"Who?" Judith frowned but Tien had shot back into the cabin. She followed but was barely able to squeeze past the door. Ketty, Ning and now Tien were seated along the couch and Birgit and Lacey sat on the floor.

Tien began as soon as Judith managed to shut the door behind her. "I told you that man was stra—"

Ketty held a hand up. "We don't mean to overwhelm you, Judith." Ketty was obviously the spokesperson. "But we're all desperate to know what happened with poor Erik."

Judith looked at each expectant face. She was surprised Carlos wasn't there but then he wouldn't have fitted anyway.

"Sit down." Ketty patted the couch beside her and Ning and Tien shuffled up to make more room.

"It's all rather sad." Judith suddenly felt heavy, as if her body had weights in it. She sagged into the narrow space. "When I spoke with Erik we mostly talked about wherever we were at the time and what was happening there. Nothing very personal. All I really knew about him was he used to mine for opals at Coober Pedy, that he was a widower, or at least I thought he was, and he'd moved away in recent years. Then this morning he did seem a bit…" Judith recalled the way he'd behaved. "Erratic. He wanted to show me his opals. That's what was in the box."

"Stolen opals!" Tien said.

"Not exactly. They were his and his ex-wife's."

"His dead wife," Ketty said.

Judith shook her head. "Evidently she's very much alive. They worked their claim for years. Had mild success but I gather it's not an easy life and a few years back they took on a partner. Long story short, the wife had an affair with the partner. Erik walked out and took the opals that they hadn't cashed in as his share of past and future earnings. Recently the wife filed for divorce and wanted half of whatever he had left." Judith eased back against the couch. "Poor Erik became very bitter. He told her she could have them if she could find them."

"I don't get it," Birgit said. "Why bring the boxful here if he didn't want her to have them?"

"Did they find the box?" Tien glanced around as if it might suddenly appear in their cabin.

"It's not on the train any more," Judith said. "The police told me he sent his wife a map with the rail between Darwin and Coober Pedy highlighted. She knew he was coming – but not that the highlighted map meant he'd planned to scatter the opals along the way."

There was a collective gasp.

"Of course he soon realised he couldn't open any windows or doors when the train was moving."

"And the box was in my cabin for the first two stops," Ketty said.

"Yes." Judith nodded. "When I came across him this morning he'd been trying to open one of the doors on the opposite side of the train. He'd planned to scatter the opal out there." Judith waved a hand. "When he couldn't do that he took the box with him to Coober Pedy and decided to tip them in a few of his old mates' mines. He didn't have a car, of course, and someone saw him and told his ex. She and the partner caught up with him as he was about to scatter some of the opal. There was a tussle and the partner lost his footing and slipped feet first into the mine."

Once more the air around her was filled with gasps.

"Is he all right?" Lacey asked.

"Luckily something disrupted his fall but he did break some bones. That was what all those sirens were about today."

A voice came over the intercom thanking everyone for their patience and letting them know dinner service would begin soon.

"What will happen to him?" Lacey asked.

Judith shook her head. "I really don't know."

"We should get ready for dinner." Ketty rose to her feet. "Will you be all right, Judith?"

"Yes. It's all been a bit of a shock. I've never had to make a police statement before. I felt a little as if I was telling on a friend."

Ning put a gentle hand on Judith's shoulder. "You were only telling the truth."

"Poor Erik," Ketty said. "He truly was a little out of his mind to think up such a plan."

"I told you," Tien said emphatically.

"We're moving again." Birgit's legs were stretched out in front of her and her hands were pressed to the floor.

"With one less passenger," Ketty said sadly.

"I wish I'd realised what he was planning," Judith said. "Perhaps I could have dissuaded him and these terrible events wouldn't have happened."

"And it may not have made any difference. Some people can't or won't change the choices they make." Ketty opened the door. "See you at dinner."

Judith gathered her things, Ketty's words ringing in her ears.

forty-one

Night Three — Travelling South

Ketty was seated in the lounge car between Val and Warren on one side and Virginia and Beau on the other. Carlos had arrived before her, having got himself ready while she'd been in the other cabin with Judith. Erik Visser was the hot topic in the lounge car, of course, and if Ketty hadn't heard his story from Judith she might have been swayed by the kingpin-of-a-drug-trade version or her personal favourite, that he was an overseas spy reporting on the viability of our rail network. Warren had told her he'd heard that story at the bar earlier and she'd found it rather amusing.

Ketty had filled them all in with a short version of the truth.

"He was a thief after all. Just not in the way we imagined," Carlos said.

"Just as well we're all normal." Virginia waved her glass around. "Some people have rather fucked-up lives, don't they!"

Beau shook his head and Val pursed her lips but Warren let out a loud guffaw. "I'll drink to that."

"Cheers." Virginia leaned past Ketty and tapped her glass against his.

Personally, Ketty thought Virginia and Warren had probably had quite a few drinks already but she wasn't one to judge. She took a sip of the gin and tonic Carlos had ordered for her. He'd drawn up a seat beside Beau and they were chatting. She studied Carlos, trying to imagine what someone who didn't know him would see. A tall, handsome man; educated, well-mannered, charming. What are you hiding behind that debonair facade, Carlos? He glanced her way, perhaps aware she'd been staring, and shifted his chair a little closer.

"I know you said you wanted dinner with me but I'll let you have dinner with your staff tonight without me cluttering up your table," he said. "I'm going to join Virginia and Beau."

She opened her mouth to protest but he put up a hand. "You can all talk business without me tonight, but I have a stipulation. I've booked us for breakfast tomorrow morning, just the two of us. So we can talk alone."

Small needles of apprehension prickled inside her. It would soon enough be just the two of them again and while she'd previously been looking forward to it, she felt uneasy now. "I've been rethinking our Adelaide stay." They'd not had a chance to talk since she'd checked her booking online at Coober Pedy. "I hadn't thought about how expensive it would be to change our flights so—"

"I'm glad you brought it up. It was one of the things I wanted to mention in the morning. Let's stick to our original plan and..." The smallest flicker of doubt crossed his face. "Perhaps we can visit South Australia again another time."

"It's my shout for drinks," Beau said. "Can I get anyone anything?"

"Another champagne," Virginia said and Beau was soon swamped with orders.

"I'll help." Carlos followed him to the bar and Ketty felt a little sad. She'd expected him to object, to say he'd organise their stay in South Australia, but he'd given in and it seemed he'd been going to suggest it anyway.

"That's a glum face, Ketty," Warren said. "You're usually the life of the party."

Ketty lifted her shoulders and put on a smile. "I'm a little sorry it's our last night, that's all. I feel as if we're only just getting to know each other." *And that I know Carlos less and less.*

"We should swap emails," Val said.

"Now that I know where you are, we'll have to call on one another." Virginia's glass wavered in the air again. "My apartment's at Coogee. It's not that far from Paddington. We can see the ocean from the balcony and we're walking distance from some great eateries." Virginia's face soured and she tapped the stick that lay on the floor with her foot. "Were in walking distance."

"You've been doing very well these last few days," Ketty said.

Warren raised his glass. "You'll be running around the block in no time."

"Oh, look, here come the rest of your crew," Val said.

Ketty smiled as the ladies from Ketty Clift Couture entered the lounge car. They all looked so happy. Tien had barely stopped smiling since she'd been to the wildlife centre and Ketty wasn't sure if it was the bright lipstick she was wearing but even Judith had an extra lift in her step. All five had changed for dinner, each dressed in their own distinctive style. They waved as they went on to the bar.

"You've all done so well dressing up each night, haven't they, Warren? I like that dress Ning is wearing. I'd have loved something like that for the wedding we've got coming up but I'm getting too old to wear that kind of thing."

"In the words of a very wise woman, what's age got to do with it?" Virginia huffed and turned her attention to Beau and Carlos.

"The girls wanted to take you shopping," Warren said.

"I've got that outfit I wore to last night's dinner. That'll do."

Ketty smiled at Val. "My whole life has been about making women feel good about what they wear. You looked lovely in that last night."

"That's kind of you."

"But if you'd like to wear a dress for a change, why not wear one? I cannot bear to hear a woman say she'll ignore a great outfit because she thinks she's too old to wear the style or the colour. If you like it and you're comfortable, go for it, I say."

"Ketty knows what she's talking about, pet. I'll be wearing my suit. We might be old but we're not dead."

Ketty pursed her lips and glanced around. No-one else was part of their conversation. "You can tell me to mind my business but I wondered if you'd discussed the problem with your son."

Val glanced from Warren to her hands clasped in her lap.

He blew out a breath. "We're going to think on it more, tackle it together."

Val smiled and took his hand in hers. "We'll sort it out."

"Might I suggest something?"

Warren grinned. "You're a trick, Ketty, you know that. Sure, suggest away."

"You might like to think about your language. Your son could be picking his cues from what you're saying."

"Warren never swears," Val said indignantly.

"Oh, no, I didn't mean that – it's other things," Ketty said quickly. "The other day you said you were getting too old to look after your grandchildren, Warren, but is that what you really meant?"

"I suppose it was more that I'd rather be on the golf course."
Warren screwed up his face. "But I can't exactly tell them that."

"You could say you're already booked for that time. It has nothing to do with your age, really, does it? And perhaps you could only accept a gang of little ones when you're free as well, Val. Do it together."

"We do."

Warren raised his eyebrows and Val gave a tight guilty smile.

"And when you forget something, why is that having a seniors moment?" Ketty thought she may as well continue. "People of any age forget or make mistakes. Just admit it and move on."

Warren and Val looked at each other then both shifted in their seats.

"I know I'm making it sound as if it's all easy and in black and white," Ketty said. "It's not that simple, but after a few bad experiences where someone's comments have diminished my self-esteem I've given it a lot of thought. Our age shouldn't determine what we do and how we live."

"I don't think we do that, do we, Warren? We both get out and about and do all sorts."

"It's more what you say than what you do or don't do. If you say you're too old to do something, or wear something," Ketty looked pointedly at Val, "that puts the idea into other people's heads that perhaps you are."

Warren frowned. "It's certainly food for thought, isn't it, pet?"

"It is."

"And speaking about age." Warren lowered his voice and leaned closer. "See that chap that's just come in."

Ketty glanced over at the man who'd just entered. "I've seen him a few times but I haven't spoken to him. He doesn't change for dinner but he puts on a very nice tie each evening."

"I had a chat to him during the tour today. He's ninety-five."
Warren paused, his eyes wide, his mouth open in an exaggerated
gape. "I couldn't believe he was that old. He looks amazing for
that age."

Val met Ketty's gaze and smiled. "It's our time for dinner,
Warren," she said.

Virginia, who'd tuned back into their conversation, leaned
closer. "You win some, you lose some."

Ketty was pleased their final dinner on the train was turning out
rather well. They'd been seated at the two very end tables so there
was no-one behind them and, apart from the staff coming past
with food, they could almost be one table. After entree they'd
rotated seats and now it was Ketty and Ning who sat at the second
table on the aisle.

At the other table Tien was explaining about her trip to visit
the kangaroos in great detail.

"I'm glad we've got a minute together," Ning said. "I have
something to tell you."

Ketty adjusted her water glass and waited, hopeful for good
news.

"Henry rang me today while we were in Coober Pedy. I nearly
didn't answer." She sighed. "But I couldn't ignore his call."

"Has something happened at home?"

"Yes." Ning's eyes sparkled. "He has been offered a post-
graduate position and he's very pleased. We all are."

"Your sons are both very talented."

"They study hard but that's only part of the good news." Ning
leaned in. "It's at Melbourne University. He's going to move out."

"Oh."

"Well, that's not good news. I will miss him but I am very happy he has this opportunity. The good news is there will be an extra room for the baby."

"I'm glad you won't have to give up your sewing room, Ning."

"Henry was too." Ning nodded emphatically. "I don't think he was as set on the idea as Peter was. So...after I finished talking with Henry I rang Peter. And I told him I wasn't ready to retire and that when I came home we would discuss how I could help them with childcare and still continue to work." Ning grimaced. "Then I ended the call and turned off my phone."

She clapped a hand over her mouth and Ketty laughed. "Well done."

"What's happening over there?" Birgit asked and Ketty let Ning explain.

"I still plan to look for an extra seamstress," Ketty said once everyone had shown relief that Ning wasn't leaving. "If we continue with our ready-made collections we'll need at least one more person, if not two." Ketty looked from Judith to Lacey, seated side by side opposite her. "I know we said we'd talk about it once I got back but perhaps we could tell everyone what we've discussed so far."

Their mains arrived. Between mouthfuls, the plan for the new collection was discussed and as soon as Lacey finished eating she dashed back to her cabin to retrieve her sketchbook. They all swapped places again and this time Ketty was seated with her back to the wall, facing the length of the dining car. Carlos was several tables in front of her and Virginia was the life of the party at that table. Ketty swallowed the sour taste of jealousy. She had no rights over Carlos – they were simply friends who lived their own lives, but she'd grown used to his more regular visits in her life over the past five months. Now there was a shadow over their easy relationship and it bothered her.

In truth she was pleased he wasn't at her table tonight. He'd been right when he'd said it would be easier for the women to talk, not just business but about their day and more personal things that had included a long rant from Birgit about swearing off men. To herself, Ketty gave it a week, maybe two. Birgit was far too social and fond of the male sex to be alone for long. Ketty hoped that wouldn't put a strain on Lacey and Birgit moving in together.

Lacey returned with her sketchbook and shared her ideas.

"Judith and I took lots of photos today. The colours at The Breakaways were very inspiring."

"Why does the model in this one have a walking stick?" Tien tapped one of Lacey's sketches.

"I don't know, really," Lacey said. "But I think I may have been imagining Virginia when I designed that coat. And I was trying to make it inclusive."

Judith's head snapped up and she eyed Lacey closely. Ketty wondered what that was about but Lacey's sketch had sparked another idea for her too.

"We've never made coats before," Ning said.

"I'm imagining a lightweight shower-proof fabric for this." Lacey glanced up, a new determination on her face. "I still need to talk it over with Ketty and Judith. These are just ideas."

"We haven't started sewing the new spring/summer collection yet," Tien complained.

"But you know how far ahead we plan," Ketty said. "Which brings me to something else I'd like to discuss." They all looked at her expectantly.

"Oh no, Miss Clift." Tien shook her head frantically. "You're not re—"

"No." Ketty cut her off a little sharply. "Once and for all I want to say I am not retiring, I'm not selling." She looked at each of her ladies in turn then her gaze rested on Judith. "Although I've realised that I haven't been as involved with the business in recent months as I should have been and for that I apologise."

"You need to slow down some, Miss Clift," Tien placated. "You're getting ol—"

"Tien," Ketty snapped. "If you mention me getting older one more time, I'm dismissing you on the spot!"

A chorus of gasps surrounded her.

Tien pressed her fingers to her lips.

"Look at your faces." Ketty laughed. "Tien, you know I'd never let you go but please stop worrying about me." She drew each word out to emphasise her point. "Each one of us is getting older."

"Amen to that." Birgit raised her glass in the air.

"We all have ups and downs but that's life," Ketty said. "Your concern has made me ponder though. And then the other day Warren mentioned a succession plan and it made me think I should have one. So that you can all feel safe in your employment and," she looked at Tien, "if I suddenly fall off the perch there's a strategy in place."

Tien gasped.

"In short it's about creating proper job descriptions for each of your roles. We've all managed in the past. I know you all know what you're doing but our business has grown and changed. I think it would work better if you had a written plan of the part you play in making sure Ketty Clift Couture continues to flourish. And I want to make you a promise that I will go back to our regular individual meetings. I most certainly liked the opportunity to discuss how things were going and I feel you did too."

There were murmurs of agreement.

"Good." Ketty nodded. "That means next week I plan to go over the bookwork, crunch some figures, make some schedules and proposals and come back to you all with more detail."

"You're not staying on in Adelaide?" Judith asked.

"That didn't work out and this is more important."

"You're not missing your friends' wedding?" Ning said.

"No. Carlos and I will still go to Celia and Jim's celebration. That's been long planned but we had thought we'd stay on some extra days after that. I've...we've postponed that for now."

"I think I speak for everyone here when I say how lucky we are to be part of Ketty Clift Couture." Birgit glanced around and everyone nodded. "So I think it's time for more champagne."

Simon appeared as swiftly as a genie from a bottle and soon everyone's drink orders were filled. Ketty proposed a toast to their future with resounding cheers that drew looks from the remaining diners.

Belinda delivered their desserts and they talked on, drank some more toasts and eventually left the dining car when every other table had been stripped and Simon had asked ever so politely if they'd move on to the lounge car. They had another drink there, then made their way to their cabins. The sleeping arrangements from the previous night were maintained, and after many whispered goodnights finally Ketty slipped into her cabin. She leaned against the door holding on to the excitement that fizzed inside her. It wasn't just the champagne – although she'd had a few, she'd swapped to water several glasses ago. It was the resurgence of joy she felt that perhaps this train journey had worked and that her ladies and Ketty Clift Couture were back on track.

She peered at the shape on the bottom bunk. Carlos was snoring very softly. Once more when she'd returned to their cabin, he was asleep. Last night she'd been disappointed because she'd hurried him off and they hadn't had the promised drink together, tonight she was disappointed because she was still buzzing from the wonderful evening she'd just had with her staff. On a high, she'd thought she'd pin him down. He couldn't evade her questions if it was just the two of them alone in the cabin.

She listened to his deep breathing, envious of his ability to slumber so soundly. Ketty was far from sleep.

forty-two

Night Three – Travelling South

"Who is it?" Judith hissed sharply in response to Ketty's subtle knock.

"Ketty," she whispered back.

Ketty glanced up and back along the corridor but there in the single-cabin carriage, the curving waves made it hard to see if anyone was coming.

The door opened. Judith hadn't changed out of her dinner clothes either.

"What are you doing here?"

"I'm not ready for sleep. I hoped you might feel like a night-cap." Ketty lifted the two glasses of scotch she'd managed to keep from spilling as she'd travelled all the way from the lounge car.

"Come in."

Ketty stepped into the narrow space between door and bed, handed over a glass and Judith shut the door behind her.

"I wasn't sleepy either and my book is back in my cabin. I've re-read all the brochures they gave us."

They tapped their glasses and sipped.

Judith coughed and patted her lips. She blinked. "I don't drink this often, only when I'm with you."

"I lead you astray."

"Hardly." Judith's smile was warm like Ketty's throat from the scotch.

Judith sat on the bed and Ketty did the same. They swayed with the movement of the train and below their feet the floor vibrated. She looked around the tiny cabin, recalling Birgit's excitement over it on the first day.

"I'm not quite ready for this journey to end," she said.

"Thank you for organising it. I must say I was a sceptic but on the whole I've enjoyed it."

"You're not too bothered by what happened with Erik?"

Judith shook her head. "I'm sorry for him, that's all. It was odd but in the little bit of time I spent with Erik I kept being reminded of Klaus."

"Good grief. I hope not. Klaus wouldn't do anything so vindictive or silly as Erik."

"It was partly his accent. Dutch and German sound similar to me. But also when I first met Erik he was..." Judith screwed up her nose as she thought about it. "Kind and interesting. It was a shame he got so bitter about his wife, although I can relate to it. I think underneath he was a nice man. I hope he won't be in too much trouble."

"So do I." Of more significance to Ketty was that Judith might be interested in Klaus after all. She'd thought all along they were well suited. "Klaus often asks after you."

Judith drew in a breath. "I don't like to be pushed towards something. Anyway, my ex was enough for me to know I don't want to go down that path again."

"Good heavens, I'm not saying you should marry Klaus."

"Good."

"I'm talking about friendship, someone who you might have similar interests with. Of course there's no saying where that might lead."

"I'm too old for—"

Ketty groaned. "Don't you start with the 'too old' business. I'm surrounded by it." She took a slug of her drink this time, gripping the glass tightly. "Who wrote the rule there's a cut-off age for enjoying life? You're never too old for friendship, companionship, even love."

Judith pursed her lips. "I'm not interested in looking for marriage."

"Fine. Neither am I."

"You and Carlos seem very close."

Ketty inspected the small piece of ice melting in the bottom of her glass then met Judith's gaze. "Carlos and I are good friends."

Judith looked as if she wanted to say something but Ketty wasn't ready for another discussion about Carlos when she had so many questions of her own.

"There's nothing more to it than that," she said emphatically.

They took another sip of their drinks. The train rattled and wiggled its way south, their bodies jostling slightly with the motion. There was an urgency about it, as if it was hurrying their holiday away. Ketty didn't like being rushed.

"I want to thank you, Judith."

"What for?"

"For your many hours of devotion to Ketty Clift Couture over the years…and to me. You were right. I had lost my way a little recently and I'm sorry that's also meant we've not talked as much as we used to."

Judith tugged at the collar of her shirt.

Ketty took a breath. "I've some ideas for making amends—"

"There's no need."

"What do you think about the job description idea? You didn't say much when I mentioned it earlier."

"It would probably be useful."

"Particularly if we employ another seamstress."

"Perhaps."

"Lacey especially would benefit from a formalised career progression. Her job has evolved and changed in the seven years she's been with us."

"She's certainly got a good eye for design."

Ketty swallowed the little speech she'd prepared to defend Lacey's work. "Did you discuss my idea?"

"A little. To tell the truth, I used it as an opportunity to quiz her about her relationship with Dean."

"I thought it was over."

"I don't think she wanted it to be, and now that I've spoken with her and thought about the way Dean's been acting I don't think he does either." Judith studied her glass a moment. "I feel a little guilty about it," she murmured.

"Why?"

"When Dean mentioned he'd broken it off with Lacey I felt...I felt glad. And instead of letting it go I...well, I said a few disparaging things about Lacey."

"I see."

"I know now I shouldn't have. Dean can easily believe he's not worthy of someone's interest and I didn't help the situation. Trouble is I didn't know what to do about it."

Ketty's jaw dropped. "I can't believe you're even thinking about doing something."

"I'm very fond of Dean. I don't like seeing him so miserable."

Ketty suppressed a smile. It was obviously too much too soon to expect Judith to want Lacey's happiness as well but if Dean's happiness was co-dependent on Lacey's…

"Do you have an idea for shaking him out of his doldrums?"

"More than an idea." Judith winced. "I've acted on it."

Ketty took a sip of scotch to cover her surprise. "What exactly?"

"I sent him a picture I took of Lacey looking out over the view at The Breakaways. She looked rather forlorn in it. I added a text saying she'd been sad and had asked after him because she missed his company and wondered if she'd done something that had upset him."

Ketty nearly choked on her scotch. "I can't believe you're meddling."

"Neither can I."

"Did you hear back from him?"

"No."

"Bother. I think those two make a lovely couple."

"Like you do Klaus and me?"

Ketty put up a hand.

Judith smiled. "In Dean and Lacey's case I'm beginning to think you might be right."

"Lacey is a bright, talented, creative person but she can be a little reserved. I think Dean is smart and outgoing—"

"He's good at putting up a front."

"Are you saying he's not smart and outgoing?"

"No, just that sometimes his effervescence is a front."

"For what?"

"Life's challenges."

"We all have challenges. Dean has never struck me as someone who becomes upset by them."

"Except when it comes to possible relationships of the heart. He's fallen hard twice before that I know of. When the women called it off he said his disability was too much for them in the end."

"Sounds like a cop-out on the part of the women."

"They weren't right for him but it's made Dean wary, as if he's waiting for the hammer to fall. Somehow I think he saw something in the way Lacey was behaving." Judith shrugged. "And if she's to be believed it doesn't sound like she did anything. She told me the last time they'd been out Dean had wanted to go on for drinks and a meal but she'd been tired and had wanted to go home…"

"Unless she used that excuse regularly."

"Excuse?"

Ketty paused. She didn't like betraying a confidence but… "Money is tight for Lacey."

"She gets a good wage." Judith huffed. "And did you know her gran left her the house? It must be worth a decent amount in the area she lives."

"You can't eat a house."

Judith frowned.

"Lacey's dad hasn't been much help to her financially," Ketty said. "There are extra costs when you own a place and I understand it's in need of repairs. Dean's older with a bigger income and fewer overheads. Eating out regularly is part of his lifestyle."

Judith's eyes widened. "I didn't realise it was that tight for her. Are you saying Lacey couldn't afford it?"

"Possibly."

"And instead of saying so she puts Dean's invitations off."

Ketty shrugged.

"And knowing Dean as I do," Judith said, "he might take that as her not wanting to be seen out with him."

"We both know Lacey's not that kind of person."

Judith's mouth twisted sideways as if she was thinking on that.

"Truly, Judith, whatever you think about Lacey, she's not shallow."

"I suppose you're right. I must admit there's a candidness about her I hadn't appreciated before." Judith snorted. "Do you know she even offered me her spare room if I needed it."

"That's kind of her, but why?"

"Another thing I haven't had a chance to tell you. My apartment building is being totally gutted and remodelled."

"Oh, my goodness. So you'll need temporary accommodation?"

"No. We've all been evicted. Dean, the man down the back and me. The other two apartments are already empty."

"I'm so sorry. I know how much you liked that apartment. What will you do?"

"I must admit I haven't done anything yet. I was broadsided by the eviction letter. I only got it a few weeks ago. Dean's been looking but he's had no luck so far."

"I wish I could offer my rental property but I've got long-term tenants." Ketty had a place not far from the shop – she'd lived in it before she'd renovated and created the apartment above Ketty Clift Couture.

"I don't expect you to find me something. I'm going to get onto it as soon as I get back."

"I'll help." Ketty lurched forward. "And we can ask Maurice. He has contacts in real estate around our area."

"That's kind of you. I was knocked by it to start with but—"

"Klaus has a rental property too. I'm sure he has tenants but who knows when that might change. We should check with him." Ketty's mind was buzzing with the possibilities. "Between us all we can find you a nice place."

Judith's smile lit up her whole face.

"It's been a while since we had a proper chat, hasn't it?"

Judith's smile fell away and once more the bottom of her glass held her interest.

"You're not still worrying about Carlos's intentions, are you?" Ketty gave her a playful nudge. "He's been nothing but a gentleman."

"I'm glad the cabin arrangements worked out."

"I think Carlos and I are the only two from our group who kept the same beds." Ketty laughed. "When I booked this holiday there was no way I imagined all the swapping and changing that's happened."

"Carlos seems to have enjoyed the train travel and the tours."

"Yes." Ketty smiled to cover her unease, not wanting to spoil her rekindled relationship with Judith with too much talk of Carlos.

"He doesn't strike me as a shopper but he had a good look at the opals today. Did he end up buying any?"

"I don't know, but I did. I bought my great-nieces a pendant each."

"Carlos was also shopping in Alice Springs."

Ketty shifted her position on the bed. Judith was being persistent. "Yes, he wanted a tie but he couldn't find one he liked."

"Perhaps he was looking in the wrong places."

"I think so, yes. He said it was all souvenir-style. Not what he was looking for."

"I don't imagine he'd have found a tie in a pawnshop either."

"No." Ketty glanced at her watch and immediately recalled her conversation with Carlos about his gold watch. She'd been worried it had been stolen and he'd said he'd put it in his bag. Judith's mention of a pawnbroker made Ketty wonder where the watch really was.

"Ketty, I know you don't want me to mention it but is everything all right between you and Carlos?"

"Of course." Ketty got to her feet. "Look how late it is. I'm sorry I've kept you up."

They said their goodnights and she slipped out into the corridor. She knew her revived friendship with Judith was on shaky ground when it came to Carlos and that Judith was probing. Ketty was most certainly not going to add fuel to Judith's fire about what Carlos was up to until she'd had time to get to the bottom of it herself.

forty-three

Day Four – Travelling South

Lacey and Birgit were the first of their group to reach the lounge car the next morning.

"Maybe they're all sleeping in," Birgit said. "Look, there's Beau. Let's see if he wants company."

The three of them had struck up a conversation by the campfire the previous night, before all the drama with Erik, and since then Birgit had mentioned Beau's name several times. Lacey trailed along behind her friend, marvelling at how quickly Birgit's swearing off men had evaporated.

"Good morning," he said, half standing as they approached. His rather reserved features lifted into a smile directed at Birgit, who slipped onto the couch beside him.

They made small talk about the scenery. Overnight the desert had been replaced by paddocks and tree lines and more regular sightings of houses and sheds.

They were joined by Virginia, who eyed the empty table in front of them. "No drinks yet?"

"I can get you a coffee," Beau said.

"Thank you, and a champagne chaser."

Birgit laughed. "That sounds good. Do you fancy one, Lacey?"

Lacey shook her head.

"It's our last morning." Birgit pouted.

"All right, but make mine champagne and orange juice, please."

The train rumbled and shook and Birgit wobbled into Beau. She giggled and slipped her arm through his and they made their way to the bar.

"Your friend is a flirt but she makes Beau smile so I like her." Virginia glanced back at Lacey. "And I like your outfit. Is this something else from the Ketty Clift range?"

Lacey glanced down at her dress. The fabric was a rusty red colour with white spots in a simple shift with a flounce well above her knee.

"No. I picked this up in an op shop and remodelled it to fit."

"Very clever. I have a wardrobe full of designer clothes. One of the perks of my job. Some of them have only been worn once. Such a waste. Perhaps you could make use of them."

"That's kind of you," Lacey said, not feeling at all comfortable with the idea. "You could sell them."

"I'm not getting caught up in that online palaver."

"You wouldn't have to. There are several great boutiques that sell preloved brand-name garments on commission."

Virginia's piercing gaze swept over her again. "Have you ever thought about modelling?"

"I wear the odd outfit when we have a photo shoot to update our website, but I prefer to design."

"Ketty said something similar."

"Will you go back to modelling once your knee is better?"

Virginia paused, mouth open, then brushed her hand across her knee. "I imagined my career was over but this last day or so...I think if I wasn't on this damn train I could manage without my stick."

"Maybe it was being on this train that's made you feel a little better."

Virginia's sharp look softened. "Maybe."

"We need models across the generations when we're releasing our new season collections. Ketty doesn't like doing it. Would it be something you might do?" Before Virginia could answer Lacey hurried on. "I'm just thinking out loud, really. We'd have to work out payment but you're the perfect model for our range and I know a few other dressmakers who'd appreciate someone with your grace and stature and..." Lacey paused for a breath. "Gosh, I'm babbling, sorry." Lacey met Virginia's glare with a smile.

"Here we are." Birgit sat a drink in front of Lacey and proposed a toast to their holiday.

"They're ready for us to go into breakfast," Beau said to his mother.

"What about the girls?" Virginia looked from Birgit to Lacey. "Would you join us?"

"Sure." Birgit was on her feet again before anyone could blink and moving off with Beau close behind.

Virginia picked up the walking stick she'd slid under her feet. "And while your friend flirts with my son, perhaps you could give me some more information on those boutiques you mentioned... and your modelling idea."

"Happy to." Lacey glanced down as her phone vibrated in her hand. She pressed her fingers to her lips as the mouthful of champagne and orange threatened to rise in her throat.

"What is it, Lacey? You've gone quite pale."

"I'm sorry, Virginia. I have to take this call. It's my dad."

Judith made her way through the train towards her original cabin. She carried the few items she'd taken with her to the single cabin, planning to drop them off so Birgit could return after breakfast to pack.

Judith had slept late, and when she woke she had immediately begun to think of her conversation with Ketty the previous evening. It had been such a release to tell Ketty about losing her apartment. Already it felt as if finding somewhere else wouldn't be as bad as she'd imagined. They'd chatted so easily together, just like old times, until the subject of Carlos had come up. Ketty didn't want to listen and Judith hadn't pushed hard, not wanting to spoil their rekindled amity.

She drew level with her cabin door as the next door on opened and Lacey stuck her head out.

"Good morning," Judith said.

Lacey's head whipped in Judith's direction, her phone clutched to her chest.

"Is everything all right?" Judith asked. Was it possible that her plan to put Dean back in touch with Lacey had worked?

"I…my dad just called." Lacey's eyes watered and she dabbed them with a tissue. Judith glanced towards the window, giving Lacey a moment to collect herself. The train was running parallel to a high mountain range, so different from the flat terrain they'd traversed for most of their journey.

Lacey sniffed and tucked the tissue away. Judith turned back, relieved to see a small smile on her face.

"He started a new job and I hadn't heard from him but he's okay. His phone fell into a sheep trough. The SIM survived but not the phone. He had to wait to get paid and get to one of the bigger towns to buy a new one."

Lacey was speaking so fast Judith had to concentrate to keep up with her.

"You must be relieved to hear from him."

"Yes."

Lacey smiled and Judith was thankful she didn't have to deal with tears.

"I'd better go. Birgit's saving me a seat at breakfast."

"See you later."

The cabin door beside Judith opened.

"Hello," Ning said. "Thought we could hear voices out here."

Tien was peering around Ning but lost her worried look when she saw Judith.

"We were just going to breakfast," she said.

"I'll put my things away and meet you there."

Inside the cabin everything was neat but for the two unmade beds. No doubt they would be stripped and packed away while everyone was dining.

Judith was surprised when her phone rang. She hadn't looked at it since the previous evening. She dug it out of her handbag and frowned when she saw Dean's name on the screen. She took a breath and answered.

Ketty hadn't seen Carlos since he'd woken her with his customary cup of tea. He'd said they had a booking for nine thirty in the dining room. She took her time showering and getting dressed. The day stretched out in front of her, creating a mixture of emotions. The train would arrive in Adelaide just before lunch and there'd be lots of farewells, and then it would be just her and Carlos. She had to admit to a few butterflies about that now. Especially since Carlos's insistence on this breakfast together – just the two of them. Then tonight it was Celia and Jim's wedding celebration, which she was looking forward to. But it was going to be a long day and she was glad she'd slept well once she'd finally closed her eyes the previous night.

After her chat with Judith she'd put herself to bed and thought about each of her staff, glad that they'd mostly found their mojos again, although she had to admit to being a little concerned for Lacey. Not her work life, Ketty was confident about that and even more so now that Judith seemed to have let down the barriers she'd built between them. Ketty had drifted off to sleep, sorry that she couldn't fix the relationship between Lacey and her dad and Lacey and Dean but she'd had an idea about Lacey's job that might make a small difference to her finances at least.

Ketty peered at her face in the small bathroom mirror. She'd taken extra care with her make-up and she was pleased with the combination of her cream linen pants again with a soft pink silk shirt this time. Dressing well gave her confidence even if she didn't always feel it. Carlos had been so insistent he wanted to speak with her alone and she thought it would be her opportunity to have her own questions answered. Her biggest worry was that this was somehow a turning point, a line in the sand beyond which their easy friendship would be irretrievably spoiled and that bothered her. She'd enjoyed Carlos's company up until these silly niggly doubts and she blamed her old boyfriend Leo for that.

When she'd gone out with him as a young woman and eventually fallen pregnant she hadn't known he was married. The relationship had ended, along with any future chance she had at bearing her own children, when her ectopic pregnancy resulted in sepsis and the removal of her womb. Ketty drew herself up. That was long behind her now but several years ago she'd met Leo again and for a short time had been charmed by him once more, until she'd discovered he'd seen her as a meal ticket. There'd been other men in her life but her love for Leo had been the greatest and his deceit had almost destroyed her.

Carlos had been her long-time friend. Having him in Australia with her had been an on-again off-again delight she would miss once he returned to Spain for good. Their friendship had always been so easy: no strings, they enjoyed each other's company, had similar interests in people, food, architecture, travel – although she knew Carlos wouldn't cruise with her, she wouldn't be averse to taking another train holiday with him, perhaps one of the famous overseas journeys. That's providing this little get-together of his wasn't going to end their friendship. After the incident with Lacey in the opal shop Ketty had discovered Carlos could lie to her, and she didn't tolerate liars.

She lifted her chin and looked herself in the eye. For the first time she had an uneasy niggle in her stomach over a meeting with Carlos. Ketty ran a brush through her hair, applied her lipstick and set off to join him.

She stepped through the door into the dining carriage, paused and momentarily forgot her troubles as she once more took in the elegance, as charming now as it had been on their first day. At the far end, Carlos rose from the last table and gave her a small wave. She made her way towards him, pausing to swap pleasantries with the people she'd shared this journey with until finally she reached Carlos.

"You look wonderful as ever, Ketty," he said and ushered her to the seat with her back to the rest of the carriage. Once she was settled he slid in opposite.

"I slept well – what about you?" Ketty asked, feeling an awkwardness between them she never had before.

"The train has rocked me to sleep each night."

Belinda came to take their coffee order and Ketty studied the choices on the breakfast menu, disappointed that she didn't feel like anything more than the selection of toasts. They made small talk about the weather, what they would do when they arrived in Adelaide. Carlos had to track down his case and Ketty wanted to visit the shops to purchase a gift for Celia and Jim. Then they'd take a taxi up to the Adelaide Hills and their accommodation in Hahndorf.

"The ceremony and dinner are at a winery. Celia says they have wonderful food and wine and spectacular views."

Their coffees arrived and their food orders were taken. Ketty looked up from her coffee to find Carlos studying her, a strange expression on his face, a mix of concern, worry, embarrassment... she couldn't tell.

"What's this about, Carlos?" she asked.

"It's about us enjoying a meal on this train journey that we planned together. I wanted to have one opportunity before we disembark to be with you, to talk, enjoy the food and the scenery."

Ketty glanced at the countryside sliding past. It was all farming country now, sprawling paddocks, cows and sheep.

She sat back against the seat. "I'm sorry, Carlos, but I don't think I can keep making small talk while there's things between us that need to be said."

"I agree." He looked her directly in the eye, his usual charming smile in place. "One of the things I like about you, Ketty, is your honesty."

She was momentarily pulled up by his response. She'd thought perhaps he'd be evasive.

"And I've always thought the same about you but you lied to me yesterday and now I'm wondering what else you've lied about."

He frowned. "Ah yes, Lacey and the money. I'm not good at deception. You caught me out."

"Why did you lie?"

He reached into his pocket, took out a small gift-wrapped package and placed it on the table between them. "I've been looking for something special to commemorate our journey."

"You didn't have to do that."

"But I wanted to. You've been so kind to me during my time in Australia and then having to share your cabin with me...this holiday hasn't been quite what either of us expected, I suspect." He glanced at his hands clasped together on the table. "I tried to buy you something in Katherine but my card wouldn't work. Then I needed a verification code and we were on tours or kept losing reception. My cousin tried to transfer me some money but same issue. It's been a nightmare. I need to visit a bank to sort it."

"I could have helped you out."

"I didn't want to ask you for money, Ketty. There were many reasons why I couldn't talk to you about it but the main one was...I was embarrassed."

"Carlos—"

"Please." He put up a hand, revealing his smart watch. "Let me tell you the rest."

Ketty recalled his lovely gold watch and Judith's mention of the pawnshop.

"Carlos, please tell me you didn't pawn your father's beautiful antique watch?"

He met her gaze, his deep brown eyes full of sadness.

"Oh, no, Carlos."

"I'll get it back."

"You could have come to me. I wouldn't charge you interest." Ketty looked at the package on the table, horrified to think he'd traded his precious watch for it. "And you spent the money on something for me. I can't accept it, Carlos."

His sorrowful look deepened. "I picked out something at the opal shop yesterday. You came back before I could pay for it so I gave Lacey the money to collect it for me."

"So this whole subterfuge has been about buying me a gift that I truly don't need."

The small box sat between them like a too-hot coal neither of them wanted to touch.

"Partly." He took a sip of his coffee. "But there's more we need to discuss."

Belinda arrived with their breakfast – Ketty's assortment of artisan toasts and condiments and Carlos's eggs Florentine. They both smiled and nodded but when Belinda left the food remained untouched.

Carlos cleared his throat. "I've thought this over and over in my head but now that I'm here with you I'm not sure where to start."

Ketty picked up her knife and took some butter from the little dish beside her. "Eat while the food is hot." She was suddenly nervous too. Once whatever he said was out she sensed they couldn't go back to the way they'd been.

They ate, glancing at the scenery but not speaking. Ketty managed one piece of toast and a bite of the next before she gave up, while Carlos ate only half of his meal.

He placed his knife and fork purposefully in the middle of his plate then once more looked up to stare directly at her.

"Ketty, I'm making plans to stay in Australia."

Her pounding heart felt for a brief moment as if it had stopped and then a huge wave of relief washed over her. How wonderful would it be to have her friend here?

"But that's such good news, Carlos." She shook her head. "I don't understand. Why all this drama?"

"I so badly wanted everything to be in place before I spoke to you. I've been working on it since I came back to stay, when you broke your wrist."

"I remember seeing some visa information spread across my table."

He nodded. "It's hard for someone of my age—"

"Oh no! Don't you start going on about age too. I've just about had enough of people being defined by their age instead of who they are."

"Tell your government, not me. Your country makes it difficult. When it comes to visas age is an important determining factor." He sat back as Belinda came to clear their plates.

"Was everything all right with the food?" she asked.

"It was, yes. I'm sorry, we were busy talking and let it go cold." Ketty smiled. "Could we have more coffee, please, and one of those pear-and-strawberry tarts to share?"

Carlos continued as soon as Belinda walked away. "I've been looking into work. It hasn't been easy—"

"Was it here in Australia you had that rejection because of your age?"

Carlos nodded and Ketty was mortified on behalf of her whole country.

"It's not just that. There are several jobs I could do. There are a few large hotels looking for people with my skills but I can't work because I'm currently here on a visitor visa. It's been complicated, and Felix has been helping me—"

"It was my friend Felix you were speaking to the other day, wasn't it?"

Carlos nodded.

"Why didn't you tell me then?"

"I didn't want...it's complicated, Ketty...Anyway, Felix has recently navigated the system himself."

"What about your cousin in Brisbane? He must have been through it."

"Yes, but it was many years ago and he was much younger, but he's been helping with what he can."

Belinda came back with their coffee and the small tart cut neatly in two. "We'll be clearing the dining room soon to prepare for our arrival in Adelaide."

Ketty glanced behind her. The carriage was almost empty of diners.

"We won't be long. I still have to finish packing."

Belinda left them to it and Ketty thought about the phone call Judith had overheard and the many calls that Ketty had seen or heard Carlos make. "Was your case really lost?" she asked.

Carlos's head shot back, his eyes dark. "Mierda, yes!"

"I'm sorry, but it seems you've been keeping a lot secret and told some lies, and now I'm not sure."

He was instantly repentant. "I'm sorry, Ketty. This is not how I wanted it to go at all. And losing my case was an added problem.

I packed in a rush when I left Spain and instead of putting my folder of personal papers in my carry-on luggage I put it in my case. I was worried I would lose the lot and have to apply for all my papers again, a new birth certificate, bank details, all of those things you need."

"Poor Carlos. I wish you'd just told me from the start."

"I'm sorry, Ketty. I've made a mess of it. The very thing I've been trying to avoid. I wanted everything to be organised before I...before I told you about my plans. I didn't want you to think I was using you to get a visa—"

"Oh, Carlos—"

He put up a hand. "I've never been quite so rudderless as I've felt these last few months, my parents dying, deciding to leave Spain, trying to get the paperwork sorted without burdening you—"

"Really, Carlos, I might not know about visas but I could have supported you and, at least, loaned you some money until you could sort your card with the bank. I hate to think you pawned your father's beautiful watch."

"I'm not sorry. I wanted to get you something to remember our trip. When you admired that set of opal earrings I was so glad there was something I knew you'd like and at least I had a way to purchase them."

Once more they both looked at the little box between them on the table. Ketty had been terrified it might be a ring and that Carlos had been going to propose. It would have complicated their lovely friendship. Then she gasped and reached for his hand, resting on the table.

"That's it. That's what we can do to sort the visa." She gripped his hand tightly. In that moment she knew she'd do almost anything for her dear friend. "Marry me, Carlos."

His eyes widened in surprise.

"It's a marriage of convenience. Nothing would need to change. Plenty of people do it, so I hear. You can live with me when you're in Sydney but you'd be free to go wherever you wanted. You could work." She placed her other hand over his wrist. "It's the perfect solution."

forty-four

The small group from Ketty Clift Couture stood together on the platform, a much more cohesive party than had boarded the train in Darwin. Carlos had taken a final group photo for them then said his farewells and gone ahead to wait for Ketty outside the station. Except for Birgit and Lacey the goodbyes had been subdued, but if Ketty's plan went ahead as she'd hoped, they'd have to get used to seeing Carlos around.

Tien had two fluffy toys tucked under her arm from the souvenir shop. She'd found a kangaroo and, to everyone's surprise, a crocodile that she was taking home for her husband. "He loves crocodiles," she said gleefully.

Ning gave Ketty a hug. "Thank you for this wonderful holiday."

"I'm glad you all enjoyed it," Ketty said.

Ning waggled the phone she clutched in her hand. "When I turned this on a little while ago there was a voice message from Peter. He's happy for me to keep working if there's a way to also help with babysitting. But after that there was a text from my daughter-in-law saying she'd already booked a place in a nearby childcare centre and any help from me would be a bonus, not a requirement."

"I'm glad, Ning. And you know that work can be flexible for you if you need." Ketty was distracted by the approach of Beau and Virginia, who was without her walking stick. "You're looking bright this morning."

"Mum has decided the train has been good for her after all," Beau said.

Virginia gave a toss of her head. "It wasn't what I'd imagined but…it turned out all right. And meeting up with you again has been wonderful, Ketty. I'm looking forward to visiting you in your shop. Beau's been showing me your online boutique this morning. I adore your range and I've a few friends who'll want to visit as well."

"Lacey's mainly responsible for managing our website but the garments are the result of the combined talents of all my staff." Pride surged inside Ketty as she reminded herself how very lucky she was to have gathered such a wonderful group of women together and that they truly were a team again. "And I'll enjoy a trip to Coogee. I haven't been that way in ages. I'm sure Carlos would enjoy it too."

"You're not letting him go then?" Virginia quipped.

Ketty smiled. She didn't think the busy train platform the right place to announce her news and Carlos hadn't actually agreed yet anyway.

Ketty stared as Birgit stepped up to Beau and he brushed a kiss across her cheek and then, as if he'd thought better of it, planted one on her lips.

"I think that young woman might be the spark my Beau needs in his life," Virginia murmured in Ketty's ear.

"I'll see you tomorrow night," Beau said as the two pulled apart.

"To be sure," Birgit said demurely.

"We've got a plane to catch." Virginia moved off and Beau gave Birgit one last loving look and followed.

Birgit turned back to Ketty and Judith. "What?"

They both shook their heads.

Lacey, who'd been standing away from the group taking a phone call, returned at that moment, her eyes wide and her fingers pressed to her lips.

"Was that Dean?" Judith asked hopefully.

Lacey nodded and Birgit gave a short squeal of delight. "He's realised what a gobshite he was being and wants you back," she said.

"Something like that." Lacey looked at Judith. "He said you made him realise he'd been reading my signals all wrong."

"Goodness, I just sent him a few photos of our travels."

Ketty raised her eyebrows.

"I may have mentioned that you appeared to be missing him…a lot."

"Go, Judith," Birgit said. "So you'll be back together. Hey, isn't he looking for new accommodation. He could move in with us." Birgit dug Lacey with her elbow. "Or you."

Lacey's cheeks glowed pink. "We've still got a lot to talk through. And he said to let you know he's found himself a new apartment, Judith, and he's got a list of possibilities for you."

"That's nice of him," Judith said.

"Dean's a fine chap all round." Ketty smiled.

"That shirt looks good on you, Birgit," Lacey said, obviously keen to change the subject.

"Where did it come from?" Ketty asked, thinking the long-line green linen did indeed look smart on Birgit.

"I spilled juice all down my last clean shirt this morning. Judith let me borrow this," Birgit said.

"It was one I purchased from an op shop but I don't like it on me. You can keep it if you like."

"Thanks," Birgit said, beaming.

"I'm not good with op shopping," Judith said.

"There is a trick to it," Ketty agreed.

"Look at the time – we'd better get off to the airport," Tien said. "We'll miss our flight."

Ketty waved them off as Birgit tried to tell Judith how to go about op shopping.

"Oh, for goodness sake," Judith snapped. "You'll be having us sell second-hand clothes at Ketty Clift Couture next."

"Funny you should say that, Judith." Lacey grabbed Birgit's arm. "We were just discussing that after a chat with Virginia about her wardrobe of designer items with hardly any wears."

The last thing Ketty heard as they turned the corner was Judith's groan. She walked on a little further smiling to herself. They'd had an amazing journey and she was excited about the future of Ketty Clift Couture.

The voices of other passengers rose and fell around her, chatter and laughter, last photos, promises to keep in touch. She paused for one last look at the huge red engine that had towed them straight down the middle of the country. The brochure had described it as an epic 2797 kilometre journey and Ketty had to agree. The jitters in her stomach dragged her thoughts to her personal future and the plans still to be made.

She turned away from the train and made her way through the terminal to find Carlos.

forty-five

Day Four – Adelaide Hills

Ketty and Carlos made their way across the winery terrace. The air still held some warmth and the late-afternoon sun cast a golden glow over everything. Ahead of them Celia and Jim were in the middle of a group of well-wishers.

"It's a lovely setting for their ceremony. Let's give them a moment and take in that view," Ketty said and they moved to the edge of the terrace. The hills were covered in the soft greens, yellows and oranges of autumn. "So different to where we've been the last few days."

"It reminds me a little of northern Spain."

"Do they have a train? Perhaps you can take me there one day?"

Ketty had been doing her best to keep the conversation light. Carlos had said very little since her offer of marriage and now she was beginning to think he was going to turn her down.

Their afternoon had been busy. He'd recovered his case, she'd visited Rundle Mall then they'd travelled up the highway to the pretty little town of Hahndorf. Carlos had been intrigued by the German influence. They'd not had a lot of time to settle into the two-bedroom apartment Ketty had booked in the main street. They'd changed for the wedding and caught the shuttle Celia and Jim had arranged to transfer them to the winery only a few minutes out of town.

Now he turned his deep brown eyes on her and she was shocked by the sadness reflected in them.

"Are you all right?" she asked.

He nodded. "We haven't had a chance to finish our talk. There are things I must—"

"Ketty!"

They both spun. Celia was striding towards them, arms outstretched. She wrapped Ketty in a perfumed hug.

"It's so good to see you. And you, Carlos."

"You're a radiant bride," Ketty said, taking in Celia's glowing smile and her elegant lace sheath dress topped with a sheer chiffon wrap. "Duck-egg blue is the perfect colour for you."

"I'm glad I get to wear it again," Celia laughed. "Our wedding was very small and quiet last year."

"Hello, Ketty, Carlos." Jim kissed Ketty's cheek and shook Carlos's hand. "We're so pleased you could make it."

"So are we," Ketty said. "It worked out perfectly with our train trip."

"You'll have to tell us all about it," Celia said. "Jim and I thought we'd go next year."

"I think the kids are ready to get the show on the road, Celia." Jim took his wife's hand.

"This is just a brief reaffirmation of vows," Celia said. "It shouldn't take long and then we'll go into the restaurant. Their food is divine here."

"We're happy to be here to celebrate with you, aren't we, Carlos?" Ketty fidgeted with her champagne glass as Jim towed Celia away. It had just occurred to her that if she married Carlos there would have to be some kind of reception with family and friends. She'd never get away with just Carlos and some witnesses.

They moved closer to the centre of the terrace where Celia's and Jim's children shared some moving words and some funny anecdotes, including how Jim and Celia met on a cruise. It was short, as Celia had said, and family and friends were soon ushered into the restaurant where they had the most divine dinner.

"I'm getting rather used to this fine dining," Ketty said as the waiter cleared the plates from their main course.

Beside her Carlos didn't answer but took another sip of the cabernet franc they'd been enjoying with their beef.

Ketty leaned a little closer. "You've been so quiet tonight."

"We need to talk, Ketty, and we still haven't had time alone."

Ketty was troubled by the sorrow in his voice. "We will," she said. "We have tonight when we get back and our flight's not until late afternoon tomorrow."

He nodded. "Excuse me." He rose from his chair and headed in the direction of the bathroom. Ketty's heart ached. Had she made the most terrible mistake flippantly asking him to marry her?

"At last we can have a few minutes to chat." Celia slipped into the chair Carlos had vacated. "I hope you've enjoyed the meal."

"Superb."

"We're having wedding cake later for dessert." Celia lifted her glass towards Ketty's. "Thanks for coming."

"You and Jim seem very happy."

"We truly are. I sometimes pinch myself, in case it's a dream. Thank goodness we both went on that cruise and that we were sat at a table with you."

TRICIA STRINGER

"I had nothing to do with it."

"Jim and I have discussed it many times. We both believe it was the Ketty charm that got us together. I was still feeling bitter towards my ex and dear Jim was still mourning his wife. You sprinkled us with your magic and opened our eyes to the possibilities."

Ketty laughed. "That's a marvellous fairy tale. You and Jim found each other at the right time. I had nothing to do with that."

They both sipped their wine.

"Your earrings are pretty," Celia said.

Ketty put a hand to one. "Carlos bought them for me. They're Coober Pedy opal."

"That's a special gift."

"It is."

"So you said that he was in Australia for a year?"

"Yes, but it's ended up being complicated." Ketty filled in Celia on Carlos's comings and goings, the death of his parents and his final dash to get back to Australia for the Ghan trip.

"So you shared a cabin?" Celia grinned.

"We're good friends."

"I can see that."

"What do you mean?"

"The way you are together. You seem so natural, as if you've been together all your lives. I thought Carlos a bit scary back on the cruise ship but he's more like a big teddy bear, although a bit of a sad one."

"Why do you say sad?"

"A few times tonight I've caught glimpses of him with that faraway look. Like Jim did when I first met him. I guess Carlos is still grieving his parents."

Ketty nodded but she hadn't seen that in Carlos. He was sad about his parents, of course, but when they'd been together on the holiday he hadn't shown it. His sadness had only surfaced today, after her proposal. She glanced around. Carlos had been gone a while.

"What's the matter?" Celia asked.

Ketty stood up. "Excuse me, Celia, but I have to find Carlos. I think I've made the most dreadful mistake."

Carlos wasn't seated at any of the other tables. She asked a man who'd come from the men's if there'd been anyone else in there and he said no. Music played and some of the guests had taken to the dance floor. She circled it but he wasn't there. It was dark outside now and below the restaurant on the terrace, in the soft ambient glow from the loops of festoon lights, Ketty saw movement. Carlos was standing with his back to the restaurant, staring out into the darkness.

She blew out a soft sigh of relief, took two fresh glasses of the cabernet franc and made her way down to meet him.

"Carlos?"

He turned abruptly at her call. And she saw the sorrow in his eyes again.

"I brought you a fresh drink." Ketty handed him one of the glasses and pulled her pashmina a little tighter around her shoulders. "Gosh, it's cool out here now the sun's gone."

"We can sit." Carlos indicated a couch with a rug draped over one end.

They sat and sipped their wine. "We should buy some of this to take back with us," Ketty said, filling the silence with her small talk.

Carlos was staring into his glass and Ketty's heart broke for him. "Carlos, I'm sorry. My proposal of marriage may have sounded flippant but it was a genuine offer. I hope—"

She flinched as he lurched forward, sat his glass on the ground and put his head in his hands. "I've made a mess of everything." He groaned.

Ketty pressed a hand to her cheek. Today she'd found herself imagining what it might be like to have Carlos in her life permanently but... "No, you haven't – I have. You must have been horrified when I asked you to marry me. It was said in haste. I was trying to be helpful and...I'm sorry, Carlos."

He dragged his fingers back through his hair and lifted his head. "I had imagined the Ghan journey would be a chance to tell you everything, explain—"

"Explain what?"

"Please, Ketty, just let me tell you what I must."

Her heart thudded hard in her chest. What terrible thing was he going to reveal? She couldn't bear it if Carlos was fallible like all the other men she'd ever known. She wanted to reach out and clasp her hand over his mouth, stop him, but she couldn't, of course.

"I'd planned it all so differently to what's happened. The trip on the Ghan was going to be the perfect opportunity but then my dear parents died." Once more a deeper sorrow filled his eyes. "You know it will happen one day but it's painful nonetheless. Then my booking was mixed up, my bag lost, and even though we shared a cabin we were so rarely alone. I'd hoped to have the basics of my visa organised, work, somewhere to live before I...before I..."

"Before what, Carlos, please tell me." She put her glass down. Her fingers shook so much it was in danger of spilling. "You're scaring me half to death."

"That was never my intention, dear Ketty." He took her hands in his. They were warm and gripped her tightly. "Do you remember our first day on the train I asked if you were lonely?"

Ketty frowned.

"You said no, that you lived alone but that you weren't lonely."

She vaguely remembered.

"Your answer made me realise lonely was what I'd become. I've been a gypsy most of my life. My marriage failed because of it. Now that I've retired, and more recently when my parents died, I realised I'm looking for something more. I've come to understand that it's not something that I'm searching for but someone." He sat back a little but didn't let go of her hands. "I'm looking for someone in my life and since those first weeks we spent together when I came to Australia last Christmas I've understood...that someone is you."

Ketty gasped and sat back but he had a firm hold on her hands.

"I planned to ask you to marry me. I know how independent you are so I wanted to make sure I had my affairs in order. I didn't want to be ill-prepared and scare you away from the idea. I've been trying to get everything sorted so that when I asked you, you wouldn't think it was because I needed money or a visa or any help..."

Ketty sucked in a breath. "So when I blurted out a marriage proposal over breakfast I ruined everything."

Carlos gazed steadily into her eyes.

"I'm old-fashioned when it comes to sharing cabins and marriage proposals. You certainly took me by surprise."

She realised the sadness in his eyes had been replaced by a sparkle and his lips were twitching. He let go of her hands and the sudden cold chilled her. He took something from his pocket and then he was on one knee at her feet.

"Carlos, what are you doing?" Ketty glanced around. The background sound of the music playing from inside and the occasional laugh or loud voice filtered out but they were quite alone.

"I'm asking you to marry me." He opened his hand to reveal a small velvet pouch. "My biggest worry when my case went missing was that my mother's ring was also with my personal papers."

He tipped a ring from the pouch to his other hand and it sparkled in the light from the festoons overhead.

"Your mother's ring – oh, Carlos." Ketty shook her head.

"It was her mother's before her. Silver filagree with small diamonds. Spectacular but not flashy. My sister and I both hope you like it."

"You discussed this with your sister?"

"Of course."

"It's beautiful, Carlos, but…I can't accept it."

"I did wonder if you might not like it or if a ring was too much. Judith said it was such a personal thing."

"Judith?" Ketty squeaked. "Please tell me you haven't mentioned this to her."

He shook his head. "We were discussing opals and I said I wanted to buy you something. I was thinking a ring then because I thought my mother's was lost."

Ketty shook her head again. "Carlos, I've lived seventy-one years—"

He pressed a finger to her lips. "As you so often say, my dear Ketty, age is not the barrier."

He got to his feet and she rose with him. Her head was a mushy mess of thoughts. She'd never had much luck with men and she didn't want to spoil the best friendship she had so keeping Carlos at arm's length was safe. Only now he was holding her to him, staring at her as if he was worried she'd disappear. The music in the restaurant above had been turned up and they began to sway to the beat of Andy Williams singing 'Can't Take My Eyes Off You'.

She allowed her head, still spinning from all he'd said, to rest on his shoulder. She had anticipated none of this and now she didn't know what to do.

forty-six

One week later – Sydney

Birgit moved through Lacey's house, exclaiming or squealing with delight at each new room. Lacey followed her, and two steps behind Lacey was Beau, who smiled at Birgit's excitement and nodded benignly.

Everyone had returned to work at Ketty Clift Couture the previous Monday and had been immediately busy catching up on the backlog of tasks and looking at the new jobs that had come in. Lacey had investigated how to formally set up letting a room and done a thorough clean of the whole house and a rearrange of the bedrooms, and by that weekend she was happy to invite Birgit to see what she thought.

Once they'd done a full tour they returned to the front bedroom.

"Are you sure you want me to have this room?" Birgit asked.

"I am," Lacey said. "If you like it."

"Like it! I love it!" Birgit held her arms out and spun around. "This room's nearly as big as the whole flat I've been sharing with my cousins." She grabbed Beau's hand. "It's brilliant, isn't it?"

"It's a great room," Beau said and kissed her cheek. "This whole house is a good one."

"You think?" Lacey winced.

"It might be a bit run-down but it has good bones." Beau tapped a wall with his knuckles.

Birgit went to the window and looked out. "My dad would enjoy getting his green thumbs working in your garden if you'd like."

"Jungle, you mean." Lacey laughed. "I'm glad you like the room. I was thinking about the lack of nice curtains…" She glanced at Beau then back to Birgit. "I think you should ask for your curtains and stuff back from…" Once more Lacey glanced at Beau.

"Don't worry." Birgit slipped an arm through his. "Beau knows about the gobshite."

"You could easily adapt the curtains, and the couch would fit," Lacey said.

"I don't know…" Birgit lost her bravado.

"Why should he have the benefit of your hard work?" Lacey said.

"I agree." Beau gave Birgit a gentle nudge. "I've got a friend with a van. I can help you move in."

Lacey heard the sound of a key in the front door. She left Birgit and Beau to chat and stepped out into the passage.

"Hello, Dad."

The man who smiled back at her seemed a younger version of the one who'd left several weeks prior.

"Hello, love."

They hugged and Lacey felt the new strength of his muscles under his shirt.

"You're looking good," she said.

"I'm feeling it, Lace. Good honest hard work in the fresh air. I only drink on weekends and," he shrugged, "I'm working on giving up the fags."

Birgit's laugh echoed from the bedroom.

"I told you I'm renting a room to my workmate," Lacey said.

He nodded then patted his pocket. "I've got some cash for you too, love. I'm sorry it's taken me so long but I've put aside what I owe you for the car and a bit more."

"Thanks, Dad." Lacey smiled. "Come and meet Birgit and her friend."

Judith knocked on Dean's door. She'd only seen him once briefly since she'd returned from her holiday. She knew he and Lacey had been communicating via phone but they were taking things slowly and hadn't met face to face again yet.

The door swung open. "Hey, Jude. Come in."

She was pleased to see his smile was genuine and warm.

"Have you come to help me pack some boxes?"

She followed him inside. His apartment was in disarray, partly packed boxes stacked around and cupboards hanging open, their contents in jumbled piles.

"I'd be happy to."

"Nah, just kidding. It's a good chance to have a clean-out."

"When do you move out?"

"Next week. But the place I've found isn't that far from here and it's newer." He grinned. "Has an aircon in good working order too. Have you got anything yet?"

"No, but I've a few people looking as well as me so I'm hopeful something will turn up soon."

"I'll invite you over for a drink once I'm settled in my new digs."

"Thanks." Judith smiled. "I'd like us to keep in touch."

"I'd ask you to stay now but I've got to keep moving. Need to tidy up a bit. I've a visitor coming later."

"Oh?"

"Isn't that why you're here? To quiz me about Lacey?"

"No."

"Come on, Jude."

"I'm glad to hear you're seeing each other again."

"Not exactly seeing each other but we've been talking, and meeting up again seemed to be the right next step."

"I think you're a good match."

"Is that so?" Dean frowned at her.

"I'm sorry. It was wrong of me to say those...those harsh things about Lacey when you were feeling unsure about the relationship. I got to know her better on the train and I realised how much I'd misjudged her. I added to your angst about her and I realised I needed to try to fix that."

"I was going to tell you off for interfering."

"I didn't interfere."

He broke into a grin. "I think you did, Jude, but I'm glad it worked out."

"I'll leave you to it then. I'm heading over to Ketty's later for dinner."

"Say hello for me."

"I will."

Judith let herself out and paused. It was a relief to know she hadn't ruined her friendship with Dean. It was important to her and even more so if he and Lacey kept seeing each other.

Returning upstairs she wandered the rooms. She'd been doing a bit of cleaning out herself. Not that she had a new place yet but she'd started going through cupboards and culling a few things.

Somehow between the train journey, the flurry of work this last week and accepting Ketty's dinner invitation, she'd lost some of her nostalgia for her apartment.

She hadn't baulked when Ketty had said Klaus would also be joining them, and Carlos, of course, but thinking of Klaus had reminded her of Erik. She'd done a google search and found a short news item. He was in custody pending charges and the man who'd been injured was making a good recovery. She hoped Erik might get some help and move on but he would have to make that choice.

Just as Judith was making a choice to let go of her old home and think positively about a new one. She'd also decided to try to do better with Carlos. She hadn't seen him since Ketty had returned from Adelaide but she knew he was still staying at Ketty's. Work had been busy and Ketty hadn't mentioned him or what his plans were.

Judith picked up the brown-paper bag she'd sat out to take with her to dinner. It contained the scarf she'd purchased at Nitmiluk. She planned to quietly give it to Carlos, an olive branch of sorts.

forty-seven

Six months later – Paddington, Sydney

The sun lowered in the sky above Sydney and once more the fairy lights blinked and sparkled to life under the pergola at the back of Ketty Clift Couture. Ketty was too busy to pause to take them in. She'd gathered a large group of friends and colleagues for an early Christmas celebration and she was making sure everyone had something to eat and drink. She'd added swatches of flowers, and her favourite jazz playlist gave some carefree background sound.

Judith was helping, of course, as she always did. Currently she was assisting Klaus. He was making fruit punch that she'd warned Ketty had some extra 'punch' to it. Judith had started seeing Klaus after she'd moved out of her old apartment and Ketty thought his influence had softened her sometimes caustic manner. Klaus had blossomed too. Judith fussed over him and he lapped it up. Even his clothing had become more contemporary. Today he looked smart in some chinos and a linen shirt, which Ketty assumed was Judith's influence. They often spent a weekend exploring a part of Sydney they hadn't been to before. The previous weekend they'd visited Glebe and had come across a wine bar that specialised in fruity punches from the nineties. Klaus had decided he'd recreate one for Ketty's party.

Judith hurried in Ketty's direction.

"Where are you rushing off to?"

"I've left the special bottle of champagne Klaus bought in the fridge upstairs and he's panicking there's not enough fruit." They both looked to Klaus, who was spilling the contents of a strawberry punnet across the table. "For a man who does such delicate woodwork and mends clocks he's all fingers and thumbs when it comes to the kitchen."

"You stay and help Klaus. I'll get the champagne." Ketty hesitated. "That's if you don't mind me going upstairs."

"Of course not." Judith waved a hand at her. "It's your place."

"Not any more. You must think of it as your home now."

Judith smiled then spun away when they heard a muttered curse from Klaus.

Ketty went upstairs to what was now Judith's apartment. Everything had fallen into place when Ketty's long-term tenants had bought a property of their own. She'd moved back to her small house two doors the other side of Maurice and Lee's. Part of her succession plan idea had been that she would move out of her apartment and it was perfect that Judith needed somewhere to go.

Judith was Ketty's main beneficiary when it came to the business. If something were to happen to Ketty, Judith would continue Ketty Clift Couture. Ketty had set up a trust for her nephew, Greg, who would be the recipient of any personal assets. Judith could buy him out of Ketty Clift Couture or pay him a regular sum. They could work that out. Ketty knew the future of her business was in good hands all round.

She glanced around the living area as she shut the door on the fridge. Judith had already made her mark with her own furniture and artwork. And Ketty had found herself enjoying making her old house into a fresh space for her and Carlos. At least while he was there. His visa was running out and she'd miss him terribly when he left for Spain the following week. She drew herself up, tugged gently at the side seams of the full-skirted coffee-coloured shantung frock she'd made especially for today. She was determined not to have any regrets.

She'd just delivered the champagne to Klaus and Judith when Maurice waved a plate under her nose, forcing her to pay him attention.

"You must try one of my arancini balls." He'd been pestering her to try them since he'd arrived. Now she stopped and took one from the plate. The tasty morsel dissolved in her mouth, releasing a surprise of salty melted cheese in the middle.

"Delicious, Maurice," she murmured.

"I told you they were good," he said. "I suspect young Dean and Lacey will like them as well. He's a good eater." Maurice drifted off to where Lacey and Dean sat talking with Ketty's nephew and his wife.

"I'm so glad you encouraged him to take those cooking lessons, Ketty." Lee glanced over at her husband, who was laughing at something Dean had said.

"I was inspired by Warren who we met on the train. Val says he cooks a Thai banquet for the family nearly every weekend since he's been taking lessons. I remembered Maurice had said something about Italian cooking."

"He cooks for us most nights now." Lee smiled. "He's been along to the 'come and try' croquet sessions and says he may take that up. And he's been asked to be a board member of a not-for-profit. It's making so much difference to both our lives, I can tell you. Oh, there's Ning. I was hoping to catch her today. Now that things have settled a little with the new baby, she's offered to do some embroidery for me."

"First you'll have to look at several photos of the baby," Ketty said.

"I won't mind that. She's the cutest little thing."

"She certainly is." Ketty smiled. Ning worked four days a week and looked after her granddaughter for one. Each day she had a new lot of photos to show. Ketty was more than happy to share her joy.

"Look, Ketty, look."

She lowered her gaze to her two great-nieces who held a bunch of flowers each. She'd given them a box full of fresh stems and asked them to make posies. There were no other children at the party so she'd lined up a few activities for them.

"They're beautiful, girls. You've done a lovely job. Don't they look pretty against your dresses?"

"That liberty print is gorgeous," Lacey said as she joined them. "Did you make them, Ketty?"

"Yes, to go with their opal necklaces." Ketty smiled.

The little girls giggled and ran off to show their chaotic posies to their grandparents.

"They're such sweet little girls," Lacey said.

"They certainly are."

"I came to see if I could help you with anything?"

"I think everyone has a drink now."

"It's a lovely party, as always."

"And you've got some extra sparkle." Lacey's dress shimmered under the pergola lights and so did her eyes. "I'm so glad you and Dean were able to work out your differences."

Lacey glanced shyly in Dean's direction. "It was easy in the end, once we both opened up about our concerns. He thought I was avoiding dinners and wine bars because I didn't want to be seen with him."

"Which is so far from the truth. You two make a lovely couple."

Lacey's cheeks glowed pink.

"And have you heard from your dad lately?"

"Yes. He's so much happier. Loving his job and made new friends. He's going to come back to Sydney for Christmas. Judith has invited us here."

"I'm glad she's going to continue the Christmas Day luncheon. It's become a bit of a tradition."

"Let me offer those canapés around." Lacey held out her hands to take the platter Ketty had picked up.

"Thank you."

Virginia stepped into the space Lacey vacated. "Look at those two." She nodded towards Beau and Birgit, who were listening earnestly to Tien no doubt filling them in on the happenings of her latest reality TV show. "I'm so glad they met, I can tell you. That young woman has changed Beau's life."

"I think it's been mutual. Beau's been a settling influence on her. Now that women can bring back a Ketty Clift outfit for us to resell I've put her in charge of that. She's so good with alterations."

"It was a great idea of Lacey's."

"Yes. Judith and I both took a bit of convincing, I must admit, but we only take items in perfect condition. It's brought in a few customers who wouldn't normally visit a couture dressmaker, and if the item sells we give the previous owner a discount on their next purchase so it's a win-win."

"And I love the sketches and swatches Lacey showed me for next year's autumn/winter collection."

"She and Judith have become quite a team. I've recently put them in charge of our ready-made collection, and with my restructure everyone's had a small pay rise and we were able to offer top rates to our two new seamstresses." Ketty sighed. "I still find it hard to believe how much my business has expanded."

"I'm glad to have been a small part of it. It was wonderful to model some of your new collection and I've had more offers of work since then. And my friends are glad I introduced them to your services, especially Marguerite. She and her husband are always attending gala events."

"Did you see the dress we made for her last charity ball?"

"It was absolutely exquisite."

"It truly was a team effort. Lacey and I designed it, Judith drafted the pattern, Tien cut it out and helped Birgit sew it, and Ning stitched all those crystals on by hand."

"And this dress you're wearing is rather divine too."

"Do you like it?" Ketty swished from side to side. "I wanted something special for this party."

"You've achieved that." Virginia eyed her appraisingly. "Are you still planning to meet Carlos in Spain for Christmas?"

"Yes, that's why I'm having this get-together now. Once Carlos leaves we'll be flat out with our festive-season orders and then I'll be getting on a plane two days before Christmas. I enjoy these special occasions."

"Where is Carlos?"

"He went around to Felix and Anna's to pick up the sweet pastries they made for me. I suspect he's stopped there talking or at one of the several places between here and there."

"He's made a lot of friends in the area."

"He has."

Virginia slid an arm through hers. "God, Ketty, you're going to miss him."

Ketty's breath hitched. Carlos came through the side gate carrying a large white box followed by a smartly dressed woman.

Ketty's heart began to thud in her chest.

"Who's this he's brought with him?" Virginia asked. "Another of his friends?"

Ketty didn't reply but crossed the courtyard to where Carlos and the woman were chatting quietly beneath an arch of fairy lights and flowers.

The woman picked up a small microphone they'd put there earlier in the day.

"Hello, friends and family," the woman said. "My name is Flora and I've been invited here today by Ketty and Carlos to let you know a few things."

A murmur rumbled around the group as expectant faces turned their way.

"They want you all to know that Carlos's visa has been approved and he will be back to stay in the new year."

The crowd erupted into cheers and Maurice slapped Carlos on the back. "Welcome to Oz, my man."

"Thank you, everyone," Flora continued, and once more all eyes turned her way. "There's another reason Ketty and Carlos wanted you to celebrate with them today."

Carlos took Ketty's right hand and below the edge of his sleeve she caught a glimpse of his gold watch. She'd been so relieved he'd been able to get it back.

"Ketty?" His whisper raised her eyes to his.

He was gazing at her, his face lit in a wonderful smile and his eyebrows slightly raised. Ketty smiled back, squeezed his hand and nodded.

"They wanted you all to be here to witness their marriage vows."

Just for a brief moment there was silence except for the soft tones of Peggy Lee singing 'Till There Was You' and then once more the chorus of cheers and happy voices drowned out the music. Carlos leaned in and kissed Ketty.

More cheers followed accompanied by wolf whistles that Ketty suspected came from Dean and Birgit. Flora gave the crowd a moment to settle, and butterflies briefly fluttered in Ketty's chest until another squeeze of Carlos's hand and the warmth of his smile reminded her how much she loved him.

"Shall we begin?" Flora said.

"Yes, please." Ketty and Carlos spoke as one.

acknowledgements

This book is dedicated to Joy and Andrew Hilder. We've had many holidays and writing retreats on their station in the Flinders Ranges and they've helped me out with writing support on many occasions. Joy and Andrew have also been with us on research trips, we've shared many adventures, and they were fellow travellers when Daryl and I took a trip on The Ghan. Thanks for all the great journeys we've had together. And here's cheers to many more.

The Ghan is high up there on special experiences and I knew I had to take Ketty on that journey to see what she would make of it. The route the train takes in this story is true to the real trip, as is most of the general information about the travel, but please forgive my poetic licence with bookings, cabin layouts, off-train experiences etc. And a big hello to the wonderful staff and fellow travellers we met on our trip – especially Anne and Tony.

If you're someone who's ever tried to get an Australian visa, I'm sure you'll relate to Carlos's experiences although once again I've blurred some of the rules and timelines for the sake of the narrative.

Ketty likes her jazz but other music gets a mention so I've made a playlist – a *Back on Track* soundtrack – for you to enjoy. It's on Spotify and my profile is Tricia Stringer and the playlist is called 'Back on Track'.

My trip to Paddington last year was cut short by a bout of covid so sadly no visits to any of the glamorous couture dressmakers I'd planned but I did manage to touch base with Robin from Nelder Jones who gave me a small glimpse into their lovely premises. And while it wasn't as many days as I'd hoped for, I did get to experience a bit of Paddington life. I'm most grateful to Dylan at Mrs Banks Hotel who shared a wealth of local knowledge and kindly made lockdown as pleasant as it could be.

I've spoken at a few VIEW clubs in recent years and I'd like to make mention of one in particular, Marion VIEW club, which I've visited several times. On my last visit to the club I'd written the bulk of this story so I was enthralled by a couple of tales shared where the women had experienced ageist remarks. We were all appalled and then able to laugh and I'm grateful to them for adding some extra breadth to the experiences of Ketty and Virginia in my book.

The World Health Organization have released a global report on ageism, providing evidence that half of the world's population think and feel negatively about getting older, older people and this phase of life. How sad is that? Of course ageism isn't only experienced by older people and can just as easily be aimed at any generation. As with any form of discrimination we each of us have it in our power to challenge it and make a change. If you google ageism and the country you live in you'll find lots of supportive information.

A very big thank you to my publisher Jo Mackay who draws out the best in me, and my editor Annabel Blay whose insight helps me hone the story. And thank goodness for the keen eyes of proofreader Annabel Adair. They are part of the crew at Harlequin and HarperCollins, and my thanks also extend to all who've played a part in the intricate job of bringing this book to life. From editing to publicity, marketing and sales, it's a team effort – thank you.

And the result of that effort is a new story for you, dear reader. I appreciate you choosing my book to fill your precious reading hours. Thanks also for sharing the news of your enjoyment. Word of mouth is still the best way to find new reads.

Thanks to fellow writers for friendship, laughter and a listening ear. And to librarians, booksellers, book reps and the book news community, your support is invaluable in sharing the love of stories, thank you.

And finally huge thanks to my dear friends and family with special hugs for Daryl, Kelly, Steven, Harry, Archie, Dylan, Sian, Jared, Alexandra and our newest member, Lawrence. Your love and support is the fuel that keeps me writing.

book club questions

- Ketty booked the train holiday hoping it would be 'some kind of magical fix-it elixir' for the problems with her staff. Do you think it was a) a good idea and b) successful?
- Ageism is a theme in the story. Do you think old-age is a use-by date? Or is it just a number?
- Judith has an instant dislike of Carlos and sees all his actions in a bad light. Why do you think that is?
- Judith, Dean and Birgit all face the possibility of being homeless. Lacey has a home but is struggling to pay for it. How does this affect their relationships with each other and other people?
- Retirement is one of life's big changes. It challenges two couples, Maurice and Lee, and Warren and Val, in different ways. What are the challenges of retirement for these couples and how does it affect these two relationships? Could they have been better prepared or done things differently?
- Ketty nearly always sees the possibility of relationships for other people and yet she struggles to see the possibility of a relationship with Carlos. Why is that, do you think?

- Which character or moment in the novel evokes the strongest emotional response from you and why?
- Have you ever travelled on the Ghan or taken another similar train journey? How did it compare to this one?
- Have you read Tricia Stringer's *Table for Eight* where Ketty Clift goes on a cruise? If yes, which is your favourite Ketty holiday and why?
- Do you think travel changes people? Are there any examples in the book?

talk about it

Let's talk about books.

Join the conversation:

 facebook.com/harlequinaustralia

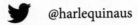 @harlequinaus

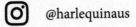 @harlequinaus

harpercollins.com.au/hq

If you love reading and want to know about our
authors and titles, then let's talk about it.